W9-BTO-009

ORANGE CRUSH

ORANGE CRUSH

A NOVEL

Tim Dorsey

wm

WILLIAM MORROW • 75 YEARS OF PUBLISHING

An Imprint of HarperCollins*Publishers*

HarperCollins books may be purchased for educational, business, or sales promotional use. For information please write: Special Markets Department, HarperCollins Publishers Inc., 10 East 53rd Street, New York, NY 10022.

FIRST EDITION

Designed by Jo Anne Metsch

Printed on acid-free paper

Library of Congress Cataloging-in-Publication Data

Dorsey, Tim.
    Orange crush : a novel / Tim Dorsey.—1st ed.
        p. cm.
    ISBN 0-06-018577-5
        1. Governors—Election—Fiction. 2. Serial murders—Fiction. 3. Florida—Fiction. I. Title.

PS3554.O719 O73 2001
813'.54—dc 21
                                                                00-143875

        01   02   03   04   05   RRD   10   9   8   7   6   5   4   3   2   1

For my mother and father

Man is what he chooses to become.

—*John Spenkelink*

ACKNOWLEDGMENTS

Thanks are owed to my agent, Nat Sobel, and my editor, Henry Ferris—two people you definitely want on your side in the alley fight that is the book business.

PROLOGUE

WITH THREE WEEKS to go in the Florida governor's race, the Tallahassee morning newspaper ran the following headline: 2 HEADS EXPLODE IN SEPARATE INCIDENTS

●

TALLAHASSEE is the capital of Florida, up in the north end of the state near Georgia. The land is less flat, more wooded; the people not as hurried or transient. In the eighteenth century the population centers of old Florida were Pensacola in the panhandle and St. Augustine on the Atlantic—too far apart to be managed under a single provisional government. Officials went looking for a spot in between. But the Talasi Indians were already on that spot, so the officials told the Indians they needed to borrow their village for about three hundred years.

Tallahassee was established the capital in 1823. East Tallahassee High School was established in 1971. On a balmy October evening in 2002, a banner hung in the high school's auditorium: GO FIGHTING SENATORS! Another hung over the stage: WELCOME GOVERNOR CANDIDATES.

A smattering of people sat in the sea of folding chairs on the basketball court. Technicians taped electrical cables to the parquet floor and checked the sound system. Agents swept the school with bomb-sniffing German shepherds. Reporters shuffled around in a tight herd, stepping on each other's shoelaces, interviewing The Man on the Street, then each other, looking for that fresh Pulitzer angle. The debate was less than two hours away.

The majestic old Florida Capitol building, with its trademark red-and-white Kentucky Fried Chicken awnings, stands proudly at the foot of the Apalachee Parkway. Behind it is Tallahassee's only sky-scraper, the new Capitol, a sterile monolith built of the finest materials someone else's money could buy.

At 5:46 P.M., a man in a dark suit and dark sunglasses stepped out a side service door of the Capitol and held it open. A platoon of ten identically dressed men jogged out of the building. The tallest one had a stopwatch and wireless headset, and just as he reached Pensacola Street, a black super-stretch limo screeched up to the curb. The man with the stopwatch opened the back door of the limo, scanned the surroundings, and turned to the rest of the men, who had taken up sentry positions across the Capitol lawn. He twirled a finger in the air, followed by a series of third-base-coach signals. A clutch of elegantly dressed men and women emerged from the service door. The array of sentries collapsed around them to form a circle of human shields, then hustled the group to the curb and shoved them in the back of the limo, which sped north on Monroe Street. A pair of forest-green Hummers joined the limo, an escort in front and a trail vehicle in back. Two small flags snapped in the wind on each side of the limo's hood. The flag on the right corner displayed the seal of the Florida governor's office. The flag on the left used to have the same seal but now read: "The Outback Steakhouse Florida Governor's Race."

Local law enforcement was worried about security. Due to the state's proliferation of military assault weapons, violent narcotics gangs and middle-aged loners in one-bedroom apartments, the capital police force reported it was no longer capable of providing what it deemed was adequate security for the governor, lieutenant governor and their families and mistresses. They said they knew of only one group who could get the job done.

The governor's office hired the people who handled security for the Rolling Stones.

The governor and staff were violently tossed left, then right as the limo slalomed the back roads of Tallahassee in textbook UN convoy maneuver. The governor and his campaign manager faced each other in the posh opposing backseats. The manager flipped flash cards.

A bright yellow card: "Wetlands Despoilment."

The governor scratched his head. "We for or against that?"

"For," said the manager. "You feeling okay? That's the third easy one you've missed."

The governor nodded, but his thoughts were elsewhere. A political world that had been second nature his entire life now seemed alien, oblique, clumsy. He felt light-headed, and the periphery of his vision dissolved with a hallucinatory tinge. He looked around the spacious interior of the limo, packed with the usual suspects. The leather bench seating seemed to go on forever, all the way up to the chauffeur's soundproof partition, like a hall of mirrors. The governor squinted and took a hard look for the first time. Who the hell *were* all these people? They stared back at him, smiling and nodding—handlers, trainers, therapists, linguists, donors, spokesmen, media consultants, speechwriters, image makers, spin doctors, crisis teams, spiritual gurus, food tasters, pollsters, pundits, wags, wonks, interstate bagmen, unindicted co-conspirators, miscellaneous hangers-on, and three bimbos who looked like the Mandrell Sisters.

The campaign manager snapped his fingers in front of the governor's face.

"Wake up! I have some people I want you to meet."

The manager patted a bald man on the back. "Governor, this is Big Tobacco." The manager then pointed to others who had wiggled their way back from the forward seats and now crowded shoulder to shoulder in the rear of the limo. "And this is Big Oil, Big Sugar, Big Insurance and Big Rental Car . . ."

The limo approached a sprawling compound north of the Tallahassee limits. A guard waved them through the twin white metal gates with musical notes that replicated the entrance at Graceland. The vehicle entered a tunnel of nineteenth-century oaks. The residence sat on an elevated bluff—ten thousand square feet, three stories, brick, with portico and columns of Federal architecture. One

hour until the debate, one last stop. Fund-raising. A high-end cocktail reception at the home of a man who needed no introduction
other than "Perry."

Periwinkle Belvedere, the most influential lobbyist and political
tactician in the state of Florida, who only drank mint juleps.

Perry would have been imposing, even frightening, if it wasn't for
his gamma-ray smile. Six-four and full head of obscenely red hair. He
was trim, but his hands and head were extra-large, and he greeted
everyone with a fluid personal manner and a handshake that—
through years of practice—precisely matched the pounds per square
inch of his guest's.

Power was everywhere in Tallahassee. Political, industrial, sexual.
Puddled up all over the city. Periwinkle simply connected the puddles
and organized the water. Soon he had a raging river on his hands,
which he dredged, dammed, reservoired and viaducted according to
his fee schedule.

But the times were changing. Laws limiting gifts, requiring disclo-
sures, a full public accounting. The fun had already started to wheeze
out of the capital balloon. Perry was mingling in the library, trying to
hide his irritation at the legislators peeking through the blinds and
curtains every few minutes, keeping an eye out for reporters like
lookouts at a safe-cracking. Journalists, thought Perry, now there's
an attractive bunch. They could put a damper on an orgy.

If ever a place had an orgy in mind, it was Perry's. The Roman
fountain in the foyer pumped Dom Pérignon. Inside the dining hall
and out on the torch-lit patio: tables almost collapsing under Keys
lobsters, beluga caviar, Périgord truffles, Peking duck and Alaskan
salmon. All top-shelf, except for the two Sterno trays at the end of
the last banquet table, specially ordered by Periwinkle to cater to the
particular tastes of the Florida speaker of the house. Pigs-in-a-blanket and Beenie Weenies.

When the lawmakers first reached the buffet tables, there was
aggressive jockeying, the bright glint of cutlery and serving ladles,
and finally a blinding piranha frenzy. In minutes, it was quiet again.
The aftermath was chilling. Salmon stripped to the spinal column.

Blue cheese chunks bobbing in the punch bowl. Beluga flung across the linen like coffee grounds. Cocktail sauce splattered mob-hit-style.

But what really inspired Perry's awe was their Light Brigade desiccation of the open bar. "My God," he said in a reverent, hushed tone. "They're worse than sportswriters."

No matter how many parties Perry threw, he couldn't get over one of nature's marvels, the sights and sounds of lawmakers at the trough, storing up complex carbohydrates for the winter in their woodchuck cheeks and distensible pelican throats. Early on, Perry learned that perks had a curious Bermuda Triangle effect on lawmakers, sending the instrument needles spinning in their judgment cockpits. It worked out to about a dime on the dollar. Fifty bucks of complimentary food, drink and knickknacks bought as much influence as a five-hundred-dollar campaign contribution.

Despite the adorable government-in-the-sunshine reforms, Perry's soirée tonight began to show signs of life, and a smile crossed his face as the foyer echoed with the hollow din of clinking glasses, self-important laughter and cell phones.

Another cell phone went off, and a half-dozen people at the petit fours checked their jackets and purses. The ones who came up with nonringing phones winced in public shame; the one with the activated phone smirked.

The smirk belonged to Todd Vanderbilt, who answered his cell phone loudly for the benefit of those around him: "It's your dime!"

Todd was Perry Belvedere's top lobbyist, and his cell phone rang every five minutes because he told his personal assistant to "call me every five minutes."

"What do I say?"

"You don't say anything."

"I don't understand."

"I know."

Between phone calls, Todd's beeper went off. So did his Palm Pilot, Sky Pager and self-correcting wristwatch, receiving microwave data from the Atomic Clock in Colorado.

Another alarm went off somewhere on Todd. He reached in his

jacket, pulled out an e-gizmo and grinned at the crowd. "Stock split!"

"Ha!" countered a rival. "The market's closed!"

"Tokyo," said Todd.

"Oooooooooooo," the impressed crowd responded, then clapped.

Todd was everything Tallahassee was looking for: young, handsome, ambitious and completely full of shit. From his wardrobe to his manicure, everything was consciously in place. Except for one puzzle piece. The girl on his arm. His date was Sally Brewster, Perry Belvedere's accounting wizard. She was twenty-three, which was right in Todd's usual kill zone, but that's where it ended. Sally had scored something like a million on her SATs and graduated magna cum laude from Princeton, where she had a full scholarship and no dating life. There were a number of reasons. Her long hours studying left little time for extracurricular activity. And she had a nose like a stromboli.

Consequently, Sally remained awkward and frumpish. Her brown hair was straight and stringy, and her clothes looked like the uniform at a Cracker Barrel. She was also sweet as they come. And when a girl is as intelligent and nice as Sally, nature—with its charming brand of whimsy—makes her have a crush on a guy like Todd.

Sally had hovered around Todd for months, running to get him coffee, baking him cookies and banana bread, laughing at jokes that were at her expense. He routinely took out frustrations on her because she was the path of least resistance, and she forgave him.

Last Friday morning, Todd checked the market action on his office computer and chewed with his mouth open. Sally stood demurely with a baking tray.

"Killer brownies," said Todd, still chomping. "Hey, you wanna go to Perry's party with me next week?"

Todd thought Sally had gone into anaphylactic shock.

He got her a chair and a glass of water. "Tell me if you're gonna be sick, okay? 'Cause I can't get anything on this tie."

Sally spent the next week shopping. She ran up charges for clothes, her hair, everything. Even was fitted for contact lenses so she could ditch the granny glasses.

It would be nice to say the change was stunning, and that Sally emerged like a beautiful swan. It was not to be. She looked as natural and graceful as a rusting robot, stiffly hobbled on high heels, blinking rapidly from new contacts and bumping into things.

Periwinkle Belvedere glanced from his watch to the doorway, waiting for the governor. Standing with him was Elizabeth Sinclair, Perry's office manager. Todd Vanderbilt may have been Perry's hottest lobbyist, but Elizabeth was the glue of maturity that held his staff together. Dignified dark business suit and pearl stud earrings. Blond hair in a short, conservative Meg Ryan cut. She was forty-eight years old, wondered why she was still single, and remembered why every time she came to one of Perry's parties.

"You certainly look nice tonight," said Perry.

"Thank you," said Elizabeth.

"Although we talked about your clothes."

"I know."

"I really wish you'd wear something a little more . . ."

"More what?"

"You know."

"No, I don't."

Perry sighed. "Why can't you be a team player like Todd?"

Elizabeth and Perry looked over to the faux fireplace, where a series of electronic beeps, pulses, tones and buzzers were going off all over Todd, who smiled and produced a device in each hand and announced: "The sound of success!" He flicked open the cell phone. "It's your dime!"

Elizabeth turned to Perry. "Your star pupil."

Perry shook his head. "Look, I'm depending on you—" Something across the room caught his eye and he perked up. "Here comes the governor. Try to be nice."

Heads turned as the state's chief executive crossed the ballroom. His campaign manager and press secretary trailed close behind, whispering over his shoulders, overlapping each other, identifying people just before the governor shook their hands.

"There's Helmut von Zeppelin, mega-developer . . ."

"And that's Marshall Bellicose Leghorn, cattle baron . . ."

"Here's 'Little Tony' Mezzanine, local organized crime . . ."

"And this is Elizabeth Sinclair, Belvedere's office manager . . ."

Sinclair smiled with professional distance. "Pleasure to see you again, Governor."

She braced as they shook hands, determined to keep grinning through anything. She remembered shaking hands with him at the last party. "Wow, lady, that's some grip you got on ya. Bet it comes in handy, if you know what I mean." Wink.

The memory made her shiver.

Tonight, the governor shook her hand deferentially and averted his eyes. "Nice to see you again."

That's weird, she thought.

Suddenly, the governor and Elizabeth were knocked off balance as Sally Brewster crashed into them. The pair steadied Sally before she could topple off her high heels.

"You okay?" asked the governor.

"New contacts," said Sally.

Elizabeth fixed Sally's bra strap so it wouldn't show. "Let's get a glass of wine." She turned back to the governor: "It was nice seeing you again."

The women moved to the bar and ordered cabernet.

"I've got some comfortable shoes out in the car," offered Elizabeth, her bunched eyebrows betraying acute sympathy for her spastic friend.

"No, I've got to do this."

"You're way too smart and pretty for a jerk like Todd. What do you see in him, anyway?"

Sally just gave her that smitten look. It reminded Elizabeth of her own youth. Easier to reason with a wild bandicoot than a crush.

"You got it bad," she said, and they touched wineglasses.

They sipped quietly next to a row of potted ficus flanking the bar. A familiar voice boomed from the other side of the trees.

"Come on, guys, fork it over! We had a bet!"

Elizabeth and Sally peeked through the leaves. It was Todd and two of his buddies, who pulled currency from their wallets and handed it grudgingly to Todd.

"Okay, okay, you win," said one of the buddies. "You definitely have the dorkiest date at the party."

Sally put a hand over her mouth, started crying and ran from the party, but not before slamming into the governor again and taking an ugly tumble down the front steps.

Elizabeth marched around the end of the trees. "You son of a bitch!"

"What?" said Todd, then turned to see people running to help Sally. "Oh, her? She'll get over it. She didn't honestly think someone like *me* would actually go out with her. You see the honker on that chick?" Something began beeping. "Hold on, I got a call." He flicked open his phone. "It's your dime!"

Elizabeth dumped her glass of cabernet on his chest.

"Hey! My shirt!"

She stomped off.

Todd stared down in horror at the purple stain spreading like a gunshot wound. Something walked by that made him forget about laundry. His eyes followed the lithe figure across the room. She was a Latin beauty with short hair and a nametag from the Brazilian embassy.

"Salsa!" Todd said to himself. He licked his index finger, touched it to an imaginary location in the air and made a hissing sound. "Spicy hot!"

He trotted after her.

In the next room, a senator from Hialeah peeked through the blinds and saw what he had been dreading all night—a reporter talking to the guard in the driveway, gesturing at the house with his notebook. The first ant at the picnic.

A minute later two more reporters arrived, then a few more, and soon a large motley throng clamored in the driveway. The senator closed the blinds and discreetly informed his colleagues:

"*RAID!*"

They scattered in all directions. People ran into each other; women lost their heels. The Florida speaker of the house stuffed a handful of pigs-in-a-blanket in each coat pocket, gripped another in his mouth, and joined the stampede spilling across the mansion's driveway.

Cars patched out, fishtailing on the lawn. Senator Mary Ellen Bilgewater was ambushed before she could get to her Saab. She came up swinging. "How dare you ruin this party! We deserve this! People don't understand the sacrifice it takes . . ."—starting to sob—". . . you don't know how hard it is being a lawmaker! You just don't get it!"

A half hour later, on the other side of town, the crowd that had gathered for the gubernatorial debate was growing restless in the auditorium of East Tallahassee High School. They began stomping their feet and singing. ". . . *We will, we will rock you!* . . ."

A network cameraman turned to a sound technician. "I hate that fucking song."

The governor's limo approached the auditorium, where a mob waited at the stage entrance: a tight flock of reporters, obsessed followers, and demonstrators with pickets. FREE CUBA! MEDICAL MARIJUANA NOW! PICK ME, MONTY!

The Reform Party candidate, Albert Fresco, was outside protesting that he wasn't allowed to participate in the debate. Fresco and his staff wore T-shirts with his campaign slogan in large type: I'M MADDER THAN A SUMBITCH!

The limo stopped as scripted a block from the auditorium. The head of Rolling Stones' security spoke into his voice-activated headset. "Send in Jagger."

A Mick Jagger impersonator got out of a sedan across the street from the auditorium and sprinted for another door around the side of the building. The mob shrieked and ran after him. The limo pulled up to the unattended stage entrance, and the governor's entourage was whisked inside without incident.

The audience in the auditorium piped down as the event's moderator, Florida Cable News correspondent Blaine Crease, laid down the League of Women Voters' ground rules for the debate.

The candidates stood at identical podiums thirty feet apart. The

Democratic challenger was the Florida speaker of the house, Gomer Tatum, a fifty-eight-year-old portly, perspiring William Howard Taft–shaped man. He had fine black hair and an emerging bald pate. During commercial breaks in the debate, his dandruff blizzard would be carefully vacuumed and tweezered off the shoulders of his navy-blue suit by a crack staff who worked him like a trauma team. But they could only do so much. Under the television lights, Tatum appeared pasty and wilting.

The Republican incumbent wore an identical blue suit, but a longer, slimmer cut. Governor Marlon Conrad, thirty-eight years old, and everything about him projected confidence, success and high poll numbers—from the sound of his name to the Richard Gere good looks and Kennedy hair. If that wasn't enough, there was the family legacy. Great-grandfather Cecil Conrad, citrus magnate whose vast landholdings north of Lake Okeechobee were still in the family, the source of its embarrassing wealth. Grandfather "Two-Fisted" Thaddeus Conrad, twenty-term congressman who earned his nickname on the McCarthy committee. Father Dempsey "Tip" Conrad, former attorney general and current state Republican Party chairman.

Moderator Blaine Crease signaled thirty seconds to airtime.

Tatum's campaign manager looked out onstage and saw something that almost gave her a stroke.

"Where did he get *that*?" The manager ran onto the stage and snatched a pig-in-a-blanket from the speaker's mouth and stormed off. The speaker glanced furtively at his manager, then produced another pig-in-a-blanket from a coat pocket and resumed chewing.

Conrad's people, along with everyone else, had considered the campaign a slam dunk. Marlon was supposed to put Tatum out like a wet cigar in the early weeks.

Then the stumbles, the missed opportunities. Conrad hadn't been himself lately. The timing was gone, and there had been no knockout punch. Tatum managed to hang ten to twelve percentage points back, a distant second, but still in range.

Tonight at East Tallahassee High, the televised debate was the first major statewide event of the campaign. Conrad's staff was hopeful.

Their man had been the stuff of vigor all day, and television was his medium. It certainly wasn't Tatum's.

As the debate opened, the governor's people stood behind the stage curtains, leaning forward on the balls of their feet, waiting for the kill. Instead, Conrad sleepwalked through the event, dazed.

Near the end of the debate, moderator Blaine Crease was handed a note by a network aide. There had been a problem at the prison in Starke. Something with the state's electric chair. Child torturer-murderer Calvin Rodney Buford had been set for execution at seven sharp. But one of the guards forgot to put the conductive jelly on the ankle strap. Also, they had failed to account for a metal plate in Buford's head, which acted as a giant capacitor and heat sink. Two big jolts. Then a third. Still alive, although much more irritable. At 7:12 they gave it everything they had for four minutes, at the end of which Buford's head let go like a stuffed pepper in a microwave.

The state of Florida had retired the electric chair two years earlier in favor of lethal injection. But in the last legislative session, a number of key incumbents faced a massive no-bid contract scandal that was only eclipsed by the revelation that they had blown thousands of taxpayer dollars on Internet pay sites involving humiliation and discipline. The issues wouldn't go away. So, in the middle of the ethics hearings, the legislature brought back the chair, and all was forgotten.

Moderator Crease recounted the news from Death Row for the candidates. "Gentlemen, in light of tonight's development, and indeed a whole series of botched executions, wasn't it a mistake to reinstate the electric chair?"

Backstage, Conrad's manager smiled and pumped a fist. "Perfect timing! This is his best bully pulpit!"

Onstage, Conrad stared at his hands. He looked up. "It's something to think about."

"What the fuck!" yelled his manager. He threw down a sheaf of papers. "It's a no-brainer! I can answer that one in my sleep: 'I hope all their heads explode! Then maybe they'll think twice before they commit crimes in Florida!"

Crease turned to Tatum. "What about you, Mr. Speaker?"

The camera caught Tatum off-guard—eyes wide, bulging in terror, a pig-in-a-blanket protruding from his stuffed mouth. He inhaled it, gulped hard and hit himself in the chest with a fist. "Uh . . . I hope all their heads explode? . . . Uh . . . then maybe they'll think twice before they commit crimes in Florida?"

The audience went wild. Tatum looked around, startled at first, then grinned.

Florida Cable News had arranged for home viewers to register opinions live during the debate with special keypads. At East Tallahassee High, the results were displayed on the auditorium's basketball scoreboard. After the electric chair question, Tatum's stock slowly began rising . . . and kept rising. . . . The audience gasped when the numbers finally leveled off.

Three weeks left in the campaign, it was a dead heat.

Four hours after the debate, the auditorium swarmed with police. Shortly after the governor and audience had left the building, there had been an explosion.

The Tallahassee police detective in charge of the scene directed forensic photographers and gloved technicians through the debris in the balcony.

A tall man in a rumpled tweed jacket ducked under the yellow crime tape at the top of the stairs and approached the detective. He flashed a gold badge. "Mahoney, homicide."

The detective studied the badge. Miami Metro–Dade.

"Mahoney, it looks like you're out of your jurisdiction."

"It's all one big, sick jurisdiction now."

"I hear ya."

"Miami sent me up here because of a case we had. Miami thinks we may have a match."

"Miami thinks a lot of things."

"What do you think?"

"I think I have a dinner at home getting cold."

"It's a cold world."

"Never heard that."

Mahoney stared down at the lumpy sheet on the balcony floor. "What's the skinny?"

"A witness says he saw the victim come up here with a young woman. My guess is he was trying to score a little nooky."

"Nooky?" said Mahoney. "They still have that around these parts?"

"If you know the right people."

Mahoney nodded. He pulled an antique silver flask from his tweed coat and took a pull, then offered it to the detective.

The detective waved off the flask. "I'm on the wagon."

"What wagon's that?"

"A big red one with stripes. What do you care? You're Mr. Hot Shit from Miami."

"Please, drop the mister." Mahoney pointed down at the sheet. "We got a make on the vic?"

The detective flipped open a notepad. "One Todd Vanderbilt."

Mahoney leaned down and lifted the sheet. The body was missing the head and right hand.

The detective held up a clear evidence bag filled with minuscule plastic chips and semiconductor shards.

"Cell phone?" asked Mahoney.

The detective nodded. "My guess would be C4 plastique explosive hidden in the speaker and wired to the answering button."

Mahoney stared off into space. "I'd say he had the wrong calling plan."

"A janitor was sweeping down below when it happened," said the detective. "Claims he heard someone say, 'It's your dime!' then *kaboom*. The victim's head took off across the auditorium like an Olympic volleyball serve."

Mahoney shook his head. "Isn't that always the case?"

"Look at this." The detective opened the victim's shirt to reveal something written on his chest in Magic Marker:

KISS ME—I JUST VOTED!

1

WHAT A DIFFERENCE a year makes.

It was the fall of 2001, exactly twelve months before the debate at East Tallahassee High. Marlon Conrad not only wasn't governor, he wasn't even planning on *running* for governor. At least not yet. Marlon was going to throw his hat in the ring in 2006, but that was a whole term away. In the meantime, he was perfectly content frittering away his days in a do-nothing political sinecure, tending to his hobbies.

It was a calm October afternoon, and a magnificent tarpon broke the surface of the water. It twisted in midair, trying to throw the hook, and landed back in the ocean with a grand crash. Then up again, tail-walking for its life.

Marlon worked fast with the joystick. He clicked the trigger, easing drag, finessing the tarpon on his computer screen in Silver King Xtreme Fishing.

There was a knock at the door, distracting Marlon, and the fish broke the line. It poked its head from the water and stuck out its tongue before disintegrating off the screen.

"Damn!" He swiveled in his chair. "Come in!"

The door to the office opened. There was gold lettering on the outside: MARLON CONRAD, LIEUTENANT GOVERNOR. In walked a buxom southern belle with poofy blond hair, Babs Belvedere, Marlon's fiancée in an arranged marriage between two of the state's most powerful families.

She wore a transparent pout and held out an index finger. "I have a splinter."

"Another one!" said Marlon, turning back to the computer and hitting the "cast" button on the joystick.

"You don't love me anymore."

"Foolishness!"

It wasn't exactly a lie. He never *had* loved her.

The fish took the bait and jumped on the screen. Marlon zigged and zagged with the joystick.

Babs set a large box on the corner of his desk. She held her injured finger in Marlon's face. He pushed her hand out of the way and tried to recover with the joystick, but the damage was done. The fish stuck its tongue out again.

"Damn!"

He turned to Babs, her finger still outstretched.

"Kiss it and make it better," she demanded. Now the pout was real.

"Oh, all right." He gave it a quick peck, and her mood boomeranged to glee. "Guess what?" she said, pulling up a chair, plopping down and slapping both her knees in excitement. "I bought a new puppet!"

She took the case off his desk and placed it in her lap and opened it. Inside was a big frog, the newest in a long line of wooden marionettes that filled the shelves in Babs's bedroom. The source of all the splinters.

"Just what you need—another puppet."

"You don't respect my *art*," said Babs, expertly manipulating the frog's strings with both hands. Barely moving her lips: *"Ribbit, ribbit, ribbit."*

"You possess genius," said Marlon, hitting the "cast" button again.

She actually did have some ability, and could now throw her voice short distances at will. The daughter of Periwinkle Belvedere, she was Miss Tallahassee 2001 and runner-up for Miss Florida. Babs easily could have been Miss Florida, too. She had become a finalist based on the strength of her ventriloquist act in the talent portion of the pageant, but she blew her final question, becoming flustered and saying she wanted to end world peace and promote illiteracy in the Third World.

The scheduled marriage was considered a deal-maker by the capital's movers and shakers. It would consolidate power and grease the skids for all kinds of ecopolitical alliances. Marlon thought she was an airhead.

He still hadn't found the proper way of telling anybody he didn't want to marry her. In the meantime, of course, he had taken the sex. Who wouldn't? What a cheesecake! But now, even that had stopped. Both knew why, and they didn't want to talk about it. Marlon had become sexually traumatized. On a recent evening, he had been going down on Babs when her vagina greeted him with the voice of Howdy Doody.

Babs made the frog hop across Marlon's desk. *"Ribbit, ribbit . . ."*

There was another knock at the door.

"Interruptions!" said Marlon, flinging the joystick aside.

Standing in the doorway with a leather organizer was Marlon's chief of staff, Gottfried Escrow. "Sorry, but your appointments are waiting. We really have to get the schedule moving."

Escrow pointed out the door into the lobby. In a row of chairs against the wall, under a giant oil painting of "Two-Fisted" Thaddeus Conrad, sat a conga line of older men in tailored suits. At the head of the line was a local construction magnate facing multiple investigations for shoddy workmanship and fraud. He arose, handed the chief of staff an unmarked envelope, and went inside.

The man took a seat across the desk from the lieutenant governor and placed his hands humbly in his lap. "I told my wife: For justice we must go see Marlon Conrad!"

"Two of your new roofs collapsed after light rain. A girl was hospitalized."

"I am but a simple businessman . . ."

Behind him, the chief of staff was giving Marlon the high sign to speed things up.

"I'll see what I can do," said Marlon, standing.

The man clasped Marlon's right hand in both of his and shook it earnestly. "Thank you! Thank you!"—bowing repeatedly as he backed out of the room.

Three appointments later, Escrow came in the office holding a large laminated map mounted on foam board.

"What's that?"

"It's the new voting district we've been working on. I need you to okay it. You're chairman of the party's redistricting committee."

"Work, work, work," said Marlon, squinting at the prop. "Details?"

"We cut a deal with the Black Caucus and cobbled together a gerrymandered district that would be ninety-six percent African-American. Surprisingly, the five surrounding districts became predominantly Republican."

Marlon glanced up at the outline of the new district as he scribbled his signature on the appropriate documents. "It looks like copulating giraffes."

Escrow turned the map around to face him. "You know, you're right."

"Who's next?"

Escrow checked his organizer. "Bond lawyer."

Five minutes later:

"But won't we get caught?" asked Marlon.

"Do you understand government bonding?"

"No."

"Neither does anyone else. The press would rather stick hat pins in their ears than try to write about it."

"Sold." They stood and shook on it.

"Who's next?"

"My brother-in-law," said Escrow. "Wants a job."

"What do we have?"

"How about Family-Values Czar?"

"There such a thing?"

"We've already got the uniform."

The in-law appeared in the doorway wearing what looked like an Argentinian admiral's uniform with giant epaulets, a chestful of medals and a cap with fat gold braiding on the visor.

"Draw up the papers," said Marlon.

The makeup team arrived, followed by press secretary Muntjack "Jack" Pimento.

Marlon hated reading. Nobody could ever remember seeing him with a magazine, let alone a book, and he ordered his staff to read the newspapers for him and write summaries, which he also refused to read. Press Secretary Pimento was finally forced to read the summaries aloud to Marlon each day while he was having his press conference makeup applied.

"Too long!" Marlon snapped after hearing a recent news summary.

The next day, Pimento pruned it down to a round robin of headlines and choice lead paragraphs.

"Still too long!"

Pimento decided to switch newspapers and condense the already condensed *USA Today*.

"Still too long!" Marlon said upon hearing the summary, which distilled the morpheme residue left by the austere editors at *USA Today* down to one noun and verb per story.

Today, Pimento pulled out his latest summary.

"Stock market is up; people are bad."

"Perfect!" Marlon stood and whipped off his makeup bib.

He headed into the Capitol auditorium and the blinding TV lights of the press conference, which was packed with government staff to applaud the lieutenant governor's answers and, if necessary, boo reporters' questions.

"Mr. Conrad," said a tenacious reporter from the *Palm Shore Daily Clarion-Bugle*. "In your short administration, you've already hired fifty-seven friends, relatives and campaign donors to newly created and arguably unnecessary positions."

"Your point?" said Marlon.

"You pledged to cut waste. We now have a Protect-Our-Children

Czar, Protect-the-Flag Czar, Fight-for-Prayer Czar, Devil-Music Czar and, as of today, something called a Family-Values Czar. What's going on here?"

"Efficient government is what's going on!" said Conrad. Staff members along the walls applauded and cheered.

"I thought Republicans were against government growth."

"This is completely different," said Marlon.

"How's that?"

"We use the word *czar*."

"But—"

"No more questions!" said Escrow, stepping up and raising his arms at the podium.

The press corps objected vociferously, then went to lunch in a large group.

2

MARLON CONRAD ALWAYS knew he would someday be governor. In fact, everyone around him thought the same thing. Anything less and Marlon's life would be judged a failure.

It just wasn't supposed to happen this quickly—the plan had been for Marlon to kick back as lieutenant governor and wait another four years. The current governor, Horace Birch, was a shoo-in for a second term and would retire in 2006, clearing the way for Marlon to run in the next election cycle.

Then—just months before the gubernatorial debate at East Tallahassee High—the unthinkable. Governor Birch was killed during a lobbyist-arranged caribou hunting trip to the Yukon when a distracted Learjet pilot turned the controls over to a corporate hooker who made a ninety-degree landing into the side of the Donjek Glacier. Birch's remains were sprinkled at midfield during halftime of the Florida–Florida State football game and inadvertently trampled by the Homosassa High School Marching Shrews.

Not only was Marlon running for governor four years ahead of schedule, he was running as the incumbent. It reeked of destiny.

As a child in Tampa, Conrad had gone to the finest schools, enjoyed every privilege. For his sixteenth birthday he got a Mercedes, prompting a tantrum until it was traded for a convertible Jaguar, which was repainted candy-apple red at his whining.

Marlon matriculated at the University of Florida in Gainesville and joined the most prestigious fraternity, which was given a twenty-thousand-dollar endowment to nominate him for student body president. Marlon was quickly offered membership in the coveted Blue Key society, the university's ultrasecret cabal of hardworking students who met clandestinely to play fort. Upon graduation, Marlon moved into Tampa's gated Excelsior community, drove buckets of range balls into swimming pools adjoining the Palma Ceia Country Club, and backslapped everyone during lunch each day in a private restaurant atop a forty-story bank.

Marlon's dad advised him that because he was a lock to be governor someday, Marlon should capitalize now and embark upon a career of taking his payoffs in advance, while there was still no illegality or nosy reporters. Marlon, fresh into the workforce, opened Inside Track Consulting, which consisted entirely of a bank account.

Business exploded.

Early on, a naive Marlon actually showed up at the corporate headquarters of Heap Big Medicine with a flimsy one-page report extolling the virtues of buying low, selling high.

"What a joker!" said the chairman, making the report into a paper plane and sailing it.

The plane hit Marlon in the left eye and he went down in a decorative waterfall.

"Geez! Sorry 'bout that! Fucker got away from me."

The chairman pulled Marlon out of the fake lily pads, and they laughed about it and spent the afternoon drinking private-stock bourbon in the chairman's office and firing a potato cannon out his eleventh-floor window.

Marlon became partner in sundry real estate and development firms. For small initial investments, which were waived, he was quietly steered into the acquisition of cheap, unusable land that, with uncanny regularity, soon had new sewer lines, interstate exit ramps, shopping centers and municipal parking garages.

In return, the Conrad family's contacts in the intelligence community alerted the real estate firms when they needed a property, then paid over market. There was never any paper trail for the press to trip over because it was all classified top secret in the interest of national security. They catered to the unending stream of deposed South American strongmen, drug-running government witnesses and

CIA-trained torture experts who had to flee to the United States when their governments tragically fell to democracy.

Marlon sat on so many boards of directors that he was in danger of being labeled employed. The presence of the Conrad family name lent a fragrance of legitimacy to the companies, and Marlon's rigorous duties were to smile for his photos in the annual reports and then shrug his shoulders at investors when the owners relocated to Pago Pago. But Marlon's checks always cleared, and he could never understand what all the fuss was about in the newspapers.

Years passed in ease and insulation. But as Marlon entered his mid-thirties, the leisure slacked off. Handlers put him out on the waterfront-mansion fund-raising circuit. Not as the draw, mind you. These were the development years. Sharpening his smile and small talk.

Marlon: "No—no plans to run for now." An aw-shucks grin. The guys in the three-piece suits and cowboy hats: "C'mon, you're a natural! You gotta run!" His handlers standing by the grand piano with vodka martinis, drooling: *This is going like glass.*

Unfortunately, Marlon couldn't be ensconced forever behind the guard shacks at capital-gains golf colonies. The vagaries of politics required that some fund-raisers eventually be held in high-risk media zones, like museums and hotel conference rooms, and reporters starting asking obnoxious questions—Has he ever had a job?—and a handler would step between Marlon and the reporter: "This is just a friendly little get-together. Mr. Conrad is here only as a concerned private citizen interested in good government." If that didn't stop the inquisition, the handler would lean into the reporter and whisper, "How about some free food?" and the reporter's eyes would spirograph as he was led to a glazed pyramid of buffalo wings.

But the unjust questions kept coming, and Marlon was forced to engage in the illusion of work. The handlers created a galaxy of phantom consortiums, which Marlon chaired with a firm, paper-jawed resolve. Team Conrad spent heavily on fax machines, watermarked stationery and lapel pins, and soon people were whipping out checkbooks and elbowing to climb aboard Marlon's Millennium Foundation, Sunshine State Roundtable, Osprey Nest Inner Circle,

Imperial Coconut Select Committee, and Florida 2000 Blue-Ribbon
Panel and Grille. For less money, there was the second-tier Royal
Poinciana Institute, the Golden Palm Think Tank and the Chinch
Bug Conservatory, which only included a box lunch. They cogitated,
consternated, wrung hands and Xeroxed position statements.

Having properly assembled a synthetic work record and a very
real fortune, Marlon was run for lieutenant governor, where there
was even less risk of work, and he landslid into office. He quickly
established a reputation as a man of principle by remaining stead-
fastly loyal to all who had bought influence ahead of time. With just
a nod or wink, building codes loosened, consumer rights floundered,
investigations of friends flickered out, and jobs and contracts flowed
like milk and honey. Sometimes he just had a twitch, and the lawmakers weren't sure whether it was a nod or wink, but they were
taking no chances. In December, Marlon stifled a sneeze, and a
chemical landfill went in next to an elementary school.

Despite his means, Marlon demanded complimentary parking,
meals and tickets to all the best events. If there was a line at a restaurant and he was unrecognized, he caused a stink. He made his
motorcade run all the red lights and cut off ambulances. In Marlon's
mind he was restoring honor and dignity to public service in the
post-Clinton era.

Marlon's big coming-out party after being elected lieutenant governor was the opening day of the legislature.

The onset of the legislative session each year is an extraordinary
phenomenon. On the eve of the session, forget going anywhere nice
in Tallahassee. Lobbyists buy up the whole town. Periwinkle Belvedere
alone books six or seven restaurants. Scotch moves out of liquor
stores on forklifts, and beautiful women materialize in unnatural
numbers. One young lobbyist was known to patrol the streets into
the wee hours, looking for impending DUIs. He once found the Ways
and Means chairman T-boned into a pine tree on the side of Thomas-
ville Road, and he quickly shoved the senator over to the passenger
seat and hopped behind the wheel just before the police cruiser
pulled up. "Sorry, officer, I must have been going too fast for conditions." From that day on he owned the senator. Word got around,

and now, whenever the legislature is in session, the Tallahassee police are outmanned on the streets three to one by lobbyists.

On the morning of Marlon's first session, a hungover legislature arrived in chambers. Their desks were modern, and their chairs high-backed and padded. . . . Except they couldn't see their desks and chairs. The place looked like Princess Di's funeral—floral arrangements of every design, piled and stacked layers deep, the entire floors of the House and Senate covered in roses and orchids and tulips. Flowers made into big hearts, bouquets in the shape of the Capitol dome, a giant horseshoe arrangement for the representative from Ocala. And not just flowers, but candies, nuts, engraved sterling gavels and a tiny glassine envelope of cocaine from a lobbyist who knew the way to one particular senator's heart.

When Marlon made his entrance in the House, they were chomping pistachios and opening gift cards. They saw Marlon coming down the center aisle and tried to get his attention. Marlon waved to the right side of the chamber. The representative from Daytona Beach grinned and held a floral race car up next to him like it was Romper Room. Marlon turned and waved to the left side, and Representative J. J. Weathervane smiled irrepressibly and flapped free football tickets at Marlon. Representative Boley "Bo" Bodacious cut in front of Weathervane and held up a fourteen-karat Space Shuttle zero-gravity pen and pencil set, and he and Marlon high-fived over it. The cheering was deafening now, and Marlon broke into a trot for the podium. When he got to the microphone, he put his hands up for quiet.

"We must continue earning the respect of the citizens of this great state. There are many challenges ahead this session. Numerous crises have arisen since last year that demand immediate attention . . ." He noticed his watch. "Hey, it's almost lunch," and Marlon led the charge downstairs to the cafeteria.

●

MARLON Conrad learned everything he knew about life from his father, Dempsey "Tip" Conrad.

Rule Number One: At any given moment, poor people, somewhere, somehow, were screwing them.

From this maxim all other rules flowed. At an early age, Marlon was taken on tours of Dempsey Conrad's barbell manufacturing plant. Dempsey walked down the assembly line greeting the workers. The bane of Dempsey's existence was three words: repetitive-motion injury.

A worker with carpal tunnel wrist braces smiled and nodded. "Good to see you, sir."

Dempsey smiled back, then whispered to Marlon: "See those wrist braces? He's trying to screw me! Never forget that."

Marlon sat in on meetings between Dempsey and the plant manager, who was worried about the increasing injuries on the line.

"Relax," said Dempsey. "That's what our employee benefit flex-plan is for."

The plan consisted of company doctors who were to patch up the workers and get them back on the line as fast as possible and, under absolutely no circumstances, certify them as disabled. The plan was based on the assumption that sixty percent of all medical conditions will fix themselves. Other conditions were so bad, fortunately, that the workers died. For the troublesome remainder, the company dispatched private investigators to dredge up personal quirks for dismissal ammunition.

"But Mr. Conrad," said the plant manager. "We're starting to see some really shitty workmanship. A whole shipment of He-Man Ultra-ZX workout machines was defective. The carriage bolts keep snapping off the weights—twenty-seven customers have already been pinned in their homes. One guy's larynx was crushed; he's taking soup through an IV."

"Sounds like someone's trying to screw me!"

"Sir, we're maiming both our employees and our customers. Our legal department can't keep up with the suits. Something needs to be done."

"You're right," Dempsey finally conceded. "Increase our contributions for tort reform."

He turned to Marlon. "Everyone wants something for nothing! Remember that."

As Marlon grew into a young man, Dempsey Conrad began introducing him to all the right people. First, there were the neighbors in their fortified neighborhood. On Dempsey's block alone lived four CEOs who needed bodyguards whenever they went outside. They had made their fortunes by firing as many people as possible: Chainsaw Charlie, Buzzsaw Bill, Hatchetman Henry and Mort the Table Lathe.

Buzzsaw Bill called to Dempsey over the hedge. Dempsey smiled and waved in return.

"Gotta hand it to you for beating back labor here," said Bill. "Stock's up thirty points. I've never seen a place where it's so easy to cut people loose and hire part-time replacements on a full-time basis."

"That's why we call it a Right-to-Work State," said Dempsey. They nodded solemnly and then broke up laughing. It was a good laugh, and Buzzsaw had to wipe the tears from his eyes. "Now, if we can just get rid of that MLK Day nonsense."

There was a disturbance at the next house. Chainsaw Charlie was berating the contractor building his addition. He demanded that a newly installed toilet be replaced because one of the painters had peed in it.

Charlie saw Bill and Dempsey, and he yelled over to them, "Next thing you know they'll want a drink from the faucet instead of the garden hose!"

Dempsey gave him a what-are-ya-gonna-do? shrug. "They won't be happy until they screw us out of everything!"

Marlon began accompanying his father on golf junkets, where he was introduced to lobbyist Perry Belvedere and future governor Horace Birch as they plotted with Dempsey to consolidate power and dominate the state.

They were on the seventh tee at the Breakers in Palm Beach. Dempsey addressed his ball, then looked up at Marlon. "Golf is the lubricant of power! Never forget that."

Dempsey topped his drive and it rolled to the ladies' tee.

"You play like a homo!" chided Belvedere.

"That's not what your mother said last night!" countered Dempsey.

They got in their electric carts and silently rolled up the course. "Every president has played golf. Ike, Nixon, even Slick Willy," said Dempsey. "Why?"

"It's the lubricant of power?" ventured Marlon.

"Exactly!" Dempsey stepped out of the cart on the ladies' tee. He took a four wood and skulled the ball again, sending it another worm-killing thirty yards.

"Golf is also a great window into a person's character. Friend or adversary, doesn't matter," said Dempsey, picking up one of the large pink spiked balls marking the ladies' tee and firing it off the side of Belvedere's golf cart as it drove past. "A person's true nature comes out."

By the time Marlon graduated from college, he had been introduced to everyone who mattered in the state of Florida.

Except one.

They were waiting until Marlon was absolutely ready.

"You keep telling me about this guy, so why can't I meet him?" asked Marlon.

"Believe me," said Dempsey, "you'll meet him soon enough."

Marlon was unimpressed. "What kind of a goofy name is *Helmut* anyway?"

3

HELMUT VON ZEPPELIN made his money the old-fashioned way. He fucked people.

Helmut always had his eye out for cheap land, which meant natural habitat. Before the last brick was mortared into Cinderella's Castle, von Zeppelin had bought up everything he could on all sides of Orlando. Then he started buying up politicians.

Von Zeppelin worked with deliberate speed. First the bulldozers. Ancient Indian burial ground? Whoops! Endangered species? Damn, didn't even see the little buggers! Then came the pavement, stud framework, cheap hip roofs, biologically engineered sod, and, finally, trusting families with high-interest loans from Zeppelin Mortgage, which were backed by Zeppelin Insurance and closed at Zeppelin Title. It was a contained-loop ecosystem. Helmut percolated every last drop from his fellowman, and he was better at it than anyone else because he knew a weakness stronger than sex.

No money down!

Helmut loved the rules and laws of society. They slowed his competition. In every regulation, Helmut saw a tiny margin to be made. A bit less drainage than required, shorter nails, thinner beams, paint that would peel a year earlier, roofs that blew away at just three miles per hour less than code. A little here, a little there, and before long Helmut was a happening guy.

At every city, county and state meeting, von Zeppelin demanded tougher regulations. He knew laws were only as good as the inclination to enforce them, and Helmut torpedoed any remaining will through broadside circumnavigation of campaign finance laws. Soft money, in-kind contributions, bundling, and—most influential of all—delivering cash from others. Helmut was the rainmaker's rainmaker. He strong-armed business brethren for a thousand dollars a plate or they'd never work again in five counties, and he brought together the worlds of politics and industry for mixers at his mansion that were like gigantic Tupperware parties for assholes.

So much money was flowing through von Zeppelin to the political parties that it shifted the paradigm. Instead of Helmut trying to gain access to politicians, they fought to get close to *him*. When party officials had a budding young candidate, they brought him in to kiss Helmut's ring. Von Zeppelin's financial imprimatur could lock up an election. More important, funding your opponent would ruin you. Nobody had ever, ever crossed von Zeppelin.

After three decades of better business, the landscape of central Florida, from Polk County clear to the Atlantic, was embossed with von Zeppelin's HO-gauge vision. The whole region moon-pocked with developments named Buena Bay, Bay Harbor, Harbor Islands, Island Vista, Vista Palms, Palm Ridge, Ridgedale, Daleville, Villa West, Westwood, Wood Lakes, Lake Shores, Shore Acres and Mayberry-by-the-Sea. Tight grids of flooding, chipping, falling-down homes slipping inexorably into Dante's circle of lower-middle-classdom, each community erected by a separate corporate entity that was promptly bankrupt after the last house was sold, a series of *jus civile* firewalls that made it harder for customers to sue Zeppelin than to travel back in time.

Now were the golden years—time for Helmut to relax and watch his empire's neoplastic growth and enjoy the good life in his dream palace. It was a fabulous residence. But Helmut hadn't built it. Shoot, he had no idea how to build a house. He brought in the most skilled artisans and the finest raw materials from Europe. And he watched them like a hawk because he suspected the builders of trying to cut corners and cheat him. People were like that.

The results were breathtaking. A courtly Tudor Revival manse with a working vineyard, meditation garden and Italian statues of Italians. The compound was the site of von Zeppelin's unyielding daily routine. Each morning Helmut would awaken at dawn in the Athenian Room, where he was served crumpets before being dressed by his valet in the Carthaginian Room. He preferred light French suits because he thought they flattered his tall but unremarkable frame. He inspected himself in the mirror, the shaved dome, the lines of sixty years in his face, the bushy gray mustache. The valet handed Helmut his monocle. Helmut had perfect eyesight, but he wore the monocle because he wanted to evoke the robber baron days. After dressing, he spent the morning in the dark-paneled Constantinople Room, consummating phone deals. At the stroke of noon, the maid served a cucumber sandwich in the Caligula Library. She stood by until he finished, then poured a half inch of Courvoisier Erté Edition I into an antique snifter. He would dismiss her and take the cognac into his favorite space in the house, the Rockefeller Room, where he sipped and talked to the life-size painting of John D. and sometimes got a wistful tear appreciating the hanging sepiatones of coolie laborers driving railroad spikes. At sunset, Helmut strolled through the meditation garden with his hands clasped behind his back, reflecting on his accomplishments. He stopped to sniff a lilac. He was nearing the rarefied peak of Mount Bastard. When Helmut walked by, even the other most vicious corporate bastards said, "Now *that's* a bastard!" There was only one more level above him, and von Zeppelin was determined to reach it.

Sport team owner.

4

IN LATE 2000, two years before the next gubernatorial election, newsrooms across Florida began buzzing. There was word a major sports story would break at noon out of Orlando.

A hundred sportswriters in sartorial squalor waited anxiously outside the locked doors of a conference room at the Hyatt.

Inside, the staff completed preparations, plugging in microphones and adjusting the temperature of the warming trays at the complimentary buffet along the back wall.

Rumors were rampant outside the doors. The story was expected to lead all newspapers and broadcasts. The stench of competition coming off the sportswriting corps was thick, everyone checking the time, ready to make their move. Stations prepared to go live at noon.

At one minute before noon, an aide neatly stacked press kits on a table just inside the entrance. Then she opened the doors. The sportswriters stampeded past the table and gang-banged the taco bar in the back of the room. The live broadcasts cut to commercials.

Twenty minutes later, the hot bar looked like an Amtrak derailment, and the last sportswriter straggled to his seat. It was quiet. Someone burped.

NFL Commissioner Pete Petrocelli stepped up to the podium, smiled and shuffled papers.

"The National Football League is proud to award the latest expansion team to Orlando."

The room was electrified.

"It is my pleasure to introduce the team's owner, Helmut von Zeppelin."

Petrocelli stepped back and clapped as Helmut got up from his chair and walked to the mike.

"I guarantee I will bring a championship to Florida in three years!"

The sportswriters scribbled furiously. One raised a hand; Helmut pointed.

"How can you make such a brash prediction?"

"Son," said Helmut, "when you die, they're going to put one of two things on your tombstone: 'Dud' or 'Stud.' "

More scribbling. Another hand went up.

"Does the team have a name yet?"

"The Florida Felons."

"Where and when will they play?"

"In a new state-of-the-art stadium, to be constructed in time for the 2002 season."

"Team colors?"

"Orange and green," said Helmut. "All this is in your press kits. . . ." He looked around and saw none of them had press kits, then noticed the untouched stack by the door.

Another hand.

"What's with the monocle?"

Helmut pushed out his chest and grabbed his lapels. They were obviously responding to his bold sophistication.

Another reporter: "It makes you look like Colonel Klink."

"You little—!"

Helmut was around the podium in a flash, but he was restrained by the NFL security assigned to all press conferences since the Bears coach went berserk last season and beat a writer unconscious with the metal lid of a warming tray.

Commissioner Petrocelli grabbed the mike.

"Any more questions?"

All hands went up.

"Great. Thanks for coming," and the NFL rushed Helmut out to a waiting limo.

* * *

Despite his inauspicious start, Helmut von Zeppelin became an instant hit inside the National Football League.

At the owners meeting the following month in Honolulu, everyone sat at a giant Lemon Pledged conference table. Commissioner Petrocelli was about to call the meeting to order. He saw von Zeppelin wave a hand.

"Yes, Helmut?"

"Can we have a lockout?"

"Why?" asked a puzzled Petrocelli. "We're in complete agreement with the players' union."

"Ah, come on," said Helmut. "Just for fun!"

The room roared.

Unfortunately, things were not going as smoothly back in Orlando. The politicians were having trouble finding a location for the new stadium. They'd also been unable to persuade the citizens that a stadium construction tax to enrich Helmut was in their best interest. They met behind closed doors.

"What's the snag? I pay you well!" complained Helmut.

"It's the word *tax*," said the chairman of the County Commission. "It's gotten a bad name. It's those damn liberals."

Helmut shook his head. "And now *I* have to suffer."

"Maybe if we call it something else," said the chairman, "something more palatable—something they actually want . . ."

They brainstormed.

"A 'prize' . . ."

"A 'bonus' . . ."

"A 'rebate' . . ."

"A 'blow job' . . ."

"Wait! I got it!" said the chairman. "How about 'Community Reinvestment Fee'?"

"That issue's settled," said Helmut. "Now talk to me about location."

"Nothing's working," said a councilman. "Everyone's heard about the stadium and jacked up the price on all available land."

"Isn't there a law against that kind of unfair business practice?"

They looked at each other and shook their heads no.

"Then make one!" said Helmut. "In the meantime, who knows the solution to our problem? Anyone?"

The youngest member of the council raised an unsure hand in back. "Uh . . . knock down a bunch of poor people's houses?"

"Ding, ding, ding!" said Helmut. "We have a winner!"

THE stadium went up in record time. It was a gleaming American testimony to all things big. Prior to leveling a dozen blocks of homes, von Zeppelin held community and church meetings, promising the neighborhood that it would share in the prosperity.

It happened just like he said. Residents around the stadium started charging five bucks for fans to park in their front yards. And tiny, withering restaurants and taverns around the stadium sprang back to life.

Von Zeppelin was outraged. Someone else was making money. He sicced business regulators on the residents for operating parking concessions without a license, and he threatened restaurants and bars with infringement suits for televising games "without the express written consent of the National Football League."

Business around the stadium dried up. Helmut was happy again. He initiated the highest season-ticket prices in the league with massive five-year deposits that grew in his interest-bearing accounts. Was there anything he was forgetting?

Oh yes, and he wanted love.

Before the first game, Helmut had walked onto the field with his biggest Cheshire grin, waving to the cheering crowd with twin victory/peace signs like he was taking off from the White House lawn.

Marching bands played. Lasers flickered. Doves were released. A man in a personal jetpack flew around the inside of the stadium. Out ran the Felonettes, the giant-breasted cheerleading squad, who fanned out along the sidelines and began jumping rope.

The Felons charged out of the tunnel from their locker room, and the fans went wild. The team showed how tough it was by running through a big piece of paper. Then they ran through dry-ice fog. The fog diminished visibility, and the man in the jetpack lost his horizon and plowed into the "Up with People" singers.

The extravaganza took an intermission to play the football game.

The Felons' defense held the Pittsburgh Steelers to just five eighty-yard touchdowns in the first half.

The Felons were losing forty-two to nothing in the third quarter when the first object struck the glass of von Zeppelin's skybox.

"What was that?" Helmut asked his personal assistant.

"Might have been a pass, given our quarterback's accuracy."

Something else hit the window.

"Okay, that was no pass!" said Helmut.

The dregs of a warm beer slimed down the outside of the glass.

Then a hot dog bounced off the window, but the sauerkraut stuck. Followed by a glob of cheese nachos. A triangle of pepperoni pizza. A tampon.

"Where's all that stuff coming from?" said Helmut, walking to the floor-to-ceiling window for a better view of the seats below. His assistant followed.

"I think they're throwing it on purpose, sir."

"On purpose? I don't understand."

"I would guess they're upset with you."

"But they *love* me. They told me before the game."

"That was before we were losing—what is it now?—forty-nine to nothing."

"That's how shallow these people are?"

The assistant nodded his head sadly. "Afraid so."

"That's pretty heartless."

Thwack, thwack. A snowcone. Sushi.

"Do you love them?" asked the assistant.

"Of course not. They're bourgeois."

Helmut and his assistant were facing each other, silhouetted against the giant window that was now completely obscured. Sunlight filtered through the mustard and ketchup, and the owner's booth was bathed in a warm, dim crepuscular glow.

They stood silent for a moment. The tempered glass muted the hollering of the crowd into a faint white noise. They began to hear soft sirens from emergency vehicles.

"You know, sir, it's actually kind of pretty. This part up here . . ."—the assistant got on his toes and indicated with a circular motion of his palm—". . . Jackson Pollock."

"I was thinking a Monet sunset over water," said Helmut, pointing to the left side.

An out-of-breath police officer opened the door to the skybox, letting in a thunder of crowd noise. People were running back and forth in the background behind the cop.

"Keep this door locked and don't open it until I come back!" The officer slammed the door shut, and the room was soundproofed again.

A rotten head of lettuce hit the window, then a giant one-pound meatball of raw hamburger.

"We don't serve that stuff," said Helmut.

"They must be ransacking the VIP kitchen now."

"Oh," said Helmut, nodding. He looked around. "It's really sort of peaceful. I could get some thinking done in here."

"Yes, sir. Very soothing."

"What's happening now?"

"I think they're trying to land your private helicopter and get you out of here, sir."

"Are we in danger?"

"Yes, sir. It looks that way."

"I see," said Helmut. He looked around the room again. "This points up a design flaw. Every owner's booth should have an escape system."

"Wouldn't that be expensive?"

"What do I care? I won't be paying for it. . . . Take a note: Bring up ejection pod at next commission meeting."

Something hit the window and burst into flames upon impact, and the condiments ignited in a blue-and-yellow flambé.

"I don't think the commission will go for it," said the assistant.

"What can they do? I'll threaten to move the team."

"Gotta hand it to you, sir."

Helmut tapped the side of his head with an index finger, indicating one smart cookie.

The door to the owner's skybox opened again and the roar came in. It was the police officer. "It's time, sir."

Helmut and his assistant walked past the officer, who was staring curiously at the burning window.

"All that food . . ." Helmut said as he left the room. "I'm hungry."

"Arby's has a big parking lot," said the assistant. "We can land the bird."

"Are they the ones with curly fries?"

"I think so."

"We're there."

The police officer closed the door behind them.

5

JACKIE MONROEVILLE HITCHHIKED into Tallahassee with a tattered backpack and a dream of being the First Lady of Florida.

Twenty-four years old, she came equipped with a high school diploma, waitress experience and thermonuclear ambition. She had the coy, freckled face and disarming eyes of Sissy Spacek, and her secret weapon was the best shampoo money could buy.

Jackie scoped out the terrain of power, window-shopping downtown restaurants at lunch for the men with the best suits. A half block from the Capitol, her gut told her she had the right place, and she asked for an employment application. Within a week, she was the best waitress at the Quorum Grille. Fast, accurate, dishing pie with a balanced amount of flirtation. On average, her ass was grabbed three times a day, her breasts double-entendred seven. It only made her more confident. The stupider they were, the easier it would be to make it in this town. At night in her garage apartment, she went through the business cards the men had tucked in her waitress apron, segregating the ones who just wanted to get in her pants from the ones who wanted to peddle her sex appeal for commercial advantage.

After two months, she bought a snappy red business suit, selected the five most promising business cards, and examined herself in her full-length mirror. Already five-eleven, she decided against the heels and kicked them off. She practiced tough facial expressions. "You are a tiger!" She did a spinning kung-fu kick with a "Heeee-*yaaaaah!*"

She addressed herself in the mirror one last time. "Go out there and *kill!*"

Three hours later, Jackie was looking at herself in the mirror again, having just landed a nontyping secretarial position at the lobbying firm of Periwinkle Belvedere. She pointed at her reflection with authority. "You are the fucking master of time, space and dimension!" Then into jogging shorts and out the door.

Jackie was a mutt, a scrappy little piece of white trash from a cruddy redneck toadstool town in the Florida panhandle. Half trailers, half broken-down cabins, the whole neighborhood stank of complacent failure and diseases that had been wiped out elsewhere. Jackie's girlfriends could plan on getting jailed, pregnant, shot or raped by a relative before twenty-one, and Jackie had no special talent or intelligence that would exclude her. Just a pile of grit. She cursed and she spat. She hustled through her shift at the cotton mill and went jogging three miles every evening, then came home and read *People* and dreamed. She had no real education. She only knew she wanted up. And that the spitting would have to go.

The polished manners of her lunchtime customers, their business suits, the professional talk—all freakishly exotic to Jackie. What she did was study people. She didn't know how to describe success, but she knew what it looked like when it walked in the diner. Jackie watched to see what they did differently. She went to the Tallahassee airport and flipped through the magazines the executive women put down. That's how she picked out her business suit. She followed one of the women into the airport's hair salon, buttonholing the stylist after the woman left—"Give me what you gave her"—paying a week of waitressing tips. On her breaks, she sat in a booth at the Quorum Grille, pretending to read, instead listening to conversations and writing down words. At night she practiced for hours—the poise, the grooming, the vocabulary—trying to lose her textile twang. She found it couldn't have been more slow and difficult if she had been raised by wolves. But Jackie's self-training was relentless: a draconian, do-it-yourself *My Fair Lady* intervention.

Jackie showed up her first day at the lobbying firm and was told by Periwinkle himself to go home. All her job required was attendance at Perry's dinners and parties. She had just learned she was decoration.

It opened up all kinds of hours during the day to hang around the Capitol and read tossed-aside newspapers. She collected the citizen's guides to good government from the "free" racks. She studied the mug shots and kept a notebook of names and titles.

In the middle of the 2000 legislative session, Jackie arrived for her first party at the Belvedere compound in the slinky, strapless black dress provided by the firm. She stood with six other attractive women in dazzling evening wear. At first Jackie thought she was outclassed. The women were obvious blue bloods. Had to be debutantes from the old Tallahassee families. No visible tattoos or needle tracks. She kept her mouth shut and smiled politely. But after listening to them giggle for a half hour, Jackie thought, What is their fucking problem!

She inched away from the women, toward the punch bowl, not watching where she was going, and bumped into someone at the end of the buffet table.

"I'm so sorry," she said, concentrating on syntax. "I beg your pardon."

The other person didn't answer. Jackie recognized him from the newspapers. It was the speaker of the house, Gomer Tatum, and he wasn't answering because he was turning purple. He reeled down the buffet, one hand at his throat and the other pulling trays of hors d'oeuvres off the table. Jackie caught him from behind at the lobster bisque. She got her arms around him and a fist up under his rib cage. She constricted her arms and thrust. Once, twice—*c'mon, you cow!*—three times, forcefully expelling a partially digested pig-in-a-blanket into an oil portrait of Horatio Belvedere III.

Jackie received a light round of applause.

"Whew!" said Tatum. "Another close one!"

Jackie did some quick brain-retrieval from the better government guides. Speaker of the house. Let's see. Third in line to be president. No, that's federal. But it's gotta be something close like that on the state level.

She checked his left hand. No ring. "You have a girlfriend?"

Tatum looked behind him to see whom she was talking to.

"I'm talking to you!"

They started dating regularly, going to all the finest restaurants where lobbyists kept running tabs.

"You ever think of running for governor?"

"Me?"

Jackie realized the first thing that would have to go was the extra pounds. He was unelectable in his present buffoon weight class.

Jackie decided to fuck him into shape.

It was a steep but noble sacrifice, which Jackie could only accomplish with the lights off and the room one hundred percent dark. Then she climbed on top and gave him the most vigorous, aerobic screwing ever experienced in an industrialized nation. She got into a precise rhythm designed to boost his cardiovascular system and burn cholesterol. The whole time she motivated herself by mentally projecting the governor's mansion inside her frontal lobe and repeating under her breath, "I'm gonna be First Lady. I'm gonna be First Lady. I'm gonna be First Lady. . . ."

After ten minutes she began hearing a wet smacking sound that she couldn't place at first. She slowed her rhythm, listening carefully until she experienced the first tremors of dread.

"Are you—? . . . Are you *eating a sandwich?*"

She heard a loud, esophageal gulp. "Wanna bite?"

"Oh! Jesus!" She leaped off him and jumped in the shower and scrubbed obsessively with an abrasive sponge and hydrogen peroxide.

IN the fall of 2001, Gomer Tatum, much like Marlon Conrad, had no idea he'd be in next year's governor's race.

But unlike Conrad, Tatum hadn't for a second been mistaken for gubernatorial timber. Since becoming speaker of the house, his biggest accomplishment was keeping ice cubes stocked in his office wet bar, which had to be camouflaged by a twenty-volume set of *Reader's Digest* condensed editions ever since the permissive lunchtime drinking of the go-go 1980s had resulted in numerous afternoons of unintelligible legislation and sprained ankles.

Speaker of the Florida House of Representatives was the perfect job for ice-cube detail, just as long as his staff kept back-dooring special-interest bills through the rules and calendar committees, onto the floor and into the governor's hands. Great pay and benefits, no qualifications required except a highly elastic sense of situational ethics. It was kind of like being maître d' at the most exclusive restaurant in the state, or, in Tatum's case, the guy with the cologne and paper towels at the urinal.

The speakership was an extremely powerful and important position, so it was awarded based on whose turn it was.

Actually it hadn't been Tatum's turn this time, but the person ahead of him in the line was, well . . . black. The Democratic leadership giggled. Yeah, we know we've always gone in order, but get real!

Since then, Tatum had retained the speakership for two reasons. One, he could be bought. Two, he went cheap. Tatum became tremendously popular with the swarm of lobbyists who worked the Capitol like bees, tending and preening Tatum, the bloated queen at the center of the hive. The only ambition Tatum possessed was to stay clear of political entanglements that might jeopardize his state pension or leisure time on the job.

When the governor's race began shaping up, Tatum had placed the safe bet and thrown his support behind the Democratic front-runner, state Attorney General Casey Underworth.

A week later, Underworth was found confused on the side of the Apalachee Parkway after a single-vehicle accident, pouring champagne in the radiator. Wearing half a tuxedo. The wrong half. An underage female in the passenger seat. Withdrew from the race for "health reasons."

The mantle then fell on house majority whip J. J. Weathervane, who a month later said he had no idea why a local building contractor broke into his house while he was on vacation and installed a new roof. Gone to federal camp for the summer.

Next up: Secretary of State Betty Luckett, whose last official act was earmarking state funds to imprint her name in a variety of vibrant colors on a whole catalog of bottle openers, key chains, golf tees, mousepads, stress balls and fake vomit. Indicted for aggravated dumbness.

And on it went . . . way down the line of succession . . . House Transportation subcommittee on fuel efficiency chairman in absentia Nick "Boom Boom" Ribbentrop, heart attack in private booth at the Gentlemen's 25-cent Executive Cinema . . .

Conspicuously passed over in the attrition was Tatum, who sweated bullets every time the party looked around for a new candidate, and who sighed in relief each time someone else was tapped.

But after Ribbentrop keeled over, the Democratic executive board finally relented, against its better judgment. Okay, okay, we'll try Tatum. Where is he?

Tatum thought he had it made in the shade. He'd just restocked his wet bar and was now wobbling blissfully though the state cafeteria in the Capitol basement.

Tatum was quite a sight in the cafeteria. A breed apart, he would eat anything, limp salad, pudding crust, like something out of a prison movie, or Belushi in *Animal House*, starting to chow down before he reached the cash register.

"Tatum!" yelled the state Democratic Party's executive chairman, Coco Robespierre, walking up behind the speaker as he pushed a heaping styrene tray along the metal rails.

Tatum was caught in the act, a large dumpling halfway in his mouth. He tried to cram the rest inside, but his cheeks were already at maximum tire pressure. He desperately poked at the clump of food with puffy little fingers. He tried to close his mouth, but it wouldn't shut all the way, and his lips tightened like a gasket around the doughy protuberance.

"Mmmmmm?!" asked Tatum, turning to the chairman and pointing at his own chest.

"Never mind," Robespierre said and walked away.

THE Democratic Party instead went with former Insurance Commissioner Wolfgang LaGuardia.

His candidacy was announced during a prestigious cookout/fundraiser at the home of a Leon County circuit judge. The elite of the Democratic power structure were out on the judge's screened-in pool patio. The press was invited because they were needed; Wolfgang's name recognition was expected to debut in single digits.

Tatum was there with his date, Jackie Monroeville, who by now was totally brazen. She had introduced herself to everyone, knew the language, the secret paths of power. She grabbed a drink and sidled up to the party chairman.

"Coco, I don't see how you could pick LaGuardia when Tatum was available. If this was the federal government, he'd be third in line!"

"What are ya doin' with that shlub?" said Robespierre. "Want to join me for a cup of coffee after this thing?"

"Only if you back Gomer for the nomination."

"Suit yourself," said Coco, smiling and waving at a donor across the patio.

An hour later, LaGuardia decided he would show the host how a future governor operates a gas grill. But something went wrong in his ratcheting of the fuel line—possibly the four Johnnie Walkers he had before making the adjustments—and when the lid exploded off the grill, it made one hole going up through the screen roof over the patio and another when it came back down and landed in the pool. The music was turned off, and there was a full ten minutes of stifling awkwardness until the judge, partial to gin himself, considered the two holes in his screen roof and said, "Fuck it! Let's have some fun!"

The music came back on, and voices rose again in merriment. The judge's wife wheeled out an old charcoal grill from the garage, and they kept LaGuardia away from it. Soon the fire was glowing at the perfect pitch, and the grill was covered with steaks, shish kebobs and baked potatoes in aluminum foil.

"Soup's on!" yelled the judge's wife. LaGuardia ended up first in line, a few more scotches under his belt, and he was having trouble gauging the earth's gravitational field. When he reached for something to steady his balance, his hand found the handle on the grill. But the grill had wheels, and it rolled into the pool.

Coco Robespierre saw it happening in slow motion and wanted to scream, but nothing would come out. The grill hit the water like a political atomic bomb. The coals went in with a loud sizzle and sent up a mushroom cloud of steam. Ash filled the air Vesuvius-style and spread out in a thin film across the pool's surface. The metallic potatoes sank, but the filet mignon floated like turds.

"Don't worry—nothin' I can't fix," said LaGuardia, on his knees at the edge of the pool, reaching for the steaks with a long-handled skimming net.

Jackie Monroeville saw the horror on Coco's face, and she realized it was now or never. Coco was standing at one end of the pool and Jackie at the other. In between was LaGuardia, kneeling and fully extended with the skimmer. The TV crews turned on their lights and zoomed tight on the candidate. Jackie sauntered along the edge of the pool toward Coco. As she passed LaGuardia, she gave him a discreet knee in the butt, and into the pool he went. The TV crews fought for position. When Jackie got to Coco, his face was in his hands.

"*Now* will you back my Gomer?"

THERE HAD TO be a first political crucible for Marlon Conrad, and it came in the summer of 2001, when Governor Horace Birch asked him to handle the dismantling of affirmative action.

It was a delicate matter the party had been trying to slip through for years. Marlon stepped up to the plate and authored the Everything's-Fine-and-Dandy-Florida plan, which was ghostwritten by his chief of staff, Gottfried Escrow, and concluded that everyone was now, for lack of a better term, white. Marlon unveiled it in time for the evening newscast.

The next morning, Marlon played video tail gunner while Escrow read aloud from his clipboard, delivering the routine roundup of the state's overnight gunfire.

". . . We had a double shooting in Fort Myers . . . a triple shooting in Bradenton . . . a quadruple shooting in Pompano . . . another quadruple in Miami, but the NRA is pressuring us to call it a pair of doubles . . ."

The phone rang. Escrow answered.

"I see . . . I see . . . thank you." He hung up.

"What was that?" asked Marlon, clicking off fifty-caliber bursts with the joystick.

"Sir, we have a little public relations problem. Customs has Babs in custody at the airport. She failed to declare five thousand dollars in rare Belgian puppets."

"Unbelievable!" said Marlon, spinning around in his chair.

"What's with the fucking puppets? I'm starting to think there's something seriously wrong with that woman!"

Meanwhile, a large contingent of African-American lawmakers, activists and students had begun assembling in the lieutenant governor's anteroom for a sit-in. Shortly before noon, an unsuspecting Marlon got up from his desk to head out for lunch. Unfortunately, network cameras were rolling when Marlon opened his office door, bugged out his eyes and yelled, "Ahh! Black people!" Then took a quick backstep and slammed the door.

He ran over to Escrow. "What'll we do?"

Escrow said he wanted a look. He ever so carefully cracked the door and peeked out, and he saw a lobby full of people staring back at him. He slowly closed the door.

"If we stay real quiet, maybe they'll go away."

It went on like that most of the afternoon, every hour or so the lieutenant governor's door opening a tiny slit and Marlon and Escrow peeking out, one head on top of the other, then the door closing silently. The protesters exchanged puzzled glances.

Near the end of the afternoon, Press Secretary Jack Pimento came bopping carefree through the lobby, whistling "Me and Julio down by the Schoolyard." He waded through the middle of the sit-in—"What's up, guys?"—and resumed whistling as he walked in Marlon's office.

Marlon and Escrow stared at Pimento in shock.

"How'd you get in here?"

Pimento looked confused and jerked a thumb over his shoulder. "The door."

"But . . . aren't the protesters still out there?"

"Yeah, why?" said Pimento.

"They didn't attack?" said Escrow. "They just let you through?"

"What's going on?" said Pimento. "You guys are acting weird."

They sat Pimento down and told him what was going on, and Pimento started cracking up.

"Just call 'em in here and talk," he said.

"We can't do that!" said Marlon.

"Why not?"

"We're scared," said Escrow.

Pimento walked over to the door and opened it.

"What are you doing?" shouted Marlon.

Pimento called out to two lawmakers he recognized. "Could you come in here a second?"

The legislators entered to find Marlon and Escrow standing rigid and alert against the back wall. They looked at Pimento as they warily took seats. "Everything okay in here?"

Pimento nodded. He turned to Marlon. "Tell 'em your side."

"Well, it's like this," Marlon began in a stiff cadence. "I don't think affirmative action is fair. All those state contracts arbitrarily set aside. Doesn't seem right."

"What would you like to do with the contracts instead?" asked a lawmaker.

"Give 'em out based on merit, to people who have actually done something to deserve it."

"Like what?"

"Well, like helping me and my family," said Marlon, sitting down and loosening up. "Some of these people have given us so much. Pointed us to good investments, offered us low-interest loans and campaign contributions . . ."

The lawmakers stared.

"You see what I'm saying?" asked Marlon. "You can't just go around your whole life asking for handouts . . ."

". . . Something for nothing," said Escrow.

". . . The free lunch," said Marlon. "You've got to do something first to *earn* it. These people who know my family—they've already put up. What am I supposed to do? Tell them, 'Sorry, I have to give your contracts to someone we've never even met'? It's just not fair. It's not fair to them, and it's not fair to me. Now, is that what you want me to do? Be unfair?"

The lawmakers were dumbstruck.

Marlon smiled. "I didn't think so."

He came around the desk and shook their hands, and Escrow ushered them out of the office and closed the door.

"They sure are pushy," said Marlon.

"No kidding," replied Escrow.

Pimento stared at them with the same look as the lawmakers. "How exactly did you get to be like this?"

"Hard work," said Escrow.

"Strong values," said Marlon.

•

CHIEF of Staff Gottfried Escrow and Press Secretary Jack Pimento hated each other's guts.

It was philosophical, it was professional, it was personal. Always trying to one-up each other and become Marlon's favorite, constantly contradicting and interrupting. Marlon once caught them in the break room slap-fighting like four-year-olds.

"Knock it off!"

Marlon asked his father for advice on which one to fire.

"No, no, no!" said Dempsey Conrad. "In palace politics you always want to cultivate a little constructive factionalism. Prevents coups, keeps your power base solidified."

Gottfried Escrow loved politics.

He had been chairman of the College Republicans at Florida State. During the presidential race in '84, he and his buddies showed up before a Democratic rally wearing Mondale buttons and volunteering for the decorating committee. The campaign was delighted. Escrow's gang gathered up all the posters and banners and even the tape and staplers and ran off and threw them in a ditch, then snickered. He thought it was a perfect micro-illustration of why the Democrats were no good for America.

Escrow was a trim five-ten. He had the baby face, short-sleeve dress shirt and disturbingly beady eyes of a door-to-door missionary, and he still viewed the world exactly as he did when he was fourteen, sitting at the dinner table listening to his father. "Watch out for the unions and the commies!"

Escrow began each morning by selecting one of a dozen starched white shirts evenly spaced in his closet on wooden hangers. He had his dark hair neatly trimmed for thirty dollars every Friday.

His chief of staff's office next to the lieutenant governor's suite was immaculate and well appointed. He buffed his oak desk every morning until it was a mirror. Machiavelli sat on the bookshelf. In stately frames along the north wall was his gallery of role models. Lee Atwater, Jesse Helms, Rush Limbaugh and Ken Starr. Behind his desk hung a poster titled *Loyalty*, with G. Gordon Liddy's hand over a candle. In an age that teemed with paranoid conspiracy buffs, Escrow was privately disappointed that he had never been asked to *join* a conspiracy.

Pimento's office was a cyclone wake, a tiny windowless room with papers everywhere and *Rolling Stone* magazines concealing lost halves of sandwiches.

Escrow stood in Pimento's doorway, unamused. "Clean this shit up. It's a disgrace!"

"You're not the boss of me."

"Actually, I am," said the chief of staff.

Pimento went about straightening his office. He had an old stereo, and he put on his cleaning music, "All Along the Watchtower," both Bob's and Jimi's versions. Pimento was six feet and thin, with a military haircut and flecks of gray on the sides. His rapidly blinking eyes were ice blue. Pimento was the dreamer—the Lennon to Escrow's spit-polished McCartney. He was a Rockefeller Republican who believed the interests of the lower class were tied to a properly regulated pro-business climate. That and more wrestling on cable.

Marlon always thought there was an invisible devil and angel sitting on his shoulders. He didn't realize it was Escrow and Pimento who were fighting for his soul.

The pair gave Marlon their own briefings every afternoon, and they always fought over who would go first.

After lunch on a Thursday, the two headed for Marlon's office from opposite sides of the rotunda. When they saw each other, they walked faster until they were trotting, then sprinting. They wedged shoulder to shoulder in the office doorway, struggled briefly, and broke free.

"I'm first!"

"I'm first!"

Marlon slapped his desk. "Don't make me come over there!"

"He went first yesterday!"

"It's Pimento's turn," said Marlon.

"But—"

"It's settled!"

Escrow grumbled as he trudged across the carpet and dropped into the sofa.

"What do you have?" asked Marlon.

"Electric chair. Press conference in an hour," said Pimento. "There's been a lot of bad publicity with all the mishaps. I thought I'd prepare a full report so you'd be ready for the questions. . . . And you know what? It's fascinating! I went way back into the science and law, the whole history in Florida—"

"Right, right," said Marlon, spinning a hand impatiently, *get on with it.*

"Okay," said Pimento. "Along the way, I found an interesting case. The guy's set for execution in a few months. You might want to ask the governor to take a closer look—"

"If they arrested him, he must be guilty," said Marlon.

"Do we have to listen to this?" said Escrow.

"Shhhh!" Marlon snapped at Gottfried, then turned back to Pimento. "Pick up the pace."

"Right," said Pimento, rubbing his palms together, looking at the ceiling, going over everything he wanted to say. "Okay, this is gonna be good! You ready?"

Both of them: "Yes!"

"Okay . . ."

7

ELECTRICITY HAD QUITE a year in 1887.

Thomas Edison and George Westinghouse waged a fierce battle over who would dominate the revolutionary new utility. Edison had DC—direct current—and Westinghouse had AC—alternating current—and they were playing hardball.

On a cool morning in February, Edison traveled to the town of West Orange, New Jersey. A crowd gathered in the square as Edison and his assistants placed a large iron plate on the ground and wired it to a thousand-volt AC generator. Onlookers pushed and shoved for better views. Edison's team placed twenty-nine dogs and cats on the metal plate. They turned on the juice.

Most in the crowd were sickened by what happened next, but a few liked it.

Edison's message: "See? AC current is dangerous!"

Across the Hudson River, lawmakers in New York State took a different view of the demonstration: "Hey, we have some *people* we'd like to do that to."

William Kemmler fried August 6, 1890, in Auburn, New York.

The electric chair was born.

•

AT the end of the nineteenth century, electrocution was in demand because the technology was so advanced. At the beginning of the twenty-first, it was in even higher demand because it was so primitive. For many, lethal injection just wasn't quite as—how would you put it?—*satisfying.* . . . Then there was the sentimentality. Over the years, the chairs in various states had acquired their own quaint nicknames: Old Sparky, Yellow Mama, the Indiana Shit-Boiler.

In 1972, the United States Supreme Court voted five to four in the case of *Furman v. Georgia* to halt executions because they were cruel and unusual. When the court changed its mind in 1976, it was as if Prohibition had been repealed. Gary Gilmore was the first to go, shot by a Utah firing squad. But he had requested to be killed—no fun in that. The country wanted someone dragging his heels a bit.

Enter punk and general screwup John Spenkelink, who stuck up a bunch of gas stations in California, escaped from prison, and stumbled haplessly across the country to Florida, right into the path of an oncoming political freight train.

Spenkelink was a skinny twenty-three-year-old in 1973 when he hooked up with a much bigger and more hardened forty-five-year-old career criminal named Joe Szymankiewicz. On February 3, Joe was shot dead in a Tallahassee motel room. He'd also been hit in the head with a hatchet. At trial, Spenkelink testified that Joe had beaten and sexually assaulted him at gunpoint.

John was poor and didn't get a good defense. Guilty: first-degree murder. Sentence: death.

Legal experts raised their eyebrows. It might well have been first-degree murder. On the other hand, given Szymankiewicz's violent record and the criminal lifestyles of people like John and Joe, the exact circumstances were not ascertainable. Not to the degree of certainty that you kill someone. A death sentence just didn't pass the smell test. With better counsel it was probably second-degree murder or manslaughter, maybe even innocent by self-defense.

John appealed. Timing was everything.

When Spenkelink's case came up, he was in line to be the first person in the United States involuntarily put to death since the Supreme Court decision. His picture appeared on the cover of *The New York Times Magazine,* with the headline THE NEXT MAN TO BE EXECUTED? The political cost to spare Spenkelink was rising. The train had left the station.

During appeals, his attorneys argued capital punishment was cruel and unusual. John couldn't believe his ears. They were using his case to attack the Supreme Court ruling. *The whole country wants the death penalty—you're gonna get me killed! Don't attack the Supreme Court—attack Szymankiewicz! He was raping and beating me!*

On the night of May 25, 1979, a Friday, they shaved John down. He couldn't stop shaking. The warden took pity and slipped him some whiskey.

John's last words: "Capital punishment: Them without the capital get the punishment."

During the Republican gubernatorial primary in 1994, one candidate bragged in a TV ad that as attorney general he had helped kill Spenkelink. Even fifteen years later, it was still good for a few votes.

●

FLORIDA'S electric chair was getting some serious wear and tear. Built in 1923, the furniture portion—the sturdy three-legged oak seat— was replaced in 1998. The electric apparatus was not.

The chair is located at Starke, in the speed-trap no-man's-land between Gainesville and Jacksonville. It costs $55.14 a day to house a condemned inmate; their cells are six feet by nine. An anonymous executioner is paid a hundred and fifty bucks.

When the legislature reinstated the chair prior to the 2002 election, the Department of Corrections immediately experienced a rash of what the official spokesman termed "minor incidents."

Gerald Samuel "The Grim Reaper" Morgenstern, serial killer of prostitutes. Last meal: Delmonico steak, baked potato with sour cream and chives, French bread, Caesar salad, half gallon of mint chocolate ice cream, two liters of Dr Pepper. For his last statement Morgenstern read a rambling seven-page condemnation of the U.S. judicial system until even his spiritual adviser began glancing at his watch. He concluded: "I'd rather be fishing." Then he seized up and the hood over his head caught fire.

Thomas "Crazy Tom" "Squirrelly Tom" Vogel, while on PCP,

broke into a private residence and disemboweled a woman in her third trimester. Barbecue beef ribs, corn on the cob, baked beans, chilled peanut butter M&Ms, lemonade. Looking around at the people strapping him in, Tom said, "I think I've seriously fucked up." He bolted straight in the chair and blood spurted out his chest.

Meredith "The Black Widow" Fricatolla poisoned four men with swimming pool chemicals. Fried shrimp, fried catfish, french fries, two fried eggs, onion rings and a diet Mr. Pibb. "I got nothing to say . . . Wait! I just rememb—" She went into spasms before what prison personnel described as "a midair static-electric discharge from the base of the seat to the foundation." The morning radio shock-jocks were more concise: "Lightning shot out her ass!"

The next case was the most interesting yet, even though the prisoner didn't die.

Electrocution opponents have long contested the state's position that death is quick and painless. They counter that because the human brain operates on tiny electrical impulses, the current from an electric chair throws normal perceptions of reality out the window. An execution that takes a second, they contend, could seem like days inside a short-circuited brain. But there was no way to prove or disprove the theory. Until Billy Joe Fahrenheit came along.

A moment after the switch was thrown and a thousand volts began dancing in the folds of Billy Joe's cerebrum, he found himself flying through the air at incredible speed, circling the earth. The sky strobed orange, green and pink each second, and his body became elastic and nine hundred miles long, stretching all the way across Portugal and part of Spain. It was actually quite pleasant. He dove into the Atlantic Ocean, his body disintegrating upon impact with the water, and he became billions of microscopic twinkling mites that swam in a school toward the bottom of the sea. Suddenly the mites re-formed and broke the surface of the water and he was flying again, this time his body made up entirely from a single element, beryllium, and Billy Joe was thinking, Can ya beat this crazy shit?

It went on that way for the longest time until Billy Joe didn't feel so good anymore. Then he started feeling extremely *bad*. Everything went dark and he began to hurt like hell all over. He heard someone yell: "He's still alive!" and the hood was pulled off his head.

Billy Joe gave extensive media interviews until he was put back in the chair the following month and dispatched on an equally interesting journey, but with a different ending.

●

PIMENTO suspended his presentation on capital punishment when he saw Marlon and Escrow starting to doze.

"Hey! You awake?"

"Absolutely!"

"Good. You don't want to miss this next part."

Pimento told Marlon he had checked the legal dockets. The next two prisoners up for execution were clearly guilty, but Marlon might want to take a closer look at lucky contestant number three, who was convicted in a case out of the Florida Keys.

●

THE Miami Dolphins had just kicked off to the New England Patriots in a blizzard in Foxboro, Massachusetts. The phone rang in the kitchen of football fan Anita Braintree of Boston. It was December 1989.

Anita's eyes stayed on the TV as she picked up the receiver. On the other end, she heard another TV tuned to the Patriots, giving her the game in stereo. She also heard rowdy drunks and a faint jet engine. She was expecting a call from her husband, but instead it was her husband's annoying business partner, Frank Lloyd Sirocco, and he sounded a little trashed.

He said he was in a sports bar across the highway from the airport. She heard a loud bang over the phone.

"What was that?"

"Toy musket," said Sirocco. Intoxicated people marched around him dressed like Ben Franklin, Thomas Paine and Nathan Hale. The

Patriots intercepted, and Mrs. Braintree heard cheering over the phone.

"My flight's snowed in," said Sirocco. "They're closing the runways at Logan—"

"Is that a flute?"

"Fife and bugle," said Sirocco. "I can't get through to George in the Keys. When he calls, can you tell him it looks like our scuba trip is off?"

"Ooooooooo," said Anita.

"Ooooooooo," said Sirocco. The Patriots had fumbled.

George had taken a flight out of Logan the night before, ahead of the front. A blizzard now raged in Massachusetts, and Mrs. Braintree threw another log on the fire. She settled in for the second quarter, planning to phone George at halftime and pass on his partner's message.

When Anita called down to the A1A Dive Center on Cudjoe Key, the caretaker was watching the Patriots and Dolphins on a portable TV on the screened porch, sweating and swatting mosquitoes under a plantation fan. He grabbed the registration book.

"Let's see, George Braintree. He's in cabin number . . . hold on a sec . . ."—they stopped to watch the Dolphins kick a field goal— ". . . cabin number five." He rang the cottage and waited. "I'm not getting an answer."

Two hours later—and precisely ten seconds after the Dolphins beat the Patriots seventeen to fourteen—Anita dialed the 305 area code again. This time she asked the caretaker to personally check on George.

When the caretaker opened cabin five, the TV was on the postgame show. George Braintree's suitcase was opened neatly on a chair, his scuba gear stacked against the wall, his red rental Taurus parked by the pool. Even a recently popped beer on the nightstand. The caretaker called Anita back and said everything looked normal. He must be at the convenience store or the pub.

He didn't tell her about the wallet he had found on top of the TV, or the twenty he took.

Anita turned off the TV. It wasn't like George not to call. On the other hand, he had been known to drown his sorrows after more than one Patriots loss. When Anita couldn't reach George on Monday, she called the Monroe County Sheriff's Office.

The deputies got the vibe the moment they stepped in cabin number five. Absolutely nothing out of order—no sign of struggle or robbery. It was all wrong. The wallet and the blaring TV. The can of beer on the dresser, warm and full.

A week later, nothing. A month, still nothing.

Anita demanded answers from the sheriff's office. She just couldn't accept it. She had driven George to the airport herself and kissed him good-bye, and he had gone to Florida wearing a loud shirt and disappeared into hot air.

MRS. Braintree was the primary suspect, mainly because she was half her husband's age—the trophy wife. They had no children, and she stood to get everything. But the detectives' audit of the Braintrees' finances revealed George was worth more to Anita alive. He was underinsured and top-heavy with debt. She would have to sell the house.

The police swung their glare to George's partner, Frank Lloyd Sirocco, who was now the sole proprietor of their business. Frank said that on the day George disappeared, he was watching a Patriots game in a Boston bar, fifteen hundred miles away. Dozens of people saw him.

Who were they?

He wasn't sure; they were dressed like Minutemen.

What set off bells with the detectives was the seven life insurance policies on George. A small one had named Anita as beneficiary, but six named Frank.

What did Sirocco have to say for himself?

"Standard business practice," said Frank. He showed them the books. The policies totaled half the company's value on paper. Partners regularly did that so if one of them died, the survivor wouldn't have to dissolve the company to pay off heirs. He showed them the buy-sell contract.

But why six different policies?

"George had a bad ticker," said Frank. "He had to purchase a bunch of small policies that didn't require physicals."

The cops let Frank go, but kept an eye on him.

Frank immediately started dating George's widow. She moved in a month later, and they married the following June.

If there's one thing cops hate, it's someone getting away with murder and yukking it up in the process. Frank and Anita weren't even trying to hide it. New cars, trips, parties, even rumors Anita was coming down with a nasty drug habit.

The police kept checking, turning up threads of information that meant little individually but together began to weave a compelling circumstantial case. Shortly before George's disappearance, Frank Lloyd Sirocco had reported his gun stolen. He made large cash withdrawals. On the weekend in question, there were three calls to Florida from the pay phone around the corner from Frank's home. They checked the log of money orders at the nearest convenience store—several large ones coincided with Frank's withdrawals. But there were no names on the log and the security tapes had been erased.

The police knew they had their man. They decided to bluff. Frank was confronted. He didn't ask for a lawyer, but he also refused a lie detector. "I saw something on *60 Minutes* about how they're unreliable."

"You took up with the widow awfully fast."

"Had to," said Frank. "Some of the life policies were screwed up. No collateral assignment. She still owned thirty-one percent of the company—was going to sell to her brother. You know what an *idiot* he is?"

They took the file to the DA. The prosecutor said he was convinced Frank was their man. But that was entirely different from winning a case, and he refused to take it to the grand jury. The police argued they had more evidence on Frank than against half the murder suspects who got indicted.

The prosecutor shook his head. "Without a body, you need twice as much."

It was all there, he said—almost. Bring him one piece of physical evidence tying Sirocco to the crime. Or a body.

"Fat chance," said the head detective. "If anyone's not going to leave a trace, it'll be someone in his line of work."

Frank and George owned Clean Sweep, Inc. "Crime scene restoration, biohazardous abatement and remediation, 24 hours, discreet." They marketed to banks and other financial institutions, and—between disgruntled workers and suicides—it was more business than they could handle. Their clients didn't care how much it cost, just make it go away, and Frank and George made a fortune scraping hair and bone off the walls of executive suites with million-dollar views. Their logo was a chalk outline.

A year quickly passed.

January was a busy month for the Monroe County Sheriff's Office. More specifically its marine patrol. From Ley Largo to Key West, thirty-seven separate incidents of tourists with no nautical experience renting boats with enough horsepower to change the weather. Add: unmarked channels, no depth charts, and Bacardi, and a lot of visitors were returning to the rental offices soaking wet without boats.

A twenty-foot twin-engine Wellcraft was found in the middle of Big Spanish Key. They estimated it was planing at fifty when it sheared through a hundred feet of immature mangrove. As deputies winched the boat back, they discovered it had plowed away the sand and muck of a shallow grave. Forensics determined the two holes in the back of the skull were from a .38, but crabs had eaten the fingerprints.

A week later and forty miles up the Keys, an unemployed marijuana addict was living off a diet of illegal seafood. He was diving in fifteen feet of water under the Long Key Viaduct when he found two lobsters sharing a coral hole with a .38 Special. The diver was in great spirits as he loaded a cooler full of crustaceans into his '75 Honda Civic. He had enough food for a week and a gun that would bring at least forty bucks. He decided to celebrate by firing up a fat one right where he was parked on the side of the causeway, which was where the police awoke him six hours later with a knock on the driver's window.

The discoveries of the gun and body remained unconnected until the monthly cold-case call from Boston.

Bam. Dental records ID'd the body, and the FBI matched ballistics with the slugs in George's head. They raised a serial number off the gun where someone had tried to burn it off with acid. Registered in Massachusetts to one Frank Lloyd Sirocco.

IN the wake of George's disappearance, Frank had turned over the active management of Clean Sweep to underlings and was now trying to manufacture glory days as coach of a local peewee football team.

It was a Friday-night game. Frank grabbed a pair of linesmen, a face mask in each hand. "You're playing like pussies! I want you to take out that quarterback. After he releases the next pass, one of you grab him and stand him up and the other roll into his knees!"

Two cops showed up.

"Frank Lloyd Sirocco?"

"Yes?"

"You're under arrest for the murder of George Braintree."

He was led away in handcuffs as a quarterback in first grade was stretchered off the field.

Frank was extradited to Florida and found guilty in a three-day trial in Key West. It took the jury four hours to come back with a recommendation of death, based upon the aggravating circumstance that Frank had been a real dick on the witness stand.

Frank Lloyd Sirocco—the newspapers always used his middle name—would spend the next decade in a cell at Union Correctional Institution in Raiford, thirty miles southwest of Jacksonville. He became close friends with the vampire killer, the werewolf killer, and the Angel of Death, but Ted Bundy didn't want anything to do with him, calling Frank "creepy."

Six months before the 2002 gubernatorial debates got under way, Frank was transferred to Florida State Prison at Starke. It was not a good sign. Most of Death Row was at Raiford, but the front of the line resided at Starke, with the electric chair. Frank wore orange T-shirts, distinguishing the condemned, and got an hour a day for exercise. Otherwise he was kept in his cell.

The worst part: no air-conditioning.

8

PIMENTO BEAMED PROUDLY as he concluded his report on capital punishment and the Sirocco case.

"Well? What did ya think?"

Marlon's and Escrow's heads had fallen back over the tops of their chairs, and their mouths were open, snoring.

"You weren't even listening!"

"Sure we were," said Marlon, waking up quickly. "Every word."

"I can go over it again if you want."

Marlon and Escrow: "No!"

Escrow looked at his watch and jumped up. "Yikes! We have to prep for the press conference!"

Marlon didn't care. He turned on his computer fishing game and called over his shoulder to Pimento, "Phone Belvedere's firm. Get Elizabeth Sinclair on the line."

"What for?" asked Pimento.

"Wouldn't you like to know."

Pimento grabbed a phone on the other side of the office and began dialing.

"Sir, the press conference," said Escrow. "You're being hammered for all these crony favors—"

"Then stop making appointments! *You're* the one who keeps sending them in to see me. What am I supposed to do? Be rude?"

"I'm not pointing fingers," said Escrow. "We just have to rehearse for some hard questions."

Pimento pressed touch-tone buttons. ". . . *Welcome to Belvedere and Associates. Please press one, all others press two. Choose from the following selections. If you know your party's extension, enter it now. If you do not know your party's extension, press three....* " Pimento pressed three. *"... Welcome to the directory. Please spell the last name of the party you wish to speak to, using the corresponding alphanumeric buttons on your touch-tone phone."* Pimento punched in S-i-n-c-l-a-i-r. *"We're sorry, your selection is invalid. To enter a valid selection, press nine-four. To enter an invalid selection, press four-nine. ... If you would like assistance, press seven...."* He pressed seven. *"You have pressed seven. If this is correct, press five. If this is not correct, press eight. Your current wait is now estimated at two minutes. Calls will be handled in the order in which they have been received. Please do not hang up and redial, as this will delay the handling of your call. To delay the handling of your call, press four-three, all others press star-five. Rotary callers, please hang up. Your current wait is now estimated at four minutes...."*

"Sir, the press conference!" said Escrow.

"Shit!" said Marlon. A tarpon stuck out its tongue. Marlon turned off the fishing game and surfed to a porn site. "Don't bunch up your pants, Escrow. Just pack the place again with my staff. Works every time."

"You'll be flying solo," said Escrow. "They've all gone on some junket."

"With *this* budget deficit?"

"Don't worry. No tax money is involved. It's all being paid for by the people they regulate."

"Good," said Marlon. "Wouldn't want to get raked over the coals for that, too."

Pimento pressed buttons. *"... Your current wait is now estimated at six minutes. Please have your account number ready. Enter your selection now, all others press star-nine. To hear your options again, press pound-two. To return to the previous menu, press star-eleven...."* Pimento pressed more buttons. *"... Hello, this is the voice mail of George Defazio. I'm away from my desk right now...."*

Pimento held the phone away from his face and gave it a weird look. "Who the hell is George Defazio?" He hung up and redialed.

"*Welcome to Belvedere and Associates. Please press one . . .*" Pimento pressed buttons. "*. . . You have entered an invalid selection. Please select again. If you would like to speak to a representative, press the pound key. . . . We're sorry, all representatives are busy at this time. If this is an emergency and you require immediate assistance, press star-one. . . .*" Finally, thought Pimento, pressing star-one. "*Hello, this is the voice mail of George Defazio. . . .*"

Pimento gritted his teeth as he hung up and redialed. "*Welcome to Belvedere and Associates. Please press one . . .*"

"Sir, these favors—" said Escrow.

"Shhhh! You're making me mess up." Marlon typed in sex chat with someone named Mindy.

"Sir, perhaps if you didn't spend so much time playing video fish—"

"I'm not fishing. I'm at Catholic Schoolgirls in Bondage."

Pimento pressed more buttons. "*. . . Your current wait is now estimated at eight minutes. You have not entered a valid selection. Enter your selection now. If you would like to hear this menu again, press star-pound. If you would like to press star, press star. Your current wait is now estimated at eleven minutes. Thank you for calling Belvedere and Associates. Good-bye.*" (click)

"They're gonna have us for lunch," said Escrow. "These press guys—you don't know 'em like I do."

"You worry too much. I'll just—"

There was a loud crash. Marlon and Escrow turned to see a broken desk phone sticking halfway out a fresh hole in the drywall. Pimento stood next to it with a red face and heaving chest.

"Sorry," he said. "I'll pay for that."

"If you want something done right . . ." Marlon grabbed his own phone. He dialed a private number to Belvedere's firm. "Elizabeth Sinclair, please."

There was a pause as the receptionist connected Marlon. He gave Escrow a knowing wink.

"This is Elizabeth Sinclair."

"Liz, Marlon. Why don't we meet at Clyde's after work and talk some business."

"What kind of business?"

"You know, *business* business."

"Thank you, but I'll have to pass."

"Your loss."

"Maybe next time."

Marlon replaced the receiver. "Frigid!"

"Sir, we're running out of time," said Escrow, tapping his watch. "You're overconfident."

"Chill," said Marlon, picking up the joystick. "I'll just say I'm a friend of business and the workingman. If that doesn't work, I'll accuse them of being against free enterprise."

"You've got free enterprise confused with capitalism," said Pimento. Marlon and Escrow turned.

"The *last* thing capitalists want is free enterprise. McDonald's and Burger King are mortal enemies, but there's one thing that'll unite them like lost brothers—a Taco Bell going up on the block. They'll do anything to keep 'em down in the fast-food ghetto."

Pimento began pacing and waving his arms.

"Capitalists don't want free trade any more than they want whooping cough. Their nature is to conglomerate, homogenate, vertically integrate and dominate until there *is* no competition. The rules? Screw the rules! They'll rig the game, spit on the ball, bribe the refs, tilt the playing field, pork the cheerleaders and kick free enterprise in the nuts."

"That's it!" said Marlon. "Random drug test!"

"But—"

"Go!" Marlon pointed at the door. "Piss! Now!"

Pimento slinked out of the office.

●

ESCROW knocked on Marlon's open door. He held a personnel file gingerly like a Dead Sea scroll.

"What now!" said Marlon, clicking "hit me" on Internet black-jack from the Cayman Islands.

"Sir, I think you need to see this . . . it's the results of Pimento's drug test."

"The what?"

"The one you ordered, remember?"

"Oh, right, sure," said Marlon. "So what's he on? Psilocybin? Angel dust?"

"No, nothing illegal. But they found traces of lithium and Elavil. To get those, you have to be under psychiatric care. He's a head case."

"We already knew that," said Marlon.

"Sir, I don't think it's prudent to have someone of questionable stability so close to the seat of power."

"*You're* the one who hired him."

Escrow recoiled. Marlon was right. If there was a psychiatric hand grenade in Pimento's past and it went off in the media, the trail would lead back to Escrow. He had to handle this delicately, get Marlon to dismiss Pimento on ostensible grounds.

"Sir, I don't think you're taking this seriously enough."

"What's in his file?"

"Just the usual—no red flags," Escrow lied. He clutched Pimento's personnel file to his chest. The file was empty except for the drug test—another Escrow oversight and another excellent reason he didn't want this drawing any attention.

Jack Pimento had begun his government career six months earlier in the mailroom without the required background check—a security breach that slipped through the cracks because of a government office laboring under the crushing hardships of overstaffing, nepotism and banker's hours.

Pimento slipped into the public affairs office a month later in the scramble to fill a spate of openings created by the discovery of rampant functional illiteracy among speechwriters. The camel's straw was Marlon's last TV appearance, when he looked as perplexed as the audience after reading "the electrical college" off the Tele-PrompTer.

As chief of staff, Escrow got called on the carpet good for that one. He was ordered to purge public affairs. In desperation, Escrow looked around and saw Pimento eating a peanut butter cup at the watercooler, and he gave him a shot at a one-paragraph press release. When that came out unmangled, Pimento got longer releases to write, then a speech, then he pinch-hit for the governor's State of the State Address. Everything that came off Pimento's fingertips was clean, terse and expositorily bulletproof. Marlon's handlers couldn't believe their luck, and in a perverse Tallahassee twist that had everyone crying foul, Pimento rapidly rose to the top of his department based on ability.

Escrow had signed off on the promotion himself without even looking at the paperwork. Now he rued the day.

"But sir," he said, standing at Marlon's desk. "I really think you should consider dismissal—"

"Nothin' doing," said Marlon, remembering his father's advice.

"Can we at least send him to a state shrink? Quietly, of course. Just to cover bases?"

Marlon swiveled his chair back to offshore baccarat. "If that's how you get your jollies."

ONE week later, a state psychiatrist paid an afternoon visit to Marlon and Escrow.

"I can't get into specifics because of patient confidentiality, but you have nothing to worry about with Mr. Pimento."

"You mean he's not dangerous?" asked Escrow. "Not even a teeny weeny bit?"

"Absolutely harmless."

"Thanks, Doc," said Marlon, and Escrow showed him out of the office.

Escrow shook the doctor's hand in the hall. "Say, about that patient confidentiality . . . c'mon, you can tell me."

"Afraid not," said the doctor. "It's a very serious oath. It's almost like religion."

Escrow handed him a hundred-dollar bill.

"He has amnesia," said the doctor.

"Amnesia!" repeated Escrow. He grabbed his forehead and fell back against the wall. "If this gets out, I'm finished! Who knows what kind of monster I have in there!"

"You got a pussycat—gentle as a kitten," said the doctor. "The odds are his memory will come back on its own anyway. I wouldn't worry."

Across town in a dingy apartment, Pimento rocked back and forth on the edge of his couch, watching a tape of *Taxi Driver* for the fourteenth time in as many days.

He got up and went in the bathroom and stared in the mirror. "Who are you?" He pounded on the mirror and it broke, blood trickling down the sides of his hands.

Pimento had drawn a blank for six months, but two weeks ago— the first day of the *Taxi Driver* film festival—he started getting flashbacks during the climactic shootout scene. Disturbing stuff. Phantasmagoria. Snippets of guns and gore, a chainsaw and severed fingers, and somewhere in the middle he was at the World Series. How did *that* fit? . . . Through it all, he still couldn't remember his name, which was Serge A. Storms, or that he had, you know, killed a bunch of people.

He came back in the room as *Taxi Driver* was ending and replaced the tape with *The Manchurian Candidate*.

9

THE SUN WAS setting in a primrose sky. Tiny mangrove humps in the Florida Keys appeared on the horizon as the South American airliner began its descent from forty thousand feet for the approach to Miami International.

The pilot and copilot were talking in Spanish about the defoliating blight that was Ricky Martin's career.

"Should have put a stop to Menudo when we had the chance—"

He was interrupted by a cockpit alarm, and they looked at the blinking amber button. "Flight attendant needs assistance."

When the copilot opened the door in the back of the cockpit, he saw what he'd been fearing. There—in the aisle between seats 27C and 27D—the man in the business suit with his necktie wrapped around his forehead like a kamikaze. Unsuccessfully trying to light a cigarette, stumbling and falling into other passengers, who shrank back in their seats with revulsion.

"How many has he had?" the copilot asked the flight attendant waiting outside the cabin door.

"Only three vodkas," she said. "Must have brought a bottle."

The man climbed on top of the beverage cart, which, because of the jet's descent, began rolling forward. It accelerated, slowly at first, but rapidly picked up speed until it veered into the back of seat 14C at fifteen miles per hour, scattering empty cans of Sprite and Mr. and Mrs. T's Bloody Mary Mix, and catapulting the businessman into the bulkhead separating first class from huddled mass.

The flight attendant cringed at the force of the impact. But the businessman soon made his way to his feet again like the Terminator. He staggered and slid his necktie back down to his collar.

"His muscles must have been all relaxed from the alcohol," said the flight attendant.

"What's his line?" asked the copilot.

"Commodities broker."

"Fits the profile."

The broker grabbed a lavender sunbonnet off a woman's head and put it on. Another flight attendant tried one last time to coax him back into a seat. He swatted her with the bonnet and shoved her to the floor. "Fuck you, too!" And he began weaving aft.

An anxious Brazilian dignitary in first class grabbed the copilot's arm. "What's going on?"

"Air rage," he said, starting to move down the aisle. "Routine. Nothing to worry about."

The broker made his way to the back of the plane and began yanking the handle on the door of what appeared to be an occupied lavatory. The door finally opened and the man went inside and slid the lock.

The copilot and flight attendant stood guard in the aisle a few rows away. "Hopefully, he'll stay in there till we land."

The pilot radioed ahead. Federal aviation agents were waiting on the runway.

"What's Ricky Martin got that I don't?" the copilot asked the flight attendant.

"You?" she said, giving him a quick up-and-down and laughing.

"Excuse me," said a passenger coming forward from the lavatories, wearing a red leather Miami Heat jacket, and the copilot and flight attendant parted to make room.

"Look," said the copilot, putting out his arms and thrusting his pelvis.

After landing, the passengers quickly deplaned. Some ran all the way to baggage. Bodyguards ushered the Brazilian dignitary into a waiting Mercedes. The federal agents boarded.

"He's still in there," said the flight attendant, pointing to the back of the plane, and agents in FAA windbreakers moved briskly down the aisle.

They opened the lavatory door.

* * *

An hour later, the agents milled in the aisle, drinking coffee and flirting with flight attendants. A disheveled man in a tweed coat walked toward them and flashed a badge.

"Mahoney, homicide."

"Mahoney, this is federal territory."

"Not while you're on *my* runway."

"Is this going to get ugly?"

"It already has." Mahoney produced a flask and offered it to the federal agent.

"That's against the rules."

Mahoney took a pull. "The rules are different here."

"That's what I heard."

"What else you hear?"

"Take the Cowboys and the points at home."

"Air rage?" asked Mahoney, pointing to the rear of the plane.

"Classic case."

They walked to the lavatory and the agent pushed the door open.

Mahoney stepped inside, bent down and lifted the sheet.

"We found him facedown in the metal toilet," said the federal agent. "Someone tied a travel alarm clock on the end of his necktie, stuck it in the hole and flushed."

"And the pressurized suction of the high-tech commode did the rest?"

The agent nodded grimly. "Must have been at least ninety pounds per square inch. Strangled him in short order. I had a hell of a time cutting him loose with my pocketknife."

Mahoney stood up and rubbed his chin. "My guess is he won't be using those frequent-flier miles."

"Take a look at this," said the agent. He bent down and lifted the victim's shirt.

"Somebody's a comedian," said Mahoney.

"My gut tells me it wasn't Lenny Bruce."

They stared back down at the words written in Magic Marker on the victim's chest.

FLY THE FRIENDLY SKIES.

10

MARLON CONRAD'S POLLS were out of sight.

Nobody had ever been as popular in Florida. He had matured as a politician, growing more handsome and charismatic all the while. It almost didn't seem fair. He wasn't just good-looking for a politician; he was good-looking for a movie star, and he had mastered the art of looking you straight in the eye with a hint of empathy, making you believe for that moment that you were the only person in the world who mattered. He soon earned the nickname "The Great Communicator," because of his unbelievably high approval rating among the people he was hurting.

The newspapers were another matter. They never bought Marlon's act. The editorials invoked Marie Antoinette and the fox guarding the henhouse. The papers' sting was swift, on-target and ignored. Not even a blip in the polls. If anything, Marlon's numbers were still going up.

It was going smooth. Too smooth. Just when Marlon's handlers were their most smug, a reporter's question came twirling into the camp like a German potato masher.

On a warm September evening just after sunset, Escrow and a bodyguard were standing outside a banquet hall overlooking Sarasota Bay near the Ringling Causeway. A peach-faced reporter fumbled with a large stack of Xeroxed public records and wouldn't make eye contact. "Uh, when did Mr. Conrad register with the Selective Service? I can't seem to find any record—" A bunch of the papers got away, blowing in a circle on the pavement, slipping over the seawall. The reporter ran around the parking lot, occasionally stomping on a document.

The bodyguard laughed and flicked a cigarette butt end over end into the bay, enjoying the looping orange tracer. Escrow called over to the reporter in a W. C. Fields voice: "We'll have to look into that one, kid," and they went back inside the banquet hall.

The next day the phone rang in Escrow's office. He listened impatiently. "We're still working on it. . . . I'll give you a ring."

He hung up. "That kid again!"

After ten days of persistent calls, Escrow was grumbling out loud. He slammed the phone. "Sick of this! . . . Can't take a hint! . . . Now I have to get up!"

A half hour later, Escrow stood in Marlon's doorway with a file. "Houston, we have a problem."

A corporate jet from Big Phosphate was dispatched to retrieve the three-headed hydra—Governor Birch, Periwinkle Belvedere and Dempsey Conrad—from a weekend spokesmodel summit in a houseboat off Naples. That night the lamps burned into the small hours at Belvedere's lobbying firm. Staff were summoned from home. The coffee kept coming.

"How could you *not* register?" yelled Dempsey.

"They don't have a draft anymore, do they?" asked Marlon.

"You still have to register! It's a federal crime!"

"I didn't see the point. If I got called up, we have a million ways to get me out of it."

Dempsey to Perry: "He's not getting it."

Birch: "They're gonna Quayle him!"

"Quayle me?" asked Marlon.

"You know the joke," said Birch. " 'Did you hear Stanley Kubrick made a movie about Dan Quayle's military service? It's called *Full Dinner Jacket.*' "

"Ouch."

"Look, we'll get the lawyers on it in the morning," said Belvedere. "Have him *nolo contendre*, pay a fine. Shit, he's too old now anyway."

"Of course he'll skate in court," said Birch. "What I'm worried about is the court of public opinion."

"Excuse me," said Elizabeth Sinclair. "I think I know the solution—"

"Oh, Elizabeth," said Perry. "Would you be a sweetie and get us some more coffee?"

Sinclair got up without reacting. As she poured Sanka in the next room, she wished she had the nerve to quit and start her own firm.

Back in the bunker, Dempsey snapped his fingers. "I got it—preemptive strike! Have him enlist in the reserves! Think of the publicity from his two weeks of active duty!"

"It'll be like GI Elvis!" said Perry. "By the time that wormy reporter prints his story, we'll have Robert Capa photos all over the place!"

Birch smiled. "You know, we might even come out ahead on this one."

You'd have thought war had broken out. The state's newspapers dutifully published photos of Marlon climbing an obstacle-course wall, belly-crawling under fake machine-gun fire, and sitting back in the barracks, writing letters to Babs on the home front. There were pictures of Babs, too, knitting, canning preserves, and staring out the bedroom window, surrounded by shelves of Belgian puppets, bravely awaiting her man's return from the hell that is Lakeland.

●

A week after Marlon completed his tour of duty, a limousine from Big Tire and Rubber picked him up on the runway at Orlando International Airport. Dempsey, Perry and Birch were already inside.

"I don't see what the big deal is with this guy," said Marlon.

"Don't get cocky," snipped Dempsey. "You were lucky on that military thing."

"But I don't even like football," said Marlon.

Dempsey grinned at the governor. "He doesn't like football." He turned back to Marlon. "Son, the three of us are all huge football fans, but today we don't give a jumping fuck who wins or loses. This is business."

"We think you're finally ready," said Birch. "We're taking you to the mountaintop."

"Helmut von Zeppelin can make or break your career," added Belvedere.

"But I thought you three guys had all the power in the state," said Marlon. "The notorious Birch-Belvedere-Conrad troika."

"Let's just say we like to stay on friendly terms."

The limo swung through a private gate at Big Auto Parts Stadium.

The four stood outside the private elevator leading up to the owner's booth. The doors opened.

Birch grabbed Marlon by the arm. "Whatever you do, don't say anything about the monocle."

They stepped in the elevator, and the doors closed.

"Hold on to your hat, son," said Dempsey. "You're about to make your first trip to the top of Mount Bastard."

●

"GOVERNOR! Damn fine of you to drop in," said Helmut, jumping up from a sofa in his skybox and striding confidently toward the group. He pumped Birch's hand like they do on the range. "And this must be The Kid!"

Helmut grabbed Marlon's hand. "I've heard great things about you! You've got an incredible future if you play your cards right. But what am I saying? Of course you will—you're a Conrad!"

They all laughed stoutly and then stopped.

"Bet you want a mint julep," Helmut said to Belvedere.

"Does a bear shit on the pope?"

"Got something new all of you should try."

Helmut walked over to an antique credenza and pressed a button. A hatch opened and a bar service ascended via hydraulics.

"That's some setup," said Dempsey.

"Only the best will do for our taxpayers," said Helmut. They laughed again and Helmut filled five glasses with a brownish-orange liquid. "Speaking of which, did you hear the property appraiser won't grant me an exemption for the stadium? Says he wants to tax it like any other business. I've never heard of such a thing! *Churches* don't have to pay . . ."

Birch turned to Periwinkle. "Destroy his career."

"Done."

"I expected no less," said Helmut, handing out drinks.

Birch held his glass to the light. "Looks good. What is it?"

"Venezuelan rum. Forty years old," said Helmut. He raised his own glass. "Death to the weak!"

"Hear, hear!"

They knocked the rum back all at once.

Marlon wasn't used to drinking straight, and he made a face.

"You're not going to puke, are you, kid?" Helmut slapped him on the back, sending a high-proof draft into Marlon's sinuses, and he had to excuse himself, prompting another bout of jocularity.

"I remember when I was comin' up," said Helmut. "Blew my guts hundreds of times." The others smiled in recollection and agreement. Yes, nothing better.

Birch sniffed his empty glass. "There's something extra special about this stuff I can't quite place."

"It's duty-free," said Helmut.

Birch nodded. "Should have known."

Marlon came out of the bathroom, and he and Dempsey sat on the couch. The others pulled up chairs and got down to business. Helmut brought the bottle of rum.

"Governor, I want to talk about the sales tax exemption for the stadium again. I've been hearing crazy talk of a move to repeal the provision. Don't think for a second I doubt you. But it's a pile of money, and I'm a count-hatched-chickens kinda guy."

"Well, I'm a bird-in-the-hand kinda guy, so that almost makes us kin." The laughs just wouldn't quit. More rum. "Look, you got nothing to worry about. It's arranged."

"I don't know . . ." said Helmut, scratching his noggin. "I already got the thirty million committed. *Seriously* committed. Guys from New Jersey."

"Helmut, here's your guarantee," said Birch, patting his chest. "As long as I'm breathing, it'll get done. And if something happens to me, there's always my lieutenant, Marlon here." Birch slapped Marlon's knee.

Helmut turned to him. "Can I count on you, son?"

"You can count on me, sir."

"Good, 'cause you don't know these Jersey guys. If it don't come through, I'm in a world o' hurt."

The afternoon wore on. More rum.

At the beginning of the third quarter, the Cowboys ran ninety yards from scrimmage, making it thirty-five to nothing. A submarine sandwich disintegrated on the window of the skybox.

On the ensuing kickoff, the Felons fumbled. A cheese steak smacked the glass, followed by soft drinks and a caramel apple with nuts that stuck like a rubber-tipped dart.

Helmut nodded at his assistant, who reached down to a console beside the couch and flipped a recessed switch, activating water jets and giant windshield wipers.

"Tough season?" asked Birch.

"You have no idea," said Helmut.

By the fourth quarter the Felons trailed by forty-five, the bottle from Venezuela was empty, and they were all gassed.

Marlon killed his drink. "Hey, Zepp, what's with the fuckin' monocle?"

Horrified silence.

Finally, Helmut reached over—"Come here, kid"—and punched Marlon in the shoulder. "I like you!"

"Ow," said Marlon, rubbing his arm.

The others exhaled in relief.

Some kind of incendiary device hit the window, setting the glass and wipers on fire, but Helmut's assistant had it out quickly with the water jets.

"I didn't know football was so exciting," said Dempsey.

"Oh, you can't just sit at home and watch it on TV," said Helmut. "It's a whole different game in person. . . . Who wants a ride in the ejection pod?"

11

THE TELEVISION WAS on porn in room 314 of the Sky Host Motel on Miami's Eighth Avenue.

"They always have the same cheesy *Starsky and Hutch* seventies music in the background of these films," said the guest reclining with the remote control.

"Know what you mean," said another, sitting on the bed next to him. "Whenever I hear it in an elevator, I get all romantic."

"Shut the hell up!" said a third man with a ponytail who looked like Willie Nelson. He sat in a rattan chair at the nightstand, thumbing through a roll of Greek currency. "I can't hear myself count!"

A jet roared overhead.

"Look!" said the man with the remote, pointing at the local TV news. He turned up the volume. "*. . . Police are on alert around the airport for the Willie Nelson Bandit . . .*"

"Goddammit! Now I gotta start over!"

"How much is a drachma worth, anyway?"

The ponytail lashed out with a large bowie knife, flicking his cheek.

"Jesus!" said the man with the remote, pressing a palm to his face, then holding it out to look at the blood. "That's gonna scar for sure!"

"It'll give you character—you won't look like such a twinkie." Back to counting: ". . . seven hundred, eight hundred . . ."

The man with the remote quietly slid his hand toward his waistband, going for a small pistol. When his hand was inches away, he reached quickly and drew. Something caught his eye. He glanced down and saw the snakeskin handle of the bowie knife sticking out his windpipe.

As he tumbled off the bed, the man sitting next to him snatched the remote from his lifeless hand. "Good! Now I get to watch what *I* want to."

"Not now," said the ponytail. He stood and picked up a sawed-off shotgun and pulled back the curtain; it was dark out. "We have to clock in at work."

A green Buick Century pulled up to the security shack at a rental car lot next to the airport, and the guard lowered the tire spikes and waved it through. The Buick turned onto Twenty-first Street. A rusted Pinto pulled out of the breakdown lane across the road and fell in behind the Buick.

Six blocks later, in a stretch of Miami that empties at sundown, the light turned red. The Buick stopped, but the Pinto didn't.

The rear-ender was five miles per hour.

"It was all my fault," said a man with a ponytail, getting out of the Pinto.

The driver of the rented Buick got out wearing a red leather Miami Heat jacket and walked back to inspect the damage.

●

A police corporal unrolled crime scene tape as red and blue lights flickered off the buildings six blocks from Miami International. Next to a Pinto were two lumpy white sheets.

A haggard man in a tweed jacket pushed his way through the crowd of onlookers and flashed a badge.

"What do we have here?" he asked the corporal.

"My gut tells me it's not the Hair Club for Men."

The tweed jacket took a pull from his flask.

"Should you be doing that?"

"We do things differently in Miami."

"That's what I hear."

"What else you hear?"

"Take Dallas and the points at home."

"I see."

"You got a name, Detective?"

"Yep."

"Wanna share it?"

"Mahoney."

"Mahoney, we just solved the Willie Nelson Bandit case."

"Dead?"

"He won't be singing 'To All the Girls I've Loved Before.' "

"I liked that song."

"Mahoney, this one bothers me."

"They all should."

"I have kids."

"Got pictures?"

The corporal flipped open his wallet.

Mahoney nodded. "You've been busy."

"I try."

"You mind?"

"Be my guest."

Mahoney lifted one of the sheets. The victim with the ponytail had his shirt ripped open, and something was written on his chest in Magic Marker.

Mahoney stared off in the distance. "I need to get my head away from this. Where's the action tonight?"

"North side."

"Wish me luck."

"Break a leg."

Mahoney pulled out his flask again as he walked away under the crime lights and a landing 747. The corporal looked back down at the ponytail's chest.

I'VE FALLEN AND I CAN'T GET UP.

SHORTLY after two in the morning, a crowd of slender, chic people jammed the sidewalk and spilled into fashionable Washington

Avenue on Miami Beach. They pressed against a blue velvet movie theater cordon keeping them back from the entrance of the hottest nightclub on the island, the Rash.

Inside the velvet cord, two bouncers stood with grave expressions, occasionally nodding that someone was properly chic and letting them in. The crowd beckoned for their attention like they were trying to catch a helicopter on an embassy roof.

The first bouncer was a stocky man with a tight fist of a body in a black double-breasted suit. Out the neck of his jacket popped a bald bronze head. His face was worn and etched, right off a buffalo nickel. Large feathered earrings brushed the shoulders of his jacket. He was the silent one. The talker was a tall, thin man in a ginger turtleneck with a blond mustache and wispy goatee, a fifth-generation Floridian who spoke with the contrived French accent of Pepe Le Pew.

Limos began arriving. Pepe unhooked the blue cord and ordered the crowd to part for the beautiful people, who gave Pepe air kisses. The *Enquirer* took photos. Rumors swept the crowd.

"Look! It's rocker badboy Tommy Lee! . . . And there's funnyman Jim Carrey!"

"It's talk diva Kathy Gifford! . . . There's controversial rapper Puff Daddy and gal pal Jennifer Lopez! . . . And isn't that the usually effervescent but sometimes enigmatic and dangerously thin Calista Flockhart?"

A Brazilian dignitary with diplomatic goon squad arrived and entered without notice.

It used to be a shoe store before Miami Beach heated up, and the interior looked the same as the day the moving vans drove off with the crates of Stride Rites, except the club had added a handful of sofas and love seats from the Salvation Army. There wasn't enough air-conditioning.

Red and purple beams of light rotated and danced across the faces in the humectant darkness, and the thumping music induced irregular heartbeats. The Brazilian dignitary grabbed a bourbon and a seat in a ratty La-Z-Boy. He gripped the wooden handle on the side and pulled it to lean back, but it broke off in his hand and the spring uncoiled inside the chair, dumping him over backward into a cinder-block wall. The lounger popped back upright without the dignitary. The bodyguards heard the noise and turned. They panicked when they saw the empty chair and pulled submachine guns. The dignitary jumped up from behind the chair with bourbon on his suit, and the bodyguards relaxed and put their guns away.

"Let's get out of here," said the dignitary. "I love America, but there's a lot I don't understand."

He did a quick head count of bodyguards. "Hey, where's Pedro? Ah, screw 'im. If he can't stand his post, he can find his own ride back."

The dignitary was Benito Juárez "Loco Benny" Pecadillo, head of the dreaded secret police known as Los Grosería Pasmados, literally the Rude, Dumbfounded Ones. Pecadillo had just been forced to flee to the United States after a group of kidnapped human rights workers escaped certain death when Pecadillo absentmindedly held a pair of metal clamps in his mouth, trying to crank-start the electric generator used to torture dissidents, and shocked himself unconscious. Amnesty International demanded action. The CIA, which had trained Pecadillo at the School of the Americas in Panama, feigned ignorance. "The Company" arranged through its usual clandestine network of ex-operatives in Miami to discreetly acquire a residential property and quietly put Pecadillo out to pasture.

A Miami police officer was investigating a rented Buick Century abandoned on the side of the MacArthur Causeway when a stretch limo blew by.

Inside the limo, Benito Pecadillo was stargazing. Benny had been expecting the old Miami Beach. Jackie Gleason, Sammy Davis, Jr., Meyer Lansky, Benny Goodman. He'd kept his face pressed to the limo's window ever since they left the Rash, hoping to recognize someone famous.

The limo turned off the causeway for an exclusive island in the middle of Biscayne Bay and soon pulled up the brick driveway of Pecadillo's new home. Benny and six bodyguards piled out of the backseat and into the mansion. There was a fantastic party going on behind the house next door, and Benny went out on his patio. He checked out the crowd over his hedge. Sly Stallone, Gloria Estefan, Madonna, Rosie O'Donnell.

"Damn," he said. "Not a single star."

The new digs were a two-story hacienda with lemon-yellow canvas awnings and twin rows of royal palms leading from the back door to the pool overlooking the bay and Miami Beach. Shortly after midnight, Benito relaxed in the hot tub next to the pool while an undocumented maid served him canapés and refilled his daiquiri. Patrolling the dark backyard were six bodyguards in sleek white Italian suits concealing black Uzis in shoulder holsters. The pool was lighted, and the cool blue ripples in the water projected tranquilizing waves of light on the palm trees and linen suits. Benito immediately felt at home.

Back at the Rash, a waif in a lime latex body tube went into the rest room to snort the newest designer drug, XGB5, which gave people the uncanny sensation of throwing money away while chewing their own lips off. It was hard to come by and everyone had to have it. She went to the last stall and opened it and screamed.

A half hour later, a Miami homicide detective in a tweed jacket barged through the crowd.

At the front door, Pepe Le Pew said he couldn't let the detective in without seeing some identification.

The detective reached out and plucked the ring from Pepe's pierced nostril.

"Ahhhhh!" Pepe screamed, grabbing his bloody nose and hitting the ground. "You're a fuckin' animal!"

"I see you recognize me now. Guess you won't need that ID after all." Mahoney walked into the Rash.

All the club's guests were being held for questioning. Mahoney moved through the middle of the crowd. An avant-garde Dutch movie director patted Mahoney's tweed sleeve. "Cool wardrobe! Shabby retro!"

Mahoney rabbit-punched the director between the eyes, and he went down. "Don't touch."

In the back of the club, a uniformed officer was guarding the rest room, and he stepped aside when Mahoney flashed his badge.

Mahoney lit a cigar stub with an old Zippo inscribed MABEL. "What do we got here?"

"Brazilian bodyguard," said the officer. "Diplomatic ID said his name was Pedro."

Mahoney glanced back at the growing confusion toward the front of the club and blew out smoke. "Didn't this use to be a shoe store?"

The officer guarding the rest room nodded yes.

Mahoney nodded, too. "Figures."

The officer didn't know what *figured.*

Mahoney nodded toward the rest-room door. "Magic Marker?"

The officer nodded again.

Mahoney frowned. "Doesn't add up."

The officer was confused.

Mahoney went inside, to the last stall, and looked down at the victim's chest.

WELCOME TO FLORIDA. NOW DIE!

Detective Mahoney finished the crime scene at the Rash just before dawn and ate ten-dollar eggs at a café two streets over on Ocean Drive. The manager tore up his check.

"Your money's no good here."

"Thanks, Louie." He took a pull from his hip flask as the sun rose out of the Atlantic.

"Go easy on the sauce," said Louie.

"Go easy on those filterless Camels," said Mahoney. "You sound like a whore gargling broken glass."

"Nice imagery."

"Not as pretty as the stiff over at the Rash."

"That bad?"

"Worse." Mahoney gazed across the street at a sunrise fashion shoot. "This is one sick city—"

Mahoney's beeper went off.

"And about to get sicker," said Louie.

Mahoney answered his beeper call at the hacienda-style mansion on Star Island. The place looked like a war zone. Seven white sheets covering bodies all over the compound. Neighbors said they never heard a thing. The evidence team was draining the hot tub and photographing the body of Benito Pecadillo, lying on its stomach.

"Okay, you can cut it off now," said the forensic photographer.

A detective with scissors snipped away the black plastic trash bag taped over Benito's head. When he got halfway done, the odor hit and knocked him back.

"Jesus! What *is* that?"

"I'd know that smell anywhere," said Mahoney, walking up from behind. "Model airplane glue."

Mahoney looked around and saw everyone staring at him.

"Oh, so crucify me for having hobbies!"

When they finished cutting the bag off, the pathologist rolled Benny onto his back, and they all saw it at the same time.

Magic Marker.

ASK ME ABOUT MY GRANDKIDS!

ESCROW stood in Marlon Conrad's office scanning the *Miami Herald*. He suddenly covered his mouth. "Oh no! Not this!"

"What is it?" asked Marlon.

"You know someone named Loco Benny?"

"Who?"

"Let this be a dream," said Escrow, tearing through the paper to the jump page. "Aaaahhh!" he screamed and dropped the paper.

Marlon spilled his coffee. "Now look what you made me do!"

Escrow pointed silently. The story's continuation covered the centerfold of the section, complete with a flow chart of information boxes and sets of mug shots that proved guilt beyond a doubt because they were grainy and out of focus.

"We're screwed!" said Escrow.

After the discovery of the body of Benito Juárez "Loco Benny" Pecadillo, the *Miami Herald* had investigated just how such a notorious human-rights violator could end up in a south Florida mansion at taxpayer expense with the blessing of the intelligence community.

The series of connecting boxes led from Loco Benny to a nearsighted Brazilian double agent who stooged for the CIA, code-named Salamander, to a gleaming ten-thousand-square-foot refrigerator outlet in Miramar run by an ex-spook who sold exactly two Frigidaires in the last fiscal year, to Periwinkle Belvedere, who had Todd Vanderbilt set up a dummy buyer through a Chapter 11'd Brickell real estate firm, which, in the mid-1990s, counted among its nominal directors a Marlon Conrad, current address: Tallahassee. Marlon's smiling campaign mug sat in the box at the very top of the pyramid.

The story was incredibly thorough and no one read it, although the *Herald* would win the state press association's first-place award for "Best Info Boxes with an Extremely Long Story."

"So what?" said Marlon. "That was perfectly legal."

The phone rang. Marlon answered.

"I'll kill you!" screamed Perry Belvedere.

"Take it easy," said Marlon. He could hear Babs in the background. She was doing that half-talking, half-crying thing: "He doesn't want to marry me! Wahhhhhhh!"

"You marry my daughter or so help me God I'll blow your brains out!"

Escrow was listening to the whole thing on the speakerphone. "Want me to call Capitol Security?"

Marlon held a hand up to Escrow and shook his head no, then leaned to the phone. "Mr. Belvedere, your daughter's confused. I would *never* think of calling off the wedding."

Marlon kept talking until Periwinkle relaxed. "Sorry. I guess I overreacted. I know how Babs can get."

"You're preachin' to the choir," said Marlon.

They said good-bye, and Marlon hung up and fell back in his chair. "What's with that family?"

"I don't know, sir," said Escrow.

"Did I tell you what she did in bed?"

Pimento ran into the room. "We've got a serious problem!"

"It's all relative," said Marlon.

"The president just activated your reserve unit!"

"Not Lakeland again."

"No," said Pimento. "The Balkans."

"What!"

"It's all over TV."

"The hell you say! I'm injured. My gout!" Marlon grabbed his left knee, then remembered and grabbed his right. "You filed my disability papers, didn't you?"

Pimento and Escrow stood silent and didn't blink.

"Please tell me you filed the papers."

Pimento and Escrow pointed at each other and said simultaneously: "*He* was supposed to do it!"

"Imbeciles!" Marlon picked up the phone and started dialing. "I'll fix this myself."

"Put the phone down."

They turned.

Standing in the doorway were Dempsey Conrad and Governor Birch. Perry Belvedere, the third leg of the tripod, would join them as soon as he defused Babs with some ice cream. They stepped inside and closed the door.

"Just got off the phone with the *Trib*. Papers already have it," said Birch. "This is a grand mal fuckup."

"You can't get me out of it?"

"Of course we can, you fool," said Dempsey, "but the political cost is unsurvivable. We're hammering some Democrats right now for dodging Vietnam. You're going with your unit."

"No way," said Marlon. "The food blows."

"We'll fly in whatever you want," said Birch. "Even arrange to keep you in the rear, at headquarters."

"What if people are mean to me?"

"You listen here, you little prick!" said Dempsey. "What's done is done! You're going! I've worked my whole life to get you where you are, and you're not going to blow it 'cause you're too much of a pansy to handle a little combat. Did I have that attitude back in the Big One? Was I scared? Fuck no!"

"You were in the steno pool, stateside," said Marlon.

"Why, you ungrateful—" Dempsey dove and tackled Marlon and they began rolling on the carpet, across the giant berber seal of the state of Florida. Escrow, Pimento and Birch tried to separate them, and one by one their arms got caught in the rolling bodies and they were sucked into the maw of state power.

Outside the office, secretaries heard the telltale sounds of a future insurance claim and came running. They saw the political blob roll one way and then the other. It slammed into a bookcase, and a row of autographed college footballs toppled from their tees and began bouncing off the men's backs. Dempsey came up with Marlon in a headlock, and he held him immobile while the others began figuring the timetable for Marlon's deployment.

Marlon looked out sideways from his father's armpit at the appointment calendar on his desk. He realized that if he went overseas, they would have to postpone his wedding to Babs.

"You've convinced me."

⬤

LONG before Marlon's C-130 troop transport left Florida soil, the Pentagon, despite the short notice, was able to put together a quagmire. By the time Marlon's plane landed in Albania, organizational chaos was epidemic.

There had been little action in Kosovo for a couple years, and even less on the horizon. But then came the refugees again. The Kosovars were afraid to return home and stayed massed at the fringes of the border countries. The Balkan allies applied pressure on the State Department, which responded by air-dropping leaflets featuring Serby, a cartoon Serb field mouse, and Alby, an ethnic-Albanian magic gnome, who embarked on a playful adventure traveling back home together through the enchanted forest. When cartoons failed, the United States tried to entertain Serbia with The Overwhelming Show of Military Force. The president deployed all available active and reserve troops not currently engaged in the fourteen other global hot spots, border clashes, ethnic cleansings and a parade at Euro Disney.

The president assured the American people not to worry—there would be no "action," not even any mopping up. The Serbian military hadn't made a peep in months. There would just be a bunch of marching around for the TV cameras to make the allies happy and get the refugees to their feet and moving in the right direction.

Marlon and thousands of other GIs had sat idle at the Albanian air base for two weeks. Nothing to do but write letters, chain-smoke and swap paperbacks. Then they had all of an hour's notice to hurry up and move out. The generals got the news over CNN during a live press conference at the White House, when the president said troops would be in the air in sixty minutes.

Nobody was ready. Pieces of units were strewn all over the place, but Washington was applying a full-court press. The brass decided that if they grouped the soldiers by state, the common bonds would promote esprit de corps and fighting will. Also, that's how everyone was rostered, and it was the only way to make deadline. Loudspeakers at the base crackled to life. The troops were ordered to muster in a large, empty aircraft hangar, where a giant map of the United States was being drawn on the floor in chalk. They were told to stand in their state.

As transport planes taxied up to the hangar, a different state was ordered onto each aircraft. At first they went alphabetically, but there was a lot of pushing and shoving, and a scuffle broke out when landlocked Colorado tried to muscle its way through the Midwest. So they went by who was closest to the door.

Back in Washington, the president deftly swatted questions like flies. He recognized the veteran correspondent for UPI, which hadn't existed for years but nobody had the heart to pull her credentials.

She stood and pointed at the president with her pen. "How many men do you expect to lose?"

The president leaned into the podium. "Our military is in such incredible fighting condition that I actually expect to *gain* men. . . . Next question! . . ."

Back in Albania, Marlon was incredulous. He ran up to a colonel with a clipboard. "But I'm supposed to stay in the rear. There has to be some kind of mistake. I'm the lieutenant governor of Florida!"

"Then stand over there," said the colonel, pointing at the chalk outline of the Sunshine State.

"But—"

"Now!"

Marlon shuffled over and stood on Lake Okeechobee.

"Hi, I'm Tex Jackson," said the man next to him, standing on Clewiston. Marlon reluctantly shook hands. He couldn't believe this was being allowed to happen to him.

The rest of the men subconsciously gravitated to their hometowns. Standing on respective parts of Florida were Lech Kluzinski, De Funiak Springs; Roosevelt Washington, Riviera Beach; Enrico Marconi, Arcadia; Dino Schwartz, Indiantown; Fulgencio Zapata, Homestead; François Bordeaux, Sebring; and Hank "Vinegar Bend" Fulbright, Inverness. Marlon looked around. Sheesh, he thought, small-town bumpkins.

The others had mutual contempt for Marlon. They knew it was a cosmic accident that he was seeing anything but light pencil duty. The exception was Tex Jackson. Jackson was nearing his fiftieth birthday and sergeant major stripes, and even the colonels secretly looked up to him. He was genial and protective of his men, and his quiet maturity could unite even the most diverse units.

Jackson was an even six feet and his physique a notch toward the weak side. His features were also a bit soft and deceptively vulnerable. He wasn't exactly the black Mr. Rogers, but it was close. What commanded respect was his judgment. Jackson's temper and patience were inexhaustible, except when tactical swiftness was required. Nobody who had served under him could ever recall a decision that wasn't fair or right. Within five minutes, Marlon thought he was a schmuck.

Three days of marching through the Balkans didn't change his mind.

Marlon sat on the stone edge of a nonrunning fountain in a town circle. It was cold and still in southern Kosovo. Marlon looked around at the bullet-flecked buildings, the shelled stores, the filthy, underfed children that appeared now and then, running doorway to doorway. A crying old woman in tatters.

"What a bunch of losers."

"We're movin' out!" yelled Jackson, and Marlon and eight other men hoisted their packs and stood.

They had been trudging through town and countryside, and Marlon was roundly disgusted by what he saw. Nobody seemed to have a job. He was just about to throw a fit and demand to be sent home when a love letter arrived from Babs. He kept marching.

At first, it actually hadn't been half bad. The abject poverty had seemed kinda pretty, in its foreign way, and Marlon took lots of snapshots. The problem was his traveling company. Everyone else in his platoon was a complete idiot.

They made camp that night in a bombed-out farmhouse near Suva Prizka. Sergeant Jackson and Corporal Lech Kluzinski sat against what was left of a low brick wall that acted as a windbreak. They opened C-rations and joked.

Marlon walked over, and Jackson smiled and gestured to the spot of dirt next to him. "Pull up a chair." But Kluzinski gave Marlon a chilly stare. He grabbed his food and got up without saying anything and left to sit with the others over by a well.

"What's *his* problem?" asked Marlon.

"Don't mind him," Jackson said with a gap-toothed smile. "That's just Lech."

Marlon cut open a dark olive plastic pouch and squeezed out cold SpaghettiOs. "I think Lech is a loser."

Marlon heard laughter and looked up. The other men were staring at him, and Lech had a sneering grin.

"Peasants," Marlon said under his breath.

There was shouting in the road. Coming from a farmhouse was an ancient man, his face shrunken and stubbled, and his clothes a rag-patchwork. He stumbled toward them in weepy celebration, waving a small paper American flag on a little wooden stick.

"Great," said Marlon. "Here comes another winner."

Marlon grabbed his camera and took a snapshot for his album of scorn.

The old man approached the group by the well and started shaking hands, bowing, profusely thanking them in a rapid language they didn't understand. He walked over to Tex and Marlon. He grabbed Marlon's hand, but Marlon pulled it back and rubbed it on his pants.

The old man gestured toward the other group at the well and picked up Marlon's camera.

"Thief!" said Marlon. He started to get up, but Jackson grabbed him by the shoulder.

Marlon turned and saw the constant smile was gone, but there was still patience.

The old man motioned for the Yankees to get together as a group, making an exaggerated clicking gesture with his index finger—*I take your picture.*

The men gathered by the well and put their arms around each other's shoulders. Marlon had started somewhere near the middle of the gang, but nobody wanted to touch him, so he slowly worked down the line until he wound up on the end, with only Jackson's arm draped around him.

The old man gestured again and yelled a happy command.

"I think he just said 'goat cheese,' " Marlon whispered.

The old man handed the camera back and overthanked everyone again and went stumbling back to his farmhouse, waving the little American flag over his head. Marlon rubbed his camera with a sock.

Marlon had been attached to a regular Army unit, but there was nothing regular about it. There were only nine of them. Marlon, a lieutenant, was the sole officer and held rank. But sergeants ran the Army, and everyone knew Jackson was the real authority. That was fine with Marlon, who didn't want the work.

Marlon sat alone near the collapsing brick wall, sopping SpaghettiOs from an entrenching tool. Jackson had gotten up and was talking with Kluzinski by an empty chicken roost. Tex pointed toward Marlon; Lech shook his head no. There was more talking. They started walking his way.

"We've gotten off on the wrong foot," said Lech, extending a hand to Marlon. The words came out like he was at gunpoint. "I'm Lech Kluzinski from De Funiak Springs."

"Don't complain to me about it."

Lech spun to Tex and threw up his arms. "I can't deal with this asshole!"

Lech stomped off, and Tex gave Marlon a look of disappointment. Marlon shrugged and cut open a plastic bag of saltines.

12

AS THE LAST light of day was leaving the Balkan sky, an Australian half-track rolled down the dirt road leading out of town. A sergeant from Brisbane inquired about the unit's identity, then rooted through some duffel bags.

Mail call.

He tossed bundles over the side of the truck, and the men swarmed them. Then they dispersed to private spaces and read letters from home. A general pall of melancholy fell over the group. The platoon's crooner, Dino Schwartz, sang a Harry Connick tune. A box for Marlon was left on the ground; Jackson picked it up and delivered it.

"Hot damn!" shouted Marlon. "Babs came through!"

He yelled so loudly everyone else turned around. They saw him reach into the box and pull out an economy-size bottle of Scope. They started laughing, and Lech made a crack about bad breath.

Marlon couldn't help but rub it in.

"For your information, my fiancée used her hair dryer to get the plastic shrink-wrap off the cap and back on again so she could slip this by the Army inspectors." Marlon held the bottle up proudly like a trophy. "This isn't mouthwash! It's Absolut vodka with green food coloring!"

The platoon could move like lightning when it wanted to, and Marlon never knew what hit him. He sat up groggy in the dirt as the men passed the Scope in a circle.

Marlon turned to Jackson. "Make them give it back!"

"You're the lieutenant."

"I can order them to give it back?"

Jackson nodded.

"Excellent!" Marlon took a step toward the men. He stopped and looked at Jackson. "Were you going to say something?"

"Nope."

Marlon took another step, then looked back again.

"Why are you looking at me that way?"

"What way?"

"*That way*," said Marlon. "Stop it!"

"I'm not doing anything."

"You think I should let them have it, don't you!"

"This is your chance."

Marlon simmered a moment. "All right!" he said. "But you're really starting to get on my nerves."

An hour later, under a harvest moon, everyone was getting a little fucked up. Marlon had let them have the vodka. He even asked if he could join their circle.

Jackson sat it out, lying in front of the farmhouse on his side, head propped up on his hand, enjoying the sight of his men finally coming together.

Before nodding off, they made a campfire and sat around telling dirty stories.

"Okay, okay, I got one," said a tipsy Marlon. He told them about Babs and Howdy Doody.

At the very end of the night, Marlon grabbed the Scope bottle one last time. He held it up against the moon and saw a few drops in the bottom.

He stood and swayed a bit and raised the shatterproof bottle in a toast. "You're all a bunch of losers!"

Kluzinski shouted back: "And you're a rich pussy!"

They all laughed, including Marlon, and then they fell asleep.

●

THEY rolled out at dawn. Another day of walking their butts off. Their orders were to head northeast through Štimlje and across the

Sitnica River, then swing back around, like cops circling the shopping mall during the holidays.

Lech and Marlon walked abreast, talking a streak.

"How does Babs do that?" asked Lech.

"She calls it her *art*," said Marlon.

"Howdy Doody, eh? I think I could get turned on by that."

"That's because you're a sick bastard," said Marlon, and he punched Lech in the shoulder.

"Hey! You had your middle knuckle out!"

"I learned it from this football owner."

"Oh yeah?" Lech punched him back on the shoulder, nailing the muscle.

"Ow!"

They marched on, rubbing their arms.

Tex Jackson strolled behind, listening to the two Chatty Cathy's. What have I created?

Others began falling back in the loose column and joining the bull session. Washington, Bordeaux, Zapata, Fulbright, arms hanging on the rifles across their backs, like scarecrows.

Soon, the whole unit was yapping.

". . . Name the Super Bowl's only MVP from a losing team . . ."

". . . Eddie Haskell was the genius behind the show . . ."

". . . How many feminists does it take to screw in a lightbulb? Answer: That's not funny! . . ."

". . . Chuck Howley."

"Who?"

"MVP. Super Bowl V, 1971 . . ."

Damn, Marlon thought, these guys were a hell of a lot more fun than everyone back in Tallahassee. And they weren't nearly as stupid as he had always thought.

"Hey, Marlon," called Fulbright. "Everyone says you're gonna be governor after old Birch retires. That true? Well, *I'm* gonna vote for ya."

"Me, too!" said Bordeaux.

"Me, too!" said Marconi.

And on it went until Marlon had a solid voting bloc.

Washington moved up next to Marlon. "Let me tell you about the struggle of the black man . . ." He said it with a grin. "Damn! I can't believe I'm talkin' to the next governor. Wait till I tell Ma!"

The rest followed Washington's lead, taking turns marching alongside Marlon, telling him what they would do if they were governor.

"Hold blowout kegathons at the mansion!" said Fulbright.

"Attack Castro on a moonless night!" said Zapata.

"Make the people at Motor Vehicles work on commission!" said Marconi.

Marlon nodded politely through it all.

"This is great," Washington yelled to the whole platoon. "Finally, we'll have a governor who represents *us*."

Geez, thought Marlon, I'm starting to like the little suckers and all, but I hate to break the news to 'em—

Marlon and Lech were pelted hard in the face with a spray of wet, warm red chunks. A second later they heard the thunderclap. Zapata toppled over without a forehead.

"Sniper!" yelled Tex, and they dove off the road into tall grass.

"Where'd *that* come from?"

Bordeaux and Fulbright lost it, shooting in all directions.

"Cease fire! Cease fire! You're wasting ammo!"

The men heard the unmistakable swish of bullets cutting the air near their heads. Tex shouted commands and led the way crawling back in the direction they'd come. A concussion wave hit, the ground shook and the air filled with dirt, then the sound of the mortar round that had landed eighty yards down their intended path. They stopped crawling. A motorized noise from a third direction, getting nearer. From every possible escape route a threatening sound. Instinctive panic. Marconi stood to run, took a round and fell dead in one step.

Another mortar. They buried their heads as the dirt fell. Sixty yards away. "They're finding their range," said Tex. "After the next round, we go for the tree line."

"We'll never make it!"

"We're dead here!"

A shell hit fifty yards off. "Now!" They jumped and bolted. Schwartz was cut down in the first ten yards, but the rest sprinted over the crest of a hill. It was a rolling half mile to the trees. The lactic acid cramped and burned in their thighs, but they ran through it. Ten yards into the forest they collapsed in the dead leaves, panting and shaking, about to pass out, the tops of trees spinning.

"On your feet!" Tex shouted.

They could see them now. Two Serb tanks on the road in the distance, heading south and passing them by.

But something else turned off the road and was coming over the hill toward the woods. A fast little vehicle bounding along. One of those renegade Mad Max jeeps with a machine-gun mount welded in back. It wasn't Army-issue. It was civilian police—local thugs emboldened by the Serb army who went raping and marauding after the tanks shelled the villages.

Tex slung his M-16 over his right shoulder and began climbing a tree on the edge of the woods. The others were surprised at how fast and quietly he ascended for his age, but he'd done it a thousand times hunting deer from tree stands north of Okeechobee in the Avon Park Bombing Range.

"Get going and make lots of noise," said Tex.

They heard yelling from the jeep, which was almost to the edge of the woods, and they took off, firing salvos as they went. They'd made it a hundred yards when they heard three distinct rifle shots.

The men looked at Kluzinski, the most experienced one left. Their eyes asked the question. American rifle?

"I just don't know!"

If the rounds weren't American, they'd better get moving. No, they had to go back for Tex. While they were arguing, Jackson silently cut through the trees and overtook them. "Let's go," he said on the run, and they raced after him.

They gave the roads and towns a wide berth, looping through the countryside. Tex wanted to head back to Suva Prizka. Another American unit was supposed to follow a day behind them, and maybe they could hook up.

The route took extra hours, but no more casualties. They reached the outskirts at nightfall. There was smoke on the horizon, and flickers of flame through the windows of a tiny stone building. They found the well where they had drunk the green vodka. In the road was the body of the old man in rags, the stick of the little American flag jammed into his left eye socket.

"Jesus Christ!" yelled Washington. Fulbright and Bordeaux cried like children. Tex looked at Kluzinski, who was in a rage. Marlon stood in shock.

"Can't stop now," said Tex, and he led the way sprinting through a pasture.

THE folks in Tallahassee had gone seismic. Calls flooded the Pentagon from the governor's office, state legislators and the Florida congressional delegation in Washington—all the same sentiment: "What the hell do you mean you don't know where he is?"

Threats were made against the defense budget. The ball rolled downhill until it crashed into a general's office in Albania. His staff pored over intelligence reports and satellite photos. Nothing on Marlon for three days.

On the fourth, the evening newscasts back in the States were dominated by the surprise Serb offensive and sketchy reports of American casualties. A private communiqué from the general's staff in Montenegro was transmitted to Governor Birch's office. A unit from Florida was reported in an area of the shelling at Suva Prizka—that's all they had.

Birch picked up the phone and called Montenegro. "Put the general on!"

"He's not available. Is there something I can help you with?"

"I'm going to take a giant dump on the general's career if he isn't the next voice on this line!"

He heard the phone covered up in Montenegro and some muffled talking, a long pause and a new voice.

"Nimitz here. How can I help you, Governor?"

"I want Conrad out of there!"

"Sir, we still really don't know what's going on. We can't just drop everything for one—"

"Shut the fuck up, Nimitz! I've got two U.S. senators who owe me, and they'll tourniquet all new weapons funding until the joint chiefs bust you down to scrubbing latrines at Fort Benning, you little shit-boring parasite!" The screaming was so loud the general had to hold the phone away from his ear, and his whole staff heard the torrent. "Go in there with everything you got and pray you can find him!"

Birch hung up.

Within fifteen minutes, bases in Macedonia and Albania had scrambled six Apache helicopters and an air-sea rescue team used to extract downed pilots. They were followed by a four-engine Lockheed gunship with water-cooled .50-caliber cannons under the wings that could cut a hundred-yard swath and put a minimum of three rounds in every square foot. Accurate too—it could paint one side of a street and leave the other untouched. The plane was classified top secret, first sent to Panama to support the Contras during the Sandinista thing. It officially didn't exist.

Jackson's platoon spent the night by a small stream outside Suva Prizka and awoke at daybreak. They came upon the edge of town before noon. The Serbs must have gone east. They spaced out and walked opposite sides of the street. Tex looked around a corner and jumped back and flattened against the building. The others saw his reaction and ran to his side of the street and pressed themselves against the same wall.

"What is it?" whispered Lech.

Tex pointed to an open doorway behind them, and they slipped inside. They went to an upstairs window, where they wouldn't be as easily detected, and looked out. Parked at the other end of street, in front of the last house, were three Mad Max jeeps. The front door of the house flew open, and there was yelling. A handful of people were shoved outside, and they cowered in the road: two women, two children and an old man. They were followed by a half-dozen young men with guns drawn. There was angry screaming from the women.

One of the armed men climbed on the back of a jeep and stood behind the machine-gun mount.

There was the sound of firecrackers, and five bodies crumpled. The men walked to the next door and kicked it in.

Tex stepped back from the window. He took a small envelope from his breast pocket. A religious medal and a family picture inside. He looked at the photo, eyes glassy.

"What are you thinking?" asked Lech.

Jackson didn't answer. He put the medal and picture back in his pocket, picked up his rifle and ran down the stairs.

"Goddamn him!" said Lech, and he ran after Tex. Marlon and the others hesitated, then followed, more out of fear of being left behind than anything else.

It was a major firefight in less than a minute. The Americans were outmanned and outgunned, and their ammo was almost gone. But Tex and Lech had the Serb cops in an L-shaped ambush as they came out the next doorway. Two civilians and two thugs died in the initial encounter, and the others dove for cover. The jeeps were useless in the tight city street, but one of the thugs had a grenade launcher and he fired it into the stairwell where Lech was positioned. Lech dove at the last second, but he lost his gun and had to crawl from the rubble. The thugs slipped out Lech's end of the ambush and headed for an alley.

Marlon, Hank, François and Roosevelt ran out of the same alley, right into the thugs. Hank was first on the draw, killing a Serb with his sidearm. After that, both groups fled for opposite sides of the street, exchanging wild gunfire as they went. It was happening in seconds. The Serbs made it around the corner of a building; the Americans dove behind the abandoned stands of an outdoor vegetable market, but Marlon wrenched his ankle and fell short of cover.

Roosevelt ran back to get Marlon and threw him over his shoulders in a fireman's carry. He was almost back to safety when three bullets slammed into his back. In a last effort that came from nowhere, Roosevelt threw Marlon over the side of a vegetable stand before falling dead outside.

The remaining three were pinned down and taking heavy fire. The wood was no protection. A round splintered through and hit Hank in his shooting hand.

From Lech's position in a doorway up the street, he saw the thug with the grenade launcher across the road, aiming for the vegetable stands. Lech looked around quickly—still no sign of his gun. He jumped up and sprinted. The Serb saw him at the last moment and turned, but Lech tackled him and they went down with the launcher, blowing them both up.

At the other end of the street, the thugs who had made it around the corner of the building were preparing a second launcher. Tex was upstairs over a bombed-out bakery. From a window, he saw the grenade launcher at the corner. Across the road, the three Americans were still pinned behind the vegetable stands. Jackson padded down the stairs and ran across the street to the thugs' blind side.

Through a slat in a vegetable stand, Marlon could see it coming together. To their left, the barrel of the grenade launcher poking around the corner. To their right, Tex running full gait, quietly gliding tightly against the front of the buildings. Five strides away, Tex pulled the pin on a hand grenade. He ran right up to the corner.

The thugs were ready to fire the launcher when Tex's hand appeared at the edge of the building, just below the barrel of the launcher, dropping the grenade at their feet. One of the thugs jumped into the open and got off a quick carbine burst at the fleeing Jackson before the grenade blew off his legs and killed the other two.

Up the street, Tex fell.

It was quiet. Eight bodies in the road. All over in five minutes. Marlon ignored his bad ankle and limped to Tex. Jackson was conscious, but he'd already bled a small pond. He labored for breath. "Go see my family—" He wanted to say something else, but died quickly.

Marlon sagged and closed his eyes and began crying softly.

Suddenly, the door of the building in front of Marlon burst open. Screaming people of all sizes spilled out. Marlon stood up. A family surrounded him and clung to his uniform, begging. Three old women, an old man and two children. All the men of fighting age had been taken off and executed months ago.

Walking out of the building behind the family were seven smiling Serb police officers with rifles. The one with the biggest smile had a tiny cigar in his mouth and a potbelly, and he'd been waiting for this day his whole life. He had spent twelve petty years on the police force bullying his neighbors, and now that he was operating under the wink of the Serb army, had graduated to torturing and murdering them with relish.

When the Serbs stepped out of the doorway and into the street, the family cowered behind Marlon. The children clung to his legs. An old woman in a shawl wept and cursed the cops.

The cops lowered the rifles to their sides and began laughing. The one with the potbelly mocked the old woman.

Marlon felt one of the children on his leg quivering. He looked over to where Tex lay. He slowly turned back to face the Serbs, straightening his spine and lifting his chin. He took his .45 pistol out of its hip holster and raised it at Potbelly with a fully extended right arm that was shaking.

A Swiss photographer for Reuters was hiding in a church steeple down the street and took a sequence of motor-drive zoom shots with a six-hundred-millimeter lens.

Potbelly pointed at Marlon and laughed and said with an accent, "John Wayne!"

The others broke up, too. But eventually they tired of laughing, and Marlon saw their eyes become vacant. They began raising the rifles.

There was this sound. The cops looked around. A deep drone rolling in from the hills. The swooping Lockheed suddenly appeared just above the building tops, and there was no place to hide. The .50-caliber cannons cut them to pieces where they stood. The strike was surgical—barely any dust kicked up on Marlon or the family.

When the rescue team landed the helicopter ten minutes later, Marlon was sitting in the middle of the road, holding Tex's hand.

13

RED-WHITE-AND-BLUE STREAMERS FILLED the terminal at Tallahassee Municipal Airport. Out on the runway, banks of TV cameras stood three deep atop a temporary stage. A red carpet led across the tarmac to an empty podium decorated with yellow ribbons.

"There it is!" someone yelled and pointed, and everyone looked skyward.

First it was a dot. Then General Nimitz's plane grew larger until it made the approach and landed on runway niner.

Marlon was coming home a national hero. The Reuters photographs had appeared on the covers of both *Time* and *Newsweek*, Marlon aiming his pistol with his right hand, his left arm swept back behind him protecting the family, facing down seven armed Serbs. And the perfect tear-jerker detail: the smudge-faced three-year-old girl peeking out from behind Marlon's leg.

"That kid alone's worth five elections," Governor Birch had said privately.

There was even talk of the presidency. Birch would soon begin hearing rumors that he would be pushed aside for Marlon to make an early run, and it would worry Birch right up until he crashed into the Yukon in a Learjet full of hookers and moose guns.

But on this sunny day in the panhandle, all was right with the world. When the hatch opened, General Nimitz appeared and waved for an inappropriate duration until his aides nudged him down the steps. Then came what the crowd had been waiting for. Marlon appeared first, then Bordeaux and Fulbright, whose arm was in a sling. They walked down the stairs as the tuba section of a local high school band played "War, What Is It Good For?" and orange-spandex nymphs threw batons high in the air.

The three returning soldiers were led toward the podium in front of a row of folding VIP chairs. General Nimitz was seated in the first chair, and a nymph's errant baton throw came down above his right eye, requiring a fuss and butterfly closures.

Conrad, Fulbright and Bordeaux waved again when they got to the microphone. The applause seemed to go on forever.

Governor Birch approached Escrow. He canted his head toward Fulbright and Bordeaux. "Get them out of here!"

As the applause petered off, Escrow grabbed the two by the arms and led them over to a pair of chairs hidden behind a giant wreath that read, "Welcome home, Marlon." He handed them single-serving bags of Ruffles.

Marlon looked out across the panorama of admiring faces. He had been here before—the night he won the lieutenant governor's race, balloons dropping from the ballroom ceiling. He smiled sheepishly and waited for the last few people to stop clapping.

"I . . ."

Marlon stopped. He looked around for Fulbright and Bordeaux and spotted them behind the wreath. He paused, then faced the crowd again.

"I want to thank . . ." He turned and gestured toward the VIP seats, where Governor Birch and his father were seated. He stopped again.

Marlon took a deep breath. "I want to talk today about a man I met. He was a sergeant . . ."

"Oh, Jesus," Dempsey Conrad whispered out the corner of his mouth to Birch. "Here we go."

Marlon stopped again. He scanned the faces in the crowd. Each pause was growing more uncomfortable. Marlon lowered his head and bit his lower lip. The crowd began to murmur.

"We love you, Marlon!" yelled a woman in back, which produced sprinkled applause and a blast from a hockey arena air horn. Marlon's eyes stayed lowered.

Governor Birch rushed to the podium and put a buddy arm around Marlon's shoulders. He leaned to the microphone. "We're so proud to have you home, Marlon!" Birch stepped back and began clapping, and the crowd came to its feet for a standing ovation.

They got Marlon in the limo quickly. Birch slipped Escrow a hundred. "Take him out and get him drunk."

The crowd broke through the police line and chased Marlon's limo down the runway.

THE next morning, Escrow appeared with his clipboard in the doorway of the lieutenant governor's office.

"What are you doing?"

"What's it look like I'm doing?" said Marlon, tucking a cell phone in a stuffed gym bag, looking around to see if there was anything else he might want.

"I hope you're not packing for a trip."

Silence.

"You can't go anywhere! You have a month of appointments stacked up!"

Marlon zipped the gym bag—"Please move"—and squeezed past Escrow in the doorway.

Escrow scampered alongside him through the rotunda. "At least tell me where you're going."

Marlon kept walking.

"Okay, if you won't tell me, I must insist that I come with you. You've been under a lot of pressure lately."

They left the Capitol for a limo waiting at the curb. As they pulled away, Escrow reached into Marlon's gym bag on the backseat between them and pulled out the cell phone.

"I have to call your dad and the governor. This is highly irregular."

Marlon's voice was tired. "Don't mess with me today."

Escrow stopped mid-dial and looked at Marlon. He quietly put the phone back in the bag and started tapping his fingers on his knees. A minute passed. "Okay, I put the phone away. Now, will you tell me where we're going?"

"Clewiston."

"Clewiston! That's eight hours!"

"Nine."

For nine hours they drove. Marlon leaned forward and stared out the window the whole time, not saying a word. Escrow fidgeted.

They pulled off Interstate 75 south of Sarasota, and Marlon went into a convenience store. Escrow watched from the limo, then he grabbed the cell phone and quickly dialed.

"Clewiston!" yelled Birch. "Bring him back! Now!"

"I'm afraid of him—he's not right."

"Of course he's not right! Something happened to him over there!"

"Can't you send people?"

"Messy. It'll get press. You have to bring him in alone. *You're* his chief of staff!"

"I think he's in search of something."

"Great! The future governor is trying to find himself. Sets a dangerous precedent for the citizens."

"But maybe it would be good for him to—"

"No buts! We don't want people to find themselves! We like 'em just the way they are! Bring him back or you're through in this town!"

The line went dead. Escrow saw Marlon coming out of the food mart with snacks, and he stuffed the cell phone back in the bag.

They headed inland, taking Route 74 at Punta Gorda. Marlon ripped open a foil pouch and offered it to Escrow.

"Bugle?"

Escrow shook his head. Marlon shrugged and looked back out the window and ate salty conical corn snacks.

They picked up US 27 and were soon deep in sugarcane country. Belle Glade, Moore Haven, Harlem and, later, Clewiston, "America's Sweetest Town." Raised causeways of packed dirt ran next to deep canals, cane fields sprawled in grids, and twisting trails of refinery smoke dotted the horizon. A sign thanked a doctor for returning to practice in the town.

"Pull over here," Marlon told the driver.

The limo eased off the road south of Palmdale, at the Cypress Knee Museum. Marlon had hoped to get a burger, but the place was deserted. A new Florida institution—the ghost roadside attraction. Marlon read a faded wooden info sign about cypress knees, the knotted roots that stick out of the swamp so the trees can breathe. He walked through the covered outdoor exhibit and contemplated. There was a yellow photo from the fifties, when the place was hopping, and another of the late owner, who collected pieces of cypress that had grown to resemble stuff. Marlon wiped dust off the display glass and saw dolphins, FDR, Stalin, Madonna and one knee with a Salvador Dalí title, *Lady Hippopotamus Wearing a Carmen Miranda Hat*. He learned that the museum's founder, Tom Gaskins, Sr., displayed knees in the Florida Pavilion at the New York World's Fair in 1939.

"Let's get out of here," said Escrow. "This is spooky."

They got back in the limo and crossed the Caloosahatchee Canal and drove along the berm of Lake Okeechobee. Their driver left the main road, taking lefts and rights through a humble residential section, and the homes looked worse and worse.

The driver found the name Jackson on the mailbox, and he turned up a dirt road to a small clapboard house. They were already on the porch, a dozen of 'em. Marlon felt sick. He knew Tex wasn't rich, but he didn't expect *this*. His widow, Inez, came forward and shook his hand.

"Our family is honored you've come. He wrote about you."

Marlon couldn't help but ask. "Are all these Tex's?"

"No, two are sons-in-law and three are grandkids. Our oldest two live with their own families up the street."

Marlon ran it through his mind: *Tex was a grandfather*.

They came off the porch in a line. They all said "sir" and shook his hand.

Inez took him into the living room. Marlon accepted a seat on the couch and sweetened iced tea and listened. Every Jackson had lived within a mile of that house for eighty years, ever since they started diking the 'glades, and every one of them had worked in the sugar fields or the plants. It was in their blood; they worked too hard for what they had, and they were proud. Her youngest boy played high school football at Cane Field, and Inez worked the taffy booth every year at the Sugar Festival. Back in the eighties, they were defaulting on the second mortgage. Tex couldn't find anything in Clewiston that paid enough on a ninth-grade education, so he did what he had to. The Army recruiter thought Tex was crazy, wanting to enlist at thirty-five. Tex sent as much home as he could. . . . Marlon told Inez every detail he remembered from the moment he met Tex in the hangar. He answered all her questions tirelessly for hours. . . .

Just before midnight, they said their good-byes in the driveway. Inez held Marlon's hand and thanked him. As Marlon went to pull away, Inez suddenly found herself squeezing his hand hard—not wanting to let go. Marlon stopped and let her hold on as long as she wanted. Her face was a pained tangle of things she wanted to say. She finally let go, put a trembling hand over her mouth and ran back to the house.

Marlon got in the limo.

"That was a very nice gesture," said Escrow. "Now we can get back to the Capitol."

"We're not going back."

"What?"

"I have five more widows to visit."

Over the next several days, Escrow made a series of furtive cell phone calls outside gas stations in Homestead, Manalapan and Indiantown.

"You're fired! No, you're dead!" shouted Birch.

Escrow pleaded for understanding. There was nothing he could do.

"Where are you? I want to come out there and strangle you myself!"

Escrow took the phone away from his face and slowly closed it shut on the small tin voice.

"Escrow! *Escrow!*"

The limo crossed the railroad tracks and Old Dixie Highway in Riviera Beach, and Marlon told the driver to turn off Blue Heron Boulevard. The limo worked its way through a neighborhood even poorer than Jackson's. When they pulled up to the small wooden house, fifty people were in the front yard in dark suits and dresses.

Escrow's nerves were starting to crumble from all the black people he had been seeing. Marlon opened the door and got out, but Escrow refused to leave the safety of the limo.

Everyone stopped talking and appraised Marlon as he walked across the lawn.

An older woman stepped from the others and met him halfway. She shook his hand.

"I'm Ethel Washington, Roosevelt's mother. You must be Marlon. Thank you for your letter about my son."

She led him into the house and they sat on the couch together. The home was from the forties, in an old section of west Riviera Beach back when the railroad-track color line was enforced.

Three men out on the lawn walked up to the limo, and Escrow ducked. They knocked on the window. "You can come out."

Escrow waited a few minutes, then slowly raised his head and peeked out the window. They were still there. He ducked again.

"We won't bite."

Escrow cautiously opened the door and walked stiffly into the house, and the others followed him inside.

Relatives brought Marlon coffee and cake. Escrow sat in the most remote chair in the room, hands in his lap, legs together, shoulders hunched, eyes darting.

A gold Cadillac pulled up, and four men in leather coats got out. Roosevelt's wayward cousins from Miami, the Overtown Posse. They walked in the front door and stopped when they saw the white faces. They grumbled among themselves. The word *honky* was said a little too loud.

Ethel Washington shot them a look. "Your manners!"

She and Marlon stood up.

"This is the lieutenant governor, Marlon Conrad, from Roosevelt's platoon. He's come to pay his respects."

The four didn't move. Marlon walked across the room to shake their hands.

"Now sit down and eat something," said Ethel.

She got out the photo albums and went through them with Marlon. "Here's Roosevelt when he was just five . . ."

The Overtown Posse went in the kitchen and filled paper plates with potato salad. They brought chairs back in the living room, and two sat close on each side of Escrow. They glared at him. Escrow stared straight ahead and made a high-pitched whine like a dog picking up an ultrasonic noise.

Marlon and Ethel went through all five photo albums, and then the family started putting on coats to go over to the funeral home.

Ethel was stoic at the casket. Marlon waited until all the relatives had finished and then he went up. He seemed to stand there for the longest time. His head gradually began lowering until he was resting his forehead on the edge of the casket.

Ethel got out of her seat and walked up and put an arm around Marlon and led him back to a chair. The Overtown Posse looked at each other.

•

THE next day, Enrico Marconi's funeral in Arcadia. Like the others, they didn't have much. Marconi's widow parked their pickup truck on the edge of the cemetery lawn. She left Enrico's trusty golden retriever, Sinatra, in the front seat with the window rolled down. After the widow closed the door, Sinatra stuck a paw out the window for her to shake.

The hearse arrived. Enrico's widow was trying to get his two young children to settle down. A few friends and relatives arrived late from the church, dabbing tears with handkerchiefs as they walked up the path to the burial site. As each one passed Enrico's old pickup truck, Sinatra stuck a paw out the window. It just made them cry harder.

Off to the side, in a separate section of chairs, sat a group of seventy-year-old men from the local VFW post who had volunteered to give Enrico a color guard. They straightened their VFW hats and looked respectful. Marlon went over and spoke with each one. He did quick math in his head. Probably Korea, he thought. Wow, the World War II guys are all but gone.

Marlon went to the edge of the parking lot to take his position as pallbearer. They hoisted the casket and followed the priest and altar boys down the path past the pickup, a paw popping in and out of the window. As the service began, one of Enrico's sisters sang a rousing rendition of the Lord's Prayer. Marlon sat on the edge of the VFW section. Out the corner of his eye, he noticed activity among the veterans, randomly taking off and putting back on their hats, over and over.

He heard whispering.

"No, we're supposed to take the hats *off* for prayers but keep them *on* for songs."

"But it's the Lord's Prayer."

"But she's *singing* it!"

The matter went unresolved, and hats kept going on and off.

When Escrow called in from the road the next day, he was surprised to find Birch in great spirits. The press had gotten hold of the story, and it was turning to gold. One of the VFWs had taken snapshots of Marlon as pallbearer, and they were printed in the tiny local paper and then picked up by the wire services and reprinted across the state. It was fabulous, said Birch. The war-hero lieutenant governor secretly visiting all the widows, shunning publicity. The reporters were a day or two behind, showing up at the widows' homes, interviewing and taking photos. They all gushed about Marlon.

"He couldn't have picked better places!" said Birch. "All these great American small towns. Mom, apple pie, a high school feel-up in the back seat of a—"

"Governor!"

"Sorry. I'm just so happy. I didn't know he had it in him. He's coming off like some kind of fucking *Man of the People*, God help us all!" Birch broke into deep laughter. "He must have had some kind of political epiphany over in Bosnia—"

"Kosovo."

"—and finally hit his stride. This whole sincerity thing. It's perfect. Fools 'em every time!"

"So you're not mad at me?"

"Mad! Absolutely not, son, you're going places!"

"But you kept telling me to stop him and bring him in."

"Will you learn to think for yourself? . . . Hold on, someone else wants to talk to you. . . ."

Dempsey Conrad came on the line. "You're doing a fine job, young man. I can't tell you how proud I am of how Marlon's turning out. He's like the son I never had."

"He *is* your son."

"Keep up the good work," said Dempsey. "Just one question. Do you know where his next stop is?"

"I don't think he wants me to tell you."

"What the hell's this?" Marlon shouted as the limo approached the Kluzinski residence in De Funiak Springs. Seven satellite trucks were parked on the street and short-sleeved reporters smoked and ate egg-salad sandwiches on the sidewalk. The Kluzinskis were barricaded inside, peeking out from the curtains.

Marlon looked at Escrow. "Did you have something to do with this!"

"Me?"

14

THE NEWS SENT a shock through the state.

Governor Birch's plane had gone missing. Then reported down. A Canadian aerial reconnaissance team spotted a Learjet sticking out the side of a glacier. The tail number matched the plane belonging to Perry Belvedere's lobbying firm that had been carrying the governor.

It took dog sleds three days to reach the site, but the temperature had preserved the bodies, and they were recovered and shipped for thawing back in Florida. A DC-3 mosquito-spraying plane flew over the wreckage, dumping a bushel of navel oranges in a poignant memorial ceremony designed to garner free publicity for one of the state's cash crops.

Flags flew at half-staff. Birch's body arrived first, and there was a somber graveside service at one of the capital's oldest cemeteries. Dempsey Conrad and Periwinkle Belvedere eulogized Birch with some homespun coondog stories. Then they went drinking for three hours before getting an urgent phone call and rushing across town to restrain Mrs. Birch, who—after word leaked out about the hookers' bodies starting to arrive at the airport—was in the process of busting out every pane of glass in the governor's mansion with a high heel.

On a breezy gray day in Tallahassee, Marlon Conrad was sworn in as the forty-third governor of Florida. There was a large, though understandably sedate inaugural crowd on the Capitol steps as the chief justice of the state Supreme Court administered the oath.

Perry and Dempsey were off to the left, behind the TV cameras.

"Terrible thing about Birch," whispered Perry.

"Tragedy," whispered Dempsey.

"On the bright side, Marlon will be running as the incumbent in five months. That's worth at least six points in the polls."

"Birch who?" said Dempsey.

They were still suppressing snickers when Escrow slid up to them and whispered out the side of his mouth, "I'm worried about Marlon. He's different ever since he got back from combat."

"Of course he's different," said Dempsey. "He's coming into his own."

"That little funeral tour last month was nothing short of brilliant," said Perry. "Best thing in the world him going over to Bosnia—"

"Kosovo."

"—and hanging out with the common man to learn what plays in Peoria."

"But he's different in other ways," said Escrow. "Acting erratic, bizarre."

"Like how?" asked Perry.

"He's started *reading*."

Dempsey nodded with concern. "Keep an eye on that."

The chief justice was also worried. Marlon still had his hand on the Bible, but he was looking around, talking to himself and not paying attention. As the justice read the oath, he thought he heard Marlon say at one point: "Blah, blah, blah . . ." When the justice came to the end and asked Marlon if he would faithfully execute the office, Marlon quietly said, "Whatever."

The justice paused an anxious moment, then decided the answer met the constitutional minimum and proclaimed Marlon governor. There was a soft, polite round of applause as if Marlon had sunk a two-foot putt.

A week later, Escrow placed an emergency call to Dempsey Conrad. "He's having these behavior swings. Now he's a workaholic."

"Growing pains," said Dempsey. "Give him some space."

Marlon was indeed erratic. One day he was staring off for hours, the next he was hyperactive. He scheduled an emergency special session of the legislature to deal with the twin crises facing the state's children that had been all over the newspapers Marlon had begun reading every morning: physical abuse and gun violence. He reactivated a half-dozen criminal probes into major campaign contributors that he had quashed the year before, and he canceled another half-dozen suspect state contracts that he had personally shepherded. He held back-to-back press conferences and told the truth. Then he spent the next day staring.

During one of his busy spells, Marlon quietly used a Republican Party discretionary fund to hire Florida journalism professor Wally Butts. Butts's job was to secretly investigate the cases of prisoners coming up for the electric chair. Marlon didn't have a problem with executing vicious killers; he had a problem killing the innocent. Butts was his death penalty goalie.

Butts opened his first case file. Frank Lloyd Sirocco. Frank didn't fit the profile of a potential miscarriage of justice. He was wealthy and white. But you never knew. Butts flew to Boston and canvassed the old neighbors, the nearby stores and business clients. Traditional shoe-leather newspapering. Everything checked out.

When Butts got back to Florida, a message was waiting on his answering machine. A woman in Boston wanted to talk to him. It was about the Sirocco case. Butts returned the call. No, she wouldn't talk on the phone.

Butts flew back to Boston courtesy of the GOP, and they met in an Irish bar. He found her alone, fidgeting by the window. She was middle-aged, gaunt and smoking like a construction worker. A waitress wearing a green felt derby served them Guinness. The woman killed hers, then bombshelled: George Braintree had molested Frank Sirocco's daughter.

She shook her head emphatically when Butts asked her to give an affidavit. Wouldn't even tell him her name. "I've said enough."

Butts pleaded.

"You don't need me," she finally said. "There are others."

"Who?"

"Give me the phone number at your hotel."

Butts wrote it on a matchbook from the bar, The Paddy Wagon, and handed it to her.

"How do you know all this?" he asked.

She chain-lit another cigarette with a shaking hand. "He molested me, too." She got up and left quickly.

Butts had planned to squeeze in a Red Sox game before they tore down Fenway Park, but now he was grounded in his hotel room for the weekend, within ringing distance of the phone.

He didn't have to wait long. He got the first call at seven that night, then two more the next day. It became a routine, meeting a string of nervous women in O'Flannery's Pub, Ye Olde Tavern and Cheers. They all said they had been molested by George Braintree, just like Frank's daughter. None would agree to come forward.

The last woman walked away from the table, and Butts called after her: "But I need someone to go on the record!"

The woman turned around at the door.

"Find the daughter."

15

MARLON WAS ON an upswing the day before the special legislative session. He had almost forgotten that he'd scheduled the thing just a week earlier. He sequestered himself in his office, drafting and redrafting legislation he planned to have introduced. He ordered Escrow and Pimento not to let anyone disturb him, and the two stood outside the door, snarling at each other.

It was late when Marlon knocked off. He had cut Escrow and Pimento loose hours ago. Marlon closed up the office, threw a jacket over his shoulder and waved at the guard as he walked across the echoing rotunda. He opened the front door of the Capitol. The scene outside was something between Mardi Gras and the day in the fall when all the students return to a university. Cars pouring down the Apalachee Parkway, people hanging out windows, honking horns. Signs at quick-lubes: WELCOME BACK LEGISLATORS!

The next morning, Marlon was in the office before dawn. Pimento had the coffee going, wearing a "Property of Miami Dolphins" training jersey. The phone was already ringing, and Pimento screened the calls and faxes.

"These just arrived," said Pimento, handing Marlon a stack of morning papers from around the state.

"Good, good," said Marlon, nodding, chewing a mouthful of bagel too fast. He skimmed the front pages, chugging coffee, spilling some on the *Post*. Pimento ran back to a ringing phone.

Marlon opened the *Orlando Sentinel* and saw a full-page political advertisement for the Reform Party. There was a large photo of a paunchy, self-styled Archie Bunker–type—their candidate for governor, Albert Fresco. He was griping about incumbents and the whole stinking bunch in Washington and Tallahassee. Across the top of the ad, in a carefully selected font, was Albert Fresco's motto: I'M MADDER THAN A SUMBITCH!'"

"Unbelievable," said Marlon, turning the page.

Escrow arrived and stood in the doorway. Marlon's desk was covered with papers, both his arms going with coffee and bagels and telephones, Pimento standing next to him with a steno pad and coffeepot.

"What the hell's going on here?" said Escrow. He pointed at Pimento. "This is all your doing!"

Pimento scratched his nose with his middle finger, giving Escrow The Secret Bird.

Marlon flipped the last newspaper closed. "Okay, let's hit it!"

●

MARLON was psyched.

So were Dempsey and Periwinkle. They had arrived early in the spectator section overlooking the House floor.

"Always knew he had it!" said Perry. "Wonder what brilliant plan he's got cooking this time."

"I smell dynasty!" said Dempsey.

Marlon marched through the rotunda with Pimento in tow. To their left, bright camera lights went on, followed by shouting and people flipping open notebooks. A press conference had broken out. It was Reform Party candidate Albert Fresco.

"I'm a say-what's-on-my-mind kinda guy, and I'm madder than a sumbitch!" Fresco yelled at the cameras. "I'm a straight shooter, a no-nonsense type. I don't beat around the bush. I say what I mean, and I mean what I say! . . ."

"Mr. Fresco, do you agree with the governor that we need to increase staffing for child protective services?"

"No, no, no!" Fresco shouted at the reporter, waving his arms. "I can't be bothered with that pointy-headed *issue* stuff! I've got common sense, and I've had it up to here! . . . Did I already mention that I'm madder than a sumbitch? . . ."

To Marlon's right, more camera lights went on. Free entertainment provided by a PAC pushing to allow power plants to burn a controversial South American fuel. A chorus line of women high-kicked their way across the south end of the Capitol, The Orimulsion Dancers.

Marlon kept walking. He entered the House chamber, where he was to address the joint opening session. Inside, everyone joked and chatted convivially, opening gift cards.

And the flowers.

An entire spring meadow. Marlon couldn't see a single desk. It seemed to get worse every session, like the lobbyists were trying to outdo themselves. People started noticing Marlon and waving, but Marlon was feeling a little weird. At first he thought he might faint. People's voices warbled and blended into swirling orchestra arrangements, everyone moving in slow motion. There was J. J. Weathervane, clutching another sterling gavel, and Boley "Bo" Bodacious, kissing a bottle of scotch with a ribbon around it.

Marlon began walking down the center aisle, faster and faster. He broke into a run. He swerved to a desk on the left, angrily sweeping the flowers to the floor. He grabbed a vase off another desk and smashed it in the aisle. He ran down an entire row with his arms out, knocking all the pots and wreaths to the ground. He grabbed the ridiculous floral horseshoe off the Ocala representative's desk and bashed it against the plate glass of the spectator section.

On the other side of the window, Perry Belvedere turned to Dempsey Conrad. "This doesn't smell like dynasty to me."

The press gallery had been braced for another marathon yawner, but suddenly there was news on the floor. The TV people fumbled for blank cassettes, and photographers loaded film.

Marlon was out of breath but not finished. He was up at the front of the chamber, by the dais, looking for a new target. He saw a handful of men in the back of the chamber, and he knew they didn't belong. Only lawmakers were allowed past the air lock of their new glassed-in chambers. But Marlon now saw these other guys in back, these *lobbyists*. How did they get in here? He knew how, the fuckers! Marlon charged.

The lobbyists saw that crazy look in his eyes and turned and ran—straight into the glass. Ow, Jesus! Where's the door? It's clear, too! We can't find it! . . . They felt along the glass sideways, looking for a knob or hinges or something, but it was too late. Marlon caught one from behind. The spectators on the other side of the window watched in horror at his silent scream, his frantic pawing against the glass in a futile attempt to find traction—Marlon grabbing him by the ankles and pulling him off the window, dragging him down the aisle and all the way to the speaker's chair. He let go of the ankles to grab some flowers, and the lobbyist tried to scamper away on his hands and knees. Marlon beat him over the head with bouquets of roses and chrysanthemums.

Dempsey and Perry couldn't believe their ears. They looked around. Everyone was cheering and whistling. They had never seen such a response from the gallery. And it wasn't confined to the Capitol. TV affiliates went live across the state. In living rooms and sports bars everywhere, robust applause. Down on the floor, the disgraced lobbyist, whimpering, trying to crawl away, all this pollen and petals and shit in his hair, and Marlon gives him a last kick-in-the-ass-to-go. Then Marlon stormed out of the chamber and was mobbed by reporters and spectators as soon as he cleared the air lock.

"Amazing. He's tapped into the whole anger thing," said Periwinkle. "Everyone's always wanted to do that to a lobbyist. Even me. And *I'm* a lobbyist."

"Let me run a radical notion by you," said Dempsey. "Maybe he's even better at this than we are."

"From now on, we don't interfere. . . ."

"No matter how crazy it seems. . . ."

16

MARLON WAS ALL over the evening news. The tabloids and England were calling.

It didn't matter.

As soon as Marlon had left the chamber, the legislature went about its usual three-toed-sloth business. None of the governor's bills got out of committee.

Marlon wasn't daunted. The next morning he decided to redouble his efforts. He was optimistic as he left his office for the gun industry hearings.

When Marlon arrived in the packed committee room, the lawmakers were crowded at the gun lobby's table, getting autographs from Jack Savage, former Hollywood semistar who now shilled for the munitions industry. Savage smiled as he signed scraps of paper and proposed legislation. He was wearing an unstrapped Army helmet, his trademark from his last nonflop, the 1959 war rhapsody *Guns, Guts and God*. Behind him, the right side of the gallery was filled with Second Amendment supporters in combat fatigues, martial arts robes and biological warfare hoods.

But Marlon had his allies, too. The left side of the gallery was full of law enforcement from around the state. They sat quietly with black bands around their badges, nodding their support to the governor.

Marlon took his seat next to committee chairman Mott Ewing. Ewing pounded his gavel, and the legislators frowned and stopped getting autographs and took their seats.

Marlon asked to be recognized. "I want to start with Tefloncoated bullets—their only purpose is to penetrate police officers' vests."

"Rubbish!" responded Savage. "They're for sportsmen. They're great for target practice."

A ninja in the audience held up a sign behind Savage: TEFLON-COATED BULLETS DON'T KILL COPS. PEOPLE KILL COPS!

"I want to follow up," said Chairman Ewing. Marlon nodded—good, an ally. Ewing paused, then broke into an embarrassed smile. "Will you sign this for me?" He held up a poster from *Planet of the Chimps*.

"I'd be happy to," said Savage.

Marlon fell back in his chair and rolled his eyes.

By the end of the afternoon, the lawmakers had addressed the crisis of gun violence in Florida by drafting laws against flag-burning, needle-exchange programs and public art involving urine.

Ewing prepared to adjourn the hearing.

Jack Savage raised his hand.

"Yes?" said Ewing.

"I think we should close with a prayer."

●

ON the third and last day of the session, Marlon was back in his office at daybreak, but he was starting to show wear. He chugged coffee, riffled the morning papers and triaged his proposed legislation, hoping to get at least something passed.

"Now I understand the old saying," he told Pimento. "Two things you don't want to see being made: sausage and law."

"Could be worse," said Pimento, pointing out a newspaper article from Alabama, where the legislature had tackled its state's rural poverty and unsettling infant mortality rate by banning dildos.

"Just hope none of our guys see that and get any bright ideas."

Escrow showed up with his clipboard. "Governor, Jack Savage is here to see you. He wants to know—and I quote—'how he can help us.' This could be a record contribution!"

"Don't think I won't hit you."

Marlon took a last slug of coffee, and he and Pimento marched passed Escrow.

"Governor—" said Savage, smiling and rising from his seat in the lobby.

"Fuck yourself, Rambo."

They stormed into the rotunda. To the right, a lobbyist for Jesus PAC was holding a press conference denouncing moral relativism as the greatest threat to intolerance that God-fearing Americans had ever faced. To the left, The Product Liability Mimes.

Marlon never broke stride.

When he hit the door of the House chamber, he was surprised and delighted. Everyone serious, reading glasses halfway down their noses, moving deliberately, reading bills. The clerk and the speaker sat at the dais, poring over upcoming business. That's more like it, thought Marlon.

Following tradition, some lawmakers brought wooden train whistles into the chamber to blow when they wanted to kid other lawmakers that they were "railroading" bills. They gave the whistles a few practice toots, then blew the spit out of them.

Marlon walked optimistically to his key legislative point man. Every governor has several point men in both the House and Senate. Their job is to introduce legislation advocated by the governor, since he is not a member of the bodies and can't do it himself. Marlon spoke urgently with his top man in the House.

"Don't worry, I understand completely," said the point man. "It's a done deal." He took the bills from Marlon and headed for the speaker's desk.

Marlon and Pimento grabbed seats in back. "Okay," said Marlon. "This is it."

At the end of the day, when House Speaker Gomer Tatum finally gaveled the special session to a close, Marlon couldn't believe what he had just witnessed.

It had been a nonstop relay race of Robert's Rules. The proceedings got off the line fast and accelerated with building efficiency. Bills rolled out. People took quick turns at the microphone. Votes came in rapid succession, tabulated on the new overhead Insta-Vote 5000. Feasibility study, Port Richey–to–New Port Richey bullet-train corridor. Passed! Five thousand dollars, Cape Sable Massacre Festival Dunking Booth. Passed! Pied-Billed Grebe, First Alternate State Bird. Passed! Hundred thousand dollars, Mulberry supercollider seed money. Passed! Increased criminal penalties for sports agents giving away Nikes. Passed! . . .

Someone blew a train whistle.

Toot! Toot!

Dominic Calabro of Florida TaxWatch strutted around the visitors' gallery in a turkey costume.

Laughter filled the chamber.

Except Marlon.

He made an end run to the clerk's desk. "What the hell is all this? The session is supposed to be about children!"

"Oh, right!" said the clerk, rustling through papers. "Your bills are coming up any minute. . . ."

Marlon went back to his seat.

His point man made it to the front of the line. He grabbed the microphone and made an impassioned plea for the welfare of the state's children.

Marlon leaned forward in his chair.

". . . So I want to talk today about our decline in moral values." He held up a newspaper. "Look what they're doing in Alabama about it!"

Marlon slapped himself in the forehead.

The lawmaker proposed outlawing oral sex. However, a legislative aide whispered something in his ear, and the lawmaker amended his bill to exempt fellatio and only ban cunnilingus.

"Cunnilingus?" Dempsey said to Perry in the onlooker section. "Heard some of my assembly-line workers talking about that. Is that some kind of repetitive-motion injury?"

"Can be," said Perry.

The bill passed.

Toot! Toot!

17

DETECTIVE MAHONEY'S WIFE had kicked him out of the house again.

"Every time you leave for work, I never know if I'll ever see you again! I can't take it anymore!"

"It's just a job."

"You love it! You're just like the guys you arrest! You all get high on the action!"

In his heart, he knew she was right. He put on his tweed coat and cocked fedora, kissed her on the forehead and headed into the night.

Mahoney went for a long walk in the city. It was where he did his best thinking. It had just stopped raining, and he bought some smokes in a corner liquor store. A Camaro full of kids went by. "Look at the weirdo!" It splashed a puddle on Mahoney's shoes.

Mahoney looked down at his soggy oxfords and shook his head. "Wrong-way kids on a dead-end street."

He turned into a doorway with a pink neon martini glass above it. The place was extra dark with red light, the way he liked it. He put his hat on the bar.

"Give me a bourbon, Louie."

The bartender set a highball glass in front of Mahoney. "The name's Sam."

Mahoney pulled out a George Washington and a handful of change.

"Your money's no good here," said the bartender.

"Thanks."

"No, I mean it's no fucking good. You gave me a bunch of peep show tokens."

"Sorry." Mahoney found some more money in another pocket and put it on the bar. "Crazy day at home, Louie."

"Why do you keep calling me Louie?"

"You look like a Louie."

Mahoney drained his drink in one long pull and set the empty glass down on the venerable bar. "Dames, Louie. One minute you think you've found true love, the next you've had your wallet lifted by a cross-dresser named Tallulah . . . Ever kissed a man, Louie?"

"What?"

"I mean by accident. Tongue and all."

"Get the fuck out of my bar!"

"You're right, sleep it off. Always watchin' out for me. Good ol' Louie."

"I said, *get the fuck out of here!*"

Mahoney picked up his hat, fit it on his head at a jaunty angle, and strolled out of the bar.

He walked another hour down Biscayne Boulevard until he ended up in the cramped lobby of the Gulfstream Inn and got a room with extra mildew for twenty-nine dollars. For another sawbuck, he had a bottle of rotgut delivered to the room in a brown paper bag. He was asleep before Letterman came on.

Mahoney was startled awake at three A.M. by a horrible scream, a gunshot and a tremendous automobile crash.

"Probably nothing," he said and went back to sleep.

The gunshot and crash were on TV in the next room, but the scream was real. It came from the room two doors down.

Inside, a young woman sat up alone in bed, panting. Over the back of a chair was a red leather Miami Heat jacket.

She threw the covers off her legs and went to the sink and turned on the light. She gazed in the mirror.

Looking back was a woman about five-eight, way too thin, tiny features much younger than her twenty-two years and black hair in a pixie cut, just over the top of her ears. A beauty mark on her right cheek, skin an elegant light cocoa. She was wearing white panties and a big Key Largo jersey. She noticed the bandage wrapped around her left hand. She had forgotten about that. It was now soaked through pink, like hamburger juice, and she began changing the dressing with disinterest.

It had been a busy week, coming in from the airport and all. Learning her way around Miami. She had ditched the Buick on the MacArthur and caught a taxi. The hack dropped her at a Walgreens and got out to help with her single bag. She tipped him, then remembered her Walkman in the backseat—not paying attention as she reached in, and the driver slammed the door extra hard, the way cabbies do.

"Holy shit!" the driver yelled.

The door bounced back open on its own. The skin was gnarled back to the bone across the four knuckles, with plenty of blood. The fingers had to be broken.

She didn't make a sound, just stared without expression at her hand, turning it over, looking at one side and the other, tilting her head quizzically. The driver panicked, ready to jump in ten directions at once. She grabbed him with her good hand as he started to faint.

The driver got his bearings and found a T-shirt in the front seat and wrapped it around her hand.

"Jesus! Doesn't that hurt?"

She looked up at him blankly.

"You going into shock?"

She shook her head no.

"I'll call an ambulance!"

He turned to run inside the Walgreens but suddenly felt electricity running along the insides of his legs. He looked down. Her good hand had him between the legs, and he saw it contract into a fist. He hit the ground. She held her bad hand to her chest and picked up her Calvin Klein duffel bag. The last the driver saw of the woman was the view from under the taxi, her bare feet on Biscayne Boulevard.

The first place she came to was the Gulfstream Inn, where she got a room on the second floor and now stood in front of the mirror.

The pink gauze fell in the sink in folds. The first long wet stretch came off. She grabbed the sports section of the *Herald* and wrapped the used bandage and dropped it in the wastebasket. She grabbed another section of the paper and set it beside the faucets, ready to take the next wad. She started to hallucinate. The nightmare that had awoken her a few minutes earlier was back again, this time while she was fully awake.

She was on a dirt street high up over the water. It was night and she could see small ships in the distance. There was a port, and cargo cranes lifted lumber and sugar and coffee at the Bay of Guanabara. To her left rose the steep peak of Mount Corcovado, with a large white statue of Christ on top. Way down below shined the city. Banks and skyscrapers, luxury shops and discotheques. But she was up in the *favelas*, the shantytowns of collapsing aluminum and cardboard, running sewage and confusion. She began to feel cold and hungry. She had a paper bag in her hands and she put it over her mouth and nose. Soon the hunger went away and she felt warm. She heard reverberating voices and there were others like her all around. Small boys and girls, six, seven years old, filthy, walking down the street with paper bags of glue. She was the smallest.

Few from outside the *favelas* ventured up the high parts of the hills. But halfway down, where the mountains sloped out into the city, the two worlds of Rio de Janeiro slammed together like tectonic plates. The street children stayed at the edge of the *favelas*, scurrying out like roaches to grab what they could before the boots came down.

She walked along the side of the narrow road that dove down toward the lights of the city. She put the paper bag on her face again. When she took it away, she saw headlights. The children began running. She turned and ran too, but she tripped, and the police van rolled over her, wheels on each side, not a scratch. The children scattering, squirting between buildings. Others began falling over, gunshots in the head. The men jumped out of the van. A big one smelling of tequila grabbed her by the arm and threw her into the back of the truck with three other children, and they were driven out to a large home in the countryside and locked in a shed and violated every night for a month after the men were drunk. But the novelty wore off and fresh children arrived. One by one, they were taken out into the

woods and did not come back. When it was her turn, the oldest, fat-
test, drunkest one took her off. He was very rough with her, and his
weight nearly crushed her rib cage. But before he could kill her, he
began snoring. She wiggled out from under him and began running
through the woods back to town. She remembered hearing the others call him Loco Benny.

The dream jumped forward, years later. She was covered with
green and black paint, shooting guns in the jungle with the guerrillas.
Blowing up things with plastic explosives.

The visions evaporated in the mirror, and the young woman was
looking at her reflection again. She squeezed out an entire tube of
model airplane glue into a paper bag and brought it to her face.
When she was good and warm, she removed the bag. She decided she
was tired and put a pistol in her mouth.

She looked in the mirror and down in the sink, then at the gauze
on the newspaper. Something in the paper caught her eye, the *Herald*'s story about the relocation of the late Benito Pecadillo. Loco
Benny. She took the gun out of her mouth, brushed the gauze off the
paper and became the first person to read the entire hundred-inch
article.

Of particular interest was the fancy flow chart of players. She got
out her Magic Marker and began circling some of the faces in the
boxes, beginning with "Todd Vanderbilt, Belvedere and Associates
Inc." and ending at the top of the pyramid with "Marlon Conrad,
Governor."

She picked up the phone and got the flight times for Tallahassee.

18

AFTER THE DISASTER of the special legislative session, nobody had seen Marlon. He had slipped back to the governor's mansion and didn't come out for two weeks, seeing no one but the pizza man.

Escrow and Pimento struck a frosty truce. They had to coax Marlon out of the mansion. The campaign was about to start.

The state trooper in the mansion's guard shack said Marlon hadn't set foot outside. Escrow tried the doorbell again and again. He and Pimento began peeking in the windows. Escrow tried the doorbell for the fifth time. "Come on, Governor! Open up! You have to come out sometime—"

Marlon opened the door. He turned and walked back into the mansion without a word.

Escrow and Pimento glanced at each other, then walked through the open door and followed Marlon to the living room. Empty pizza boxes and trash everywhere.

The governor flopped down on the sofa and grabbed the remote control. He was wearing sweatpants and a T-shirt, and he needed a shave. *Dr. Strangelove* was on the big-screen TV.

"Gentlemen! You can't fight in here! This is the War Room!"

Pimento got the coffee going and Escrow rounded up the pizza boxes. Under the boxes were some books and folded-over magazine articles.

"Pimento, look at this. . . . *Robert Kennedy and His Times . . . Eyes on the Prize . . .* He's reading again!"

Escrow set his briefcase on the coffee table and flipped the latches. He removed a videocassette and went over to the TV. Slim Pickens was flying through the air on an atomic bomb.

Escrow hit "eject" and put in his own tape.

"Governor, we have some work to do. The first debate is only a week away."

Footage from a vintage Florida debate came on TV. A decidedly younger Jeb Bush at one podium and Governor Lawton Chiles at the other. The year was 1994.

"Okay, now pay close attention," said Escrow, like they were watching a football training film.

On the screen, Chiles wore an avuncular smile. *"The old he-coon walks just before the light of day."*

Marlon got a funny expression. He spoke for the first time. "What's *that* supposed to mean?"

"Nobody knows," said Pimento. "But what it effectively translated to was: 'Sit down, son. You ain't finished learnin' from the Old Man.' "

"Check this out," said Escrow. He fast-forwarded to Chiles at a press conference: *"We've got to go to the lick log."*

Marlon scrunched up his face. "He won with that stuff?"

"Every time."

THEY slowly got Marlon going again, brought in the barbers and manicurists, put him back on a pizza-free diet.

By the night of the campaign's opening debate at East Tallahassee High School, Escrow and Pimento thought they had their man turned around.

A half hour into the debate, they were crestfallen.

Then the moment of truth: electric chair or lethal injection?

Marlon stared at his hands and pooch-kicked it. Escrow cursed and threw papers. Then he watched as Gomer Tatum got a running start at the question, did a triple lutz and nailed the landing.

Pimento yelled out to Marlon: "Go to the lick log!"

Escrow gave him an elbow. "Shut up with the fuckin' lick log already!"

"You shut up!" They started shoving until the Rolling Stones people pulled them apart.

Up in the closed-off balcony, lobbyist Todd Vanderbilt was putting the moves on a fetching Brazilian woman he'd picked up at Perry's party. It was a little chilly, so she wore a Miami Heat jacket. She pushed him away coyly. "I have to make a quick phone call. Can I borrow your cell phone?"

"But what if I get calls?"

"I'll only be a minute." She winked and ducked into the ladies' room and began puttying plastic explosive into the phone.

Down below, Marlon was rushed out to a waiting limo and back to the governor's mansion. He walked around the living room in a trance, said he was feeling a little down, and headed off to bed. Escrow and Pimento slept on the couches.

Shortly after two in the morning, Marlon sat up in bed. He thought he heard something. There was a tapping at his door. "Pssssst!"

He got up and opened it.

It was Pimento. "Governor, let's get going."

"I'm not going anywhere except back to bed. I'm depressed, and you're crazy."

Pimento opened a large brown envelope. As press secretary, he was responsible for all photographic work. He had routinely sent the film from one of Marlon's cameras through the developing lab months ago.

He didn't say anything as he removed a black-and-white eight-by-ten and handed it to the governor.

Marlon had to sit down. It was the group photo of his platoon in Kosovo, the one the old man had taken by the well.

"You gotta pull out of this," said Pimento. "The people need you. . . . Come with me."

Marlon put on some jeans and a USF Bulls T-shirt. They crept down the back staircase without waking Escrow and waved to the state trooper as they tiptoed to the garage.

Fifteen minutes later, Marlon was standing next to Pimento as he tried to jimmy the lock on the back door of the state archives.

"What are you doing that for? I'm the governor. I can go in there twenty-four hours a day. All I have to do is call the Capitol Police . . ."

"Wouldn't be the same," said Pimento. "Keep a lookout."

A few more seconds with the slot screwdriver and Pimento had them inside. Their footsteps echoed down a marble hallway between rows of display cases bathed in moonglow from the skylights.

"Look at all this stuff," said Marlon. "I didn't even know this was here."

They took their time. Spanish doubloons. A stuffed panther. A swimsuit Marilyn wore on vacation with Joltin' Joe. A mess kit used during training on Useppa Island before the Bay of Pigs. Alan Shepard's space helmet. The barefoot mailman's bag. A mermaid costume from Weeki Wachee.

"Over here!" Pimento whispered urgently, waving Marlon down to the last display case. "This is what we came for."

Marlon caught up with him and peered into the case. It was empty except for a single pair of worn-out old shoes in a soft golden light. Pimento picked the lock with a nail file and slowly opened the glass door. He licked his lips and rubbed his palms together. Then he carefully reached into the case and began lifting the shoes off their pedestal.

"Are you keeping a lookout?" he asked Marlon.

"Yeah, here comes an Indiana Jones boulder."

Pimento handed the shoes to Marlon. "Try 'em on."

Marlon sat down on the cold floor and kicked off his sneakers. He slid on the old brown shoes and laced them up. He stood and took a few practice steps.

"How do they feel?" asked Pimento.

"A little big."

"You have to grow into 'em."

"How far did you say he walked in these?"

"One thousand and three miles, from Century in the northwest tip of the panhandle to Key West. It slingshotted him from nowhere into the U.S. Senate in 1970," said Pimento. "That's how he got the nickname Walkin' Lawton Chiles. He was elected governor in 1990 and died in office in 1998."

Marlon closed his eyes and clicked his heels together. "There's no place like home. There's no place like home. . . ."

Pimento patted him on the back. "Follow the yellow brick road."

They returned the shoes to the case and snuck back out the jimmied door.

Pimento climbed behind the wheel and checked his watch. "We gotta hurry. Sun's coming up soon."

They drove across town and parked next to a large treed lot and hopped a fence. Pimento ran a short burst and Marlon caught up.

"This is far enough," said Pimento. He got down on the ground and Marlon followed his example. They crept a few yards until they were perched behind a large stone slab. Marlon looked around. There were stone slabs everywhere. Nothing but oak trees and tombstones.

"We'll do the stakeout here."

"For what? The Great Pumpkin?"

"Shhhhhhh!"

Marlon lowered his voice to a whisper. "What are we looking for?"

"That's his grave over there."

"Whose grave?"

"Who else? Walkin' Lawton's."

They sat and waited in silence. Marlon was nodding off as the sky started to turn light. Pimento nudged him and pointed. "There he is! There he is!"

"Where?"

"Right there! Look!"

"You're making this up. I don't see any—wait. What's that?"

In the dim gray light, a small hunched silhouette slipped silently across the grave.

An old raccoon.

19

"WHERE HAVE YOU been?" shouted Escrow. "I was just about to call out the National Guard!"

Marlon didn't answer. He and Pimento ran for the master bedroom. Escrow appeared in the doorway and found the two darting around the room, dumping dresser drawers into suitcases.

"You two are bad chemistry," said Escrow. "I want you both to stop and sit down. You're scaring me."

"No time," said Marlon. "Got a campaign to catch." He ran to the living room.

Escrow looked at Pimento. "What did he say?"

Pimento smiled. "I think he's ready to make a serious run."

Fifteen minutes later, Escrow was in the back of the eastbound limo going over his clipboard. "Sorry about my reaction back there, sir. Yes, activity is the best thing. Keep your mind occupied. Good to see you're with the program again. . . ."

Marlon leaned forward and turned up the stereo until he couldn't hear Escrow. It was Johnny Cash. *"Well, I'm going down to Florida, and get some sand in my shoes. . . . I'll ride that Orange Blossom Special, and lose these New York blues."*

"Does it have to be that loud?" yelled Escrow.

"What!"

"I SAID, DOES IT HAVE TO BE SO—"

Marlon killed the stereo.

"—LOUD? . . . Thank you." Escrow looked down at the clipboard. "Okay, we head east to your next stop in Jacksonville, then back to the capital for a fund-raiser . . ."

"No," said Marlon.

"No, what?"

"We're not coming back. We're going all the way."

"All the way where?"

Marlon didn't answer.

Escrow pointed at his clipboard. "We have a tight schedule to keep."

Marlon leaned and tore the paper off the clipboard, wadded it in a ball and tossed it on the floor.

Escrow glared at Pimento. "What are you laughing at?"

"Nothin'."

Marlon saw something out the window as they were leaving Tallahassee. "Take this turn," he told the driver.

They pulled into a Winnebago dealership.

"What are we doing?" asked Escrow.

"If we're going to win this election, we'll need the right wheels," said Marlon. "In a perfect world, we'd make whistle-stops in a caboose on the Orange Blossom Special. But it ain't around anymore. This'll have to do."

They walked across the lot, turning a corner at the end of the showroom. And there it was. The moment Marlon saw it, he knew he had to have it.

The salesman smiled. "I don't think we'll need to worry about that credit check, Governor."

Marlon sent the limo driver back to Tallahassee, and they climbed into their new campaign vehicle.

"This is more like it," said Marlon, sitting high up in the fighting chair behind the steering wheel.

Pimento was riding shotgun and Escrow was in back, in the rest room.

The RV had previously been traded in following a country music tour sponsored by a soft drink bottler.

As the Winnebago bounded across Florida for the Atlantic Ocean, the other drivers on Interstate 10 saw the colorful artwork on the side. Slices of citrus spraying glistening droplets, and big bright letters in a tangerine script running the length of the RV.

ORANGE CRUSH.

20

"CHECK OUT THE cool bridge!" yelled Pimento.

He and Marlon had great views from the front of the RV. The *Orange Crush* started across the historic Main Street Bridge, and the pair leaned to look out their windows, down through the old blue girders at the barges and ships in the sweeping St. Johns River far below.

"There's the former Independent Life building," said Marlon, pointing. "You can always recognize a picture of Jacksonville's skyline by that glass skirt."

"Hey, Escrow, you're missing it!" Pimento called back.

Escrow sat at the mobile kitchenette, checking his watch and fuming. "We're going the wrong way! We were supposed to meet the security people an hour ago!"

"Relax and enjoy your life," said Marlon. "We'll get to the convention center."

"But you won't have time to change!"

"You worry too much."

The *Orange Crush* arrived at the Prime Osborn Convention Center only moments before the second gubernatorial debate. The Rolling Stones security was in a tizzy. Marlon was supposed to have arrived at an undisclosed location three hours early, so they could send out a decoy convoy, create a diversionary mock disaster, then make him suddenly appear onstage in a puff of smoke to the opening chords of "Jumping Jack Flash."

Instead, Marlon pulled right up to the front entrance and was mobbed. Albert Fresco tried to get the attention of the cameras. "I demand to be allowed in the debate. I'm not highfalutin. I'm a working stiff, down-to-earth and madder than a . . ."

House Speaker Gomer Tatum was already at his podium in a new suit, and he didn't know what to make of Marlon climbing up onstage in jeans and a T-shirt.

The Jacksonville debate was going with the town hall format. Audience members would ask questions, either candidate could jump in, anyone was allowed to follow up and roll with the topics wherever they went, no time limits. If everything went according to plan, the network would have a free-for-all on its hands.

Jackie Monroeville was onstage, dabbing extra makeup off Tatum's face with a Kleenex. "Just keep hammering him on the electric chair. It's his soft underbelly!" She held another Kleenex under his mouth and made him spit out some last-second food. A network technician in a headset held up three fingers, then two, one, and finally a fist. He swung his arm and pointed at the moderator's table.

"Good evening, this is Florida Cable News correspondent Blaine Crease, and welcome to the second Florida gubernatorial debate. . . ."

A homemaker from Atlantic Beach planted by the Democratic Party asked the first question. "Governor, at the last debate you didn't seem to make your position clear about the electric chair."

"We should have lethal injection," said Marlon.

"But last summer you said you'd love to throw the switch yourself, even jiggle it."

"That was a year ago. You gotta grow. . . ."

Another plant: "Governor, people are getting fed up with the two-party system. What do you think about the Reform Party candidate? He had a fresh message."

"He's the south end of a northbound horse."

Scattered laughter. Escrow paced in the stage wings, bumming cigarettes.

The local chairman of the Southern Baptist Convention asked Marlon why he hadn't returned the group's litmus test questionnaire on moral values.

"Because you're busybodies."

The man bristled. "Just what I thought! I saw in the paper where you opposed our boycott of Disney for giving homosexuals health benefits!"

"Come, join us," said Marlon. "There's plenty of room in the new millennium."

More laughter.

"You mean the thought of them doing that doesn't make your skin crawl?"

"I don't know," said Marlon. "I don't think about it. How often do *you*?"

The crowd was laughing pretty good now. The man's head turned bright red and someone yanked him back down into his chair.

On the side of the stage, Jackie was pulling out her hair. She yelled to Tatum: "You're letting him run away with it!"

He couldn't hear her over the applause for Marlon. Jackie wrote quickly in big letters on a chalkboard and held it up: "JUMP IN!"

Tatum jumped in. "I'll fry 'em until they're good and dead!"

But the question was about day care, and Jackie smacked herself with the chalkboard. She started scribbling again on the board and held it up.

Tatum stared offstage as he read the sign haltingly into the microphone. "What . . . are . . . we . . . going . . . to . . . do . . . about . . . welfare . . . and . . . quotas?"

That grabbed the crowd's attention. A lot of grumbling and heads bobbing in agreement.

Jackie looked at Tatum with expectant eyes. Remember what we rehearsed?

"No more free ride," said Tatum, a little less stiff. "We're sick of the people who sit at home watching TV and having babies, sponging off those of us who get up every day and go to a job!"

Tatum didn't so much get applause as angry shouts of alliance. "Yeah!" "Sick of it!"

Tatum's voice gained confidence and volume. "I'm tired of unqualified people getting the promotions that we've earned just because of some stupid law!"

The shouting from the audience increased. "Hell, yeah!" "We've had it!"

"I'm sick of criminals on weekend furloughs in our neighborhoods!"

"Right on!" "You tell 'em!"

Tatum was at full throttle. "I'm sick of the handouts! I'm sick of the constant attacks on the family! And I'm sick of the godlessness!"

The whole auditorium cheered and yelled. Tatum turned to Marlon. "Do you agree with me?"

"No."

The audience gasped. There was a thud backstage. Escrow had fainted.

Marlon grabbed the microphone from his podium and jumped down from the stage. He walked up the middle aisle, stopped and looked around.

"Why are we so angry?"

He continued up the aisle, looking at individual faces.

"We're all blessed. We're living in a wonderful place in a bountiful time—the luckiest people on earth. . . ."

He turned and walked back toward the stage.

"Do you know why we have it so good? Because many of our parents and grandparents left their bodies in faraway places, never to see their families again. Normandy, the Chosin Reservoir, Dong Ap Bia, Suva Prizka."

He stopped and raised an arm.

"Who here lost a relative in World War II?"

Several hands went up.

"Korea?"

More hands.

"Vietnam?"

The place was so quiet you could calibrate a sound meter. Marlon climbed up and sat casually on the edge of the stage.

"We owe them everything, and we can never pay them back. But there's one little thing we can do to honor their memory. . . . What do you say we cut each other some slack?"

Marlon set the microphone down on the stage. The debate had barely begun, but he walked down the aisle toward the exit.

"Where are you going?" Blaine Crease shouted from the moderator's table.

Marlon turned. "I'm goin' to the lick log."

The press corps flipped through slang dictionaries. The Rolling Stones security tried to keep the crowd back, but Marlon was mobbed again as he left the convention center. People yelled out questions as he climbed up to the driver's seat of the RV.

"Any campaign promises?"

"I promise not to tell you what you want to hear."

The *Orange Crush* pulled out of the parking lot.

21

THE DEBATE LED all newscasts for the next cycle.

Marlon was on the move.

Escrow freaked out in the back of the RV. "You're out of control!"

"I'm having fun," said Marlon.

"Fun's important," said Pimento.

"No, it isn't!" said Escrow.

"What's the map say?" asked Marlon.

Pimento ran his finger down the chart in his lap. "Castillo de San Marcos."

"We can still go back to Tallahassee," said Escrow.

No response.

"You're having a midlife crisis," said Escrow. "That's okay. Perfectly understandable. Most guys get Corvettes. You get a Winnebago. . . . Let's go back."

"Tunes!" said Marlon.

"Check!" said Pimento, finding an FM station.

"Is everyone on drugs?"

"*. . . You say you want a revolution, well you know, we all want to change the world . . .*"

●

BACK in Tallahassee, the press was in disarray. Nobody knew where the candidates were. The flak lines at the campaigns went unanswered. Reporters stared in speechless torpor at empty press-release slots in the mail room of the Capital Press Center.

A columnist for the *Tampa Tribune* yelled down the hall, and the others came running to a television set. A news helicopter had picked up the Winnebago on A1A south of Jacksonville and was cutting in live. TV correspondent Blaine Crease shouted above the whap-whap-whap of helicopter rotors about the ultimate Capitol insider turning outlaw with a Bolshevik charge down the coast in an RV.

Blaine Crease was the star correspondent of Florida Cable News. He had been selected moderator of the gubernatorial debates because FCN, the lowest-ranked network in the state, was the only one that would agree to telecast the traditional ratings-killer. But now that Marlon had apparently gone off the posttraumatic deep end, the rights to the debate were an unexpected gold mine, and Crease smelled a shot at national stature. A former stuntman, Crease had made his name with the newsman-as-fearless-participant feature story, and he regularly placed himself in needlessly dangerous situations that were constantly getting the network sued.

Hovering just feet above the Winnebago as it cruised down A1A, Crease ordered his pilot to get even closer, and he would hang out the helicopter with the TV camera for a better shot. Crease opened the door and activated his microphone.

Back at the press center, more reporters crowded around the TV.

"Is Governor Conrad on some kind of renegade crusade, fighting the system, or is this just another cheap political trick we've come to expect from that same old crowd in Tallahassee?" said Crease. He zoomed in on the driver's window. "God only knows what kind of high-risk, high-stakes discussion is going on inside the Winnebago!"

"School bus!" Marlon called out, sliding a little plastic window over a square on his highway bingo card.

"Fire truck!" said Pimento, sliding his own window.

A massive object suddenly swooped across the windshield.

"Whoa! What the hell was that?" yelled Pimento. "Looked like a helicopter!"

Marlon jerked the steering wheel, and they went off the right

shoulder of the road. He corrected, but the RV's high center of grav-
ity took them all the way across the highway and off the left shoulder.

The helicopter pilot did an emergency pull-up.

"The Winnebago's gonna crash! The Winnebago's gonna crash!"
Crease yelled on-air, still filming as the *Orange Crush* kicked up
clouds of sand, careening from one side of A1A to the other, rocking
perilously on its suspension.

Marlon fought with the steering wheel and finally brought the RV
back under control.

"Wow! That was incredible!" said Crease. "Marlon Conrad has
survived the first major test of his breakaway campaign! But who
knows what harrowing obstacles still lie ahead? . . ."

The TV audience loved it. Calls poured into the network from
around the state, viewers wanting more. The network stayed live for
almost an hour until the *Orange Crush* entered a thunderstorm and
the pilot refused to fly any farther.

In a Jacksonville motel room, Jackie Monroeville and Gomer
Tatum sat on the end of the bed, watching saturation TV coverage of
the *Orange Crush*. Jackie grabbed Tatum by the collar and shook
him. An éclair went flying.

"He's stealing your momentum! You gotta get out ahead of this
thing!" she yelled. "We have to reinvent you!"

"How do we do that?"

"We're hitting the road!"

●

THE miles below Jacksonville are mostly undeveloped, the highway
running along the shore. The thunderstorm let up, and Marlon and
Pimento resumed sightseeing. There were a few clouds left over land,
but it became a clear day on the Atlantic, warm and blue. An occasional cabin cruiser with deep-sea rigs popped over the horizon.

Two state troopers on motorcycles pulled them over near the
Guana River State Park. "Governor, please wait here until a security
escort can arrive."

"No!" said Marlon. "No escort!"

"You have to have an escort. We've been given orders."

"No! I'm the governor, the chief law enforcement officer in the state, and *I'm* giving you an order: no escorts!"

"Please stay here," said the trooper. "This is over my head. I'm going to call it in."

The trooper phoned headquarters in Tallahassee, where the head of the department—a political survivalist—in turn knew where to call.

The phone rang in the lobbying office of Periwinkle Belvedere.

"I see," said Perry. He held his hand over the phone and called to Dempsey. "It's the troopers. They say Marlon's refusing escort."

"What about the Rolling Stones people?"

"He fired 'em in Jacksonville."

"Tell him to put Marlon on. I want to talk to him."

Perry handed Dempsey the phone.

"Son, this is a bad piece of judgment. They still haven't caught the person who killed Todd Vanderbilt."

"So?" said Marlon.

"You *do* know what happened to Vanderbilt, don't you?"

"I read the papers."

"That's right, you're one of those *readers* now. So you know a bomb went off right where you were debating not an hour earlier. That's too close for comfort. We need to find out what's going on."

"Sorry."

Dempsey looked at Perry. "Won't budge."

"Remember what we said?" replied Perry. "No interference."

Dempsey held his breath a few seconds, bulging his cheeks, then let it out. "Yep, 'No matter how crazy it seems.'" He told Marlon to put the trooper back on the line. "Let him go. No escort."

The motorcycle trooper stood in the gravel and waved as the RV pulled off the shoulder and back on the highway.

Marlon drove the speed limit and was passed constantly on the two-lane road. Someone threw a bag of trash out the window, and it blew apart on the edge of the pavement next to a crying Indian. In Marlon's rearview, a red Ferrari weaved erratically around other vehicles until it was on his bumper, then blew past at ninety. It had a vanity tag: DAY-TRADR. Speedboats and Jet Skis roared along the shore, flushing wading birds into the air.

They began to detect development on South Ponte Vedra as they hit the outskirts of St. Augustine. There was no bridge over the inlet, so A1A took them on an inland detour.

The shadow of a blimp crossed the road in front of them.

Marlon stuck his head out the window and looked up; he saw a TV camera pointing back down. They followed a winding route along the Intracoastal Waterway and into the heart of St. Augustine.

"There's the fort!" said Pimento. "Castillo de San Marcos! It's made of coquina!"

Marlon pointed at two old statues. "And there's the Bridge of Lions!"

"Look!" said Escrow. "There's an election slipping away!"

Pimento turned around. "Did the other kids not play with you when you were a child?"

They pulled over at Flagler College and got out with cameras. Marlon and Pimento took snapshots of the Spanish Revival architecture at the old Hotel Ponce de León built by Henry Flagler. Then they got back in the *Orange Crush* and whipped around town visiting the oldest *everything*.

"St. Augustine was founded in 1565, but did you know Pensacola is actually older?" said Pimento.

"Really?" said Marlon.

"It's true. Pensacola was founded a few years earlier, but there was a break in the occupation, so St. Augustine gets the crown as longest *continuous* U.S. city."

"You realize there's absolutely no way to make any money off that information," said Escrow.

"The governor needs to know that sort of thing," countered Pimento.

"Does not!"

"Does too!"

"Knock it off!"

They ended up at dusk atop the St. Augustine Lighthouse. Marlon and Pimento stood on the caboose-red porch wrapped around the lamp, taking pictures of the ocean and the inlet. Clouds moved in and the wind picked up with an invigorating nip and stinging raindrops. Escrow brought up the rear. He panted and grabbed the balcony railing after taking the last of the two hundred and nineteen steps up the tower. "This is ridiculous! What does all this sightseeing have to do with an election?"

Marlon raised his camera for another picture. "You're gonna have to be more cool if you want to hang out with us."

As they emerged from the lighthouse's base, a blimp was putting down in the parking lot, and the cabin door opened.

"We want more debates!" said Blaine Crease, hopping out. "Normally they're a ratings write-off, but this new *truth* thing of yours—it's hot!"

Marlon stowed his camera.

"We caught Tatum a few miles back at a Dairy Queen," said Crease. "He's agreed. We booked the speedway for tomorrow. What do you say?"

"We want to negotiate ground rules," said Escrow.

"We'll do it," said Marlon.

Hours later, after sunset, the Winnebago rolled south along the ocean. It was dark inside except for the green instrument lights. Escrow was asleep in back. Marlon and Pimento sat up front talking quietly. There were no other cars on the two-lane road.

"Know what I remember?" asked Marlon. "My playpen. We were on vacation and my mom set it up on the beach under a big green umbrella."

"No kidding."

"That vacation is my earliest memory," said Marlon. "I remember this sign with an alligator wearing a sombrero pushing a shopping cart."

Pimento snapped his fingers. "That's at the Grator Gator grocery on Singer Island! We used to go there when I was a kid." Then: "How'd I remember that?"

"Weird what sticks with ya," said Marlon.

The moon had just risen over the Atlantic, and they rolled the windows down to hear the surf.

•

SHORTLY after the campaign got under way, a time-honored journalism ritual resumed. News vans and satellite trucks were dispatched to a modest neighborhood of ranch houses in Tampa.

Not all the state's reporters could be assigned to the most important, diamond-hard news stories. A certain percentage worked the feature beat. It was the most vicious beat in Tampa Bay. There were only so many ways you could write about giraffe births at Busch Gardens and the oldest cigar roller.

But elections were different. They were spaced far enough apart so that veteran reporters had no problem dusting off their clip files and going back to the same well over and over.

It started ten years ago with one reporter and one feature story. Her name was Patty. She was assigned the "man-on-the-street" article for the election. It would be a challenge. There had been many memorably forgettable men-on-the-street from years past. The old guy in the barbershop getting a crewcut, complaining about the Beatles and kids "all hopped up." The farmer in Mom's Diner eating meat loaf and blasting Saddam Hussein, wearing a baseball cap with plastic shit on the visor that read, "Damn pigeons!"

In a brilliant stroke, Patty grabbed a telephone book and discovered that there really was a local resident who had the misfortune of walking through life with the name Joe Blow.

Patty went out and interviewed Joe. She learned he had a wife, two kids, a cat, a dog, a high school education, a three-bedroom house with a big mortgage, and two cars (one paid off). He drank sixteen gallons of beer a year, mostly on a sofa watching 3.4 hours of TV a night. He lived within a hundred miles of where he had grown up. He had read no books in the last twelve months, during which time he had eaten seventeen meals at McDonald's and nine at Burger King, with the rest of the chains eating up the remaining slice of the pie chart. In politics, he favored Republicans for president and Democrats for local office, although he didn't vote more often than he did. He had never won anything, but the Blows had once been a Nielsen family.

Joe had answered all of the reporter's questions faithfully and with good humor, and he eagerly awaited the article in the paper the next morning. He had no idea what was coming.

A decade later, it had long since ceased to be amusing. Every election, more and more reporters showed up and camped out in Joe's yard like he was the Rosetta stone.

In a way, he was. That first reporter had unknowingly tripped over something. But after enough articles were written, the pattern became clear. Everything, absolutely everything, Joe Blow was or did in this lifetime was completely, invariably average. Not just within the standard deviation, but dead-on-the-money mediocre. It started to get to him. The incessant articles only confirmed Joe's notion that he would never achieve anything of note. On the other hand, he wasn't such a bad guy.

Joe looked like . . . well, it was kind of difficult describing Joe. The more reporters thought about it, the more they realized it was impossible. He had no distinguishing features whatsoever. It was like interviewing robbery witnesses who didn't get a good look. "Average height, average build, really don't remember anything about him—just like a million other guys on the street." If police ever asked people to create a composite of Joe's face with a computer program, they'd point at the original generic mug the computer started with. "That's him!"

This time around, the reporters had begun showing up three weeks before the election, carefully charting everything Joe did. The stress was getting to be too much. His wife couldn't go shopping without being tailed by test marketers from Kellogg's and Frito-Lay. His children came home crying, saying their classmates were calling them "lukewarm," "pedestrian" and "pablum."

Joe Blow would head out to his car each morning before work with a mug of coffee.

"What did you have for breakfast, Joe?"

"Please leave us alone! I'm begging you!"

"How much coffee do you drink a day?"

"Is that perk or crystals?"

Joe lurched out of the driveway and raced off to his job as an orange juice taster at the Tropicana plant.

The shopping habits of the Blow clan may have been intriguing, but it was Joe's political views that drew the most attention. Because he was so average, he instinctively gravitated toward the candidates who would ultimately poll a majority of the electorate, and he began predicting races with oracular certainty. At first it was novel; then it became scary. Joe accurately called twenty-six consecutive races before the street filled up with TV trucks and he refused to give any more predictions, but the genie was already out of the bottle.

Joe Blow came home from work. He got out of his car carrying his lunch pail.

"How was your day at work, Joe?"

"Who do you like for governor?"

"How many times did your bowels move?"

"Fuck off!"

22

FIRST THING THE next morning, a state trooper pulled the *Orange Crush* over again.

Marlon rolled down the window. "I thought we'd settled this."

"Mail call," said the trooper. He passed a small cardboard box through the window and left.

"I asked them to do that," said Escrow, taking the box from Marlon. "If we're gonna be on the move, we have to stay plugged in."

Escrow sat down on the floor behind the driver's seat and began sorting the cards and letters.

Marlon pulled back onto the road, and Pimento came up front with a stack of newspapers and climbed into the passenger seat.

"The *Times-Union* is leading with your unorthodox campaign in a Winnebago and the disgruntled gunman rampage. The *Herald* is leading with your campaign and the Willie Nelson Bandit. The *Times* is leading with your campaign and the shoot-out at the kindergarten. The *Tribune* is leading with your campaign, a quadruple shooting and the discovery of a head in a crab trap in Tampa Bay. The *Sentinel* is leading with the campaign, a triple drive-by and a shocking exposé revealing that students are drinking at college football games."

"My turn," said Escrow. "You got a lot of mail. It generally falls in three categories—donations, requests and insane rants. . . . Here's ten thousand dollars from Big Insecticide, five thousand from Big Trial Lawyers, another thousand from Big Nursing Home, five Gs from Big Lap Dance, and, what's this? Two-fifty from Little Businessman?" He tossed it out the window. "Three thousand from Big Asbestos Removal, five K from Big Indicted Highway Contractor—"

"Toaster Strudel?" offered Pimento.

Escrow waved it off, but Marlon took one.

"Time to pay the piper," said Escrow. "Here are the requests: '*Get the charges dropped against my company,*' '*File charges against my competitor,*' '*Loosen smokestack rules,*' '*Give us the bridge contract,*' and '*Come to my daughter's wedding.*' I don't know about that last one—sounds a little presumptuous."

The shadows of two blimps criss-crossed each other on the highway.

"The rants are basically still the same," said Escrow. "The first one is the standard '*You suk!*' and a few more cover the same ground: '*Bite it!*' '*Eat it!*' '*Suk it!*' Here's another '*You suk!*' followed by '*No UN in the U.S.*' '*The Trilateral Commission Suks!*' '*When will you wake up to the Jewish world conspiracy?*' '*Stop lying about the flying saucers!*' and '*You suk!*' "

Marlon turned on the radio.

"Sir," said Escrow. "I want to pick out something to listen to."

"I don't know . . ." said Marlon.

"C'mon. If we're going to have fun, like you say, then you have to let me play, too."

Marlon relented, and Escrow turned the knob until he came to a station playing John Philip Sousa military marching music. He swayed side to side and smiled.

"Aaaauuuhhh!" screamed Pimento, heat-butting the lavatory door. "Make it stop!"

"He's right," said Marlon, changing the station. "Don't take it personally."

They crossed the bridge over the inlet at Fort Matanzas and soon saw a blue arch on the left.

"Is that Marineland?" said Marlon.

Pimento nodded. "Opened in 1937. World's oldest marine attraction. You'll never again see one built in such an incredible location, just a ribbon of land between A1A and the ocean. It's like a museum of old roadside Florida."

"I've never been," said Marlon.

"You're kidding!" said Pimento. "Then we absolutely have to stop!"

"By all means," said Escrow. "Let's stay a week."

They pulled over in a gravel lot and parked next to a red Ferrari with a vanity tag, DAY-TRADR. A man got out of the sports car talking on the phone. He wore a tight-fitting golf shirt, tighter slacks and loafers without socks. "Sell the bonds! Put an eighty stop-limit on the IPO! . . ."

Marlon and the gang went inside. Things didn't look good. The gift shop's air-conditioning had been cut off, and the shelves were nearly empty. Marlon flipped through a few sun-bleached postcards from the sixties, and Escrow picked up a seashell toilet seat and stared through the opening at the others.

They went out to the dolphin tank and had the whole thing to themselves. Ten dolphins lay around the water, no shows, nobody to perform for, listlessly pushing a basketball around the pool with their noses.

One dolphin flicked the basketball up to Marlon. He caught it and threw it back. The dolphin got its bottlenose under the ball and flicked it up again.

"Where is everyone?" said Marlon, catching the ball, throwing it back.

"This is a tragedy," said Pimento. He clapped his hands, and the dolphin threw him the ball. "We'd better take a good look—it might not be here much longer." He threw the basketball back.

"Hey, it's market forces," said Escrow. "Sink or swim."

Pimento caught the ball again and threw it back. "Escrow—try real hard not to poop on this moment."

The dolphin flicked the ball again, and it went wide.

A young woman in a wet suit caught it. She made a clicking sound with her mouth, threw the ball back in the water and dove in after it.

The men stopped talking and watched her. She swam around and caught rides from the dolphins. One dolphin spun on his side, and she rubbed his belly. She didn't smile once—almost a frown the whole time. She was chewing gum.

They guessed her age at around twenty. She was tall and fit, with developed shoulders from swimming, and she had dark hair in a tomboy Buster Brown cut. Her posture was fiercely independent, but her face seemed vulnerable. It was a corny picture of everything that was right in America. Marlon and Pimento felt hopelessly paternal.

The woman rolled on her back and grabbed a dorsal with her left hand. She closed her eyes, and the dolphin took her around the tank, over and over.

On the sixth lap, there was shouting. They turned and saw a man hanging over the side of the tank.

"Why haven't you returned my calls?"

Her eyes opened fast, and she let go of the dolphin.

She swam to a ladder, and the man followed her, walking along the tank railing and yelling. "I asked you a question! Nobody treats me like that!"

She climbed out without a sound and started to walk away.

"Did you hear me?" He grabbed her by the arm. The others recognized him. It was DAY-TRADR. "How come you don't want to go out again? Too good for me?"

He shook her. She didn't resist, just let him yank her back and forth and gave him an empty stare.

"You think you're a tough little bitch!"

She finally spoke. "L-l-l-l-let g-g-g-go. You're h-h-h-hurting m-m-m-me!"

He slapped her across the face.

Out of the blue, Pimento erupted with a wild aboriginal scream and charged. The man saw him coming and released the woman's arm just as Pimento tackled him high. They fell into the life preservers. Pimento had the upper hand, but the man pulled a gaff hook off the wall.

So Marlon dove in.

He wrestled the hook away, and he and Pimento began punching the piss out of the man's kidneys.

Escrow jumped up and down. "Oh my God! Oh my God! Oh my God! . . ." He looked around for tourists, but the place was still empty.

If the woman hadn't pulled them off, Marlon and Pimento might have cashed out DAY-TRADR.

"We have to get out of here!" yelled Escrow.

Marlon and Pimento seemed to be taking their time, having trouble registering what they'd just done. Pimento rubbed his scuffed knuckles, and Marlon pulled one of his fingers, popping it back into joint.

"What are you waiting for?" shouted Escrow, pushing them in the direction of the exit.

The woman was also lollygagging, standing over her unconscious assailant.

"You've got to come, too," Escrow told her. "We need to debrief you."

She didn't respond at first, but when the man started regaining consciousness, she turned and ran after them.

They sprinted down the steps and across the street to the Winnebago and took off south.

The woman was sitting up front with Marlon. He went to say something but stopped. He looked at her profile. Gentle features except the cheekbones, which were high and sharp. There was a small scar on her chin. Her wet suit was black-and-aqua and getting the seat damp.

"What's your name?"

She didn't answer.

"You want something to eat?"

He looked over at her, but she stayed facing forward.

"I'll stop anywhere. Just say the word. We got your Checkers and your Pizza Hut . . ."

She pointed.

"That's more like it."

Marlon looked to see where she wanted to go. "Hey, that's not a restaurant. Those are batting cages."

She pointed again, more emphatically.

"You're the boss," he said. "Batting cages it is."

There were five machines in ascending order of velocity. Marlon got out some quarters and walked to the first machine, but she grabbed a bat and helmet and went right for the last one. She squared off at the plate and looked over her shoulder impatiently, waiting for Marlon to put in the quarters. When the last coin fell, the twin wheels began spinning and the balls fell into the chute.

The pitches smoked. Marlon had never seen anything that fast. She fouled off the first three, then found her rhythm and clobbered the next seven. The machine stopped. She turned and stared.

"Okay, okay!" Marlon put in more quarters. The machine began firing again. She kept her streak going, hitting eight in a row with the meat of the bat, most ending up high in the net.

A ball misfed into the wheels and came curving through the batter's box, knocking her down.

She jumped up, tore off her batting helmet and slung it at the machine. Then she crowded the plate and crushed the bat handle in her grip.

The next pitch was another curveball inside, and she opened her stance and pulled it with authority. She stomped away from the plate, handed the bat to Marlon and left the cage.

Pimento waited until she was out of earshot, then came up to Marlon. "What the hell was *that*?"

"I think it's what's called 'unresolved issues.' "

23

THE YOUNG WOMAN from Marineland was sleeping in a bunk in the back of the *Orange Crush* as it continued south along the shore. Escrow tapped on his laptop. Pimento sat up front with Marlon.

"Volkswagen! I called it!" said the governor. He slid an orange window over the Beetle on his card. "I almost have bingo."

"No fair," said Pimento. "I want to draw another card. I got a silo, a snowplow and a mountain on mine."

"Did she say anything?" asked Marlon, pointing over his shoulder.

"Nope. Went right to sleep."

"I don't get it. Won't tell us her name, address, anything."

"She's probably still shook up. Can't say I blame her after what we saw."

"Speaking of which, what happened back there?" asked Marlon.

"What?"

"Jumping that guy. Not that he didn't deserve it. It just isn't you."

Pimento paused awhile. Finally: "I don't remember."

"Don't remember what?"

"Everything."

"What do you mean?"

"I don't know who I am."

"We're all trying to discover ourselves."

Pimento shook his head. "That's not it."

"What are you saying?" Marlon chuckled. "You have amnesia or something?"

Pimento nodded.

"Forget about it!"

But Marlon saw it wasn't a joke.

"You're serious, aren't you?"

"For months, the only thing I could remember was all these history facts and trivia. It was the damnedest thing," said Pimento. "But recently I've started to have these little flashbacks. It can be triggered by something that reminds me of my childhood. . . . Or it can be from The Dark Side, when something makes me angry. Then I start remembering bad things, and I black out. Like back at Marineland, I can only remember that guy yelling at the girl. The next thing I knew he was unconscious and I was standing over him."

"Why didn't you say anything to us?"

"I was afraid you'd fire me. This is the best job I've ever had. Then again, how would I know?"

"I can't believe this!"

"So you're not going to fire me?"

"Of course not."

"Someone I know would."

"Escrow thinks you're dangerous," said Marlon.

"Escrow's dangerous."

"So your memory's on the hazy side. So what? It doesn't change your character. I've been around you long enough to know you're good people."

"I'd just like to remember. Sometimes I find myself in the bathroom for like twenty minutes staring in the mirror . . ."

"Don't worry—I'm sure it'll come back eventually. Meanwhile, you're my best speechwriter. You're my *only* speechwriter. I can't fire you."

"Thanks."

"Just don't attack any more people."

"Deal."

Escrow came forward to report an urgent phone call.

"Sir, we have to move on the tax exemption for the new stadium in Orlando. Von Zeppelin's starting to call people. It's getting nasty."

"I'm going to block the exemption," said Marlon.

Escrow became nervous, then laughed. "Okay, you got me. Good one."

"I'm serious."

"You're starting to scare me," said Escrow. "The joke's not funny anymore."

Marlon was quiet.

"Sir, you've been doing a lot of crazy things. But this one you don't want to mess with. He'll crush us. He could even have us killed."

"There are a lot better uses in Florida for thirty million dollars," said Marlon.

"I'm sure there are. But that's irrelevant."

"Why does he need an exemption, anyway?" asked Pimento.

"He *doesn't*," Escrow said like he was talking to the simple. "That's not the point. The point is that he can get it."

"Not this time," said Marlon.

"What is the fucking *problem* with sports team owners, anyway?" said Pimento. "It's like they took business classes on the Death Star."

"What are you, some kind of Trotskyist?" said Escrow.

"They're not warm-blooded," said Pimento. "I'm convinced they hatch from subterranean membrane pods."

"There you go again—blame it all on the businessman," said Escrow.

"I just want them to show a smidgen of humanity, something we can examine under the microscope to prove there's a few platelets carousing through their arteries instead of that phosphorescent green Prestone ooze I saw when the Buccaneers' owner was riding on a parade float and accidentally cut himself on a money clip suffering from metal fatigue."

"Are you hearing this?" Escrow asked Marlon.

"Play nice," said the governor, trying to concentrate on driving. "Don't make me pull over."

The argument awoke the dolphin woman, and she came forward in the RV rubbing her eyes. She was wearing some unflattering clothes they'd picked up along the way at a strip mall. Jeans, sneakers and a 3 FOR $10 T-shirt from a defunct serpentarium.

"You ready to stop for something to eat now?" asked Marlon.

Escrow checked his watch. "Not enough time, Governor. The debate's set for nine at the speedway, and it's still a long way to Daytona."

At the word *governor*, the woman turned and looked at Marlon, and her eyes flashed with recognition.

"I know," said Marlon. "Don't that beat all?"

Marlon made up time behind the wheel, and in less than an hour they began seeing the bars, college kids and motorcycles that signaled Daytona Beach's orbit. Everyone shifted to the left side of the Winnebago and stared out the windows as traffic thickened and slowed. Outside was a tropical Coney Island, people jamming the boardwalk and the midway, riding the Space Needle, bungee-jumping and driving on the beach to a thousand stereos.

"Right there!" Pimento pointed. "That's where Sir Malcolm Campbell drove two hundred and six miles per hour to set the land speed record on February nineteenth, 1928. The car was called the *Blue Bird*, powered by a Napier aircraft engine."

"More news you can't use," said Escrow.

Marlon turned west, away from the hubbub, and crossed a bridge to the mainland.

"Turn up here on MLK," said Pimento. "I remember something else."

"We don't have time!" said Escrow.

They turned.

Minutes later, they were standing on the edge of an old campus. Pimento whispered, and Marlon nodded.

"Big deal, it's a school. And now we've seen it," Escrow shouted from a window in the RV. "Can we finally go? I mean, if that's okay with you. It's not like we're going to be on TV or anything tonight."

They got back in and headed east.

Marlon was still a few blocks from the Daytona International Speedway when he first saw the turmoil. A giant traffic jam. Cars, lights, people, chaos. The Winnebago pulled into the parking lot next to a row of satellite trucks. Vendors sold corn dogs and fried dough.

News of the wild campaign had spread, and now anyone who wanted any piggyback media exposure was showing up. It was a long, deep ballot this year. Dozens of fringe-party candidates and constitutional amendments, and they were all represented at the speedway. There was the Communist Party and the Socialist Party and the New Socialist Party, which had splintered from the Socialists because it thought they were soft on Communism. There were the Fascists, the Nazis and the Whigs. There was the Libertarian Party, which refused to meet, and the Anarchist Party, whose goal was to disband. There were two parties that wanted to preserve the Confederate flag, the Metaphysical Party, which was selling lucky crystals, and Parrot Heads for Economic Progress.

Every one of them had a candidate for governor, and they stood with megaphones, competing in a cacophony of tortured rhetoric, all packed tightly together except for the Immolation Party candidate. The angry Reform Party nominee, Albert Fresco, was even madder than usual, now having to jockey for the spotlight with a whole cast of quarrelsome paranoids.

As the candidates shouted each other down, highly paid petition-takers canvassed the audience, signing them up for a menu of constitutional amendments that would legalize casino gambling, cap millage rates, penalize the sugar industry, regulate campaign finance, deregulate utilities, and make tax-free e-mail a birthright. Amendment 16 was incomprehensible, and Amendment 33 would repeal Amendment 16.

Marlon and company got out of the *Orange Crush* and worked their way through the noise.

"Ah, democracy in action," said Pimento.

"How do we ever win any wars?" said Escrow.

They passed Albert Fresco, who was yelling at the Fascists. "I was mad first!"

Guards cleared Marlon through the security checkpoint and into the speedway. It was like a rock concert inside. Gomer Tatum was taking water and oxygen under the Democratic tent.

Just before nine o'clock, the candidates made their way to the makeshift stage from opposite sides. Each was given a few minutes for opening remarks and rebuttal. Tatum spent his allotment talking about the electric chair. "We have an execution coming up. The guy's name is Frank Lloyd Sirocco. You watch—I'll bet anything Marlon Conrad weenies out of it! . . . So a lot of things can go wrong with the chair—good!"

The ovation was off the meter. Tatum looked over at Jackie, and she smiled and gave him an A-OK. Perfect—just like they'd rehearsed!

It was Marlon's turn. He stepped up to the microphone.

"I don't wanna talk about the electric chair anymore. It's sick, and everyone who just applauded is sick, too."

That shut them up.

"I want to talk about things that move the spirit. Great achievements don't just happen. People need to be inspired. Many things can inspire you, something as small as a really good movie. I remember watching *Rocky*—the first one, not the others, and especially not the one with Dolph Lundgren. You remember how you felt coming out of the theater?"

There was a lot of nodding. Of course they remembered!

"I know how *I* felt. I was ready to take on the world! I had stallion blood in my veins"—Marlon stopped to throw a few jabs in the air. "No more taking it from the bullies!"

There were hoots and whistles now. People shouted from the beer line. "Yeah, fuck the bullies!"

Marlon raised a hand for them to quiet down. "Things that can inspire us are all around, and we don't even notice. Today, a friend took me to a place just a few miles from this very spot. It's a place here in town you've probably driven by a hundred times. It's a story that may never be made into a movie, but it's much bigger than *Rocky*."

The crowd couldn't believe it. What? Bigger than *Rocky*?

"That's right, bigger than *Rocky*. Because it's true and it's about this great country. . . ."

Escrow whispered to a sound technician, who began playing "Eye of the Tiger" over the PA speakers.

"Turn that crap off!" yelled Marlon. The music stopped. He

looked back at the crowd. "Talk about your against-the-odds story. Her name was Mary. She was the fifteenth child of former slaves. And she wanted to start a school. She only had a dollar-fifty and five students and a small piece of property that used to be the city dump, but she also had something inside that I'd be proud to have just a small piece of. The world was against her, but she made it work. The Klan even showed up. Bunch of brave men! She just sang songs. Her full name was Mary McLeod Bethune, and that school is now Bethune-Cookman College."

He raised his arms and voice for the finale. "Bless you, Daytona, for giving us Mary! . . . I yield the rest of my time to my worthy opponent. Thank you and good night!"

The crowd went wild. They surged the stage. "Eye of the Tiger" came back on as Marlon ducked off the rear of the scaffolding and disappeared.

The *Orange Crush* rolled south in the darkness. They cruised through Titusville after midnight. Marlon looked out his window across the Indian River and saw the mammoth Vehicle Assembly Building at Kennedy Space Center. A few miles beyond it, down by the ocean, something glowed in bright spotlights.

"Must be a shuttle on one of the pads," said Marlon.

"*Endeavour* on Thirty-nine-B," said Pimento.

The woman from Marineland was in the passenger seat, but she still wasn't talking.

They passed Port Canaveral and the subtle Ron Jon Surf Shop in Cocoa Beach and the guard shacks at Patrick Air Force Base.

Marlon thought he'd try again. "What's your name?"

She wouldn't answer.

"Please, just a first name."

"J-J-J-Jenny."

Marlon smiled over his shoulder at Pimento. "She's got a name." He turned back to her. "Jenny, I think both our luck's about to change."

24

"RISE AND SHINE!"

Marlon opened the motel-room door, letting in the morning sun, and Escrow pulled the covers over his head.

Pimento sat up in bed half awake and grabbed his watch off the nightstand. "Eight o'clock! Where are we?"

"Vero Beach."

Marlon tossed the morning papers on Escrow's chest, and Escrow swatted them off.

"Get the lead out. I've been up for two hours," said Marlon. "Got your coffee here."

"Where's Jenny?" asked Pimento.

"Still asleep in the RV."

Marlon opened the lids on three steaming cups in a cardboard McDonald's tray. Pimento grabbed one of the newspapers off the floor. "Hey Escrow, look at this headline: SENATOR INDICTED IN BRIDGE-GATE."

Escrow pulled the covers off his head. "Lemme see that!"

The chairman of the transportation committee had used his influence to get a bridge built out to his investment property, squaring the value of the land.

The paper quoted the senator as he was taken into custody: "I've earned this! You just don't get it!"

Every few days the media christened a new -*Gate*. This week it was *Bridge-Gate*, last week *Lottery-Gate*, the one before that *Cable TV–Gate* and *Emission-Gate*. There was even a scandal at the water plant. The press called it *Plant-Gate*. . . . Escrow was crushed. Another conspiracy and he wasn't involved.

Marlon went out to the RV. It was unlocked and quiet. She must be somewhere getting breakfast. Marlon climbed in.

Jenny didn't hear him as she stepped out of the tiny walk-in shower. She had her back to Marlon as she grabbed a towel.

He was about to apologize and avert his eyes. But before he could, he saw something he'd never forget, and it just blurted out.

"Holy Jesus! What happened?"

Jenny spun and saw him. Her mouth opened and her eyes betrayed shame. Her secret. She ran to the back of the RV.

Marlon knew the sight would bother him for a long time. Across the top of her legs and up her buttocks, a solid pile of scars. Mended, striated flesh, line upon line. God only knew how many times the same spot had healed and been flayed open again.

Marlon ran to the back. He had no idea what was appropriate. "Who did this?"

She was curled in a bunch on the floor, hiding her face in the corner. He put a light hand on her back and she flinched hard, so he took it away.

Marlon returned to the motel room. "Consider this a day off, guys. Go shopping or something. I'm going to stay with Jenny."

"I gotcha," Escrow said with a mischievous grin.

"You're an asshole." Marlon left the room.

Escrow turned to Pimento. "I was just trying to be one of the guys."

"Ain't what it's cracked up to be."

Escrow and Pimento split up for the day. Pimento headed for the beach, and Escrow went straight to the local campaign headquarters of "Tatum for Governor!"

A bell jingled as he opened the door.

"Hi! I'd like to volunteer," Escrow told the young woman in a VOTE TATUM! plastic straw hat. "Got any campaign material you need passed out? . . . And can I have a hat?"

Escrow left with a bundle under his arm. He went to a news rack and bought a copy of the *Press-Journal*. He folded the paper over to the Senior Citizens Activity Bulletin Board and called a taxi.

Escrow tipped the cabbie outside a local retirement park, then went into the office and bribed the activities coordinator. . . .

Four hundred seniors sat in the bingo hall of Puerto Lago Boca Vista Isles East, enjoying baked goods and juice at their regular Thursday-morning installment of Canasta-Mania.

The activities coordinator tapped the microphone on stage. "May I have your attention? This morning we have a special guest with us. He's a top political official who's going to discuss issues affecting senior citizens."

Sounded important. They put down their sticky buns.

"He's come all the way from the capital, so please give a warm Vista Isles welcome to Phil Striker!"

Escrow smiled and waved to the crowd as he passed the electric bingo board on his way to the podium. His suit was blue, shirt white, tie red. On his lapel, an enamel American flag; on his head, a VOTE TATUM! straw hat.

"My name is Phil Striker," said Escrow, "and I'm with the Tatum campaign. What I want to talk to you about today is the future. And, let's face it, you're not the future. The future is youth, but how are they ever going to get anywhere if you won't take your bony little fingers off Medicare and Social Security? . . ."

The auditorium went silent.

"Why don't you stop being so selfish and accept the inevitable? I say we slash benefits and use the money to cut the capital gains tax so those out there still actually contributing to society can make some money and get this country moving again! Who's with me?"

The first thing to hit Escrow was a cinnamon roll. Followed by slices of cantaloupe and papaya, blueberry muffins, crescent rolls and a crumpled-up Styrofoam cup weighted with a rock that had somehow made its way into the auditorium.

"Wait!" Escrow yelled. "Would you for once think of the poor young executive instead of your incontinent butts?"

They charged the podium with canes and electric scooters.

"Kill him!" someone yelled. A metal folding chair flew up onstage.

"Go ahead, live in the past!" he yelled and threw a batch of VOTE TATUM! campaign brochures at the mob and escaped off the side of the stage.

●

ACROSS town, another group of senior citizens sat in another hall, their coffee cups long since empty, doughnut crumbs on the tables, napkins wadded and rewadded dozens of times. They fidgeted painfully.

The group was ninety minutes into a high-pressure time-share pitch that had been guaranteed to last "no more than a half hour." That was the price they had to pay for all the breakfast pastry and beverage they could hold. The time-share people knew their audience. To retirees, free doughnut holes and orange juice were like crack.

A hunched old man in a Pearl Harbor vet baseball cap got up to leave. The salesman blocked his path.

"But I want to go."

"Just a little while longer."

"You said it would only be a half hour."

"Sit down!"

The man sat down.

There were about fifty of them in the audience, all at least sixty-five years old. Except one guy. He was fortyish and making his ninth trip to the food table. He was on the thin side, with blue eyes and short hair that had touches of gray at the temples.

"Must have a high metabolism," one senior whispered to another.

A second retiree got up, this time a woman.

"And where do you think *you're* going?" asked the salesman.

"I have a doctor's appointment."

The salesman pointed at her seat. She sat back down.

Everyone was distracted by a loud rattling noise in the back of the room. During his latest trip to the food table, the younger man had wrapped his arms around the massive plexiglass orange juice sprinkler-dispenser and was tipping it forward to get the last drops. Then he drained the tiny paper cup and headed for the door.

"Not so fast," said the salesman, stepping in front of the man.

Pimento pointed back at the juice machine. "But it's empty."

"Nobody leaves until I say so."

Pimento grinned and gave the salesman a solid head butt to the face that broke the man's nose, and he punctually went to the floor yelling and bleeding.

The seniors erupted with a big "Hurray!" and charged out of the room like a slow-motion storming of the Bastille.

Escrow and Pimento arrived back in the motel room at the same time. Marlon was watching the evening news. The anchor desk had just wrapped up a pair of segments involving local seniors. First was a small uprising at a local bingo hall—some broken windows, a lounger set on fire. Then the station cut to an assault at a time-share seminar. Nobody would identify the assailant, but a Pearl Harbor survivor had taken responsibility, and the anchor desk joked about his becoming a hero for the second time.

Marlon eyed the pair as they walked in the room. "Guys?" he said suspiciously, pointing at the TV.

"Look at the time!" said Escrow. "We're going to be late for the book-signing!"

"Whose book-signing?" asked Marlon.

"Yours!"

"When did I write a book?" Marlon asked as they drove over to the Vero Beach Book Center.

"It just came out," said Escrow. He pulled a copy from his brief-case and handed it to Marlon. "I've been meaning to tell you."

Marlon examined the impressive hardcover. The front had a soft-focus picture of Marlon walking barefoot on the beach at sunset, with an inset of the famous Reuters photograph from Kosovo. He read the title.

A TRUST RENEWED: GIVING GOVERNMENT BACK TO THE PEOPLE
AN OUTSIDER'S BLUEPRINT FOR BOLD NEW REFORM
MY OWN COURAGEOUS JOURNEY
by Marlon Conrad

Marlon bounced the book in his hand, gauging the heft.

"Pretty heavy—lot of pages," said Marlon. "Who wrote it?"

"I did," said Escrow.

"I see," said Marlon. "Where'd you get the title?"

"Standard stuff. It's how all campaigns are run now. Just keep promising change and reform out the wazoo . . ."

"And then get reelected and keep giving them the same old thing?"

"Exactly."

"I can see how you got to be where you are."

"Can't take all the credit," said Escrow. "They teach it in college now."

The Winnebago pulled into the bookstore parking lot. An impressive line of book-toting people spilled out the door and snaked around the building. Across the street, protesters waved signs behind a police barricade.

Marlon read the placards as he climbed down from the RV. BOOK OF SHAME! VILE VOLUME! BOYCOTT THE OPPRESSIVE WRITINGS OF CONRAD! CHARACTERS HAD NO DEPTH!

The bookstore's author liaison came out and shook Marlon's hand. "I'm a big admirer," she said, leading him inside. "Love what you're doing on the campaign."

"What did you think of the book?"

"Your economic theories are quite impressive, but . . ."

"But what?"

"Don't take this the wrong way, but your day-care ideas seemed a little, well, heartless."

"Is that so?" said Marlon, scowling at Escrow.

Marlon took a seat at a table in the back of the store and was soon signing books at a furious pace. The people were gracious, requesting a variety of inscriptions to themselves, relatives, friends and pets.

"Make it out to 'Debby, the hottest account representative I've ever laid my eyes on.' "

The line went on forever. People smiled and shook his hand and heaped on the compliments. A man in a camo hunting cap handed Marlon a book. His T-shirt read FLORIDA MILITIA JAMBOREE '99. He patted Marlon on the back and winked. "Good to see you're with us!"

Marlon looked up puzzled. "Oh, right. Sure thing."

There was a commotion at the front of the store. An Orthodox rabbi had broken through the police line and burst in the doors. "I can't believe what you wrote about the Holocaust!" The police caught him from behind and wrestled him back outside.

Marlon grabbed Escrow by the arm. "What did I write about the Holocaust?"

"I'm gonna get you some more pens," said Escrow, pulling away. "You never know when you could run dry."

●

TRAFFIC was insane as the *Orange Crush* rolled down Interstate 95 after the book signing. Not the volume. The people. Every fourth driver speeding and weaving like a maniac, darting between other cars with barely enough room, starting in the far left lane and cutting across three vehicles for the exit ramp. Ahead of them, Marlon saw a gun momentarily pointed out the window of a Camaro, a traffic gesture which, due to its frequency in Florida, is ignored.

Marlon took exit 51.

"Where are we going?" asked Escrow.

"West Palm airport. Have to pick up someone for Jenny."

"That reminds me," said Escrow. "You never told us about your day."

And he wasn't going to.

He had left Jenny in the Winnebago most of the morning but kept an eye on it through the motel window. At noon, he picked up a sack of fast food and knocked on the RV's door. No answer. He went inside. She was still in the back, so he left the bag on a fold-down table.

Back in the motel room, he dialed the phone.

"Belvedere and Associates," said the receptionist.

"Elizabeth Sinclair, please."

Marlon was told she was no longer with the firm. "I'm not supposed to do this," said the receptionist, and she gave him a new number.

Marlon dialed it.

"Sinclair and Associates. This is Elizabeth Sinclair."

"Ms. Sinclair, this is Marlon Conrad. I'm in Vero. I'd like you to join the campaign."

"Thank you very much, Mr. Conrad, but we're completely booked with clients." She was lying. She had only a couple of small local candidates and was wondering how she would pay the electric bill.

"Name your price. We really need help."

"I appreciate it, but I'm sorry . . ." She started to hang up.

"Look, I know how I used to be. This isn't like that. I have an emergency and I don't know who to talk to."

Marlon told her about Jenny.

"This is out of my league," he said. "You're the only mature person I know."

"You don't even know me."

"There are five Learjets at the Tallahassee airport and five corporations just drooling to give me one. I've called ahead and said you're our top campaign adviser. They'll do anything you say. . . ."

"I don't know."

"Please do this and I'll never bother you again. We'll pick you up at West Palm International."

A Learjet from Big Pharmaceutical landed after dark at the executive hangars in West Palm Beach. It had a giant gelcap on the tail.

Elizabeth Sinclair stood at the top of the stairs and looked around for her ride, but all she saw was this goofy Winnebago. Then she saw Marlon, Escrow and Pimento get out. They were all in shorts and rumpled T-shirts. Escrow's shirt had a pointillist rendering of Newt Gingrich's face above a motto: GO NEGATIVE EARLY!

God, she thought, is it too late to go back?

Marlon ran to the bottom of the stairs. "Thanks for coming. . . . She's in the *Orange Crush*."

"In the *what*?" asked Elizabeth, climbing in the back of the RV. Marlon drove off the runway and picked up Southern Boulevard.

Fifteen minutes later, Elizabeth came up front and flipped open a cell phone. She interrupted a college friend at the Royal Poinciana Playhouse. It was an emergency. The friend left her date and climbed in her black Jag.

They met Sinclair's friend, a world-class psychiatrist, at her Mediterranean home on the north end of Palm Beach, near the inlet. The *Orange Crush* was rousted twice by police in the swank neighborhood before it pulled through the twelve-foot box hedge that formed an arch over the driveway.

Sinclair introduced everyone, and then they left Jenny and the psychiatrist in the house and waited in the Winnebago, playing the Florida version of Monopoly.

The psychiatrist came out of the house two hours later as Escrow was putting hotels in the Everglades.

"Rory, can I talk to you a minute?" she asked Sinclair. They walked back to the porch.

Marlon and Pimento looked at each other. Rory?

"She's traumatized," said the psychiatrist. "She shouldn't be going anywhere, but I can't get her to cooperate. She says she'll run away if I try to take her off that bus or whatever it is. She's developed a dependence on those guys."

"She *is* messed up."

"Something happened back there on the road, but she won't say what. I've written a prescription in case she becomes agitated. You'll have to keep the bottle—she's in no condition to self-medicate."

"Hold on. I'm not riding with those guys!"

Her friend gave her The Look.

Marlon watched the two old college buddies hugging in the driveway, and Sinclair got back in the Winnebago. The governor looked at her as she settled in the passenger seat. "Rory?"

"Nobody calls me that!"

As the psychiatrist watched the Winnebago pull out through the shrubbery arch, she thought she could hear the men inside chanting something.

"Ro-ry! Ro-ry! Ro-ry! . . ."

25

DETECTIVE MAHONEY'S WIFE hadn't taken him back, and he was paying by the week at the Gulfstream Inn on Biscayne Boulevard.

The Gulfstream had three stories, and Mahoney was on the second. The first was taken up by the Sailfish Diner, a smoky short-order grill favored by cops and cabbies on the lobster shift, and the staircase was next to the cash register. On the wrong side of the water from Miami Beach, the Gulfstream was one of the few art deco holdovers that hadn't been renovated. It had a white, curved, streamlined facade with window AC units and rust streaks. There were clusters of filthy glass blocks and a buzzing green GULFSTREAM neon sign. The *F* flickered.

Mahoney's room was in back, with a view of the alley. It was a tiny dump, but he made himself at home as best he could. He brought a black-and-white TV, a portable hi-fi record player and a stack of jazz records on the old Verve label. He put a photo of Broderick Crawford on the dresser.

Mahoney sat at the modest writing desk watching TV in a white tank top. Also on the desk was an open can of Vienna sausages and a large jar of Mr. Mustard with a butter knife sticking out. There was a glass of straight bourbon, no ice. He lit a Chesterfield and set it in a plaid beanbag ashtray.

The TV showed a huge wave rolling toward a beach, and the theme music to *Hawaii Five-O* came on. Mahoney smiled for the first time all day.

"McGarrett, Five-O!" Jack Lord barked into a phone. Mahoney grabbed a case file off the bed and opened it in his lap.

Mahoney had been obsessed with the case for years. He studied the smiling mug shot for the thousandth time and read the name on the fingerprint card: Serge A. Storms. It was the biggest fugitive case in Florida that nobody had ever heard of. Serge was a suspect in several murder cases, including two at the 1997 World Series in Miami. Mahoney had once tracked him down to a rental home on Trigger-fish Lane in Tampa, and there had been a chase and a showdown. Serge escaped.

Mahoney had gotten so close to the case that he'd developed a grudging admiration for the guy. Serge was a regular encyclopedia of Floridiana. It was one of the many ways he was a genius and insane at the same time. Storms traveled in low-life circles, and his victims were mostly dirtballs, scam artists and predators. The people started rooting for him. Everywhere Mahoney went looking for witnesses, he found people who revered Serge like a folk hero, a tropical D. B. Cooper. At one point, Mahoney began getting postcards from the guy. He expected the usual taunts a detective receives when a criminal learns he's on the trail. Instead, he got travel tips and a suggested reading list. Mahoney checked all the books out of the library, in case there were any clues. But all he found was a bunch of novels that were now on his all-time favorites list. Willeford, MacDonald, Buchanan, Garcia-Aguilera—Florida crime fiction supreme. Right after he arrested the guy, he was going to thank him and borrow some books.

Hawaii Five-O ended and the news came on. Mahoney put down the file and adjusted the antenna. The first story was about the string of bodies turning up with a bunch of pithy slogans written on them with Magic Markers.

The anchorman dubbed them the Bumper Sticker Murders.

"Great," said Mahoney. "Here come the copycats."

Sure enough, over the next few days stiffs would start turning up all over the state with clichés scribbled in Magic Marker. A road rage victim in Jacksonville: FORGET ABOUT WORLD PEACE . . . VISUALIZE USING YOUR TURN SIGNAL! A hooker in Pensacola: SEX IS LIKE PIZZA.

WHEN IT'S GOOD, IT'S REALLY GOOD. WHEN IT'S BAD, IT'S STILL PRETTY GOOD. A psychiatrist strangled by a patient in Sarasota: DOES THE NAME PAVLOV RING A BELL?

Mahoney went over to the window. He cranked it open and stuck his head out into the alley. Down the north end of the street he had a glimpse of the skyscrapers in the Miami skyline. His new sidekick, a stray cat he'd named Danno, jumped up on the sill, and Mahoney gave him a Vienna sausage.

Mahoney stared down the alley at the city lights and petted the cat. "Book 'em, Danno!"

⬤

THE roadways were getting cluttered. Political posters and signs on sticks everywhere—roadsides, front yards, tacked on utility polls, hanging from overpasses.

The marketing techniques were getting refined. There had been a trend away from conventional political consultants and the traditional campaign philosophy of "getting our message out to the people." Surveys showed the people were allergic to messages and refused to listen, even if the president was on TV saying the water supply was radioactive and giant spiders were running the government.

The strategy shifted from "the message" to brand recognition after it was learned that most campaigns were decided during the selection of color scheme, typeface and logo. Campaigns began aggressively head-hunting at Coca-Cola and Procter & Gamble. They spent heavily on focus groups and test markets. Conference rooms full of average citizens ate potato chips and pickle spears while campaign workers auditioned fonts and swatches.

It was discovered that simple equaled good. A maximum of two colors, and icons less complicated than a trapezoid. Also gone were the slogans. Now just one word, usually nonsense, that bypassed the conscious and treble-hooked the brain stem. Candidates saw their polls rocket.

Gomer Tatum and Jackie Monroeville were a day behind Marlon, driving down US 1 in a limo. They had just entered Indian River County. Tatum stared at the political picket fence in the median.

A green-and-white sign. Garamond typeface. A starfish. JACKSON FOR MAYOR! SHAZAM!

A blue-and-yellow sign. News Gothic type. A musical note (b flat). VOTE O'MALLEY! FARFEGNÜGEN!

A red-and-black sign. Bodoni sans serif. Bowling pin. REELECT WILLIAMS! BIBBIDY-BOP!

Between debates, Tatum was on a frenetic schedule of rubber-chicken gigs and impromptu drop-ins.

They crossed the Vero Beach city limits.

"What's this coming up?" said Jackie. "Stop here!"

Tatum's driver pulled into the parking lot of Vista Isles East, and Gomer got out with a fat, cheerful expression. The residents recognized the magnetic TATUM signs on the door, and the limo was pelted with rotten fruit and smooth landscaping stones.

"Unfriendlies!" yelled Tatum. He dove back in the limo as a fetid eggplant splattered on the tinted window.

"Look at you!" Jackie shouted at Tatum in the backseat of the stretch, smacking him in the gut. "No wonder they're throwing produce! We need to bad-ass your image!"

They continued down the coast on A1A. Jackie saw a sign. JENSEN BEACH DEAD SLEDS. "Stop here!"

The driver pulled into a dusty parking lot, and Tatum got out.

Two men emerged from a dilapidated aluminum building, a four-hundred-pound biker named Tiny and a rail-thin speed freak named Fats.

"Hi, fellas—"

They grabbed Tatum by the collar and lifted him off his feet, pinning him against the side of the limo.

The chauffeur turned back to Jackie. "Want me to call the police?"

"I'll handle this," she said, quickly changing into leather hot pants. "These are my people."

The bikers were pushing a lug wrench up Tatum's nose when

Jackie's door opened. Two slender, taut legs swung out of the limo. A pair of white cowboy boots settled in the dust. Jackie stood up in her shorts and a fringed suede vest, and she put her hands defiantly on her hips.

"Which one of you shit-kickers is man enough to strap me on a hog?"

26

BY LATE OCTOBER, the expansion Florida Felons football team had carefully assembled a ten-game losing skid.

During the third quarter of a forty-point ambush by the Redskins, Helmut von Zeppelin's skybox was gutted by a carbide-tipped firebomb that shattered the shatterproof window and set the polar bear rug ablaze.

For security reasons, Helmut had to view the next game through binoculars from a greater distance. He bought one of Goodyear's backup blimps, and von Zeppelin watched his team *from* a zeppelin.

"They can't touch me up here!" Helmut declared during halftime of a fifty-point drubbing from the Saints, a moment before a rifle shot pierced the dirigible's skin near the tail.

The pilot heard a hissing sound and checked his gauges.

"I have to take her down."

"We'll miss the second half!"

"Sir, I think they're shooting at us."

"Amazing," said Helmut, standing behind the pilot with his binoculars. "What kind of gun can reach us way up here?"

"Maybe a Tac-Ops Tango-51."

"What's that?"

"Sniper rifle."

Helmut leaned with an elbow against the back of the pilot chair and shook his head in respect. "I'll have to get me one of those."

The pilot struggled with the controls, but he couldn't hold the yaw. He checked the gauges again. The blimp had begun to rotate clockwise.

"Hey," said Helmut. "This isn't the way back to the airfield."

"We're not going to the airfield," said the pilot, letting go of the steering yoke. "The puncture must be spewing air sideways. Too much torque. I've lost attitude control."

"What now?" asked Helmut.

"Ride it out—nothing else we can do."

"How long till we're down?"

"About a half hour."

"Are we going to crash?"

"Yes."

"Will we be killed?"

"Possibly."

Helmut looked out the window. "Hey—I can see my house!"

The impotent blimp swiveled slowly in the breeze across the central Florida landscape as it lost altitude. News vans began to converge from eight counties, forming a convoy behind the blimp's shadow in the road.

A phone rang in the blimp. Helmut answered. It was from New Jersey.

"You'll get your thirty million!" shouted von Zeppelin. "It's hit some kind of political pothole!"

At 4:37 P.M., a bank of fail-safe computers tripped a sequence of alarms, and corporate jets were scrambled as the blimp crossed into Disney World airspace.

The news vans stacked up at the entrance to buy tickets, then raced to Pleasure Island. A small Japanese child pointed at the sky. Everyone looked up. A giant vulcanized air bladder came flatulating across the treetops in a slow spin.

"You have to give me more time!" Helmut told New Jersey on the phone. "These politicians are a pain in the—"

Helmut heard a low-syllable-count death threat.

"You don't intimidate me!" yelled Helmut. "I was threatening people when you were—"

The phone call was cut off as the blimp crashed into the side of Planet Hollywood, and Helmut was saved when he was thrown through the ruptured side of the cabin and into a Barcalounger once owned by George Gobel.

In the parking lot, Florida Cable News correspondent Blaine Crease was weeping on live TV.

"The humanity! The humanity!"

27

IN THE HIGH-RISE offices of the *Palm Beach Daily Intelligencer-Picayune,* overlooking fabulous Lake Worth, the newspaper's editorial board heard a rumbling sound. It grew to a thundering racket, and they all ran to the window.

Down in the parking lot was the biggest Harley they'd ever seen. The rider set the kickstand and climbed off. A second, larger rider crawled out of a sidecar. They went in the building.

The editorial board turned and watched the elevator and waited.

The doors opened and out stepped Gomer Tatum, head to toe in leather, with a little Prussian helmet perched atop his bulbous head. The editorial board didn't give a shit. They craned their necks to see around him. Tatum finally moved and Jackie stepped out of the elevator, wearing her cowboy boots and hot pants again. Oh, and she still had her leather riding gloves on. The editorial board liked that.

Tatum shook hands and walked to the front of the boardroom, and Jackie took a seat by the window, propping her feet up on the sill and cracking her knuckles inside the gloves.

"Gentlemen!" boomed Tatum. "Governor Conrad is soft on the death penalty!"

Tatum looked over at Jackie. She nodded in approval. The editorial board also looked over at Jackie. She nodded at them, too.

Tatum continued: "While our schoolchildren are forced to eat stale pizza squares and fish sticks for lunch, murderers have been treated to a five-star menu of last meals under the Conrad administration. Just listen to this list: Delmonico steak, lobster, ribs, Cajun blackened mahimahi"—Tatum began salivating—"rack of lamb with curly fries, Denny's Grand-Slam breakfast . . . Gentlemen, if I'm elected, I won't just fry 'em. I'll fry 'em *hungry*!"

●

THE *Orange Crush* headed south on US 1. It was a weird stretch of road. People living permanently in motel rooms, arguing at bus stops. Boarded-up restaurants. Body-piercing joints. A sign: "Psychic on duty 24 hours."

Gottfried Escrow had an "action item" that he just couldn't seem to clear from his clipboard. "Get Frank Lloyd Sirocco's death warrant signed."

Marlon kept putting it off.

"Tatum's killing you on this. You have to get an execution in," said Escrow. "If you don't warrant Sirocco soon, we won't be able to smoke another one until after the election."

"I'm still ahead," said Marlon. "I can win without it."

"Tatum's in your margin of error! Every day he hammers on this, he chips away at your lead."

"I have faith in the people."

"I give up," said Escrow. "Here, sign this other crap."

Escrow fanned a stack of papers on the dashboard of the *Orange Crush,* and Marlon scribbled quickly at stoplights. Official proclamations. Appointments to ceremonial boards. Don Knotts Appreciation Day. The last item on the bottom of the stack, with just the signature line showing, was Sirocco's warrant.

Escrow checked his clipboard. "We got nothing for the rest of the day except your commercial shoot."

"That thing's today?" Marlon said with apprehension.

"You're not going to back out, are you?"

"No, I gave my word."

"Good," said Escrow. "I'll call Ned and tell him we're on."

●

NED Coppola was the undisputed king of the thirty-second political TV spot.

Single-handedly, he had reinvented the medium. Nobody but nobody could strike a chord so deeply with so many people in so short a time. The images, the words, the emotions—they flowed and built and exploded in operatic grandeur. All in a half minute. Wham bam, in and out, leaving some viewers weeping, others in the glow of a religious experience—but all compelled to rush out and vote with a blind fervor. Sometimes Ned produced commercials for both sides in a race. Viewers would see one spot, then the other, and were left severely conflicted and often gained weight.

Ned was outrageously expensive, and everyone gladly paid. To hire anyone else was to automatically forfeit a deciding chunk in the polls. Ned wasn't just the leader in his field; he was deity.

He hated every moment.

Ned was an extremely distant stepcousin by divorce of Oscar-winning director Francis Ford Coppola, and all he ever wanted was to follow, however far behind, in his famous semirelative's footfalls. He aspired to produce celluoid art, not the manipulative schmaltz that all the campaigns called genius.

But while Ned was without peer in the political world, he couldn't get arrested in Hollywood. Not a toe in the door. And with good reason. Ned's talents hit a kind of a ceiling at the thirty-second mark. Anything longer than a Bicentennial minute would come off the reels with stupefying results. Ned flourished at MTV sprint distances, but he had no cinematic endurance whatsoever. It was almost mystical. People who saw the rare footage couldn't believe it. How could this be the work of the same person?

It was the source of unrelenting bitterness for Ned, who poured his frustrations into the campaigns, which only improved the quality of his work and made him that much more popular and pissed off.

Ned's business office was a condo penthouse that occupied an entire fiftieth floor on Collins Avenue in Miami Beach. His studio was in an office park just over the Broward line in—where else?—Hollywood, Florida. He spent the mornings in the penthouse taking calls on his portable phone and the afternoons directing at the studio.

On this particular morning, Ned paced around his penthouse balcony in a white terry-cloth bathrobe with the monogram NIC. *I* for Ingmar. His hair was dark, shaggy and unmanaged, because he was going for "The Oliver Stone." He was inexplicably tanned for someone whose nebbish accountant looks suggested a lot of scurrying around under fluorescent lighting. He was tall and lean, but his features were on the small side and heavily weighted toward the vertical axis of his face, leaving his cheeks and jaw without a whole lot to do. Although not unattractive, the overall result prompted suspicion that his mother had been on something during the pregnancy.

The penthouse's tiled terrace wrapped all the way around the building, and Ned made hyperactive laps as he talked on the phone. The views were astounding, and Ned saw none of it. To the east, the clear Atlantic; north, waterfront golf courses; west, Biscayne Bay and uptown Miami; south, the art deco jewels Delano and Dilido. He snapped the phone closed in frustration, then opened it and dialed again.

"Chad, Coppola here, what did ya think of my new treatment? . . . I see . . . I see . . . Well, did you read the whole thing? . . . I see, just the title . . . But the title is the hook, *Thelma and Louise II*. . . . Of course I know you can't have a sequel when the main characters are killed—so get this: They had parachutes! . . . Hello? Chad? Hello? . . ."

Ned hung up and dialed the number for Paramount Studios.

"Is Brad there? This is Coppola."

The studios had stopped returning Ned's calls months ago, and recently had stopped accepting them as well. So Ned started introducing himself simply as Coppola.

"Brad—Coppola here . . . No, *Ned* Coppola, Frankie's cousin . . . Hello? Hello? . . ."

He dialed MGM.

"Harrison, Coppola here . . . Yeah, I know you told me not to call anymore, but you're going to thank me after you hear this . . . Okay,

I'll make it quick. Four words that will slay the Academy: *Apocalypse Then and Now*. Martin Sheen opens a health food store in Monterey. . . . Hello? You still there? Hello? . . ."

He dialed Universal.

"Isaac, Coppola here. . . . Right, the Coppola you never wanted to hear from again. . . . Just hear me out. Hoffman goes for his master's in *The Postgraduate*. . . . I disagree. No, it is *not* the stupidest idea in the world. . . . Okay, try this one on: *More Terms of Endearment*. . . . Hello? Hello? . . ."

Ned threw the phone in disgust on the sofa, and it bounced off a stuffed pillow into his hundred-gallon saltwater aquarium. The wall phone rang.

"Coppola here . . . Oh, hi, Escrow . . . Yeah, we're set for this afternoon . . . See you then. . . ."

The *Orange Crush* arrived at Eagle Studios a few minutes ahead of schedule, and Ned gave everyone the quick tour. Most of the studio was taken up by the set, where stagehands wheeled away a backdrop of Washington crossing the Delaware and replaced it with the 1980 Olympic hockey team. There were movie cameras everywhere, arrays of lights and boom microphones, makeup trays, and an old-fashioned cone megaphone next to a tall director's chair with COP-POLA stitched on the back.

Ned showed them the prop room. On one wall, shelves of baseball gloves, American flags, high school trophies, priests' collars, facsimile bills of rights, plastic apple pies, plastic hams, plastic mashed potatoes, plastic cocker spaniel puppies, cowboy hats, crutches, baskets of combat medals, Norman Rockwell paintings and Gutenberg Bibles. On the other wall, the racks of costumes: police officers, kindergarten teachers, firemen, crossing guards, soldiers, varsity lettermen, nuns, Boy Scouts, factory workers, Red Cross volunteers, grandmothers and Abe Lincoln.

A director's assistant approached. "Ned, it's time to get Marlon ready."

Marlon was taken to a small room with a star on the door, where he was dressed in a sky-blue long-sleeve shirt and sky-blue pants.

"Are you sure this is right?" Marlon asked, lying back in a chair as the makeup went on.

"Shhhhh!" said Escrow. "Ned's very temperamental about his work."

Marlon was taken to wait in the green room, where Ned's stable of actors sipped champagne from plastic cups and snacked on trays of cold cuts and Triscuits. Everyone else was pacing, reciting lines. A bad English Shakespearean actor, a bad Hollywood Method actor, an off-off-Broadway stand-in, a waitress with dreams, a bell-hop with migraines, a chorus line floozy, a body double, a foul-mouthed octogenarian, child-size midgets smoking cigars and Erik Estrada.

Marlon was finally brought to the set, which now had a plain sky-blue backdrop that matched his shirt and pants.

Ned sat in his director's chair. He clapped his hands twice, and a stagehand placed a large box on the set and directed Marlon to sit on it. He handed Marlon a Gutenberg Bible. They started filming.

"Cut! Cut!" Ned yelled. "Hate it!"

The stagehand took away the Bible and put the plastic cocker spaniel on Marlon's lap, and they started filming again.

"Cut!" Ned yelled. He got out of the director's chair and began marching back and forth with his hands behind his back. He grumbled and insulted his crew and invoked the names of Hollywood greats.

The stagehand took away the puppy and handed Marlon a beach ball.

"Cut!" Ned yelled. "This ain't fuckin' Olin Mills!"

The stagehand took away the beach ball and put an Army helmet on Marlon's head.

"Make him stand," said Ned.

Marlon stood. They filmed for thirty seconds.

Ned smiled and bunched together the fingertips of his right hand and kissed them like a chef. "Perfect!"

Marlon looked down at his light-blue pants and shirt. "The helmet doesn't go."

"Trust me," said Ned.

"What about the background?"

"We add all that later with computers." Ned raised the cone megaphone. "That's a wrap!"

Everybody shook hands as they prepared to depart, and Pimento asked Ned to autograph his scrapbook. "I'm a huge fan. Loved watching you work."

"Why, thank you," said Ned, faking humility. He signed Pimento's book boldly.

"You were incredible," said Pimento. "Very *Godfather*."

Ned looked up. "*Godfather!* That's my favorite movie! My step-cousin made it!"

"It's obviously in the blood," said Pimento.

"You really think so?"

Ned was so touched by Pimento's praise that he invited everyone back to his penthouse so he could spend more time with Pimento and hear more praise.

"We'll have to pass," said Escrow. "We've got a full schedule."

"Marlon, please," said Pimento. "Just for a little bit."

Escrow fumed as he sat with folded arms in a fiftieth-floor penthouse on Collins Avenue. He glanced at the fish tank and saw a tiny skeleton popping in and out of a bubbling treasure chest, next to a phone.

"The studios are run by yes-men entrenched in a *Titanic* mentality!" Ned told Pimento as they sat in Coppola's office. The walls were covered with family photos, mostly of Ned as a child on the sets of his famous cousin's movies. "Everything has to be a big-budget action film! You'd never get a *Last Picture Show* made today!"

"I hear ya," said Pimento, studying a photo of little Ned shaking hands with James Caan, covered with bullet holes.

"You appreciate film. Tell me what you think," said Ned. "*Midnight Cowboy II*. After Ratso Rizzo's funeral, Joe Buck opens this wacky delicatessen on Miami Beach."

"It's got comeback vehicle for Jon Voight written all over it."

"That's what I keep telling them, but I can't get the time of day."

"Hollywood-types."

"I got a million of 'em. Every one, solid gold. *Citizen Kane II*—

some kid pulls the sled out of the furnace, and get this: It's a *magic sled!* ... *Kramer vs. Kramer, K2: The Next Generation*—not even a nibble!"

"They're too busy cranking out *The Flintstones, The Mod Squad* and *Lost in Space*." Pimento stopped to admire a photo of little Ned in the Philippines, sharing a banana split with Brando. A lightbulb came on. "I got an idea! Why don't you come with us?"

"What for?"

"Bring some cameras. Film the whole campaign from the bus. It'd be like a Merry Pranksters thing."

"You may have something," said Ned. "I've been waiting years for a project like that. A close-to-the-bone docudrama. I'm sick of this political hackwork."

"I'm the press secretary, so consider yourself credentialed."

"Great. Give me a couple of days to wrap up here, and I'll meet you on the road."

"I think this is the beginning of a beautiful friendship."

28

THE NEXT MORNING, a high-performance Bell Jet Ranger helicopter lifted off a rooftop helipad above Miami and headed north along the coast. It traced the condo canyons and hotels from Ocean Drive to Bal Harbor, then headed inland over funky Dania.

FCN correspondent Blaine Crease pointed down at another condo. "Didn't that use to be Pirate's World?"

The pilot said he didn't know.

Marlon wasn't getting enough sleep. He yawned at the wheel on I-95. The morning drivers weaved, flipped birds and darted around the *Orange Crush*. Escrow brought a box of letters to the front of the Winnebago.

"And here's the mail. A hundred dollars from some nobody, another hundred from nobody, another hundred . . ." Escrow flipped fast-forward through the checks in disbelief. "They're *all* a hundred dollars! And I've never heard of any of these people!" He kept flipping.

"Maybe I've struck a nerve with the common folk," said Marlon. "Maybe that's all they could afford."

"Then why are they giving it to the GOP?" said Escrow. "You know the saying—'There's no dumber animal than a poor Republican.' "

Marlon hugged the shoulder of the road as a Beemer flew by, shot between two semis and skidded onto the exit ramp.

"And now we move on to your fan mail," said Escrow. " 'You

suk,' 'You suk big time,' 'We should call you Hoover you suk so much,' 'I think you're great! Just kidding—you suk!' and *'Why did you implant the transmitter in my head?"*

Another car began passing on Marlon's left. A convertible. The driver raised a pistol at the Winnebago. The other drivers saw it, changed lanes and sipped coffee. The car advanced slowly, moving up along the side of the *Orange Crush*, a convertible red Ferrari with a vanity tag. DAY-TRADR. It was nearly to Marlon's window.

"There he is!" shouted Blaine Crease. The Bell Jet Ranger swooped down over the morning traffic on I-95, made a hard bank and came up the southbound lanes until it was hovering over the *Orange Crush*. A rope ladder unrolled from the side of the helicopter.

"Look what I bought!" said Pimento, holding a tiny, pocket-sized TV with a three-inch crystal screen. "Isn't this an incredible gadget? I picked it up at Wal-Mart so we could watch Marlon's commercials on the road." Pimento looked at his watch. "His first should be airing any second."

Right on schedule, Marlon's spot opened with a soft fade-in on a playground, followed by a Veterans Day parade and an old woman in a rocking chair looking at a picture of herself as a young girl. There were violins and a mellow flute. A police officer on horseback as sunrise broke through elm branches. Children chasing an ice-cream truck. A church picnic. Finally, a ground-level shot looking up at Marlon Conrad in an Army helmet. The camera pulled back to show Marlon in a soldier's uniform with a big-ass medal on his chest that said "Hero." Behind him a massive American flag unfurling in gossamer slow motion. Fade-out.

"Genius!" said Escrow.

"That's it? No words?" said Marlon. "Where's my message?"

"The medium is the message."

"So get Marshall McLuhan to run the state."

After the commercial, ABC broke in with a simulcast from Blaine Crease's helicopter. A news caption read: "Live—Interstate 95."

"Hey, check it out!" said Pimento, pointing at the tiny TV. "It's that dude from the debates. What the hell's he doing? Must be some kind of cool stunt—he's trying to climb down onto that RV." Pimento looked out the window at their surroundings. "I'll bet that's going on right around here somewhere."

The red Ferrari gained on the *Orange Crush* and finally pulled even with Marlon's window, and the gunman stiffened his arm in aim.

"He's at the bottom of the ladder!" said Pimento, pointing at the tiny TV. "He's letting go!"

They heard a loud thump on the roof of the *Orange Crush*. They all ducked and looked up at the ceiling. "What the hell was that?" said Pimento.

The sudden noise distracted Marlon, and he swerved left, then noticed he was about to collide with a red car in the next lane, and jerked the wheel hard the other way.

"Uh-oh," said Blaine Crease.

He was catapulted from the roof of the *Orange Crush* and onto the windshield of the Ferrari, which veered off the left shoulder of the highway and began bounding down the median.

"Ahhhhhhhhh!" screamed Crease.

"Ahhhhhhhhh!" screamed DAY-TRADR.

They crashed through a palmetto thicket and kept going, Crease screaming and hanging on to the top of the windshield with both hands. They finally slowed and sank in wet sawgrass.

Back on the highway, Marlon had overcorrected and was straddling the shoulder, the right wheels bouncing through rough gravel. He carefully eased the wheels back onto the pavement.

"I hate driving in Broward County," said Marlon.

Pimento remembered his tiny TV. He looked down at the small screen. The helicopter was pulling away from traffic with an empty rope ladder swinging in the wind. No sign of Crease.

"Hey, we never got to see what happened," said Pimento. "Hope everything turned out okay."

"Are you guys finished fooling around? Can we get back to business?" said Escrow. He folded over a newspaper and showed Marlon an editorial entitled "Let 'em eat cake!" It endorsed Gomer Tatum's proposal to execute prisoners on empty stomachs. There was a comparison chart of last meals and school lunch menus.

"But I liked those pizza squares," said Pimento.

"This isn't funny," said Escrow. "The race is getting too close!"

In truth, Escrow didn't need to worry anymore about Marlon's dedication to the campaign. He was starting to push himself plenty on his own. The more people he met, the guiltier he felt. It had begun as a lark, but now Marlon wanted to win more than anything. He soon passed The Point of No Return. He bought a Woody Guthrie tape.

"... *Well I rode that ribbon of highway . . . and saw above me that endless skyway . . .*"

Marlon had been putting in eighteen-hour days swimming against the conventional wisdom. He fought fatigue with the idealistic energy of a college student as he went home to home seeing how his fellow Floridians lived, listening to their dreams and fears. He began shunning the closed fund-raisers and political tribute visits and— most terrifying of all to Escrow—refused to select campaign stops based on how they would play to the cameras.

Instead, he went to places that had never seen a candidate: inner cities, rural trailer parks, even a prison, where Escrow kept haranguing him about the political illogic of spending time with people who weren't allowed to vote. He saw kids in hospitals and AIDS patients in hospices and the bedridden in nursing homes and the homeless at roadside.

"Look at this clipboard! I don't see any votes anywhere in today's schedule!" said Escrow. "You're spreading yourself too thin! Have you seen the bags under your eyes? Thank God we're not doing any TV today."

Marlon just smiled.

But even Elizabeth and Jenny were growing concerned. They found Marlon asleep in a running shower one night and again the next day, slumped over a slide-out desktop in the back of the Winnebago with his Guthrie tape still playing.

"... *This land was made for you and me. . . .*"

* * *

The cell phone rang and Escrow answered. He held the phone away from his ear, and everyone in the RV heard the shouting on the other end.

It was Helmut von Zeppelin, calling from his estate, and he was demanding to know whether the rumor was true—that Marlon had canceled his thirty million dollars of corporate welfare to help him pay for a stadium someone else had already paid for.

"How can you really answer a question like that?" said Escrow. "Words are such tricky things. You've got your synonyms, your homonyms, semantics and syntax. And don't forget the ono-matopoeia—"

"Get your pecker outta my ear, boy!"

Escrow held the phone away from his head again for another stream of invective.

He handed the phone to Marlon. "It's for you."

"Marlon Conrad here."

Von Zeppelin introduced himself with colorful language.

"Helmut! Good to hear from you! How's the team doing?"

Escrow desperately shook his head no, running a finger across his throat in a slashing gesture. Football was a bad subject right now with Helmut.

"Helmut, you'll have to talk slower. I can't understand all your threats."

"You come here right now!" yelled Helmut, pacing furiously in a neck brace from the blimp landing. "My house! On the double!"

"I'm on the campaign trail," explained Marlon. "Did I tell you I got a Winnebago?"

"You listen to me, son! You turn that shitbox around right now and drive here as fast as you can and hope my mood improves!"

"No can do."

"What?"

"I'll be glad to talk to you if you want to come to one of the debates," said Marlon. "We usually have a question-and-answer period at the end that we open up to the public. Of course you'll have to get in line—"

Marlon heard a maniacal screaming, followed by a number of

unidentified, inorganic sounds. Helmut strangled the phone receiver with both hands and then started banging it on his desk in the Charlemagne Room. He finally grabbed a medieval mace off the wall and smashed it to tiny phone pieces.

Marlon heard the line go dead. He tossed the phone to Pimento.

"You have no idea what you've just done," said Escrow.

"I've got the basic sketch in my head," said Marlon. "There's a chance I could lose the election."

"No, you don't understand," said Escrow. "You'll be lucky if you *only* lose the election."

"You worry too much," said Marlon, turning inland. He drove west across Palm Beach County until he got to a migrant labor slum near Lake Okeechobee.

Acting on an anonymous tip intended to embarrass Marlon, immigration officials followed him into the camp and began rounding up illegals. The crowd smelled a double cross and started jeering Marlon, who began shouting at the immigration people and ultimately tussled with two officers. He was arrested.

They took him downtown in the same van as the aliens, right into a nest of TV cameras. He was quickly released when higher-ups in Immigration were squeezed by the GOP. Marlon was cheered outside the jail by human rights activists and plastered across the nightly news as a champion of the people.

"Damn!" said Jackie Monroeville. "I never should have called in that tip."

The polls went schizo, and Mason & Dixon had their field people recheck the data. Bleeding-heart liberals were crossing over to Marlon. Self-righteous conservatives jumped to Tatum. The smart business money stayed put. After the dust cleared, Marlon netted a ten-point gain.

The newspapers started picking up on it. There were long debates in the editorial offices. At first they couldn't get past their skepticism that Marlon was some kind of political genius making cold calculations. No, said the reporters who were observing it on the ground. The guy's for real. The editors dropped their cynicism. Marlon wasn't a genius; he was a fool.

They invited him to speak to their editorial boards.

An editor in a bow tie shook Marlon's hand and introduced the rest of the opinion-makers.

"Why do you aspire to power?"

"To share it with those who don't have any."

"What do you want to change most about Tallahassee?"

"The bullshit."

And on it went.

Marlon's reputation for goodwill and honesty began reaching such mythic proportions across Florida that it caused many to start remarking, "Someone ought to shoot that motherfucker!"

29

EIGHTY MILES AWAY, out in the Atlantic Ocean, the tiny island of North Bimini was dark and quiet. An ocean breeze blew through the coconut palms, and bright constellations filled the Bahamian sky.

The main road on the island is called the King's Highway, but it's nothing majestic. Narrow and bumpy with mostly golf cart traffic. As it reached its south end in Alice Town, a raucous noise rose above the surf, and red light filtered through the trees.

It was a modest old wooden bar built in the 1930s, the kind that would be called a roadhouse if it were on a mainland. The door was propped open. Faded photos, yellow newspaper clippings and stuffed fish covered the walls.

There was a sign outside, THE COMPLEAT ANGLER, and it was one of the world's finest dives. It was so secluded and expensive to get to that it had become the perfect hideaway for politicians. They had been making the quick yacht runs and seaplane hops from Florida for years, ever since Congressman Adam Clayton Powell began showing up and ordering his "usual," scotch with milk chaser. On the wall was an old celebrity photo, Gary Hart on stage doing karaoke, shaking maracas with a nonwife companion. Then there was the literary world. Ubiquitous tropical barfly Ernest Hemingway arrived in 1934 with a Colt pistol and a severe thirst and, with impressive alacrity, somehow managed to shoot himself in both legs. He waited to heal and left without fanfare.

On this calm October night in 2002, Crosby, Stills, Nash & Young was on the jukebox, and Dempsey Conrad and Periwinkle Belvedere were belly to the bar, heads bobbing to half mast from a full day of island drinking. The phones hadn't stopped ringing back in Tallahassee. Major contributors, captains of industry and special interests wanting answers, demanding to know just what the hell Marlon was up to.

"Relax. He's a political genius. It'll work out. You'll see."

They weren't buying. They wanted Marlon to back off his attacks on the "fat cats."

"But you *are* fat cats," Dempsey joked.

They weren't in the mood.

Conrad and Belvedere instructed their staffs to say they were out of town, but that only made things worse. You can ditch the press like that, but donors have ways of finding out where you really are, and they remind you the next time you ask for a check.

It was getting too hot in the cockpit. Time to bail. Dempsey and Perry ordered up a Learjet. Give it a few days to fade away.

They started taking liquid lunch at the End of the World Saloon, which had a sand floor and an elderly woman with tongs pulling conch fritters from an oil vat. They met a waitress who had served Richard Nixon and Bebe Rebozo.

"Nixon always had the same thing. Grilled ham and cheese, potato salad and a Beck's. He was real nice. I had a picture taken of him hugging me, but the CIA grabbed the camera."

Dempsey and Perry discussed the options. Get drunk billfishing in the Gulf Stream or run the table. They decided on the latter, rented a golf cart and made it a mission to visit every bar on the island.

They hit the Big Game Club and the Red Lion and Sandra's before tipping the golf cart into Porgy Bay. They walked back to Alice Town in the dark, catching occasional whiffs of ganja from the breeze. There was a glow on the edge of the western sky, the lights of Miami Beach fifty miles away, over the horizon. The pair made it back to their rooms at the Blue Water Resort, changed into dry clothes and headed for the Angler.

Dempsey stood at the bar downing a Kalik, and Perry—with considerable difficulty—had acquired a mint julep.

"... *Tin soldiers and Nixon's coming* ... *We're finally on our own . . . This summer I hear the drumming . . . Four dead in O-hi-o . . . "*

Dempsey and Periwinkle heard someone calling their names over the music. Their Lear pilot had his hand over the phone. "You got a call!"

"We're not here!" said Dempsey.

"*You* tell him." The pilot held out the phone receiver.

Dempsey heard the shouting before he got the phone to his ear. It was Helmut von Zeppelin.

"What the hell's going on? We had a deal!"

"Calm down—"

"Eat me! I've given your boy soft money, hard money, everything! Now he's refusing to even see me!"

"He's got a plan. Trust us."

"I don't trust my mother!" Helmut started strangling the phone and throwing it around the room again, and Dempsey waited patiently until Helmut's voice came back on the line.

Belvedere watched Dempsey's face turn grim as he listened to what von Zeppelin said next. Dempsey hung up the phone and threw a pair of twenties on the bar.

"We've got to get out of here!" he told Belvedere.

"What's wrong?"

"We have to find Marlon."

●

MARLON'S Road Warrior act was still topping the newscasts, and the highlights replayed over and over.

At a Federal-style mansion north of Tallahassee, in a pink upstairs bedroom filled with lace and puppets, Babs Belvedere sat on her bed untangling Punch's and Judy's strings. She watched Marlon on her bedroom TV. There was footage from Daytona and Vero. Babs zeroed in with missile-lock radar on Jenny climbing aboard the RV behind Marlon in both segments. The tears came in buckets. With wet eyes still on the TV, she picked up her princess phone and called her father, who wasn't answering because he was in the Bahamas. She left a tearful message on his machine. Then she dialed a few more numbers, the last one for the airport.

She packed a small overnight bag and went down to her father's gun cabinet.

30

JOE BLOW WALKED out to his car with his morning cup of coffee.

"Who do you like in the Senate race?"

"How do you feel about the casino amendment?"

"When was the last time you had your teeth cleaned?"

He sped out of the driveway, sideswiping a Florida Cable News van.

Joe Blow had finally had it. He decided things would be different from now on. The press corps didn't know it yet, but they wouldn't have Mr. Average to kick around anymore!

The next day, Joe set about deliberately and radically changing his entire existence. He bought an electric car, paid off his credit cards, canceled his cell phone and stopped patronizing fast food. He went to a thrift store and bought a Beta-format VCR.

The media tracked his every move. Soon, financial analysts began noticing new consumer trends and fundamental changes in lifestyle across the country. They mirrored Joe's transformation.

Joe was frustrated. He was frustrated he couldn't escape the middle-of-the-road, and he was frustrated he couldn't find any tapes for his new VCR. So he turned off the TV, began talking to his family, stopped drinking beer and went to bed early each night reading a book.

The country followed.

Whether power of media suggestion or paranormal phenomenon, every attempt Joe made to depart from the mainstream quickly became the norm. He was changing the way we lived. And, with the exception of the VCR, it was all for the better.

It only brought more media attention. The hounding was relentless, the glare too intense. Joe came home from work, and the street was filled with the reporters' new electric cars. The *Tampa Tribune* began running a standing box on the bottom of the front page every day, chronicling Joe's daily activities. It was called "Blow by Blow."

ANOTHER long day. It was after midnight. Escrow had just taken everyone's orders for sodas and was now rooting around the cooler in the dark. Pimento had locked himself in the tiny lavatory again, staring at his reflection in the mirror: "Who *are* you?"

Marlon saw something ahead in the road and leaned over the steering wheel. "What the heck is this?"

"What's what?" asked Elizabeth, looking out the windshield.

Up ahead on a dark, open stretch of US 1, a pair of sheriff's cruisers sat in parking lots on opposite sides of the road. They faced the highway with their high beams on.

Bright light filled the RV as it drove through the crossfire of headlights. Marlon pulled the Winnebago over in front of a closed drugstore. "Escrow! Get the sheriff on the phone!"

"It's after two in the morning."

"Goddammit, Escrow!"

Escrow grabbed his cell phone and dialed. He got information, which patched him through to dispatch, which told him there was no way in hell they would call the sheriff at home at this hour.

Escrow covered the receiver with his hand and relayed the message.

"Get the shift commander!"

Escrow got the shift commander, who told Escrow the same thing.

"He says the same thing."

"Escrow! You tell him that if the governor isn't talking with the sheriff in two minutes, I'm gonna fuck him for ten generations!"

Escrow uncovered the receiver. "This request comes directly from the governor, who would personally appreciate your help in this matter of utmost political urgency . . ."

Sinclair was startled. Marlon was half crazy, veins popping and heart pounding.

"What is it?" she asked.

Marlon pointed at the Atlantic County sheriff's cars in the driver's-side mirror. "They're looking for motorists DWB."

"DWB?"

"Driving While Black. That's how they park when they're race-profiling. Shine headlights in cars to see what color they are."

The sheriff came on the line. Escrow handed Marlon the phone.

"Sheriff Corrigador here. How can I help you, Governor?"

"Call off your boys! They're shining their lights across the road!"

"I don't follow . . ."

"Don't play the country hick! They're profiling!"

"Now, Governor, there's no such thing down here." He said it with a lazy patronizing drawl.

Marlon caught himself and took a full breath and matched the sheriff's poise. "Of course there isn't such a thing. But for some crazy reason your campaign manager told me last year that you do it all the time. He even made a joke that there was no way to prove it in court, and he laughed. And you know what? I laughed, too."

"Then where's our problem, Governor?"

"Pull 'em off, Sheriff."

"Now you listen here. We're polite enough in this county, but you're quite a ways from home. You can come down and visit and we'll be sweet as pie, but we don't take to it when you start actin' like you know what's better for us than we do."

"Pull 'em off or this is your last term."

The sheriff broke into a big laugh. "Oh, how precious. You're still just a boy. This here's an elected post, and we have a nice, well-oiled machine in place that takes care of things like that, so don't you go worrying your little head about it." He laughed again. "Son, you just don't seem to understand how things work."

"I'm not your son, and I'll explain exactly how things work," Marlon said evenly. "There are four veteran circuit judges in your county who are going to retire in the next three years. Instead of serving their full terms, and risk the party losing the seats in open elections, they're going to resign three to twelve months ahead of time. That way I can appoint their successors from our party, who will be virtually unbeatable running as incumbents. How am I understanding things so far?"

The sheriff didn't answer.

"Now, I have a list of four very powerful party members in your county—possibly even members of your oily machine—who are just dying for those juicy judgeships. In fact, Governor Birch even privately promised them the seats last year. But I'm gonna have to call 'em and say, 'Fellas, there's an unfortunate situation in the sheriff's office that threatens to embarrass the state party as a whole, and I'm afraid I'm not going to be able to get around to those appointments for a while because I'm too busy trying to fix that problem—unless of course there's something the local party can do to expedite the process.' . . . So you tell me, Sheriff. Does this *boy* seem to understand how things work?"

There was silence on the line and then it went dead. Marlon turned to his side mirror. A minute passed. The squad cars cut their lights and backed off the street.

Marlon started up the RV again and pulled onto the highway.

"I don't have a good feeling about that," Escrow said with an armful of sodas.

"I'm with him," said Elizabeth. "You did the right thing, but you should have gotten some allies together first instead of sticking your neck out alone. You spent a lot of political currency."

"As Lyndon Johnson said, what good is political currency if you can't spend it?"

Jenny was sleeping a lot from her medicine, and Marlon's yelling on the phone had awakened her. She slowly made her way up front with the others and sat down next to Elizabeth and yawned and smiled at her. Elizabeth smiled back.

Escrow handed out sodas. "Mountain Dew. Pepsi. . . . Who had the Surge?"

Pimento raised his hand.

Elizabeth was still smiling at Jenny, but her expression changed as she studied her face. "You remind me of someone." She suddenly got a startled look. "Jenny! . . . You're *Jenny Springs! THE Jenny Springs!*"

Jenny looked away in embarrassment.

"What happened to you?" asked Elizabeth. "You vanished from the face of the earth!"

"Who's Jenny Springs?" asked Escrow.

Sinclair looked at Pimento. "You're the fact guy. Tell him."

Pimento told him as they rolled south on US 1. He finished his Surge and was about to crunch the soda can.

"I'll take care of that for you," said Escrow. He held open a clear plastic litter bag.

"Why, thank you."

Only it wasn't a litter bag. It was a Florida Department of Law Enforcement evidence bag. Escrow sealed it and wrote in grease pencil: "Fingerprint analysis."

The streets were so deserted at three A.M. you could hear the mechanisms in the traffic lights clicking as they cycled. The RV ran a yellow near Pompano Beach. One of the RV's windows was down and the stereo on. "Age of Aquarius" wafted through the intersection as they headed for Miami.

The music faded out until only the clicking of the traffic light could be heard again in the intersection.

Ten minutes later, there was a whoosh of wind through the intersection. A red Ferrari blew through a red light at a hundred, and its illuminated vanity tag disappeared toward Miami.

●

THE rising sun was large and orange, still near the horizon, and out of its center came a snow-white seaplane with lavender trim, a Grumman G-73T Turbine Mallard, the first flight of the day from Bimini. It flew low over the art deco hotels on Miami Beach and belly-landed in Biscayne Bay. A woman on a Jet Ski raced next to the left pontoon, then angled away as the plane taxied to the ramp at Watson Island. A limousine waited on the side of the MacArthur Causeway.

Dempsey Conrad was on his cell phone before his feet touched ground. "Where are you?"

"Pompano, I think," Marlon said on the other end. The call had awoken him.

"We need to talk. Meet you in two hours on top of Pier 66."

Marlon grabbed the alarm clock off the nightstand and looked at it. "Oh, man." He fell back against the pillow. He reached to replace the clock but missed, and it fell on the floor.

Ninety minutes later, Marlon and the gang were at the front desk, booking a block of rooms on the sixteenth floor of the Pier 66 Hotel in Fort Lauderdale.

The concierge became flustered. "You're Jenny Springs!"

He ran up with a pen. "Here, sign my arm. I'll have it tattooed."

Jenny blushed and wrote.

They got in the elevator. As the doors were closing, two arms came through the opening with a pen and piece of paper and got stuck. The doors bounced back open. "Jenny. Can I get your autograph? 'To Ernie.'" The doors closed again on the arms, and bounced back open.

Jenny signed her name, the arms withdrew and the doors closed.

They rode up to the rooms, and Marlon opened his with a magnetic card. They were awestruck by the views. "You blew the wad," said Escrow. "I'm impressed."

Pimento fiddled with the plastic sign on the doorknob. "'Do not disturb!' 'No molestar!'—ever get the idea some things aren't translating right?"

They unpacked and regrouped at the elevators, and caught one to the revolving bar another floor up on top of the hotel. There were some empty cocktail tables facing Bahia Mar. Marlon sat next to Elizabeth.

"Have you thought about it some more? The campaign could really use you."

She smiled. "Answer still has to be no. . . . Besides, you already have Escrow."

They glanced at Escrow, tapping a swizzle stick to the Muzak, wearing a FREE ERLICHMAN! T-shirt.

Elizabeth looked back at Marlon. "Deepest sympathies."

Pimento stood at the window, hands on the glass. "I remember these views. The strip, the marina, the Yankee Clipper, Port Everglades. My folks must have brought me up here when I was a kid. . . . I wonder if they can make this thing spin faster. I'll go ask."

A new voice: "There you are!"

Everyone at the table turned.

Dempsey Conrad and Periwinkle Belvedere marched deliberately from the elevators.

"Marlon, who are all these people?" asked Dempsey. "I recognize Escrow and Pimento, but who are these two—these *women?*"

Belvedere chimed in with a sideways grin. "That's Elizabeth Sinclair, my former top aide. We had a disagreement on her style of client relations, so she left and started her own firm. Now she's trying to put me out of business."

Dempsey laughed. He took Elizabeth's hand and gave it a genteel kiss. "Honeypie, you got moxie, I'll give you that. But why would you want to go up against Perry?" He winked at Belvedere. "That just ain't where your talents lie."

"Where would they lie?" Elizabeth asked with a poker smile.

"Well, like at Perry's parties. I've seen you—you're a terrific hostess. You look great!"

"Thank you."

"Seriously, it's not that easy. You should be very proud you've made it this far, so don't take it too hard when your company fails. I'm sure Perry will take you back—you put women half your age to shame."

"Thank you."

"And who's this?" asked Dempsey.

"This is Jenny Springs," said Elizabeth.

Dempsey went to kiss her hand as well. "Nice to meet you, Jenny Spr— Wait. Not *the* Jenny Springs?"

"That's her," said Elizabeth.

"I was one of your biggest fans!" said Dempsey. "What happened to you?"

Belvedere cleared his throat.

"Sorry," said Dempsey. "Almost forgot why we're here."

He turned to Marlon. "Son, first I have to say I'm awfully proud of you. *Awfully* proud. But I think you're handling von Zeppelin all wrong . . . Perry and me understand what you're doing, but Helmut's a different story. You need to go visit and make nice-nice with that asshole. And while you're at it, maybe ease off a couple of other things."

"Like what?"

"Like the issues, for example. All I'm saying is give 'em a little rest. Stick to personal attacks and photo ops. Just for a few days. You don't want people's heads to start hurting."

"Can't do it."

Dempsey smiled at Belvedere. "A fighter, just like the old man."

Belvedere broke in. "Marlon, your father and I agreed early on not to interfere, since you've obviously got the Conrad instincts. But now big money is coming into play. . . ."

Dempsey tapped Perry's arm. "The boy's got a head on his shoulders. We've made our point. I'm sure he won't let us down. Isn't that right, Marlon?"

"I promise I won't let you down."

"See? There ya go!" said Dempsey. "Y'all have nice day."

He smiled again at Elizabeth and gave her hand another kiss. "You take care, sweetie, and don't bankrupt Perry too fast. He'd look kinda funny wearing suspenders and a pickle barrel."

They laughed all the way out of the bar at that one. Then Dempsey started coughing and fell in the elevator. Perry pressed the button and the doors closed.

31

THAT AFTERNOON, JOURNALISM professor Wally Butts carried a briefcase up the elevator at Pier 66 and got off at sixteen. He knocked on Marlon's door.

Escrow answered. He studied his clipboard. "Sorry, you're not on the list."

"Get the fuck outta my way, you troglodytic twit."

Escrow bounced off the doorjamb.

"Marlon, I think we have a problem with the Sirocco case. It looks like the victim raped Sirocco's daughter."

"So it wasn't insurance?"

"No, this brings in passion. He still killed him, but it's not first-degree murder, maybe not even murder at all depending on state of mind."

Escrow was turning blue. "Sure sounds like murder to me."

"Shhhhhh!" said Marlon.

"The problem is, we don't have anything to hang a hat on," said Butts. "I'm having trouble finding the daughter—time's running out."

"No rush," said Marlon. "I haven't signed the warrant yet."

"Yes you have," said Butts. "I've seen it."

Marlon turned. "Escrow!"

Escrow began sniffing. "You smell something? I think I left the coffeepot on in my room."

BUTTS thought he'd locate the daughter in a matter of days, but it was the damnedest thing. He had tracked her through elementary schools in Massachusetts. Then, when Sirocco was extradited to Florida, his new wife and daughter followed. They moved into a modest ranch house near the jail, to visit. And the trail ended cold. Butts drove to the address. Neighbors move in and out so often in Florida that nobody even remembered there being a girl. Or a mom. The house had burned down years ago. It was like they'd never been there.

Butts was clutching at straws. He drove out to the state prison at Starke.

Frank Lloyd Sirocco sat at a flaking metal table. We wore a bright orange shirt, handcuffs chained to his belt, and ankle cuffs.

"Do you know where your daughter is?"

"She's got nothing to do with this."

"George raped her, didn't he?"

It was like Frank had been slapped. He stared coldly at Butts but didn't speak.

"If he did," said Butts, "you can probably get out of the electric chair."

"Interview's over," said Frank, turning around. "Guard!"

The guard opened the door and began leading Frank out of the room.

"You're going to let yourself be killed just to keep the rape a secret?"

Frank stopped and glared back at Butts. "She's my only daughter."

●

AT ten P.M., they were all in their rooms, Jenny in 1604, Elizabeth in 1605, Marlon in 1606, and Escrow and Pimento fighting over the remote control in their pajamas in 1607. Marlon banged on the wall. "Don't make me come in there!"

Escrow and Pimento lowered their voices. "It's my turn!" "Mine!"

Elizabeth skimmed a magazine in bed, unable to concentrate. She was mad at herself. She was way too together to let those creeps get

under her skin. "Honeypie," "sweetie," "when your company fails."
She always demanded composure, but now she couldn't stop their
words from repeating inside her head. The phone rang.

"Hello?"

"You're working on Marlon's campaign, aren't you?"

"Who is this?"

"That's not important. I was talking with some friends in the capital today, and I threw your name out for a PR project. Pays a hundred thousand—"

"I said, who is this?"

"—but it starts right away. You'd have to come back to Tallahassee. You wouldn't be able to keep working on the governor's campaign."

"I'm not on the campaign."

"Good, then there's no conflict."

"I'm hanging up."

"Think about it."

She hung up.

Elizabeth sat on the side of her bed and clenched her fists. Her
breathing became shallower and more rapid. She rummaged through
her purse and found a .25-caliber pistol. She pushed it aside and
grabbed an old pack of Salems and lit the occasional cigarette she
allowed herself.

The phone rang again.

"Hello!" she snapped.

"It's me, Marlon."

"Oh, sorry."

She opened the courtesy bar in her room and twisted the cap off a
Dewar's as she talked.

"Hope I'm not getting on your nerves, but I have to keep trying.
About the campaign—"

"It would be my pleasure."

"That was easy. Must have caught you in the right mood."

"The wrong mood."

"What?"

"Good night, Marlon."

ELIZABETH deserved credit. She gave absolutely no hint that her business was indeed failing, and it had nothing to do with her yeoman effort. It had to do with the male blacklist Periwinkle had invoked against her getting any clients. That's why Dempsey wasn't just guessing when he said she was going under.

An hour later, she was sitting up in bed, back against the wall, remote-controlling over to the Discovery Channel. I'm not going back to Perry or anyone else, she told herself, no matter what. But she couldn't stop fuming. Nothing was working and she had broken all her rules. The ashtray was filling up and there were two empty scotch miniatures on the nightstand. She started thinking about the campaign she had just agreed to join. Wonderful. Now I have to play den mother.

There was a man's scream, behind her, on the other side of the hotel-room wall, and she jumped.

She ran out in the hall, praying it was what it sounded like—a nightmare. She tried the door, but it was locked. She knocked. "Marlon, you all right?" No answer.

She went back in her room and tried the pass-through door between the rooms. To her surprise, it was unlocked. She pushed it open and looked around. "Marlon?"

No Marlon.

She saw a light under the bathroom door. Her heart pounded as she slowly pushed it open.

She was relieved. It *had* been a nightmare. Marlon was sitting on the floor in his briefs next to the toilet, staring down, crying silently. Lying on the tiles was the eight-by-ten group photo of his Army unit.

He never looked up. Elizabeth watched him for a long time. Such a boy. He was ten years younger than she was and, factoring maturity, even younger. But he was so much different now.

She reached and grabbed him by the arm. "Come on."

He was distant as she walked him over to the bed and laid him on his back. She covered him up and sat in a chair next to the bed, trying to find something on TV.

Marlon fell asleep for a short spell. When he awoke, he found Elizabeth nodded off in the chair. She never fully awoke as Marlon coaxed her out of the chair and into his bed. Then he sat in the chair and checked channels with the remote. He fell asleep sitting up.

Marlon was awakened at two A.M. by Elizabeth kissing him. The TV and all the lights were off—only night reflections from the water were coming through the window.

She pulled him into the bed, and he realized she didn't have any clothes on. He started to talk, but she put her hand over his mouth.

They were perfectly still for five minutes. Then Marlon slowly began sliding toward the foot of the bed. Elizabeth reached her arms up behind her and grabbed the headboard and closed her eyes.

●

"WHERE is he?"

Babs Belvedere was drunk and hysterical, weaving down the sixteenth-floor hallway of Pier 66, waving a large automatic pistol.

Before leaving Tallahassee, she kept calling her father's office. She left several messages and finally got through to his personal secretary, who said he was meeting Marlon at Pier 66.

It would be another six hours before Perry got back to the capital and checked his voice mail and heard Babs: "Daddy! Marlon's cheating on me! I saw him on TV with that little hussy! Wahhhhhhhh!"

So Babs had packed one of her father's pistols in the check-through luggage and caught a Delta flight to Fort Lauderdale. Now she was roaming the sixteenth floor of Pier 66 in the middle of the night, mascara all over herself.

"Where is he?"

Marlon was inside room 1606, halfway down Elizabeth Sinclair. He stopped and turned his head sideways. "I thought I heard something."

"It's nothing," said Elizabeth.

Babs was out of her head, stumbling all over the hall, sobbing. "I just don't fucking care anymore!" She bounced off a fire extinguisher and trampled through room service trays that had been left out. Then another long, crying wail. One hand held the pistol and the other dragged a marionette by the strings.

A bleary-eyed Pimento stuck his head out of his room to check on all the freakin' noise. Babs staggered toward him, blinded by tears, and bumped into him.

"Sorry."

"Hey, you're Babs Belvedere!"

Babs stopped and opened her eyes; she dropped her gun hand to her side.

"Yes, I am."

"I knew it!" said Pimento. "Miss Tallahassee. You should have been Miss Florida except for that bullshit lightning round at the end."

"It was a trick question."

"You should have won just on the puppets. That was so artful!"

"You really think so?"

"Absolutely."

She broke into a pitiful smile and wiped away the tears as she lifted her puppet out of a room service tray. "Would you like a demonstration?"

"Sure," said Pimento. He looked down at the puppet. "But I think you fucked up Charley McCarthy there dragging him through all those plates of beef Wellington."

"All I need are some socks."

"You got it!"

Escrow awoke from a sound sleep when Pimento and Babs came in the room and turned on the lights.

"What's going on?"

"You wanted to go see that late movie at the all-night theater."

"What theater?"

"Am-scray!"

The next thing Escrow knew, he had been shoved out into the hall in his bare feet and his Watergate pajamas. He turned around and took a step back toward the room, but a pair of shoes came flying out the door, and it slammed shut.

For the next half hour, they sat up in bed, Babs entertaining Pimento with a sock on each hand, cocking her head side to side as a different character spoke. Ten minutes later, the lights were out and there was a pile of clothes on the floor. Pimento was sliding toward the foot of the bed.

He was greeted by Howdy Doody.

And he liked it.

It was Pimento's secret fantasy to talk dirty politics in bed.

". . . And then two members of the Hillsborough County Commission were indicted!" Pimento told Howdy Doody.

"Were they bad boys?" asked Howdy.

"Oh, they were very, very baaaaad!"

On the other side of the wall, Marlon began losing his virility.

"What's wrong, baby?" asked Elizabeth.

"I don't know," said Marlon. "I thought I heard a voice. . . . Naw. Can't be."

". . . And then the judge threw out Xavier Suárez's victory in the Miami mayoral race."

"Tell Howdy all about it."

"Oh, he was *very, very baaaaad. . . .*"

"There's that voice again!" said Marlon. "But there's no way . . . I'm starting to have sonic hallucinations. I think I have some kind of permanent sexual hang-up."

"We need some music to get your mind off it." Elizabeth bounced out of bed, and Marlon watched her pert silhouette move across the room in the half-light. She flicked on the stereo under the TV set and tuned it until she found a station she liked.

"Perfect," she said.

"Black Sabbath?" asked Marlon.

"Back in the seventies I could fuck all night to Sabbath."

Marlon was simultaneously aroused and frightened as Elizabeth ran back to the bed with bounding steps like she was making the runway approach to a vaulting horse. He sank back in the pillows with a startled look on his face, and Elizabeth growled as she pounced.

32

THE NEXT MORNING there was a knock at Marlon's door. He opened it, and his jaw fell.

"Who is it, Marlon?" Elizabeth called from the bathroom.

It was Babs.

"I'm sorry to break this to you," she said, twirling her hair with a finger, "but I'm going to have to call off our engagement. I'm in love with someone else. . . . Well, see you around." And she skittered away.

Marlon closed the door with his mouth still open.

"Who was that?" asked Elizabeth, coming out of the bathroom rubbing her hair with a towel.

Marlon threw his arms up in triumph. "Yaaaahhhhooooo!!!!!!"

Everyone had agreed to meet for breakfast in the hotel restaurant. Escrow and Jenny arrived first and got a table by the window. A paddleboat steamed up the Intracoastal. A hundred-foot yacht from Rome fueled at the marina.

By the time Marlon and Elizabeth arrived, there was a small line waiting to get autographs from Jenny.

"You were the greatest!" "Where have you been?"

They ordered waffles. Pimento arrived with a giggling Babs snuggled on his arm.

Marlon's mouth fell open again. *"Him?"*

"Try not to make a scene," said Babs. "I'm sure you'll find someone nice yourself someday."

Elizabeth cracked up.

"What can I say?" offered Pimento. "I'm soft for artists."

A crowd had gathered on the street, looking in the window and pointing at Jenny.

A local TV crew entered the restaurant and started filming Jenny eating breakfast until Elizabeth stood up and put her hands on the lens.

People from the network arrived. Suits, briefcases, contracts. A man with a ponytail and stubble pulled a chair up.

"Jenny, I'm sure you know what's going on in Miami this weekend. Normally this would be way too late to get you in, but after all, you're Jenny Springs. We can bend the laws of physics."

Jenny looked down at the floor in embarrassment.

"Please, leave her alone," said Elizabeth. "Give her some privacy."

"Stay out of this, grandma!"

Jenny spun around to the ponytail, and just like that she was a blast furnace.

"I'll d-d-d-d-do it!" she said and reached out and poked him in the eye with a stiff finger.

"Ow! Jesus Christ!" He grabbed his face. "What they said about you is true!"

The other suits helped him away from the table.

"Look!" said Pimento, pointing at the restaurant's entrance. "Ned made it!"

Ned Coppola smiled and waved. He came over to the table wearing shorts and a double-stitched photographer's vest with seventy-four Velcro pockets. He clapped his hands. "Let's get this show on the road!"

●

IT was a big day at Wacky Waldo's Guns and Explosives on US 1 in Hallandale. Strings of colorful pennants flapped in the breeze over the parking lot. A large inflatable .44 Magnum was tethered to the roof. A dancing chicken served hot dogs.

The parking lot was jammed. A red Ferrari with a vanity tag backed out as a rented yellow Mustang pulled up. The driver wore a Miami Heat jacket.

Inside, low-grade swimsuit models circulated with trays of bacon-wrapped Cheetos and champagne flutes of Coors and Busch. It was elbow-to-elbow at the glass display cases. People in trench coats, hunting jackets, rubber waders, Top Gun jumpsuits, bomb-disposal armor and a T-shirt: 3RD ANNUAL MIAMI ARMAGEDDON PAINT-BALL DEATH MATCH AND BAKE-OFF.

A thin young woman from Brazil was at the counter examining the sights of a Tango-51 just out of the crate. She dry-fired it.

"Music to my ears," said the salesman.

The woman shook her head in disagreement. Something was off. She calmly but swiftly disassembled the rifle. She located a small spring and stretched it to restore the memory, then reassembled and dry-fired again in under two minutes.

The adroit demonstration caught the attention of several customers. A trench coat nudged a Top Gun. "That just gave me a woody."

The woman was satisfied with the new sound. She paid with consecutive hundreds, never saying a word. She left the store and placed the rifle in the trunk of her rented yellow Mustang. The Mustang pulled out of its parking slot, and a 1931 baby-blue Stutz Bearcat roadster pulled in. The driver stepped out wearing a long scarf and a monocle.

Von Zeppelin went inside and approached a salesman. "I'd like to see something in a long-range sniper rifle, maybe a Tango-51. And I'd like to get an unassuming travel case for it—something I can sneak into a place with a lot of people."

"No problem," said the salesman, taking a rifle off the wall. He handed it to Helmut and smiled. "Must be something big planned. I've already sold two today."

THE *Orange Crush* was in the high-occupancy lane on I-95 when they first glimpsed the skyline.

"Miami!" yelled Pimento, pointing out the windshield. "I love driving into this city. I get all goose-bumpy!"

Marlon passed the Palmetto Expressway and kept going, deeper. The traffic became thick and Darwinian. Unlike northerners, who learn to drive on ice, Miamians have no genetic familiarity with surface traction. There had been a light rain, and cars sat crunched into the median's retaining wall every few hundred yards. The skyline grew closer.

"There's the Centrust Building!" said Pimento.

The *Orange Crush* kept on going, all the way to the crumbling spaghetti interchange at exit 5, where Marlon took the Venetian Causeway to Miami Beach. They turned onto Meridian Avenue.

"What's that?" asked Escrow, pointing at the top of a giant green hand sticking up out of the palm trees.

"That's where we're going," said Marlon. "Pimento told me about it."

They pulled over at Dade Boulevard and filed out of the RV into the hot, quiet afternoon. They started walking, and the hand grew larger. It was a big oxidized-bronze sculpture, the centerpiece of the Holocaust Memorial. They stopped and looked at it across a still pool. Escrow was a little restless, checking his watch, but he knew it was a place to show manners. Then they went around the back to the memorial wall, to all the photos and the names and the sculptures of the children, and even Escrow felt like he was having trouble getting enough air.

Marlon looked at him at one point. "Hey Escrow, are you about to cry?"

"Oh no, no, no. I . . . have something in my eye."

They got back in the *Orange Crush* and nobody felt much like talking right away as they headed across town.

Another ten minutes, another universe. Ned stuck his camera out the window as they entered Little Havana and turned onto Calle Ocho.

The *Orange Crush* pulled over and they called a cab. Pimento and Babs had decided it would be best if she went back to Tallahassee until the campaign was over. Pimento promised that he wouldn't wait a second longer before rushing back for another puppet show. Until then: "Where I'm going, you can't be any part of."

"My hero," she said, waving out the window as her cab pulled away.

Ned Coppola ordered an espresso at a lunch window, and Pimento joined him. Marlon ate yellow rice and bean soup at an outdoor table, next to a pair of old Cuban men playing dominos. Ned pointed his camera at a building with a religious mural of Elián and dolphins. He pulled a second camera from a shoulder bag and handed it to Pimento, and they both began filming Marlon from artsy angles. Marlon had finished his food, so Ned told him to imagine the best meal in his life and pretend to eat.

"Stop fooling around!" Escrow yelled from the doorway of the Winnebago. He pointed at his clipboard. "All this filming is making us fall behind schedule."

"Tension on the campaign trail!" said Ned. "I'm getting it all!"

They drove through residential neighborhoods until all the homes began to have the same exquisite orange barrel-tile roofs and tropical landscaping. Even the modest ones had killer yards of coconut palms and bougainvillea. Lots of old stucco and Spanish flourishes.

"Where are we?" asked Ned, half out the window with a camera.

"The Gables," said Escrow. "We have a book signing at noon. It's a biggie."

"Gotcha," said Ned. "I'll reload."

They turned the corner a block off the Miracle Mile, and it was bedlam. A line of people with books snaked around the historic building. Police held back protesters across the street.

Marlon parked at the curb and jumped down.

"A pleasure to meet you," said the store's owner. "You're all set up inside."

Marlon sat at a table and began signing again.

An old man in a guayabera crawled under the police barricade and charged into the store. "I can't believe what you wrote about the Cubans!" The cops jumped him and dragged him out.

Marlon grabbed Escrow. "What did I write about the Cubans!"

"I think I forgot to feed the meter."

Next up: Liberty City, then Overtown, a couple of the most blighted and dangerous neighborhoods in the nation. The rare times politicians visited was after riots and before elections. Marlon told the media he was going to one church—then went to another instead. He remembered the tactics of the Rolling Stones security and sent the *Orange Crush* out as a decoy.

A limo pulled up in front of a small, eighty-year-old clapboard Baptist church. Marlon went inside with Ned and Pimento filming all the way; Escrow stayed behind and hid in the limo.

Marlon addressed the congregation and spoke of compassion and unity. The residents had heard it all before, but they listened anyway. Soon Marlon was talking about his admiration for the civil rights movement. He knew all the references. The Sixteenth Street church bombing, Andrew Young and Julian Bond, the earthen dam in Mississippi, SNCC, Malcolm, Stokely. The Lorraine Motel. He finally moved them by quoting at length from "Letter from Birmingham Jail." It wasn't the sort of thing you could fake with last-second cramming.

Marlon was still shaking hands with the congregation when he and the minister opened the front door of the church. Outside, a mob was rocking the limo back and forth up off its wheels.

The crowd was dozens deep—no way for Marlon and the preacher to reach the car. They overheard conversations in the back of the crowd. Some white guy in the limo had been playing John Philip Sousa too loudly on the stereo.

A gold Cadillac pulled up to the curb across the street, and the Overtown Posse got out. Word swept the crowd, which hushed and parted. The posse walked through them and up the church steps, got Marlon and escorted him back to the limo.

Two of the posse got in the limo with Marlon, and the other two said they'd follow in the Caddy until they were safely away.

Marlon, Ned and Escrow crowded into the backseat. Pimento sat with the two Overtowns on the facing seat and exchanged complex handshakes. The Overtowns noticed Escrow, curled and shaking in the corner. "What's with him?"

"He's keepin' it real," said Pimento.

They pulled up in front of the Miami Arena on Biscayne Boulevard, and Marlon thanked them and shook hands all around.

33

AT FOUR P.M., TV sets across the nation began receiving a live feed from the sold-out Miami Arena.

"Good afternoon, this is Dick Enberg, and NBC Sports is proud to welcome our home viewers to what promises to be an incredible afternoon of women's tennis. This is just the first year of the Miami Cup, but what unbelievable stories we've seen so far."

"That's right, Dick," said Chris Evert, "but the one story everybody's talking about is the surprising reappearance of Jenny Springs. She literally came out of nowhere."

"The real story is how blind the linesmen are!" said John McEnroe. "I could make those calls from up here wearing a scuba mask!"

"Jenny easily disposed of her early opponents in an impressing string of six-love matches," said Chris.

"But today's match won't be anywhere near as easy," said Dick. "Jenny faces number-one seed Tanya Svenson, the gritty sixteen-year-old wunderkind from Boca Raton, Florida."

"Both are products of Nick Boleterri's tennis academy over in Bradenton," said Chris. "But the crucial difference is age. Tanya is at the height of her conditioning, but Jenny hasn't played or even been heard from since she was a fourteen-year-old phenom. That was eight years ago. Now she's twenty-two, and in tennis that's almost over the hill."

"You should know," said McEnroe.

The TV camera panned across the front-row VIP section. Jack Nicholson, Spike Lee, Marlon Conrad. A cheer went up when Jenny walked onto the court carrying her tennis bag. She wore a cute skirt with thigh-length bicycle pants underneath.

"And there's Tanya Svenson," Enberg said as Jenny's opponent emerged from the opposite side of the court in pigtails.

"Size is another factor," said Chris. "Jenny is almost six feet and now carrying a hundred and forty pounds. But Tanya is a tiny five-four, and she should be all over the court like a hummingbird. Then there's the mental game. Can Jenny handle the intense media onslaught she's been subjected to all week?"

McEnroe yawned. *"Bor-ing!"*

"Tanya hasn't been without her distractions, either," said Enberg. "Her controversial father-coach has been arrested three different times this week, the latest in a drunken brawl at a Fort Lauderdale sex club . . ."

". . . But he made bail and is with us here today to cheer for his little girl."

The camera zoomed in on Tanya's father at courtside, shirtless with orange and blue body paint, wearing a gorilla mask and sloshing a jumbo mug of beer. "Woooooooooo! We're number one! Woooooooooo!"

The two players met at midcourt to shake hands. Tanya beamed her cutest Shirley Temple smile for the camera. Then she turned and smirked at Jenny. Tanya had caught a glimpse of her getting dressed in the locker room. "What's with the bicycle pants, Scar Legs?"

That set the tone.

The first few games were coated with a film of latent violence. Instead of placing shots away, many were hit full force right at the opponent. Both players held service and Tanya won the set on the tiebreaker.

"The Jenny Springs story has had people buzzing all week," said Enberg. "Even before she disappeared, it was quite a saga."

"That's right, Dick. Her whole life has been shrouded in secrecy. All we know was that she was adopted by a foster family in Sarasota shortly before she turned pro and was touted as the next *me*," said Evert. "Everything before that has been tightly guarded. State law prohibits the release of any information about children placed in protective custody."

"There were a few ugly rumors," said Enberg, "but her family maintained a wall of silence. Not a shred about her before she turned up on the tour. Then a few months later she disappeared without a trace, adding another chapter to the deepening mystery."

"I'll tell you what's a mystery," said McEnroe. "Seven bucks for a beer!"

"Hey! Keep that away from the control panel!"

The second set started like the first ended, both women tough on service. Tanya was more mobile, but Jenny had the strength, and they were wearing each other down. Tanya would stagger Jenny with baseline shots, and Jenny would come back with a powerful slicing forehand that Tanya couldn't do anything with but hit into the net. They were drenched in sweat and snarling. Even the home audience could detect the growing venom. Each broke service in the third and fourth games. It took on a boxing flavor, two heavyweights beating each other stupid in the late rounds.

"This is great!" said the network producer. "They're ready to kill each other. Turn up the volume on the courtside mikes. I want the TV audience to hear every grunt!"

In the ninth game, Jenny's forehand overpowered Tanya, who put three in the net and had her service broken again. After the game, they switched sides of the court, breaking the rules by walking around the same end of the net. They elbowed each other.

"Slut!"

"Whore!"

The mikes picked it up perfectly.

"Whoa!" said Enberg. "Now that's spunk!"

"You idiot!" Tanya's father screamed through the gorilla mask. "That old maid's kicking your ass! Why can't you do anything right! You're a disgrace! . . ."

Jenny's serve was only getting stronger. She started the next game with an ace that froze Tanya on the baseline. Five minutes later, she won the second set on another wicked overhead.

Both players dragged to the sidelines and collapsed in chairs. They panted and poured water over their heads.

Tanya's father was seated five feet behind his daughter.

"What are you, a loser? You disgust me! You're letting that skanked-out crazy old bitch beat you! . . ."

Jenny walked briskly across the court and swung the side of her racket into Mr. Svenson's Adam's apple. His eyes poked out, and he fell back in his seat clutching his throat. The crowd cheered.

"Ooooooo," said Enberg. "That must have tickled."

"Thanks," said Tanya.

"M-m-m-my treat," said Jenny.

The third set was brutal. Halfway through, neither player had anything left—the boxers too tired to block any blows, just taking and returning punches. It was worse for the older Jenny. Tanya was exhausted, but Jenny was starting to see black around the edges. Spirit and adrenaline carried her.

After the seventh game, Jenny fell into her chair and thought she would never get back out. She put her head between her legs and strained like a fighter pilot in a six-G turn to get more blood to her brain. The network went to a commercial break.

"I'm so proud of Jenny," Elizabeth told Marlon.

"I've never seen anything like this," he replied. "I can see now why she was so famous."

Out in the parking lot, someone was arriving late in a red Ferrari with a vanity tag.

The players staggered back onto the court. Each still had strong serves and first returns, but after that it was painful to watch. Jenny lunged for a backhand she would have easily reached in the first set, but this time she went sprawling. On the next point, Tanya got turned the wrong way going back for a lob and fell.

Up high in the arena, in the maintenance room with the electrical fuses, the bolt of a Tango-51 slid shut, and the end of the barrel rested on the lip of a small observation widow. Marlon's head filled the bull's-eye of the scope.

Jenny reached back with everything she had and aced Tanya to even the set at six-all. They switched sides for the tiebreaker.

In the rifle scope, Marlon turned silently and smiled at Elizabeth.

Tanya ran to the net for a drop shot and took the lead.

The rifle's safety was clicked off.

Jenny fired another ace that bounced off the rim of Tanya's racket.

A finger began to squeeze the trigger.

Jenny fell down again diving for the ball, and it rolled into the net.

The door opened in the maintenance room. The man with the rifle turned around. "Who are you? . . . *Nooooooo!*"

Tanya dove for the ball, then Jenny, back and forth, giving every shot their all.

Tanya was up, serving, match point.

She placed it wide, then came to the net for Jenny's return and hit it crosscourt. Jenny ran for it and dove and fell again. Just out of reach. It was over. Game, set, match.

Tanya fell to her knees and started crying in a burst of emotion and exhaustion. Jenny stayed where she had fallen on the court and closed her eyes. The crowd went nuts. They stood and applauded and wouldn't stop.

Jenny finally got up and walked to her chair, staring at the ground the whole way. Her mouth quivered, but she refused to break. She fell in the chair and buried her face in a towel. After a few moments, she felt someone hugging her. She looked up. It was Tanya.

Tanya pulled her to her feet, and they put their arms around each other and waved to the crowd. The standing ovation shook the arena.

"I think I'm going to cry," said Enberg.

"Me, too," said Evert.

McEnroe wiped his eyes. "I've always loved Bjorn."

SIX hours later, the Miami arena was dark and quiet. Only a few people left, investigators up high in a maintenance area. A yellow crime tape sealed the doorway to the electrical fuses.

Detective Mahoney arrived on the scene.

The head of arena security shook his hand. "Cleaning woman found him."

"Dead long?"

"Long enough so he'll never play Carnegie again."

"He got a name?"

"Yes, but we don't know it."

"I see."

"His femur was contused, clavicle fractured and thorax crushed."

"You a doctor?"

"No, but I slept at a Holiday Inn Express."

"You're a real funny guy."

"Funny ha-ha or funny strange?"

"That's what everyone wants to know."

"I see."

Mahoney ripped the crime tape and walked into the room. DAY-TRADR was facedown on the floor.

"What have you been hearing?" asked the head of arena security.

"I hear you should take Dallas and the points at home."

"What else you hear?"

"I hear your wife is loud in bed."

Mahoney rolled the man onto his back and unbuttoned his shirt. There was Magic Marker.

"Just what I was afraid of."

"What's that?" asked the head of arena security.

"We have a copycat."

"How can you tell?"

"This one's reading a more interesting brand of bumper sticker. Also, the handwriting is different. Almost unnoticeable to the untrained eye."

"I see what you mean. The descenders slant more to the left."

"That and he dots his *i*'s with hearts."

JESUS SAVES . . . BUT GRETZKY GETS HIS STICK ON IT, HE SHOOTS, HE SCORES!

34

•

THE LAST WEEKEND before the election, the campaign went into the final turn. The *Orange Crush* swung across the Everglades and up the Gulf Coast home stretch.

They were a half hour out of Miami on the Tamiami Trail, surrounded by swamp, and Pimento was counting alligators sunning on the banks next to the road. They came upon a massive, glitzy Vegas-like complex that rose by itself in the middle of nowhere at the crossroads of Route 997. An Indian bingo palace.

"When did *that* go up?" said Marlon.

The gang was really coming together, falling into the roadtrip groove.

Jenny and Elizabeth sat cross-legged on the floor in back, laughing together as they went through magazines. Pimento and Ned were at the kitchenette playing a Hollywood board game. Ned picked a card.

" 'Pay no attention to the man behind the curtain!' "

Marlon was content.

Escrow was in a wad.

"There's no discipline in this campaign! Look at all these people!"

"Lighten up," said Marlon. "You're missing your life."

Escrow grumbled and went back to the morning papers. The *Post* had a big front-page article about the upcoming execution of Frank Lloyd Sirocco. Escrow looked sideways out the corner of his eye as he slid the paper under the seat. Next was the *Tribune*. Escrow's eyes widened. He held the paper out to Marlon.

"Look at this! They found someone murdered at the Miami Arena just hours after the tennis match!"

"So?" said Marlon.

"So your dad's right. You've gotta take a security team. First Todd Vanderbilt, now this."

"You worry too much."

Ned came forward and began filming out the windows, miles and miles of untouched sawgrass. On the horizon, islands of palms bloomed under billowing white clouds trailing off to the sea. They passed an Everglades-style country store with a bleached tin sign advertising frog legs and gator tails. Marlon turned up the radio.

"... *Some folks are born silver spoon in hand ... Lord, don't they help themselves, oh ... It ain't me! It ain't me! I ain't no fortunate son, no ...*"

The *Orange Crush* passed the Big Cypress ranger stations and Micosukee chickee huts and made the wide turn north up through Naples.

Twenty miles back, a westbound Lincoln Town Car doing a hundred and ten passed four cars at once on the two-laner, barely missing a gasoline tanker.

Ned and Pimento were accumulating a tremendous amount of footage, and they'd been FedExing the daily rushes to Hollywood each evening, but they hadn't heard anything back yet.

"They're fools not to jump all over this," said Pimento, filming Escrow throwing incoming mail in the "*You suk*" pile.

Much of the footage, however, was dubious. They had kept the cameras rolling without selectivity. There was a lot of bumping into things in the tight quarters of the RV, shaking the cameras. Also, plenty of off-center candid shots, and, when Ned started drinking, wholesale bad angles and wrong focus. It was all shipped unedited.

Ned's drinking had increased, and each night he ended up on his soapbox, cocktail in hand, delivering long-winded tirades against the packaging of candidates and the idiot-elite running Hollywood into the ground recycling the same predictable tripe. "Meryl Streep can't carry that town forever!" He noticed Pimento filming him and took a swipe at the camera. He missed and fell on his face and farted.

Later that same night, Pimento brought the camera with him and accidentally left it running when he locked himself in the bathroom again. He banged his forehead on the wall several times, then looked in the mirror. "Who *are* you?"

Marlon took the second Naples exit off I-75, and the gang checked in at the nerve center of Gulf Coast culture—a convenience store. They pulled up to the pumps at an Addiction World. At the next pump, a carload of midwestern students had laundry piled in the back of a Plymouth with KEY WEST OR BUST! written across the back window in shaving cream. A group of shirtless, sunburned men towing a boat came out of the store with four twelve-packs of Old Milwaukee. A hyperactive family tried to regroup in a minivan— "We're almost there!"—kids covered with grape Slurpee.

Elizabeth and Jenny were happy as kids, standing barefoot on the cigarette-butt-littered black tar next to the RV, smashing up ten-pound bags of ice for the cooler. Marlon got a ham sandwich and an Arizona iced tea. Escrow thumbed through *Fortune* and *Forbes* at the magazine rack. Pimento bought a croquet set.

Ned stayed in the RV, making calls on his cell phone. He dialed an East Side Address.

"Woody, Coppola here . . . *Ned* Coppola. . . . What do you mean, how did I get your number? . . . Listen, Woodman, this is your lucky day. Clear some space on the bookshelf for another Oscar. Are you ready? *Annie Hall II,* starring that Oriental chick you've been seeing . . . Hello? Woody? . . ."

Pimento climbed back in the *Orange Crush.*

"What's with the croquet set?" asked Ned.

"I'm feeling British today."

Ned's cell phone rang. He looked at Pimento. "Who could this be?"

He pressed the answer button.

"Coppola here . . . *Spielberg?*" He covered the phone and whispered excitedly to Pimento. "It's Spielberg!"

Pimento gave him an enthusiastic thumbs-up.

Ned uncovered the phone again. "What can I do for you, Steven? . . . Oh, *Felix* Spielberg. . . . Yeah, Felix, look, I'm kinda busy right now. . . . I know I said we'd do lunch. . . . My people tried to reach your people. . . . I forgot you don't have people. . . . No, I'm not trying to rub it in. . . . I gotta run Felix. . . . I gotta run. . . . Bye, Felix. . . . I'm hanging up, now, Felix. . . ."

He hung up.

Ned gave Pimento an exasperated look. "How *Schindler's List* could come out of the same gene pool is beyond me."

The cell phone rang again.

"What now!" He flipped the phone open. "Coppola here."

"Ned, this is Isaac out in Hollywood. . . . What the hell is all this stuff you've been FedExing me?"

"Isaac, I'm not in the mood—"

"I love it!"

Ned went mute.

"Everyone out here is dazzled! It's what we've all been looking for. The rawness, the energy, the edgework. All the bad camera angles, abrupt editing, horrible lighting. It's so . . ."

"Scandinavian?"

"Exactly! And it was a stroke of genius getting a bunch of unknown actors! Adds to the realism. Who's doing the screenplay? Sid? Murray?"

Ned looked at Pimento. "A new guy."

"I don't want another studio talking to him. Tell him he can name his price. Can you send the rest of the script over?"

"It's in revisions."

"Well, don't tinker with it too much. The writing's immediate! It's now! The scene with the guy banging his head on the bathroom wall—it had my guts in knots! 'Who *are* you!' Very existential. Nobody's captured that kind of intensity since *Raging Bull!* . . . And that cameo of yours! The whole *Days of Wine and Roses* thing. I didn't know you could act. Forget Nicholas Cage in *Leaving Las Vegas*—your portrayal of a drunk has just raised the bar. And that was a nice tongue-in-cheek touch, calling the Motion Picture Academy one big circle jerk . . ."

"Thank you."

"Gotta run, Ned. . . . I'm overnighting the contracts. Keep those dailies coming! This is going to be blockbuster!"

Ned closed his cell phone.

"What is it?" asked Pimento, filming him.

"In technical terms, we're hot."

It was after dark, another long day of campaigning. It started to rain. They were already on the north side of Bonita Beach, and Marlon decided to shoot for Fort Myers and put up for the night.

The drive was relaxing. They abandoned the Tamiami Trail and headed to the coast. The *Orange Crush* crossed a bridge to the barrier islands, where they picked up the thin road along the shore, one of the least-populated beachfronts left in Florida.

It was dark inside the Winnebago except for a couple of reading lights in back.

Marlon now knew the group had gelled. They were so comfortable with each other that they had become themselves. They were together, and yet they were all doing their own thing in their own space.

Jenny and Elizabeth sat at a small table in back, sipping cocoa. Jenny was asking Elizabeth her advice on men.

"The key is to underestimate them."

Escrow was in the passenger seat reading a book under the map light, *The Life and Times of the Nixon Plumbers*. Ned paced in the middle of the RV with a glass of vodka, holding court on the travesty of a colorized *Casablanca*. Pimento had locked himself in the bathroom again, raving in the mirror. Marlon felt like he was driving the bus for the Partridge Family on acid.

There were no streetlights for long stretches, and no other cars. Just the *Orange Crush*'s high beams catching occasional gusts of sea mist and a dog trotting along the side of the road. They entered Lovers Key State Recreation Area and crossed the bridge at Big Carlos Pass onto Estero Island. Marlon could see the lights ahead on Fort Myers Beach.

Pimento came out of the bathroom a little drained. He sat down on the floor behind Marlon and Escrow and chugged some Gatorade to restore needed fluids.

"You all right?" asked Marlon.

"Fine," said Pimento. "Listen, we're gonna be in Fort Myers tomorrow, right? Can we go to Thomas Edison's house? I've always wanted to see it."

"No," said Escrow.

"Don't see why not," said Marlon.

"Why am I even here?" asked Escrow.

"So we can rub off on you," said Marlon.

They slowed as they passed the strip on Fort Myers Beach. They heard Ned yelling in back. "Bogart looks like he has scurvy, and Peter Lorre's wearing lipstick!" Then something got knocked over.

The cell phone rang. It was for Marlon.

"Son, you gotta accept some security," said Dempsey Conrad. "You know another body turned up in the Miami Arena?"

"I read the papers. Just a coincidence."

"Coincidence my ass."

"I'm perfectly safe," said Marlon, hanging up.

Back at Big Carlos Pass, a Lincoln Town Car flew over the hump at ninety, and the muffler bottomed out and showered sparks.

The women were asleep and Ned was passed out when Marlon finally pulled into Lazy Shores RV Park, which was nowhere near any water. He paid a night attendant, who had broken parole in Michigan and was hooked on cough syrup. The attendant held a spoon in his mouth as he handed Marlon sticky dollar bills in change.

Escrow and Pimento were already snoozing when Marlon got back from the office, and he was hard asleep in minutes, too. Lazy Shores may not have had a shore, but it was definitely lazy. By midnight there was no sound but frogs, crickets, bug zappers and a light patter of rain.

A little after two, the rain had really begun to come down. A Lincoln Town Car pulled into Lazy Shores and turned off the headlights.

Periwinkle Belvedere had gotten his daughter's first tearful messages, but he had missed her later ones—where she said the wedding was back on. She would just be marrying Marlon's press secretary instead.

Belvedere got out of the Town Car and cursed alliteratively. "Jilt my daughter like she's some tawdry two-bit Tallahassee tramp—I'll kill the son of a bitch!"

Lightning crackled across the sky as he retrieved a Tango-51 from the trunk.

Inside the *Orange Crush*, Pimento suddenly sprang upright in his bunk from a deep sleep.

He got out of bed silently and pulled up his trousers. He grabbed his movie camera, put it in a watertight bag and slipped out the side of the RV into the driving rain.

THERE was a big commotion at the Thomas Edison Museum the next morning.

The *Orange Crush* was at a crawl, and Marlon was having trouble negotiating the Winnebago on the tight, jammed street. Ambulances, fire trucks, news vans. Police set up barricades and waved people around the block. Crime scene tape went up around the expansive lawn in front of the famous inventor's winter residence.

Escrow and Pimento rubbernecked as police motioned the RV past Edison's white picket fence.

The officer also waved on the beat-up Chevy behind the *Orange Crush*, but the Chevy angled for the police barricade and knocked it over and parked. The officer ran around the driver's side, ready to let him have it. The driver wore a tweed jacket with an upturned collar, and he took a pull from a flask.

"You're under arrest!" yelled the officer, going for his gun.

The driver opened a wallet and flashed a gold badge. "Homicide, Mahoney."

The officer took a half step back. "Sorry, Detective . . ." He looked over the car and the tweed coat and the flask. "I didn't realize . . ."

"None of us do," said Mahoney. "Watch my wheels."

He left the car on top of the barricade and climbed through the shrubs into the front yard. There was a sheet over a body. From under the sheet came a long string that stretched across the lawn and into some trees, where it disappeared.

"What have we got here?" Mahoney asked the Fort Myers detective in charge of the scene.

"A nice day spoiled by a corpse."

"I see."

"The vic's name was Periwinkle Belvedere."

"There's a mouthful. Try saying that three times."

"Periwinkle Belvedere, Periwinkle Belvedere, Periwinkle Belvedere."

"I was being rhetorical."

"We don't go for that around here."

"What do you go for?"

"An antacid that works when you need it."

"Belvedere have enemies?"

"Nothing but."

"Who doesn't?"

"These had money and knew how to use it."

"I hear that comes in handy," said Mahoney.

"What else you hear?"

"We got ourselves a spree killer, maybe a copycat, too."

"What else you hear?"

"You like women's underwear."

"Who doesn't?"

"You have a pair under your hat right now."

"You do your homework."

"May I?"

"Be my guest."

Mahoney whipped the sheet off the body like a tablecloth from under a set of china.

The heavily scorched body of Periwinkle Belvedere lay on its back. The arms were straight out from the body, and the legs were

spread. Each limb was pinned to the ground with several steel croquet wickets.

Mahoney bent down and unbuttoned the shirt. He could make out
Magic Marker words through the singed chest hairs.

I ♥ THE THOMAS EDISON MUSEUM!

Mahoney noticed the string on the lawn, and it led into Belvedere's
hip pocket. He reached into the pocket. The end of the string was
tied to Belvedere's car keys. Mahoney stood up and followed the
string across the lawn with his eyes. It stopped at the edge of some
woods, where a police officer was climbing out, carrying a burnt-up
kite tied to the other end.

"We had a pretty vicious electrical storm last night," said the Fort
Myers detective.

"The metal wickets must have grounded him."

"My guess is Belvedere discovered electricity."

"Two hundred years ago that would have made him famous."

"Now it just makes him dead."

●

"IT'S looking like the Edison tour is scrubbed," said Marlon, turning
onto a side street after the police barricade.

"I was really looking forward to it," said Pimento. "But you
know, for some odd reason I feel like I've already been here."

"Maybe you're thinking of Whitehall or Vizcaya."

"Those are a bit nicer," said Pimento. "Maybe it's because I've
read so much about the place. Did you know it was actually built in
Maine and brought down by boat?"

"Can't say I did."

A police officer waved a rented yellow Mustang past the house.
The Brazilian woman at the wheel cruised by slowly before acceler-
ating. Moments later, a 1931 Stutz Bearcat roadster was waved on,
von Zeppelin grumbling behind the wheel and trying to unsnag the
bolt of a Tango-51.

Ned Coppola stood behind Marlon, dialing California.

"Isaac, Coppola here . . . I wanted to get back with you about your call the other day and our movie deal . . ."

"What call? What movie deal?"

Ned was mortified.

"Gotcha!" said Isaac, and he laughed with extensive self-amusement. "Ned, received the latest overnight footage. It just gets better and better. Who's doing your special effects? . . ."

"Uh . . ."

"That lightning business with the kite—one word: inspired!"

"Thank you."

"Forget about the script. Don't want to see it. Just keep surprising me each day."

"We'll try."

"You're a modest little mensch. . . . Fly out when you're done. Lunch at Spago on me. *Ciao!*"

Ned closed the phone and looked at Pimento. "Do you know anything about a kite and lightning?"

Pimento shook his head. "Just what I read in the history books."

The phone rang again.

"Coppola here. . . . Oh. . . ." Ned walked forward in the RV and handed the phone to Marlon. "It's for you."

"Son, Perry's dead," said Dempsey Conrad.

"What?"

"It just happened. Found him at the Edison home."

"So that's what that was about."

"I'm sending a security team out."

"Don't!"

"I can't stand by any longer. You're leaving bodies everywhere you go. State police don't know what's going on. Until they do, we're putting you under protection."

"No way. It isolates me from the people."

"I'm sending them. We'll fight about this later."

Dempsey hung up.

Marlon made his usual low-profile rounds in Fort Myers and decided to skip the Daughters of Restricted Country Clubs luncheon. When the TV people heard Marlon wasn't coming to the lunch, they snapped their tripods shut and jumped in their vans and chased him, leaving Gomer Tatum alone at the head table with a napkin in his collar and a bread stick in each fist.

The *Orange Crush* passed the old Edison Theater downtown and took the towering Edison Bridge north across the Caloosahatchee River. They crossed another big bridge over the Peace River at Punta Gorda and took the Tamiami up through Port Charlotte and Venice. They got to Sarasota, and Marlon pulled over in the parking lot of the historic brick Sarasota High School, Pee-Wee Herman's alma mater. He spread a map out on the steering wheel and ran his finger down it. "Vista Isles is just north of here."

"Vista Isles?" asked Pimento.

"Yeah," said Marlon. "It's the sister park of Vista Isles East on the other coast, where bright boy back there pulled some funny stuff. I won't sleep well until I fix the damage and set the record straight." He called ahead to the park on his cell phone, then the TV stations.

Shortly after two, Marlon exited Interstate 75 near a factory outlet mall and pulled up to the community hall at Vista Isles. The park's manager had said it was the best time to catch most of the residents in the same place. Marlon entered the hall filled with retirees for the weekly meeting of the World Wrestling Federation Fan Club, Gulf Coast Smash-Mouth Chapter.

Marlon took the stage next to a big-screen TV, and the manager turned off the replay of a grudge match, drawing a chorus of groans. Marlon bent the flexible microphone on the podium toward him. Camera lights for three TV stations and Ned Coppola came on in the back of the hall.

"As you may have read in the papers, there were some campaign irregularities at Vista Isles East last week. I want to apologize and say that the negative representations against my opponent, Gomer Tatum, were dishonest and completely false. He is a very worthy opponent. I believe I am the better candidate, but that's not the way I want to win. Are there any questions?"

A shriveled old man wearing a GORILLA MONSOON T-shirt raised his hand.

Marlon pointed. "Yes?"

"Should Stone Cold Steve Austin be allowed back in the ring after his recent disqualification for attacking Triple H with a claw hammer?"

"I . . . uh . . ."

Pimento leaned toward Marlon and whispered, "I know this one." He leaned to the mike. "Absolutely! Triple H had it coming!"

There was a lot of nodding in the crowd. "That's how I feel," said the old man.

"Anything else?" asked Marlon.

A delicate old woman with a walker and a SEXUAL CHOCOLATE T-shirt raised her hand.

"Yes?"

"Will we ever see the Road Dogg paired with D-Generation X in tag-team competition?"

Marlon turned to Pimento.

"That's mine, too," he said and stepped to the mike. "Not as long as the blood feud continues. It would be much too volatile—the governing body wants to keep the sport clean."

The woman smiled and said thank you. Another hand went up—a man using oxygen and wearing black RAW IS WAR! elbow pads. He pulled the oxygen mask away from his face.

"Can we expect more of that cool dancing from Grandmaster Sexy and Scotty 2 Hottie?" The man released the oxygen mask just as he was passing out, and the rubber bands snapped it back to his face.

"Cool dancing? You mean like this?" said Pimento, breaking into an urban two-step. The audience began applauding.

Ten minutes later, Marlon and Escrow were standing on the side of the stage in amazement. Pimento had everyone's arms in the air, swaying them from one side to the other. "Hey! . . . Ho! . . . Hey! . . . Ho! . . . ."

Jackie Monroeville had the TV set on in their motel room, watching Marlon at Vista Isles.

"He's doing it again! We can't win for losing. We have to get to Vista Isles and steal his thunder!"

"Vista Isles!" exclaimed Tatum. "Don't you remember what happened at the last one? We almost got killed!"

"That was then. Everything's changed!" said Jackie, slapping the pecan log from his hand. "Marlon just admitted the whole thing was a hoax."

Marlon and company were in the parking lot at Vista Isles, piling back in the Winnebago.

"I think I forgot my sunglasses," said Escrow, and he ran back to the hall.

The audience was milling around at the refreshment table, and Escrow jumped onstage and grabbed the microphone. "I just want to reiterate all the things the governor said about Gomer Tatum. He is a worthy opponent, and there's room in democracy for everyone's beliefs. I'm sure he has good reasons for advocating that all senior citizen driver's licenses be screened with rigid eyesight tests . . ."

Heads in the audience turned.

". . . And that your reflexes be tested at night on a banked race track in rain-slick conditions with exploding obstacles . . ."

The grousing got louder.

". . . and so what if he's a fan of the Brooklyn Brawler?"

Jackie turned her Harley right onto Vista Isles Boulevard. They could see the spire on the community hall in the distance.

A hundred yards ahead, a Crown Victoria pulled out from a side street. A little ways back, an Olds 88 pulled out. The Crown Victoria was going ten miles an hour, and the Harley was soon on its tail. More cars pulled out. Buicks, Chryslers, Cadillacs. The Olds 88 closed the distance behind the motorcycle.

"What's the holdup?" Jackie yelled, gunning the bike.

In the sidecar, Tatum pointed ahead at the Crown Victoria. "There doesn't seem to be anyone in there."

He stood up in the sidecar and lifted his goggles, and he saw a puff of white hair even with the top of the seat.

"I'm gonna pull around and pass!" said Jackie.

Before she could, the Cadillacs and Buicks pulled alongside, boxing them in. The Harley suddenly lurched. Then it lurched again, harder. Tatum and Jackie were jerked forward.

"What's going on?" said Tatum, lurching again.

Jackie turned around.

"They're ramming us!"

35

JOE BLOW'S LIFE was graphed, plotted, timelined, and rotated in a 3-D computer model. It was recapped during a biographical special on Fox.

Blow paraphernalia was everywhere. T-shirts and baseball caps with Joe's face above a variety of mottos. IT ALL AVERAGES OUT, SHIT HAPPENS TWO TO THREE TIMES A WEEK, ORDINARY FOLKS DO IT IN THE MEDIAN.

The cameras went to his high school, where he graduated two hundredth in a class of four hundred.

"He always seemed to follow the crowd," recalled a teacher. "His grades were nothing special."

"He didn't stand out," said an old classmate. "Who would have ever thought he'd become this big?"

During the three months before the election, reporters collected 1,657 pounds of trash before dawn from the curb outside the Blow residence. They rented a small warehouse, where they spread it out on the floor like an FAA team trying to determine the cause of an airline disaster.

The debris was segregated in piles and rows. Bills, letters, receipts, beverage containers, cleaning products, steak bones, junk mail. The discoveries were mundane but consistent. Joe didn't eat the crusts from bread or the fat from pork chops. He had an enormous use for D and AA batteries. His razor blades still had some life left in them. He threw away warranty cards, didn't separate aluminum from glass, preferred paper to plastic. Joe could do better on his long-distance plan. The Blows went through peanut butter at an alarming rate. Chunky style.

On the fifth day, a breakthrough. "What's this?" asked a TV reporter from *Entertainment Tonight,* wiping mayonnaise off a Polaroid photo. It was a picture taken in the Blow bedroom. Mr. and Mrs. Blow in a compromising position wearing beaver costumes.

It was as though the reporters had stumbled upon the missing link. A spike on the seismograph. Finally, Joe had deviated from the norm. It led all the newscasts.

That night, however, Dr. Ruth said on CNN that the average person in America has at least one secret little twist they like to throw into the bedroom routine. What's more, it's healthy.

"It's the *abnormal* person who tries to suppress such tendencies, and the resulting internal pressure can lead to dangerous and dysfunctional behavior, like joining the Religious Right," said Dr. Ruth. "I applaud Joe Blow for helping America come to terms with its sexuality."

Joe Blow opened the front door the next morning and picked up the newspaper. He screamed when he read the top headline: PERV GOES MAINSTREAM.

He ran back in the house and collapsed on the living-room floor, trying to bury his face in the carpet.

"What is it?" asked his wife, timing an egg.

"They know about the beaver suits! They all know! Oh, God! This is so humiliating!" He rolled on the floor, squealing. "I can't face anyone! I can never leave the house again!"

Mrs. Blow looked out the window. Animal rights advocates arrived, wanting to know whether the costumes were natural or synthetic. A *Rocky Horror* fan club showed up with signs of support. FETISH RIGHTS NOW!

"Please, God, kill me!" said Joe.

The family decided it would be better if Mrs. Blow and the children went to stay with her parents in Ohio for a while until the beaver thing blew over.

That night Joe turned off all the lights in the house. He sat alone in the dark for hours. He could see reporters on his lawn with flashlights. He came to a conclusion.

"I have nothing to lose."

THE Tatum campaign rolled into Tampa in a taxicab.

They were a day early and their room at the Sheraton wasn't avail-able yet. They drove across the causeway, past Pirate's Cove Cabanas, Gasparilla Resort and Tennis, Buccaneer Bay Lodge, Pegleg Inn, Bluebeard Suites. The taxi rolled under the crossed cutlasses at the entrance of Shivering Timbers Motor Court.

Tatum got a room with cable and a refrigerator. Jackie ran errands.

She was back in an hour with two dry cleaning bags, and she threw them on the bed. Tatum was in his underwear, eating Mexican and watching *The Beverly Hillbillies*. He waved at the screen with a fajita. "That Jethro could act!"

"Shut up and try this on. . . . And don't get any picante on it!"

Tatum inspected his new outfit in the mirror.

"I don't feel too good about this. Seems like a big gamble."

"That's the whole idea!" said Jackie. "It's just like football. We're behind at the two-minute warning. He's playing a conservative pre-vent defense, so we have to throw the bomb."

She opened one of the bags and started wiggling into her own new outfit. "I got you this far," she said. "Now stand up! I still have time for alterations."

THE morning before the election, the *Orange Crush* turned off I-75, taking the Crosstown Expressway. When they got to the tollbooths, the skyline of Tampa appeared in the distance above the trees.

Pimento checked the time and turned on his portable TV. On-screen was the second ad Ned Coppola had produced for the Conrad campaign. It opened with a stark black-and-white photo of Gomer Tatum with a red slash through it. "Tatum—running negative ads again! Using the same old tired personal attacks and slander because he's too afraid to run on his own atheist record of being soft on child pornography and an enemy of the elderly . . ."

After the commercial, the news. Footage of firemen outside Vista Isles spraying down the smoldering chassis of a Harley and sidecar.

Escrow climbed in the passenger seat with the box of morning mail.

"... 'You suk!' 'You suk!' 'You suk!' 'Boy, do you suk!' 'I feel a breeze—must be you sucking!' and 'Free trade is for faggots!' ..."

Escrow grabbed the newspapers. He looked at the front of the *Miami Herald*, and his face brightened. He jumped up and started dancing. "I'm the man! Hooooo-hoooooo!"

He ran around the inside of the RV, doing a Charlie Brown nose-in-the-air dance.

The others gave him a weird look. Pimento picked up the newspaper Escrow had dropped. On the bottom of the page, a story about an impostor who had appeared before an audience of retirees at Vista Isles East, pretending to be from the Tatum camp. The headline: SENATE INVESTIGATES SENIOR-GATE.

"What is it?" asked Marlon, Escrow dancing with a broomstick in the background.

"He finally got his -*Gate*."

"What?"

"I'll explain later." Pimento reviewed the rest of the headlines. "Everyone is going big with Sirocco's execution tonight at Starke. The *Times,* the *Sentinel,* and the *Herald* are all leading with it— everyone except the *Tribune,* which is leading with the WWF *Raw Is War!* show tonight at the Ice Palace. . . . Oh man, we have to go! Wrestling rules! Can we?"

"Actually, that's not a bad idea," said Marlon. "You know how many people watch that show? They always introduce local notables on the air. . . ."

"It's probably some of the best exposure we can get," said Pimento.

"Kind of surprised Tatum didn't think of it first," said Marlon.

The midday news cut to a commercial on Pimento's little TV. It was a campaign ad for Gomer Tatum.

"Turn it up," said Marlon.

Tatum appeared on the screen in dark sunglasses and a sequined cape. He had a walking cane topped with a carved ivory skull. On his arm was Jackie, looking hot in a bustier and Xena the Warrior Princess outfit.

Tatum pointed at the camera. "I want you, Conrad! Tonight! Ice Palace! Lights-Out Cage Match! No-Time-Limit Gubernatorial Smackdown for the Whole Enchilada!"

"So this is where we've evolved," said Marlon.

"Actually," said Pimento, "it can't help but add dignity to the process."

Marlon drove over to Ybor City for lunch. He looked up and down Seventh Avenue.

"Where'd the Silver Ring go?" he said. "This country's falling apart."

They decided on Carmine's instead. Marlon didn't realize how tired he was until he sat down. He sank heavily into the chair like a sack of mercury, and he ordered crab cakes and Cuban coffee.

It was near the end. Events were starting to back up and overlap. The polls fluctuated by the minute, Marlon averaging a two-point lead with a three-point margin of error. Sirocco's execution was tonight. Tomorrow the polls opened. Marlon and Tatum were beyond fatigue, both running on fumes now, ready to drop—Marlon from an incredibly ambitious pace, Tatum from a cardiovascular system laboring like turbines at Hoover Dam.

They were both marathon runners in the twenty-sixth mile. They had entered the stadium, reeling and staggering, and the crowd shouted them on. Marlon's brain montaged through the last weeks, all the people he had met across over the state, all the differences and the common ground, the cultures morphing as he moved from region to region. The southerners in the north part of the state, the northerners in the south. The inland crackers, the outlying migrants, the Latins, the Jews, the Irish, the Germans, the blacks. The old migrating for their health, and the carpetbaggers migrating to feed on the old.

Marlon was tired and depressed. He had started thinking dangerously—that he could actually make a difference. He regretted being so cavalier at the beginning of the campaign. He just *had* to win.

Escrow anxiously awaited the lab report on Pimento's fingerprints. The suspense was making him a head case.

He had extra worries about Pimento that he had never shared with anyone.

Escrow locked himself in the RV's tiny bathroom with Pimento's personnel file. He opened it.

It was completely empty except for the results of the drug test and a new document, a single sheet of paper. Nobody had discovered it until two months ago, when Escrow went snooping into Pimento's background, trying to learn his real name.

The fingerprints were taking forever. Escrow decided to read the document again—maybe he had overreacted the first time he saw it and nearly passed out.

The piece of paper was Pimento's new-employee questionnaire, to be used for the in-house newsletter to introduce recent hires.

It had a sentence of instruction at the top, and the rest of the page was left blank for the employee to complete: "In your own words, describe who you are, so that your new colleagues can get to know you better."

Beneath the typed question were stanzas neatly printed in No. 2 pencil.

Please allow me to introduce myself,
I'm a man of stealth and waste
I've been around for a long campaign,
stole many a man's vote and slate

And I was 'round when Gary Hart
fought the *Herald* and took the bait,
Made damn sure that Donna Rice
Hopped on his lap 'n' sealed his fate

Pleased to meet you. Help me guess my name.
But what's puzzling you is how I never face the blame.

I stuck around St. Petersburg
when the benches had fresh green paint,
Killed the next drug czar's service tax,
And Martinez screamed, "Hey, wait!"

I rode a float,
'sposed to look like a boat
When the Orange Bowl raged,
"Can I buy your vote?"

Pleased to meet you! Help me guess my name!
But what's puzzling you is how the voters got so lame!

I watched with glee (Hoo-Hoo!)
all the duplicity (Hoo-Hoo!)
as the lies piled up (Hoo-Hoo!)
in the primary (Hoo-Hoo!)

I shouted out (Hoo-Hoo!)
"Who killed the Everglades?" (Hoo-Hoo!)
When after all (Hoo-Hoo!)
It was you and me (Hoo-Hoo!)

Let me please introduce myself (Hoo-Hoo!)
I'm a man of stealth and waste (Hoo-Hoo!)
And I made ads for nominees (Hoo-Hoo!)
who sold their souls before they reached Palm Bay (Hoo-Hoo!)

Just as every citizen's a criminal (Hoo-Hoo!)
And all the candidates saints (Hoo-Hoo!)
As heads is tails, I'm with the Governor (Hoo-Hoo!)
And I'm in need of some restraint (Hoo-Hoo!)

So if you meet me, see the irony (Hoo-Hoo!)
the hypocrisy and the hate (Hoo-Hoo!)
Use all your well-learned politics (Hoo-Hoo!)
or I'll lay your vote to waste. . . .

Escrow hit his head on the towel rack as he passed out.

36

TAMPA'S ICE PALACE was packed to the rafters. People waved homemade signs and wore T-shirts of their favorite wrestlers.

Marlon and his entourage were sitting in the front row. Pimento's seat was empty. Escrow looked around. Where the hell was he?

The crowd erupted when a ring announcer in a tux finally appeared.

"We're about to go live on the USA Network, so I want everyone to get ready to give the country your biggest Tampa welcome!"

Viewers at home watched a campaign commercial showing small children playing in a field of daisies, families filing into a country church, a grandmother serving the Sunday ham. The ad was for casino gambling.

The commercial ended and viewers nationwide were taken inside the arena, where the camera panned over thousands of cheering people.

A microphone descended from the ceiling, and the ring announcer grabbed it.

"Welcome, America, to the Ice Palace in Tampa, Florida, for Monday-night *Raw Is War!*"

The crowd went bonkers.

"We have an extra-special surprise in store for you. We've already seen Jesse Ventura leave the ring and successfully defend his title at the ballot box. Tonight, we're going to take it a step further. We may see the nation's first governor's race actually to be decided *in the ring*."

A cell phone went off in the front row. Escrow answered it.

"This is Major Banks with the Florida Department of Law Enforcement. I'm calling back with the results of that fingerprint sample you sent us. Mr. Escrow, where did you get the sample?"

"Routine security check."

"Do you know where this individual is?"

Escrow glanced at Pimento's empty chair. "No idea."

"Whatever you do, stay clear of this guy. Do not, I repeat, do not attempt to apprehend him. Don't even let local police try. He's way too violent. If you know where this guy is, we're standing by with a specially trained commando unit."

Escrow lost all color. "Who is he?"

"He's wanted in connection with a string of grisly murders in south Florida. Unarmed, he took out a three-man hit squad all by himself."

Escrow trembled. "Are you sure you have the right person?"

"Lean, six feet tall, ice-blue eyes? Short hair starting to gray on the sides?"

Escrow felt faint.

"We lost his trail in Cocoa Beach a couple years back. What makes him so dangerous is that he's borderline genius and totally insane. He can appear perfectly normal for weeks and function at high levels of society, even excel. Then—BAM!—he snaps and we're bagging bodies for days. . . ."

Escrow was trying to get his jaw to work.

"Hello? You still there?"

"Uh . . . I'm here. What's his name?"

"Serge A. Storms. You'll call us if you ever see him again?"

"You got it."

Escrow closed the phone and slipped it back into his coat.

"Are you all right?" asked Marlon. "Geez, you look awful!"

"I think I got a bad sausage."

"For a second I thought you were having a heart attack. Look— you're all flushed and clammy. You're soaked right through your shirt."

"I'm okay."

He was not okay. He was suffering a monster anxiety attack. How could I have done this? he thought As soon as it gets out, there goes the election! Guess who they'll all blame? Me! They'll gang up like they always have!

He squeezed his fists in self-anger and crunched his eyes shut. I'm such a dipshit! I'll be featured in political science textbooks. My name will live in infamy. I'll have to be buried in an anonymous grave so the Young Republicans can't dig me up and pee on my bones.

Okay, you're completely freaking out now. Calm down. Calm down. That's better. You're looking at this completely wrong. All that unthinkable stuff will only happen if someone finds out. And if you keep your mouth shut, how will anyone ever know? Pimento's been acting perfectly normal up to now. Sure, the governor will be in danger, but just for another twenty-four hours. After that, it won't matter. In fact, I'll be the hero, the chief of staff who held the rudder steady through the storm, then single-handedly drugged and apprehended the incredibly dangerous fugitive the day after the election. He made a mental note to get hold of some drugs to dissolve in a beverage. He smiled. All Escrow had to do now was cross his fingers and hope Pimento could hold it together one more day. Piece of cake. Speaking of the devil, where was he, anyway?

Marlon looked up. "Dad?"

Dempsey Conrad was moving down the aisle with six men in satin jackets, BRIDGES TO BABYLON '97 WORLD TOUR. They took the row of seats behind Marlon.

"I told you no security," said Marlon.

"What security?" said Dempsey. "We're wrestling fans. Isn't that right, guys?"

Outside, a 1931 Stutz Bearcat roadster pulled into the Ice Palace parking lot. Von Zeppelin got out with a long leather pouch.

Inside the arena, giant rock concert flashpots exploded, and Gomer Tatum emerged from behind the curtains with Jackie at his side. They strutted down the gangway to the ring. "Bad to the Bone" boomed from the sound system. Overhead, the Jumbo-tron played video clips of Tatum debating in the legislature, interspersed with footage of burning skyscrapers, earthquakes, hurricanes, mushrooming H-bombs, and a biplane flying into the side of a barn.

The crowd cheered wildly as Tatum handed Jackie his cape and started bouncing around the ring.

The announcer then introduced Marlon Conrad in the front row. Marlon stood and received his own standing ovation.

As rehearsed, Tatum snatched the microphone from the ring announcer. "Get in here, you coward!" he yelled at Marlon.

The crowd let loose again. Yeah, Marlon, get him!

Marlon just kept smiling and waving.

"Girlie-man!" yelled Tatum. He held the ring ropes open for Marlon to climb in, but Marlon shook his head no. The audience started to boo. Tatum began prancing around the ring, whipping his arms in the air, inciting the crowd to boo more.

"This was a mistake," Escrow whispered to Marlon. "We've been ambushed. This is exactly what he wanted."

"Relax," said Marlon.

The ring announcer took the mike back. "We're very disappointed in our governor. It looks like we have a new champion by default!"

Tatum had started climbing out of the ring when the announcer spoke up again. "Wait! What's this?"

Everyone turned to see someone bounding down an aisle on the far side of the arena wearing a white silk boxing robe.

"Holy Jesus!" said Escrow. "This can't be happening!"

Marlon and Elizabeth broke up laughing.

The announcer held the ropes open, and Pimento jumped into the ring and started doing the Ali shuffle. The crowd went wild.

The announcer covered his microphone and leaned over the ropes to Marlon. "Who is this guy?"

Marlon was still laughing. "My press secretary."

The announcer nodded and uncovered the microphone. He stepped back into the center of the ring.

"Ladies and gentlemen, we have a late change on tonight's card . . ." The announcer looked over at Pimento, facing his corner and limbering up at the turnbuckle with deep-knee squats. He read the name on the back of Pimento's robe.

". . . Representing the governor's office, weighing in at one hundred and sixty pounds and hailing from Parts Unknown, *The Florida Phantom*!"

Pimento threw off his robe and spun around. He was now, under both legal and clinical definitions, completely unhinged. He wore an orange 1950s-style high school wrestling uniform with the two little straps over the shoulders, and he crouched in a menacing Greco-Roman stance.

Jackie yelled across the ring: "What the hell do you think you're doing?"

"Fighting for truth, justice and the American Way!" He sashayed side to side.

Tatum was frantic. He turned to Jackie. "You said I wouldn't have to fight! You said Marlon would refuse, and I'd only have to perform a little victory dance! What do I do now?"

Jackie shoved him out into the ring. "Wrestle!"

The bell clanged.

Pimento charged across the ring, and Tatum screamed and tried to climb over the ropes. Pimento caught him by the back of his shorts and gave him a wedgie so brutal it made people queasy all the way to the third balcony. He pulled Tatum into the middle of the ring by his shorts. He grabbed him by the legs and began spinning in a circle, swinging Tatum around and around with enormous centrifugal force. He let go. Tatum flew through the ropes and crashed into a set of folding metal chairs kept on hand at ringside for wrestlers to bash each other over the head with.

Jackie ran to him.

"I'm hurt! I'm seriously hurt!" said Tatum.

"Get back in there!" yelled Jackie. "It's gonna take more than this to stop me from being First Lady!" She propped Tatum up at the side of the ring, crouched down to get her shoulder under his butt, and with a great *ooooomph!* sent him back onto the canvas. "Kill him!"

Tatum stood up and was swarmed immediately. Pimento raked his eyes. He gave him a Dusty Rhodes elbow to the skull. He punched him in the stomach. He kicked him in the groin. He bounced him off the ropes and caught him in the neck with a forearm. He gave him the atomic knee drop. He climbed up on the turnbuckle to administer the flying guillotine.

Jackie stood in the corner, grabbing the top rope and screaming. "He's killing you! Stand up and be a man!"

Tatum was down on the mat—bloody, blinded, disoriented—crawling in a circle. "Jackie! Where are you? I can hear you, but I can't see you!"

Pimento marched around his victim in the ring, doing a Mick Jagger rooster strut. The crowd loved it.

"Heeeee-yahhhhh!" Jackie came off the top ring rope and caught Pimento by surprise with a scissor kick, flattening him. She sat on his chest and pounded him over and over. "Don't you *ever* do that to my Gomer again!"

The referee slapped the canvas once, twice. But before Pimento could be counted out, he did the patented "body shake" that always removes an opponent before the third slap.

Now Pimento and Jackie were face-to-face, the fallen Tatum on the canvas between them, moaning and wiping the blood out of his eyes. They started circling each other warily, both hissing.

The rest of Tatum's campaign staff became concerned. They were sitting in the first row, on the opposite side of the ring from Marlon, and they got up and approached the officials' table.

"I think he's really hurt," said the chief of staff.

"Nonsense!" said the ring announcer. "This is great television. Listen to that crowd!"

Behind them: "Heeeeeeee-yaaaahhhhh!" Jackie grabbed Pimento's head between her legs in The Vise of Death. He started turning blue. As he was about to pass out, Pimento pulled a foreign object from his trunks, hit Jackie in the nose with it, then threw it out of the ring before the officials got wise. Jackie released her hold and fought to her feet. The blood returned to Pimento's head and he struggled to stand up on the other side of the ring. Tatum crawled and collapsed in the middle of the mat.

Jackie was feeling her nose with both hands. "I think you broke it!" she said in a nasal voice. "It's gonna look all fucked up! I'll kill you! Ahhhhhhhhh!" She charged across the ring, running over

Tatum's back and mashing his face into the mat. She leaped for a flying dropkick and took Pimento down in the corner.

"I'm pretty sure Tatum's hurt," the chief of staff told the ring
announcer. "I want you to stop the fight."

The announcer laughed. "Are you kidding? We're live on national
TV! Do you know how much money we're making?"

"Stop the fight!"

"Forget it!"

The rest of Tatum's staff was now out of their chairs, and a major
brouhaha ensued at the officials' table.

"Stop the fight!"

"No way!"

"I'll stop it myself!"

The chief of staff went for the ring. The announcer tried to block
him but was shoved to the ground. Tatum's entire camp blustered
past the officials' table and started climbing into the ring. Several
WWF wrestlers saw the ring announcer get shoved, and it offended
them. They came pouring in from backstage—Stone Cold Steve
Austin, The Rock and The Undertaker—and they began beating the
tar out of Tatum's people. The staff tried to use its sheer numbers
and pile on Austin and The Rock. More wrestlers came running out.
The Mean Street Posse, X-Pac, and Taka & Funaki. The entire ring
was encircled in pandemonium. The folding metal chairs came into
play. Wham! There goes an aide-de-camp. Wham! There goes an
undersecretary. Wham! There goes the chief of protocol, his face a
crimson mask.

The play-by-play man and the ring announcer sat at the press
table, yelling in their respective microphones.

"I've never seen anything like this! The officials are trying to
restore order!"

"It's a donnybrook! It's a donnybrook!"

Inside the ring, Pimento had Jackie in a hammerlock but left himself open for an elbow to the solar plexus. Jackie turned the tables.
She immobilized him by constricting his head between her athletic
thighs. Six separate struggles raged outside the ring.

"It's a free-for-all! . . ."

"It's all-out war! . . ."

Someone in the audience came running down the steps toward the ring, screaming like a maniac.

The ring announcer looked up and saw something so bizarre and unnatural that it could only be part of the official wrestling script. He was afraid he had missed something in one of the meetings, so he improvised.

"Oh, my God! Ladies and gentlemen! It's the Puppet Lady! It's the Puppet Lady! . . ."

Marlon looked toward the aisle. "Babs?"

Babs was both crying and screaming as she climbed into the ring with her large, wooden Punch-and-Judy set. "Let go of him! You're killing him! . . ."

Jackie had Pimento in an upside-down hold. She slowly stood up, gripping him around the waist with his head still between her thighs, preparing to drop him on his skull in a classic piledriver.

"She's going for the piledriver!" shouted the play-by-play man. "She's going for the piledriver!"

Babs was crying her makeup off again as she planted her feet, grabbed the ends of the puppet strings in her hand and began twirling Punch-and-Judy in a circle over her head like a Mexican bola. When the marionettes had reached a ferocious velocity, Babs slammed them into the side of Jackie's head. Jackie was staggered. She dropped Pimento mid-piledriver.

Babs ran over and hugged Pimento and stroked his hair. "Are you okay, baby?"

Wham!

Jackie hit Babs over the head with a chair.

Babs went skidding across the canvas facedown. She pushed herself up and slowly turned around. The crying had stopped. Her face was twisted and her teeth bared. She pointed at Jackie and said a single word: "You!"

"Come and get it!" said Jackie.

The two women charged like bulls from opposite corners and met in the middle of the ring in a savage, bone-crunching collision. They began to fight with such fury and speed that the human eye couldn't keep up with it, spinning across the ring like Tasmanian devils.

"It's no-holds-barred! . . ."

"It's a death match! . . ."

The wrestlers outside the ring stopped and watched in horror when they noticed what was happening. Stone Cold, The Rock and X-Pac winced and tightened their sphincters.

Tatum's Tallahassee staff used the diversion to organize a pincer attack.

Wham! A tax attorney caught Stone Cold in the back of the head with a tortoiseshell briefcase. From the opposite direction, a team of state auditors made a flanking move and charged the other wrestlers in the flying-wedge formation.

"It's bedlam! It's bedlam! . . ."

Meanwhile, Pimento and Babs had gained the upper hand. They had simultaneously bounced Jackie and Gomer off opposing ring ropes, then switched off and caught their opponents in twin sleeper holds. The crowd went bananas. When Jackie and Gomer were neutralized, Pimento and Babs slung them through the ring ropes, taking out the flying wedge of accountants before they could do any more harm to the WWF.

The crowd had never been louder. Rolls of toilet paper flew. The network's switchboard lit up, wanting to know if the Florida Phantom and the Puppet Lady would become regulars.

Stone Cold Steve Austin and Tampa native The Rock climbed into the ring and raised Pimento's and Babs's arms in triumph. They were joined by the rest of the wrestlers, who hoisted the couple on their shoulders.

Marlon and Elizabeth laughed and applauded ringside. Marlon looked over at Escrow, who was ashen and hyperventilating, and gave him a playful nudge. "See? I told you everything would work out. You worry too much."

As Pimento and Babs were carried up the gangway, Pimento got a strange feeling, the same one he'd had in the Miami Arena. He looked up toward the rafters. Something wasn't right. . . .

Other wrestlers took the ring as the regularly scheduled prelimi-
nary matches began. Crew members had to bring out a new set of
folding metal chairs because the others were all bent.

Escrow was in the rest room. He had his coat over his arm; his collar was open and tie loose. He bent into the sink and splashed cold
water on his face. A distant roar from the arena echoed into the rest
room. The man at the next sink had a shaved head tattooed on top
with a flaming pentagram.

"Dammit! I'll bet they just gave the match to the British Bulldog. I
hate the Bulldog!" He punched the metal paper towel dispenser,
creasing it deeply. He turned to Escrow.

"You look like a Bulldog fan!"

Escrow cowered and shook his head no.

"You sure?"

This time he nodded, rapidly.

"We've got to do something about the Bulldog!" The man pulled a
baggie of heroin from his pocket. He tapped some into his hand and
snorted. "That's better. Now I can handle the Bulldog."

"Say," said Escrow. "Can that stuff knock someone out? I mean
like if you slipped it in their drink?"

"Can drop a rhino if you use enough."

"Would you sell me some?"

"I have a few dime bags."

Escrow opened his wallet and the man grabbed a fifty. "That
should get you started." He handed Escrow five tiny packets of white
powder, and Escrow stuffed them down a hip pocket.

Back in the arena, Marlon, Elizabeth and Jenny laughed and
applauded as Too Cool did a synchronized jive dance after knocking
out the Bulldog.

The barrel of a Tango-51 poked out through a small window high
up in the arena. Inside the room, a man sat on boxes of scoreboard
lightbulbs, scanning the front row through the rifle scope. Jenny . . .
Elizabeth . . . Marlon. The rifle stopped. The safety came off.

More flashpots ignited, and electric motors began lowering a steel
cage over the ring.

A sweaty index finger twitched on the trigger of the Tango-51.

Suddenly, the door to the lightbulb room opened. The gunman turned around.

"Who are you? . . . Wait! No! I can explain! . . . *Aaaahhh!*"

The shirt on the man's limp body was unbuttoned. A Magic Marker scribbled across his chest. The *i* was dotted with a heart.

Someone stepped out of the lightbulb room and silently slipped away on a catwalk. He wore a robe with a name on the back.

THE FLORIDA PHANTOM.

●

"HOMICIDE, Mahoney," said Mahoney, flashing a badge. "Metro-Dade."

"You're a long way from your sandbox," said the head of Ice Palace security.

"It's all one big sandbox now."

"Amen."

"What have we got here?"

"A stiff. Crushed monocle next to the head. Magic Marker on the chest."

Mahoney lifted the sheet. Written across the nipple line:

TAMPA: AMERICA'S NEXT GREAT CITY!

"You've seen it all, haven't you?" asked Mahoney.

He nodded. "I got a week till I retire. But now they're teaming me up with some rookie who wants to throw away the rule book and do things his way. He's gonna get me killed."

"We've lost a lot of good men just before retirement like that."

Mahoney pulled out his flask and took a hit, then offered it.

"I'm on the wagon."

"Wanna fall off?"

"Makes sense to me." He took a slug.

"What else makes sense?"

"Not putting foil in a microwave."

"What else?"

"The victim was no wrestler."

"How's that?"

"Top of his skull flattened."

"Sounds like the piledriver."

"Easiest hold in the world to get out of. No reason at all he had to die."

"You know what that makes this then?"

The security agent nodded sadly. "Another senseless killing."

37

JOURNALISM PROFESSOR WALLY Butts couldn't get through to Marlon. He broke the speed limit all the way from Starke to Tampa. Three hours till execution.

He drove to the Ice Palace and spotted the *Orange Crush* in the parking lot just as the wrestling match was letting out.

Butts knocked on the door of the RV, then pushed Escrow aside. "Governor, he's protecting his daughter."

"Who is?"

"Frank Lloyd Sirocco."

Butts's cell phone rang, and he pulled it out of his jacket. "Hello? . . . Yes, it is. . . . I see. . . . I see. . . . Why can't you just tell me right now? . . . I see. . . . Yes, we'll be there." He hung up.

It was an out-of-town attorney. He said he was representing the daughter of a Death Row inmate, whom he was not prepared to identify on the phone. He said he had to see the governor and Butts in person. He was driving over from Lakeland, and they agreed to meet halfway, to save time. The attorney said he'd bring the daughter.

The state troopers were the first to arrive at the Hillsborough River State Park, thirty minutes east of Tampa in the middle of nowhere. It was after dark and the park was closed, but the troopers unlocked the gate. A black Lexus came around a lonely bend and pulled into the park. The troopers waved them over to the picnic tables just inside the entrance.

A man and a woman got out. The troopers frisked them and used handheld metal detectors.

The *Orange Crush* pulled in the park.

Elizabeth and Jenny were asleep in back. Escrow and Pimento were up front, but Marlon told them it was a confidential legal meeting and they would have to wait in the Winnebago. Marlon and Butts climbed out and took seats at one of the picnic tables, opposite the man and woman. There were no lights in the park, and no moon. One of the troopers parked his patrol car facing the table and put his high beams on.

The attorney held up a hand in the surreal light. "Before anyone says anything, I need to have immunity for my client."

Butts: "What for?"

"You're interested in the Sirocco murder case? If my client has information that she hasn't divulged earlier . . ."

"Right," said Marlon. "Obstruction. Accessory after the fact."

"I need it in writing," said the attorney. "Blanket immunity for anything my client says here. I've prepared the papers."

The lawyer pulled a document from his briefcase, and Butts pulled a video camera from his.

"What's that?" asked the attorney.

"We need to get this on tape."

"We didn't agree to that."

"A man's life is at stake." He looked at his watch. An hour left. "We don't have time to fool around!"

The attorney looked at the woman. She nodded.

"Okay, you can tape." The attorney handed the document to Marlon. He signed it on his lap and handed it to Butts for the witness signature.

When the attorney got the paper back and made sure everything was in order, he nodded at the woman. "Go ahead."

"I'm Angela Sirocco, Frank's daughter." She stopped and looked at the attorney. She had trouble going on.

"I know this is hard," said Marlon, "but did George Braintree rape you?"

She nodded.

"So your father's trying to protect you?"

She nodded again.

Marlon and Butts shook their heads at each other. "Jesus."

"Your father's willing to die to protect your reputation?"

"No," said Angela.

"What?" asked Marlon, confused.

"He's protecting me, all right. But not my reputation. . . . *I* killed George Braintree."

Bang. The answer almost gave Marlon and Butts whiplash. Of course. It all fell into place.

The attorney held up the document. "We had a deal now—anything said here . . ."

Marlon nodded, still stunned.

"But what about all the evidence against Frank?" asked Butts.

"He was telling the truth when he said his gun was stolen. I took it," the woman explained. "I forged checks at the bank and got money orders for the trip. Made the calls at the pay phone. I was the only one who knew what I was planning."

Butts and Marlon were kicking themselves. How could they have been so dense?

●

ANGELA Sirocco and her attorney drove away in the Lexus, followed by the troopers. The *Orange Crush* waited behind. Marlon had an urgent phone call to make before he was going anywhere.

Marlon's head was racing. He grabbed his cell phone and punched in the prison number. It beeped and turned itself off. Dead battery.

They came to get Frank Lloyd Sirocco. His head was shaved, and his knees knocked. A priest told him he was going to a better place.

Escrow was on his own cell phone when Marlon told him to get off—he had an important call to make.

"Sirocco's innocent. I have to call off the execution."

"You can't!"

"Gimme that!"

"How do you know he's innocent?"

"New evidence," said Marlon, holding up the videotape.

"Well, he probably did something else wrong."

"Give me that phone!"

"I won't let you!" said Escrow, clutching the phone to his chest. "You're gonna blow the election!"

"What's wrong with you?"

"I'll get it," said Pimento, and the two began struggling.

"No! No! No! We're going to lose the election!" Escrow started crying, then made a heaving expression. "I'm going to be sick."

Pimento let go and Escrow jumped out the door. He ran to the front of the Winnebago and opened the hood.

"What's he doing?" asked Marlon. "Throwing up on the engine?"

The next thing they knew, Escrow was sprinting into the woods, cell phone in one hand and distributor wires in the other. They were too far out in the dark countryside to walk to another phone in time.

"Get him!" yelled Marlon, and he and Pimento jumped down from the *Orange Crush* and dashed into the woods.

Ned grabbed his camera and ran after them, bounding through the trees, taking branches in the face. "I love it! This is so *Blair Witch*!"

They had almost caught up to Escrow when they came to a clearing, and the ground dropped away quickly. They tumbled down the bank of the Hillsborough River. Escrow got up and went to throw the phone in the water, but Marlon dove from his knees and tackled him. Marlon held Escrow down, and Pimento pried the cell phone from his hands.

"Call the prison!" said Marlon, restraining the struggling chief of staff.

"No!" yelled Escrow.

"Hurry!" yelled Marlon.

"Emotion!" yelled Ned.

Pimento punched numbers on the phone.

"You have reached the Florida State Prison at Starke. If you know

your party's extension, enter it now. If you do not know your party's extension, enter it now.... For further assistance, please call back during regular business hours. To hear our regular business hours, please stay on the line. To not stay on the line, press star-three. All others, press the pound key...."

"What's taking so long?" said Marlon.

Pimento pressed buttons at random. "*... You have entered an invalid selection. Please try again.... Due to an extremely high volume of calls, we cannot process your request at this time. Please do not hang up, as this will delay the processing of your request....*" Pimento pressed more buttons. "*... Hello, this is the voice mail of George Defazio. I'm away from my desk right now ...*"

"Aaaaauuuuuu!" screamed Pimento. He reached back and hurled the phone into the river.

"Brilliant!" yelled Ned.

The guards walked Frank Sirocco down a bright hallway. A door swung open and Frank saw the chair. His legs went, and they had to grab him by the armpits to keep him up. The curtain was lowered to block the witnesses' view as they carried limp Frank to the chair.

Marlon and Pimento made it back to the edge of the woods and ran to the park entrance on the dark country road. Headlights came around the bend. Marlon ran into the street and put up his arms, and the car skidded to a stop.

Marlon ran around to the driver's side. "Do you have a cell phone?"

Frank was in the chair, arms strapped fast against oak. The drill was to get the prisoner trussed up as quickly as possible and start the juice; they wanted everything moving so fast that there was no idle time for the prisoner to think about it and make a scene. Frank's head twitched around like a scared rabbit. Two men pulled the leather buckles tight on his legs and another pulled the hood down over his head.

As soon as the phone rang, the warden yelled for everyone not to move a muscle. He took the governor's call.

The warden hung up. "Get him out of there!"

They unstrapped Frank and took him back to his cell, and he fainted.

38

ELECTION DAY.

The Parrot Heads for Economic Progress were all jazzed up. Their biggest event of the year was only hours away. Months of preparation and thousands of dollars spent. They had their assembly permits from the city council, and the stage was already set up on the Franklin Street pedestrian mall in downtown Tampa.

Blaine Crease arrived early in a bright floral beach shirt, preparing to moderate the final debate of the campaign. A debate had never been held so late, but the race was a statistical dead heat, and Crease smelled a ratings coup. He'd made the campaigns an offer they couldn't refuse. If either turned him down, the other would show up alone and get an hour of free airtime and a crucial bounce in the polls. The showdown was set for noon sharp.

"Quite an impressive gathering you've got planned," Crease told the event chairman.

"And it isn't just Florida," said the Parrot Head official. "We've got Jimmy Buffett disciples coming from all over the country."

"What's this whole Parrot Head phenomenon about, anyway?" asked Crease.

"It's kind of like AA in reverse."

A giant banner went up over the stage.

THE MILLION PARROT HEAD MARCH.

A hair trimmer buzzed in room 308 of the Gaspar Motor Lodge on Tampa's Kennedy Boulevard. Tufts of freshly cut hair fell and clumped in the bathroom sink.

Pimento looked in the mirror and inspected his fresh Mohawk.

He had finally remembered who he was. His name was Serge, and he'd lost all communication with the tower.

Serge slipped on dark sunglasses and pointed at his reflection.

"*You* talkin' to me! . . . You *talkin'* to me! . . . You talkin' to *me! . . .*"

Serge left the bathroom and went over to the window. He pulled back the curtain. On the street: crack deals, male prostitution, people pushing baby carriages filled with trash, screaming at invisible enemies. "Everything's okay now," he said to himself. "You're home again."

Serge pinned a MARLON! button on his shirt, locked up the room and started walking the fifteen blocks to the Franklin Street Mall.

●

REFORM Party candidate Albert Fresco sat in his kitchen madder than a sumbitch, watching a TV program showing preparations for the gubernatorial debate in downtown Tampa.

"By God they're gonna let me participate in *this* one," Fresco said to himself as he loaded a .38 Special at the kitchen table. He stood up and grabbed his car keys.

●

THE reporters showed up at dawn for Joe Blow duty. They knew something was wrong as soon as they turned onto Elm Street. That can't be the same house, they thought, but they knew it was.

Overnight it had been painted completely black, with dripping bloodred letters across the front: HOUSE OF PAIN!

The reporters massed at the end of the street and cautiously approached the residence like they had come upon a big glowing crater. When they were all in front of the home, a powerful sound system began playing "Thriller" by Michael Jackson.

Joe Blow suddenly appeared at the top of the roof, tap-dancing. He was naked except for a beaver head.

The reporters flipped open their notepads.

"I think the streak is over," one of them whispered. "I can't see this catching on."

Joe wasn't through. He climbed down from the roof, got dressed in beach clothes and carried a tote bag out to his car. The reporters gave Joe a wide berth as he pulled out of the driveway and sped off toward downtown Tampa.

●

A young Brazilian woman stood over the bed in room 17 of the Buccaneer Lodge, breaking down a Tango-51 and packing it into a padded attaché case. She stuck the briefcase in the trunk of a rented yellow Mustang, drove onto I-275 and headed south for the downtown Tampa exit.

●

MARLON couldn't sleep. He was the first one up that morning in the *Orange Crush,* and he sent a fax to the prison at Starke just before dawn. A half hour later he followed up with a phone call to the warden. "I'm granting clemency."

"I just got your fax. We should have the paperwork done by Friday."

"Release him immediately!"

"But—"

"Twelve years on Death Row for something he didn't do? Every minute now is a further injustice. Release him!"

It was an hour before the others got up. Marlon was scrambling eggs in the RV kitchenette when they began spilling out of their bunks.

"W-w-w-what's this?" asked Jenny. She had found Butts's videotape on the dashboard. SIROCCO'S DAUGHTER was written on a piece of masking tape on the side.

"That's a statement by Frank Sirocco's daughter," said Marlon.
Jenny began shaking.

"What's the matter?"

She didn't answer. She ran to the VCR and stuck the tape in.

"Are you okay?"

Still no answer.

The tape began. "Who's that?" said Jenny, pointing at the woman in the video.

"That's Frank's daughter."

"No she's not!"

Marlon noticed she wasn't stuttering. "What do you mean?"

"*I'm* Frank's daughter."

"What!" said Marlon.

"He's a monster! He did *this* to me!" She slapped the back of her thighs. "The beatings only stopped when he went to jail for murder. My coked-out stepmom picked up where he left off, throwing things at me, singeing me with cigarettes. We moved to Florida. When she finally burned down the house, the authorities found my scars, and they got me out of there. I was adopted by a family in Sarasota and they changed my name. My records were sealed under the law protecting juvenile abuse victims."

Marlon's stomach was a free-falling elevator.

"Then who's that in the tape?"

"My stepmom."

"But she's so young," said Marlon.

"She was the trophy wife!"

Marlon dove for the phone and called the warden back at Starke. "Don't let Sirocco go."

"Too late."

It didn't matter anyway. Clemency is clemency; no double jeopardy.

He called the lawyer from the night before. "You son of a bitch!"

"Now, now, we have a deal."

"Deal's off. She lied."

"No she didn't. She was Frank's hired gunman. She *did* kill him. They split the insurance. And *you* gave her immunity."

"She perjured herself! I'll put her away! And I'll have you disbarred for suborning that perjury!"

"You got us there. . . . Wait—I can't remember. You did put her under oath, didn't you? Well, we can always check the video you took. . . . Oh, did you hear? We have a book deal, and Frank and Anita are going to renew their vows. If you don't know what to get them, they're registered at Saks."

"I'll get you!"

"Here's the best part," said the attorney, starting to laugh. "I'm a Democrat. Have a nice *victory* party tonight. . . . Gotta run. I need to call some TV stations."

Marlon and Jenny were silent in the front of the *Orange Crush*.

Escrow walked up combing his hair. "You guys need to get moving. We have to start over to the debate."

39

SERGE CHECKED HIS watch. Almost noon.

Police had set up barricades in a twenty-block perimeter around the stage on Franklin Street, and they were overwhelmed by the thousands of people pouring into downtown Tampa on foot. The crowd jammed the pedestrian mall and spilled down the side streets. SWAT helicopters circled the high-rises. Sharpshooters on top of the Amsouth Bank Building passed a thermos of coffee. Serge approached from the south.

Two grinning young executives stood at the rear of the crowd. Serge stood next to them, dark sunglasses and Mohawk. The executives noticed Serge's MARLON! button. They waved their Gomer Tatum signs in his face. YESSSSSSSSS! MARLON'S GOING DOWN!

Serge smiled and grabbed them by the carotid arteries until they fell to the ground unconscious. He tore their signs to confetti.

That was an interesting encounter, Serge thought as he continued on. They had absolutely no life experience to tell them that was coming. Such are the hazards of privilege.

Serge spotted someone else with dark sunglasses at the corner of Zack Street. The man wore a black suit and had a small transistor earphone with a wire trailing into his collar.

"You're security, aren't you?" asked Serge. "I'd like to join you guys. I think I'd be pretty good at it."

"Sure thing," said the agent, opening a notepad. "What's your name?"

"Travis Bickle."

The agent waved over a security cameraman to take a photo, but Serge had disappeared into the crowd. As the agent craned his neck to find Serge, a young woman wearing a Miami Heat jacket walked behind him with an attaché case and turned into the lobby of an office building.

There was a shout from down the street.

"Hey, you can't park there!" yelled a young police officer.

"Sumbitch!" muttered Albert Fresco, backing his pickup out of a loading zone.

Serge continued deeper into the mob. Everyone wore tropical shirts and sandals. Some had large plastic parrots on their shoulders. Some had parrots. A bank of kiosks with battery-powered boat blenders did brisk business in front of the landmark Tampa Theatre. Corona beer babes gave away T-shirts and can coozies. The lines were twenty deep outside the row of Port-O-Lets. A man went inside one of the johns with a parrot on his shoulder, but the bird got claustrophobia and went berserk, crashing into wall after wall, its owner grabbing drunkenly at empty air a foot behind the bird. Colorful pieces of feather flew out the side vents, and the Port-O-Let began to rock back and forth.

Serge looked up at the stage. A crane lowered a massive plexiglass bowl onto an eight-foot reinforced plexiglass stand. The world's largest margarita glass. Fire hoses began filling the bowl. Officials from the *Guinness Book of World Records* took notes.

Serge stopped and stared up at the tall buildings around him. Something wasn't kosher. He began picking up a frequency.

The crowd exploded as Jimmy Buffett took the stage and began strumming the six-string intro to "Son of a Son of a Sailor." He was backed up by Stephen Stills, who had gone to high school in Tampa and was a big Tatum supporter. Behind them, stagehands scaled ladders and placed a small canoe in the margarita. Then they steadied the little boat and helped Blaine Crease climb aboard.

Thirty minutes later, Buffett ended the set with "A Pirate Looks at Forty." He bowed to thundering applause and trotted off the stage. Crease turned on his portable microphone in the canoe. "Is everyone having a good time?"

Serge threaded through the crowd.

"I've been known to get a little crazy myself from time to time . . ." said Crease. He tried to stand in the canoe, but it began rocking and he had to sit back down. ". . . Made more than my share of visits to Margaritaville, if ya know what I mean!"

"What a dork!" said a man in an iguana suit.

". . . So put your hands together and give your biggest Parrot Head welcome to Marlon Conrad and Gomer Tatum!"

Marlon climbed the steps on the right side of the stage and waved.

On the other side, Jackie Monroeville snatched a chalupa from Tatum's mouth and stomped on it.

"Hey! That was ninety-nine cents!"

"Get out there!"

Marlon was still waving to the crowd when Dempsey Conrad arrived with a platoon of men in satin jackets with big lips and tongues on the back.

"I'm not even going to discuss it anymore," said Dempsey. "They found another body at the Ice Palace after the wrestling match. It's gotten way too dangerous! We're staying with you to the end—I don't care what you say—"

BANG!

Dempsey Conrad reflexively ducked at the sharp noise and spun around. A Port-O-Let had fallen over, and a parrot flew out. But the Rolling Stones people were already in motion. They tackled Marlon and formed a pile of human shields.

"Get off me!" yelled Marlon.

By the time he got up, Tatum was already at the microphone.

"Did y'all hear Marlon pardoned a Death Row prisoner late last night?"

Most shook their heads no.

Tatum pulled a sheet of paper from his jacket and held it up. "This just moved on the Associated Press wire. The prisoner's attorney has admitted to the *Miami Herald* that his client really was guilty. Here's a picture of the killer holding up a MARLON FOR GOVERNOR sticker and drinking champagne!"

The crowd booed.

Tatum looked stage right. "What have you got to say for yourself?"

Marlon walked to the microphone with his chin up.

"I made a mistake. I thought we were about to execute an innocent man."

The booing increased.

"I'm sorry. I was trying to do the right thing . . ."

The jeering became so loud, Marlon had to stop.

Ten floors above Franklin Street, a rifle barrel poked out a closet window. Marlon's head appeared in the scope.

Serge was in the middle of the packed street. He began tingling again. He looked up at the buildings. Nothing. . . . Wait! What was that? Something about an old 1930s brick hotel that had been converted into law offices. He scanned window by window. His eyes got to the tenth floor, and he began tearing through the crowd.

He got to the sidewalk and darted into the building's lobby.

The law office was empty for the rally. Only a receptionist. He pressed the up button on the elevator next to her desk.

"Hey! You can't just go—"

Serge jumped into the elevator behind the unconscious receptionist and took it to the tenth floor and began checking room to room. The first two were empty. One to go. He grabbed the door handle.

Tempers had started to flare. Marlon's people and Tatum's people were yelling across the stage at each other over political points. The Parrot Heads argued musical taste with the Rolling Stones security. The Parrot Heads were laid back, but the Stones security screwed together portable pool cues and began smacking them around. A major skirmish broke out in front of the stage.

Marlon grabbed the microphone and urged calm. "Brothers and sisters, cool out! We don't want another Altamonte!"

Jackie Monroeville stood off the side of the stage holding up a chalkboard. Albert Fresco came up from behind. He jammed the .38 Special into her back. "You're my ticket onstage. Florida is finally gonna hear my message. Start walking!"

Jackie stiffly climbed the steps and moved across the stage.

Tatum saw the gun first, and he backed away. Fresco kept the pistol in Jackie's back. He had her around the neck with his free arm and dragged her toward Tatum's microphone. When the Stones security saw the gun, they piled on top of Marlon again.

"Get off me!"

Twenty cops pulled their own weapons on Fresco.

"Don't shoot!" yelled Tatum. "You'll hit Jackie!"

A standoff.

Serge opened a closet door on the tenth floor of the law building. A thin young woman was at the window, bracing a rifle on a stack of boxes. She clicked off the safety and wrapped a finger around the trigger.

Serge dove and knocked her over. He grabbed the rifle around the trigger guard and clicked the safety back on. He slugged her. She was much smaller, but made use of leverage and guile. She elbowed and bit. Boxes flew. She clicked the safety off again and ran to the window and aimed quickly. Serge caught her from behind and dragged her back. She stomped on his instep and ran to the window again.

Ten floors below the struggle, Joe Blow was sitting behind the stage, sipping his seventh kamikaze from one of the kiosk vendors. He had been waiting since eight that morning, and he struggled to his feet and started up the stage steps.

Albert Fresco got to the microphone. "It's a rigged political system and I demand to be heard! I've got street smarts, walkin'-around sense, and I've been to the school of hard knocks. I'm a meat-and-potatoes kinda guy. I put my pants on one leg at a time, and I'm madder than a sumbitch! . . ."

And with that, Jackie snapped her head back as hard as she could, catching Fresco in the teeth. He shrieked and released Jackie and grabbed his bloody mouth.

Jackie spun and judo-kicked him in the chest. "Don't you ever, *ever* pull a gun on me again!"

Fresco was knocked off balance, and police charged up the stage steps.

In all the drama, nobody noticed Joe Blow weaving across the stage. He bumped into the back of Fresco.

Fresco grabbed Joe and put the gun to his head. "Back off!"

The police backed off.

Fresco snatched the microphone again. "I'm a straight shooter, and I say what's on my mind. . . ."

"Yak, yak, yak!" said Joe Blow.

"What did you say?"

"I wish you'd shut up."

"I'm madder than a sumbitch!"

"I'm madder!"

"I got a gun!" Fresco cocked the hammer and pressed the barrel harder into Joe's temple.

Joe ripped open his shirt, revealing sticks of dynamite strapped around his chest.

"You win," said Fresco, letting go and walking backward.

Joe Blow stood alone in the middle of the stage. He looked around. Everyone was silent, staring at him. An orange lanyard hung from the side of the dynamite, attached to the detonator. Joe grabbed the cord and got ready to pull.

"Good-bye, mediocre world!"

A shot rang out from the tenth floor of a law office.

Everyone looked around. They heard a creaking sound. The shot had hit the margarita glass, and hairline cracks snaked out in five directions. Then a chunk of plexiglass broke loose from the lip and a stream of margarita gushed out and hit Joe Blow just as he yanked the detonation cord.

The sticks of dynamite were now damp, and instead of blowing Joe to smithereens, they blew out their end caps in a brilliant stream of sparks that knocked Joe down and spun him across the stage like a Chinese pinwheel.

"Watch out! He's coming this way!" yelled Escrow. He and Marlon timed their jump perfectly, and Joe spun under their feet and down the steps.

After Joe had finally burned himself out in front of the Port-O-Lets, people's eyes began to return to the stage. Fresco was aiming his gun at Marlon.

"Looks like the ball is back in my court!" He began squeezing the trigger.

"Whoooaaaa!" yelled Blaine Crease.

The rest of the margarita glass had chosen that moment to give way, and Crease came flying out in his canoe, running over Fresco and cascading off the stage into the crowd.

The injured lay everywhere. People screamed and stampeded from the stage. Others ran toward it with plastic cups, to catch the runoff. Smoke rose from the side of the stage. Joe Blow reignited and began spinning again in the crowd. Marlon was yelling for the pile of Stones security to get off him. Hundreds of shoulder-borne parrots took off in confusion and pooped and flew into buildings. One of the cops turned to another. "I hate these Buffett things."

Serge had been able to dive and knock the woman's arm as she squeezed off a shot, resulting in the shattered margarita. Then he kicked the rifle away and pinned her to the floor and began to pummel.

Something was wrong. She wasn't resisting. Just lying there limp, taking the fists. She didn't make a sound and didn't seem to feel pain. Serge stopped, and the woman angled her head, looking at Serge with a flicker of understanding.

Serge studied her face, too.

He sat her up.

"You want to tell me about it?"

40

FOR ELECTION NIGHT headquarters, Marlon rented Centro Asturiano, the old Latin cultural hall. Tatum's people were waiting it out in a hall at the Convention Center. The scene was the same at both. Balloons and streamers. Hats, political buttons, noisemakers, liquor and Doritos.

The candidates themselves were nowhere to be seen. They sat ensconced in their respective hotel rooms with only their closest supporters. Staff members had laptops plugged into the phone lines, getting a direct feed from the secretary of state in Tallahassee. The candidates remained still, but everyone else was involved in nervous activity. Elizabeth gave Marlon a shoulder rub.

Centro Asturiano erupted when Marlon took the lead on a bunch of small-town returns.

The Convention Center shook when Tatum pulled ahead on big-city precincts.

Then Marlon, then Tatum, back and forth, deep into the night.

Various controversies arose. Ballot irregularities. Missing signatures on absentees. Fisticuffs were reported outside churches and VFW halls. Then all hell broke loose.

A shaken Jimmy Carter appeared on CNN outside a post office in Palm Beach, flames in the background. "I've never seen anything like this!"

Carter had been scheduled to observe elections in a remote mountainous region of Central America controlled by death squads, but he was rerouted instead to Palm Beach County because the election there was expected to be more primitive and unstable.

Precincts kept trickling in, the lead seesawing.

SERGE made excellent time racing across the state. He arrived in Miami an hour after sunset and pulled over on the side of the MacArthur Causeway. He pointed to a waterfront property on Star Island, not too far from Loco Benny's old place. It was set back from the seawall, and a single house light twinkled through the palms.

"They're all there," said Serge.

The Brazilian woman nodded.

Inside the home, Frank Lloyd Sirocco, his wife, Anita, and their attorney-agent were nearing the bottom of a bottle of Smirnoff. The TV was tuned to election returns, and they fell apart laughing every time Marlon fell behind. They also had a tape recorder running, in fulfillment of their $1.2 million book contract.

"What about those four women who told the journalism teacher they'd been molested?" asked the lawyer.

"Addicts. Friends of mine. We paid 'em with skag right after their interviews," said Anita. "Remember, he didn't find them canvassing the area. They called *him*. And they met at neutral sites. He didn't do his homework."

"How did you two team up in the first place?"

Frank and Anita grinned at each other. "That's really a funny story," said Frank. "Anita and George were going through a divorce, and I realized we'd screwed up the contracts. We would have to dissolve the company just to pay off Anita's share of the split."

Anita chuckled and picked up the story. "So Frank goes to George and starts hinting around about killing me. And George gets all mad and tells Frank, 'We may be getting divorced, but I still love her, and I'll kick your ass if you ever say anything like that again.' "

Anita and Frank got the giggles. Frank caught his breath: "I go to plan B. I call Anita and say, 'Let's kill George,' and she says, 'Fine by me.' "

"We all flew down to the Keys together," said Anita. "George didn't know it, but Frank and I got tickets under assumed names. I killed him in the room, and then Frank came in and cleaned it up with his professional expertise. We flew back to establish our alibis during the Patriots game."

The TV showed Marlon falling behind again, which was hysterical.

Back on the causeway, Serge kept a lookout while the Brazilian woman put on a mask and snorkel. He pulled into traffic as she slipped into the black night water of Biscayne Bay.

•

IN a twentieth-floor hotel room overlooking downtown Tampa, Escrow sat on the edge of a bed typing on his laptop. He jumped up and ran to Marlon.

"We need to lodge a protest. Reform Party candidate Albert Fresco has polled ten thousand in Palm Beach. Those are *your* votes. The citizens got confused by something called the Reticulated Lawn Beetle Ballot."

"No protests," said Marlon. "That's how the ball bounces."

"But—"

"Forget it!"

Escrow fumed. "I need to get out of here." He left the room in disgust.

The returns updated at ten P.M., the numbers rolled over. Marlon took the lead, 2,876,352 to 2,876,021. Jackie Monroeville got on the phone to Tallahassee, demanding they skip the regular count and go directly to a recount.

Escrow burst back into the room in a panic. He ran up to Marlon carrying two blue canvas bags marked PALM BEACH and held out his arms.

"Hide these!"

"I hope you haven't done what I think you've done."

"Who would have thought they'd ever miss them?" said Escrow. "How was I supposed to know they'd have Jimmy Carter?"

There was a knock at the door. Escrow looked around in panic again and then jumped inside a closet with the canvas bags. An agent from the Florida Department of Law Enforcement walked in the room. "Is there a Gottfried Escrow here?"

A whimpering sound came from the closet. The agent opened it.

"What are those?" asked the agent, pointing at the blue bags in Escrow's hands.

"Never seen them before."

"You're under arrest," said the agent, frisking him.

"You're making a mistake!" said Escrow. "I'll have your job!"

The agent felt something in Escrow's right hip pocket, and he reached inside and pulled out several packets of heroin.

"What do we have here?"

"I can explain. I was going to use that to drug a dangerous fugitive and then turn him over to you."

"Of course," said the agent. "That's what everyone uses it for."

Escrow's body went flaccid, and they had to carry him out of the room in a bedspread.

The eleven-o'clock returns came in. Tatum pulled ahead by nineteen votes. At midnight, it was Marlon by twelve, then Tatum by seven, then Marlon by one. At three A.M., nobody watching a computer screen or TV set could believe their eyes. With a hundred percent of the votes counted: Marlon 2,942,726, Tatum 2,942,726.

The constitution of the great state of Florida left only one option in such an unlikely event. The race would be decided by media circus. Every available TV camera in the state was turned on and began searching for anything with a pulse and a law degree.

Then, at four A.M., the shocker.

An agent with the Florida Department of Law Enforcement walked in the front door of the Palm Beach courthouse with the missing bags of ballots he had recovered from Gottfried Escrow. The ballots were dumped on a giant, flood-lit table in the elections office. TV cameras began rolling as the nail-biting count got under way.

They were almost finished but had to start over after the Republicans successfully filed a protest against a Democratic observer standing behind one of the counters going, *"Forty-two! Seventeen! Twenty-nine! Six! Nine hundred and eight! . . ."*

The count had almost been completed again when a press conference was hastily arranged in Tallahassee. The Florida secretary of state was about to step in front of the cameras, but the drama had been too stressful for her, and she had overdosed on rouge.

The networks switched back to the scene outside the Palm Beach courthouse. Sirens wailed. Martial law had been declared, and police moved in with riot gear to disperse an angry mob hanging a chad in effigy.

Just after sunrise, a weary volunteer held up the very last punch card, made a hash mark on a tally sheet and placed the ballot on a tall stack. Officials crowded around to see the results. This time it wasn't a tie. The networks broke into breakfast programming with the name of the next governor.

JACKIE Monroeville ran out of Tatum's hotel room and skipped up and down the halls in her bare feet, screaming her head off.

"I won! I won! I'm First Lady! Fuckin' A!"

Jumping around, swinging her arms. "I knew it!"

Guests poked their heads out of the other rooms. Jackie ran down the hall shaking their hands and leaving them baffled.

"I won! Say *hel-looooo* to the First Lady!" She fell on her back in the hallway and pedaled her feet in the air. "Yahooooooooooooooooo!"

Tatum stepped into the hallway with a drumstick. "What about me?"

"Oh, you're governor."

He took a bite and went back in the room.

POCKETS of supporters were crying as Marlon walked up to the podium at Centro Asturiano. A hush fell as he arrived at the mike. A balloon popped somewhere.

"I want to say how very proud I am of all of you, and how much your support has meant to me . . ."

People began clapping, and the applause built until Marlon had to step back from the microphone. They kept cheering. Marlon began looking at them face by face. He started thinking of all the people he had met on the campaign. He thought about his platoon, and his sergeant, Tex Jackson.

He stepped forward to the mike again, and the cheering subsided. He stared at his shoes.

"I'm sorry. I let you down." He walked away.

Some started cheering again, but it was awkward and trailed off. A woman yelled, "We love you, Marlon!" like that day at the airport in Tallahassee, but he was already out the door.

EPILOGUE

ONE YEAR LATER.

Everyone had become famous.

The documentary film *The Last Campaign* by Ned Coppola was the sleeper hit of the year at art movie houses. The soundtrack, with the Phil Collins title tune, was also a surprise chart-topper. In the summer, the movie was rereleased for wider distribution on six hundred screens nationwide. The updated film featured new footage at the end, showing what had happened to all the characters since the election.

Marlon and Elizabeth kept the *Orange Crush*. They had hooked up with an Airstream caravan and were in the process of visiting every state except Hawaii. They became a husband-wife team of guest political commentators on CNN. The film's epilogue showed them squaring off for charity against Al and Tipper Gore on a special edition of *Survivor*.

Gottfried Escrow went to jail for campaign fraud and drug possession. He was serving a two-year term in the maximum-security state prison at Starke, surviving under the protection of jailed members of the Overtown Posse, who had recruited Escrow for a black supremacist gang. The movie showed him being raffled off as a bitch for cigarettes.

Gomer Tatum became one of the best governors in Florida history. He streamlined government, cut taxes and rammed through a slate of lobbying reforms that closed loopholes for food and drink. He became an expert microbiotic chef, lost eighty pounds and wrote a best-selling celebrity cookbook. The film showed him standing in front of the governor's mansion in a pair of his old pants, smiling and holding the waistband a foot away from his body.

Jackie Monroeville was secretly calling all the shots in the governor's office. She continued her education with night classes at Florida State and blossomed into one of the most erudite and sophisticated first ladies in the country. The film showed her in Paris, where she was the toast of the town, charming everyone and wooing two dozen international businesses to the state against a backdrop of paparazzi flashbulbs.

Jenny Springs won several Lipton tennis events, then married her new coach and retired. She permanently lost her stutter when she got the results back from her pregnancy test, and was now happily expecting her first child in February. The film showed her in maternity clothes carving decorative gourds on the porch of their secluded horse farm near Ocala.

Detective Mahoney's wife had taken him back and thrown him out again three more times. He later resigned from the force, dramatically flinging his badge onto a major's desk in protest of a "candy-ass" department crackdown on police brutality. He currently resided in an efficiency over the Biscayne Boulevard pawnshop he was managing. The film showed two bouncers eighty-sixing him from "Louie's" bar.

NED Coppola sat in row 37 of the Shrine Auditorium in Los Angeles. Midway through the Seventy-sixth Academy Awards, Julia Roberts opened an envelope and called out Coppola's name for best documentary. The camera cut to a flustered Ned receiving slaps on the back before finally standing and heading for the stage.

Ned wiped away tears as Julia handed him the gold statuette. He began thanking all the people in the film, but he broke down again and had trouble regaining composure.

Billy Crystal tried to lighten the moment. "Frankie Coppola warned me about you. That's why he never lets you do the toasts at the weddings."

Ned put a hand up to signal he would be okay. He looked out into the audience and waved an arm for someone to join him. "Get up here! This is your moment, too!"

Serge bounded onto the stage with Babs Belvedere on his arm. They jumped up and down with endless excitement.

"What the hell is this?" quipped Crystal. "The kids from *Fame*?"

In Miami, ex-detective Mahoney was eating cold Chef Boyardee out of the can and watching the Academy Awards on his small black-and-white TV. He dropped the ravioli on the floor when he recognized who was on stage. Mahoney grabbed his gun and ran out the door without turning the set off.

On the screen, Serge gripped the Oscar tightly in his fist and pumped it in the air. "Thank you, America! Until next time! . . ."

A NOTE ON THE TYPE

The text of this book was set in a face called Leubenhoek Gothic, the versatile eighteenth-century type developed by Baruch Leubenhoek (1671–1739), the Dutch master whose serif innovations last to this day. However, unsubstantiated accounts attribute Leubenhoek Gothic not to Baruch Leubenhoek, the stalwart traditionalist, but to the Hungarian Smilnik Verbleat (1684–1753?), the iconoclastic rebel of typography whose use of upper and lower case set the typesetting world abuzz. It is indeed a compelling inquiry, since Leubenhoek Gothic is widely accepted as the most stunning example of the sturdy hot-face designs typified during the last golden age of typesetting, when the accomplished typemasters were nothing less than international celebrities. Stories abound of Leubenhoek unveiling a new typeface, setting fire to the neoclassical world, only to have Verbleat trump it later that week, triggering celebrations of Romanesque proportion. Such revelry often saw Leubenhoek and Verbleat become quite drunk and take nasty falls that would have sidelined men of lesser constitution. And of course women were always available; Baruch was no slouch, but Smilnik's reputation for three-ways was unsurpassed. Soon, new fonts appeared, each more daring. The reading world was ecstatic. Then tragedy. In 1739, both were rumored to have been suffering from late-stage gonorrhea when they met up in Antwerp and pitched a heated argument about whether Smilnik's *S*'s really looked like *F*'s and Verbleat crushed Leubenhoek's skull in with a clavichord.